TURN
UP THE
HEAT

MARIE HARTE

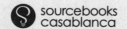
sourcebooks
casablanca

Published by Sourcebooks Casablanca, an imprint of Sourcebooks
P.O. Box 4410, Naperville, Illinois 60567-4410
(630) 961-3900
sourcebooks.com

Printed and bound in Canada.
MBP 10 9 8 7 6 5 4 3 2 1

To DT and RC

Chapter One

MACK REVERE WANTED TO BELIEVE THAT THE WOMAN HAD hit him by accident. He couldn't chalk up the incident to alcohol, a joke gone wrong, or the fact he'd been flaunting the rules. He hadn't. For once, he'd been playing clean and fair.

Yeah, and look where that got you.

Winded and flat on his back, he blinked up at the clear November sky. Seattle remained cloudless yet cold. The forecast predicted clear skies for the next week, but with the way the weather could turn on a dime, he hadn't put aside his umbrella just yet. Too bad the rain from the past week had turned the soccer field into a mud bowl.

He grimaced as the cold, wet muck seeped into the back of his jersey and shorts. Ew. Talk about a wet start to his Saturday morning.

A head interrupted his field of vision. Bright-gray eyes dominated an unforgiving face that smirked down at him. A dark ponytail swung over the woman's shoulder as she tilted her head, studying him like a cockroach. Police officer Cassandra Carmichael, in the flesh.

She stared. "That tumble you took must have hurt."

"Ya think?" he snarled, trying to ignore the ache in his tailbone. Her slide tackle had done most of the work, but the mud sure the hell hadn't helped. "Totally unnecessary."

"Yet we have the ball, so maybe it *was* necessary." She glanced over at her teammate, who kicked a goal, then turned back to him and shook her head. "No wonder your team is losing. If they're smart, they'll move you from midfield to offense. Put you out where the ball *isn't.*"

Before he could say something cutting, witty, and God-willing sarcastic, she flounced away to congratulate her teammates.

He wanted to grab her by that ponytail and roll *her* around in the mud. Then, maybe, the ref would call a time-out for a mud fight. Everyone would get involved. Carmichael would get wet and dirty. *Oh, so dirty.* Then she'd have to take off that nasty uniform to showcase that tight, toned body…

He glanced over at her. She didn't look back, completely ignoring him. Or maybe she'd forgotten she'd nearly broken him on the soccer field.

So much for a family-friendly game.

"I could use a little help here," he yelled out to her, annoyed to still be so attracted to the woman who just a week ago had given him a speeding ticket. Well, a warning, but still.

"Sorry, can't," she yelled back without looking at him and said something he couldn't make out that caused her nearest teammates to laugh.

"You don't sound sorry," he muttered and flipped off her buddies, who promptly sneered and sent the gesture right on back.

The bastards. He absolutely loathed playing against the Top Cops, no matter what the sport.

Tex, fellow firefighter, teammate, and one of Mack's best friends, helped him to his feet.

"She did that on purpose," Mack said.

"Of course she did. Duh." Tex raised a brow, his Texan accent thick as he responded, "If your brains were leather, you wouldn't have enough to saddle a june bug."

"What the hell does that mean?"

"Well, my uncle likes to say it every now and again to the stupid cousin everyone hates."

"Not helping, Tex."

But Tex had already turned to yell, "Nice illegal tackle, Officer."

To Mack he said, "Gotta say, though, that tackle was totally bitchy. She added an evil laugh there at the end."

"Agreed." Mack wiped gobs of mud from his legs and backside and glared at the woman who should have been penalized with a red card. Or at least a yellow warning. He raised his voice. "Maybe if the refs would quit leering at a certain someone they'd make the right call!"

The tall referee who couldn't seem to take his gaze from Carmichael's ass ignored him.

"I feel for you." Tex shook his head. "Our fans are giving you a pity clap just for standing up."

Mack glanced to the stands to see Tex was right. A thumbs-up from Tex's girlfriend. And a "You can do it, Mack!" from... Oh God. His mother.

Mack seethed with embarrassment. For all of five seconds. Then he decided to get even.

On the Top Cops' next breakaway down the field, Mack switched with the left halfback. "I got this." He proceeded to steal the ball from one of the Top Cops' lead scorers and sent it downfield to Tex.

"Lucky break," the scorer sneered.

Mack waited until the refs turned away before shoving him aside. Talk about annoying.

"Hey!"

"Whatever."

"Prick."

"Momma's boy."

Mack dodged when the guy took a half-hearted swing at him. Which brought several comments from the stands: protests from the Burning Embers' fans and cheers from the Top Cops' side.

The idiot Mack had just shoved eyed Mack with clear derision. "*I'm* a momma's boy? Really?" He nodded to the stands.

"You can do it, Mack!" Their mother frowned. "Xavier, be nice to your brother."

Xavier smiled wide. "Sure thing, Ma." Then he punched Mack in the arm.

Mack frowned, punched him back, and narrowly avoided a soccer ball to the face. Xavier wasn't so lucky. He took the ball to the side of his head.

"Gee, that must have hurt." Mack grinned at his brother swearing and shaking his head, no doubt to clear the ringing between his ears.

"Sorry, Xavier," Carmichael called.

Mack chuckled, took the ball, and dribbled down the field. He pretended to pass to the center and juked Carmichael into tripping over her own feet. She went down in the mud.

Still laughing, Mack yelled over his shoulder, "Officer down!"

"Jackass!"

He passed to an open player and cheered his delight when their team scored, evening the game.

Turning, he found himself surrounded by muddy, burly police officers, Carmichael among them.

"What?"

"That was cheap," she argued.

"Was it the 'Officer down' part or the part when you fell over your own feet? And wow, are you dirty."

Out of the corner of his eye he saw one of the cops grab a handful of mud. Mack ducked behind Carmichael just as the guy slung it. He heard her gasp and saw she'd been hit in the chest. And what a sorry sight that was, obscuring anything so fine.

She glared at the offender, who startled whistling and quickly walked away.

Deciding that would be the smart move, Mack followed. But not before his brother tackled him to the ground and shoved his face in wet dirt and grass.

Mack retaliated. The rest of his team joined him, and the soccer game turned into a real free-for-all. Laughter, swearing, and a lot of mudslinging went both ways. Unfortunately, both teams ended up being disqualified for unsportsmanlike behavior—but only because some smartass had decked both refs with mud as well.

―――――――――

"What a great game," Mack said as he and the guys joined their friends at the bleachers.

"Great but messy." Brad, his buddy and part of their tight, four-man firefighting crew, looked down at himself with a frown.

His girlfriend rolled her eyes. "It's just dirt, Brad."

Brad blinked. "Oh?" Then he chased her around the field laughing maniacally.

"Don't even think about it," Tex's girlfriend warned.

"Darlin', I have half a brain. Not much, but it's the half that works." He didn't even try touching her as the pair made their goodbyes.

Reggie, the last member of their four-man fire crew, stood next to Mack's mother in jeans and a jacket. He sniffled a few more times for effect. "This cold is just awful. Too bad I couldn't have joined you."

Considering the guy had been just fine the night prior over beers and darts, he wasn't earning any loyalty points for not playing this morning.

"I'm so disappointed in your weak lies." Mack shook his head.

Reggie apparently felt no such upset because he just grinned. "Gotta go. I promised Maggie and Emily doughnuts this morning."

"Fine. Go. Not like we could have used you or anything."

"Great. Bye."

Reggie left.

And then there was one…

"Oh, Mackenzie. Monkey-face, you're a mess."

He cringed. "Ma, not here." Where too many witnesses might overhear and use that name against him at work.

She huffed. "Please. It's a fine name. After your great-grandfather."

"Not Mackenzie. That nickname." He lowered his voice. "You have no idea what the guys—"

"Oh, Mon-key-face..." Xavier, older by two years but always so much more immature than Mack, called in a singsong voice. "There you are." He walked up to his brother and mother and grinned. "Buddy, you look awful."

"Right back at ya, moron." Mack couldn't help grinning back. The youngest of four, Mack loved his family. Even if they didn't always seem to understand him. Or like him. But today, Xavier appeared in a decent mood, and their mother had cheered for Mack, the lone firefighter in a family of cops.

Perhaps soon he'd see pigs fly.

Mack made small talk, watching as the crowd dispersed while subtly looking for one particular dirty player—pun intended. There. He saw Carmichael wringing the bottom of her shirt by the parking lot.

"Be right back." He left before his family could corner him. "Hey, Carmichael."

She flipped her head back, slapping herself in the face with a wet ponytail, and glared at him. "Well, if it isn't Mr. Pushy."

"Oh please. You pushed me first. I didn't even touch you. It was my fast moves and amazingly handsome face that caused you to go down, hard."

Her lips twitched, but to her credit, she didn't laugh. "You are so full of it."

"I really am."

Ha. There. She smiled. Her expression turned sour once more, and she said in a crisp, cold tone, "What do you want, Revere?"

Excited she remembered his name, he nevertheless tried to

play it cool. "Just wanted to let you know I was okay, that my tail-bone is still in one piece, you know, in case you were wondering."

"I wasn't."

"Yeah, I'm feeling loose." He rolled his neck and pulled a knee to his chest, carefully balancing as he stretched his glutes. "Everything still works." He set his foot down before he fell over and ruined all his careful posturing.

"Am I supposed to be happy for you?"

"Yes, you are." He smiled. "So, you busy tonight?"

"Seriously?" She spread her arms wide, bringing unintended attention to her full breasts. "I'll be spending the next week washing the mud from my body."

As soon as she said it, she stilled, blinked, and watched him.

Don't say it. Don't say it.

Her eyes narrowed, as if reading his mind.

"So…you want any help with that?"

"Unbelievable," she muttered, turned on her heel, and stalked away from him.

But Mack would swear he saw a grin on her face before she left.

Amused and granting himself permission to treat today as a victory, he rejoined his mom and brother, in the mood for a family breakfast after all.

———

Cass stomped back to her car, glad she'd had the foresight to bring a towel with her. At least she'd keep her car seat fairly clean while she drove home.

"Yo, you coming over later?" her partner asked.

She turned to see Jed standing by his car, his wife and the twins already inside and no doubt buckled up. "Who's cooking? You or Shannon?"

Jed frowned. "Why the hell does that matter?"

She just looked at him.

He sighed. "Shannon's cooking, okay?"

"I'll be there." She gave him a thumbs-up.

He glowered before entering his car and driving away.

Cass chuckled. Her amusement lingered on the drive home. Though she'd never admit it, she thoroughly enjoyed the competitive games she played as a Top Cops team member. Challenging—and usually beating—the other teams in their countywide sports league was so satisfying. Cass played to win. Why else bother playing?

The Burning Embers, those arrogant no-neck men and women firefighters, always gave as good as they got. She could respect that. Even though they'd both lost today, they'd put up a heck of a fight.

She particularly liked the very handsome, sarcastic, and frustrating Mackenzie Revere, though she'd deny it 'til her last breath. From the first time she'd seen the guy, she'd been dumbstruck.

Short, dark-brown hair framed an unforgettable face. He had amazing cheekbones, a straight nose, a square chin, and bright-blue eyes. And when he smiled... *good night*, but he could stop a girl in her tracks. He'd surely stopped hers. That was to say nothing of his perfectly proportioned, muscular, long-legged body. Or of his seasonal tan that said he liked the sun. She'd once seen him with his shirt off during softball season in the summer... *Whoa, momma.*

Even the fire department agreed. They'd used him as their poster boy for Station 44. She'd seen Mack on public service advertisements and in the paper and on TV, informing everyone about the new fire station that had opened earlier in the year.

Unfortunately, he was a Revere, one of the many cop families working for the city. His father, mother, and three brothers had all worked or continued to work in law enforcement. Heck, Xavier Revere worked in her precinct. Since Cass never mixed business with pleasure, she'd had to strike the sexy, firefighting Mack off her hottie list. She didn't date friends of work friends—something she continually told her partner's tenacious wife.

As much as Cass genuinely loved Shannon, Jed's wife could be pushy. For some reason, a year ago, she'd decided to put her matchmaking skills to work finding Cass a boyfriend.

At first, Cass had wondered if Shannon might be jealous of all the time Cass spent with Jed on the job. But after a frank conversation with the woman, she'd learned that, no, Shannon trusted both Cass and her husband. She had every right to, but Cass had dealt with many spouses of fellow officers on the job, and none of them seemed to like her much. Just Shannon with her wacky sense of humor and adorable, troublemaking twins.

So why was Shannon so keen on setting Cass up for a love connection?

A question that still plagued her, but Cass knew better than to bring up the subject. Lately, Shannon had been laying off, so Cass said nothing about being dateless. Or about how she'd started to feel as if she might actually be missing out on a part of life. Loneliness could be a real bitch.

As Cass pulled into her driveway, she tried to forget about the path her dating life hadn't taken and focused instead on what she needed to get done on her days off. She worked a four-on, two-off rotation with her partner. So she had one more day until she went back to work.

And that laundry wasn't going to do itself.

———————

Seven hours later, she arrived at Jed and Shannon's wearing a nice pair of jeans, a warm navy sweater, and her favorite boots. She parked in the back, per Jed's orders, and raised her hand to knock on the door, startled to hear several people inside, along with music and laughter.

That sounded like a party.

Oh, hell no. Time to go.

As she turned, the door opened.

"No, you don't. Get your ass in here." Faster than should be humanly possible, Jed grabbed her by the shoulder and spun her around. He pulled her inside and shut the door behind her. Then he shifted places with her, blocking her from exiting.

"You asshole," she swore in a low voice, conscious of the twins, who always seemed to appear out of thin air. "What the hell is this?"

Noise from several adults, alternative rock music, and children's laughter promised a cacophony of trouble.

Cass hated crowds, parties, and, according to her father, fun.

"Not my idea." He held up his hands in surrender. "Shannon told me nothing until about an hour before she forced me to change into 'company clothes.'" He grimaced and plucked at his button-down shirt.

"And you couldn't text me?"

"She hid my phone."

That did sound like something Shannon might do. "Oh, come on." Cass took a look around at the clean kitchen, decorated dining space, and mingling adults. "Your house is never this clean. Not one pair of shoes for anyone to trip over in the doorway, and you didn't notice until she told you to expect company an hour ago?"

"It's cleaning day." He groaned. "I know. I swear, though, I had no idea. And I'm a little concerned. Shannon really wanted you at this party. I hope she's not—"

"Cass! There you are." Shannon shot Jed a death glare and put on a wide smile for Cass. Despite Shannon's petite stature, beauty, and dainty appearance, the woman had a death grip when she wanted something. The hold she had on Cass's forearm actually hurt.

Cass shoved the six-pack she'd brought at Jed and reluctantly followed—*was dragged by*—Shannon into the crowded living room. "What the hell—"

"Quiet, you." Shannon pulled her toward a tall, handsome guy who looked familiar.

"Hey, Carmichael. What's up?" the man asked, his smile widening as he looked her over.

Josh Newcastle. The new guy. Her groan turned into a cough when Shannon elbowed her. "Sorry, Newcastle. Something in my throat. Ah, not much going on with me. Great party, Shannon," Cass said with feigned enthusiasm.

"Isn't it?" Shannon chirped. "So, you two know each other from work, I take it?"

Newcastle nodded with enthusiasm. "I started last week. Transferred from Spokane."

"I love Spokane." Shannon smiled.

Cass stood there, dying for a beer and pretending to be unaware of Newcastle stripping her naked with his gaze while Shannon and he chatted like besties. Over her shoulder, she spotted Jed fast approaching with a beer in each hand. He mouthed, *Hold on, I'm coming*, or something to that effect.

But just as he neared, Shannon cut him off by taking the beer meant for Cass. "Oh, thanks, honey. I was just coming to get you. Cass, can you and Josh talk while I take care of something?"

"Er, ah…"

"Sure," Josh said, beaming.

Shannon yanked Jed with her, leaving Cass at the mercy of Officer My Eyes Are Up Here.

"I hear you're single." Josh sipped from his drink. "Me too. We should go out some time."

Who? Me or my breasts? Cass sighed, waiting for him to make eye contact.

It promised to be a long, long night.

Chapter Two

"CASS, I'M SORRY," JED SAID FOR THE FIFTH TIME THAT EVENING. "I swear. I had no idea Shannon had plans for you."

"First Newcastle, then Handleman? Seriously? What did I ever do to Shannon to make her hate me so much?"

"She was taken in by a pretty face and a great body."

She blinked at him, surprised to hear those words coming from her partner.

His cheeks pinkened. "*Her* words, not mine." He cringed. "I think Newcastle looks like a gecko, and Handleman should be named handle*bars* for that tire around his waist. He barely fits in his uniform. But what do I know?"

"Not romance, that's for sure," she muttered as he pulled up to a house that could use some maintenance. The streetlight overhead showed it needed a new coat of paint, a screen door that closed properly, and maybe a car with actual wheels in the cracked driveway.

She got out with Jed and waited while he knocked. Next door, a woman could be heard shouting at a man for stepping out on her with her sister. So, not much had changed since the last time they'd swung by just a few weeks ago.

"Not my fault," Jed repeated, adding, "But I guess maybe I owe you one. For Shannon's sake."

"Owe me one? More like your soul for not breaking Newcastle's jaw. He wouldn't stop staring at my boobs."

"Gross."

"What? They're nice. But not for him to be looking at."

"Still gross. Stop talking."

She grinned. She and Jed could talk about anything. Except sex. They both drew the line at hearing about the more intimate details of their private lives. Jed considered her a sister, and she liked him and Shannon too much to wonder about what they did in their personal time. Still, grossing him out was always a pleasure.

"Since you owe me, you take point."

He sighed. "Fine. It's my turn anyway since you talked last time."

As one, they put on their game faces and waited to deal with Mrs. Cleary. The older woman was exceedingly polite, followed the rules, and called them *at least* once a month. She seemed to follow a pattern of complaint, whereby she had something to report about the latest man in her twenty-two-year-old granddaughter's life.

The last time Cass and Jed had been by, they'd found nothing to support a case of domestic violence, when said abuser was busy with his tongue down the alleged victim's throat and the victim had her limbs wound around him like a constrictor about to enjoy a meal. Upon questioning the pair, Mandy and her boyfriend had been surprised and amused.

Horny, yes. Violent, no.

Cass *always* paid strict attention to any such accusation, but in Mrs. Cleary's case, the woman honestly just didn't like the men her granddaughter had been dating. Though at the rate Mandy Cleary seemed to be going through boyfriends, the odds were she'd end up with at least one rotten apple and find herself in real trouble.

Still, Cass and Jed had a duty to serve. And serve they did because Cass wanted to think if she were the one calling in a problem, she'd be treated with respect and taken seriously.

The elderly woman who opened the door smelled like day-old doughnuts and whiskey. Her rheumy brown eyes looked out from a wrinkled face that had seen too much sun and smoke, her skin a permanent yellowed-white, like a wall tarred with nicotine. But she was always sweet, slightly stooped over, and soft-spoken. Until she coughed and sounded on death's door.

"Hello, Officers. Thanks so much for coming."

Jed and Cas nodded, and Jed said, "Sure thing, Mrs. Cleary. What can we help you with?"

While Jed spoke, Cass looked for evidence of trouble but didn't see or hear anything out of the ordinary.

"Please, come inside." The elderly woman motioned for them to enter. "It's so cold out."

They followed her into the foyer and shut the door behind them.

The house smelled stale, like watered-down depression, and Cass wanted nothing more than to leave. Instead, she stood alert, letting Jed figure out what the heck was really going on while she scanned for danger.

"Coffee?" Mrs. Cleary offered.

"No, thank you," Jed declined. "Mrs. Cleary, you told dispatch a male suspect broke in then left in a hurry. Do you know where he went? In what direction?"

"Sorry, no." She sighed.

"Can you tell us what's missing?"

"My granddaughter, for one. Mandy left with the boy when I got on the phone. But I don't know that anything else is missing exactly."

Cass could almost feel Jed biting back a sigh.

"Oh?" He waited with extreme patience.

Looking at him, one would never think Jed had a heart. He looked like a cross between a modern-day Viking and the Terminator. A big, muscular white guy with a face carved from granite and a laser-like focus that saw everything, Jed dispensed justice fairly. With so many problems lately between the police and civilians, Jed was one officer who strove to make a difference, working diligently to earn people's trust.

Community projects, constant communication training, and a need to serve the people as a whole had made him someone Cass respected more than she could say. That they both had the same outlook on life and sense of humor helped them remain a solid unit as well. So when he bit his lip, she knew he found Mrs. Cleary both amusing and tiring. But he would put the older woman's needs first because that's what Jed did.

"Well, I can't say *for sure* anything's missing," Mrs. Cleary corrected herself and frowned. "But he's a felon. I'm sure of it."

Jed scratched his temple. "He is? We looked him up last time. I thought Mandy was dating a"—he paused to glance at the notebook he took out of his pocket—"Larry Skoll. He's got a few misdemeanors but nothing serious."

"No. Larry's gone. That was a while ago."

Cass and Jed had visited three weeks ago to hear about Larry.

"I'm worried." The sweet older woman's expression grew stern. "If he doesn't have a record, he should. He breaks into my house all the time."

Jed's eyes narrowed. "Have you reported him before for that?"

A break-in was something they could investigate.

"I tried, but I was told that if he's using a key, it's not breaking and entering. Leastwise, that's what the other officers told me last Thursday."

Cass and Jed exchanged a glance before Jed said, "We want to help. Where did he get the key? Did he steal it?"

"Mandy gave it to him." Mrs. Cleary huffed. "Girl's addicted to Dick."

"I—." Jed blinked. "What's that?"

Sweet little old Mrs. Cleary answered, "My little one likes Dick. More like Dick the weasel. He's a limp, lame Dick, you ask me. I don't like that boy."

Cass and Jed gaped, and Cass didn't think she'd ever seen Jed turn so red.

Mrs. Cleary studied Jed and blinked. "Oh my. I don't think that came out right. Dick is short for Dickerson. Owen Dickerson, who goes by Dick. So when I said Mandy's addicted to Dick, I meant…" She flushed. "My goodness. That really came out wrong."

Cass did her best not to grin because if she started, she didn't think she'd stop laughing.

Jed cleared his throat. "We'd like to help you, Mrs. Cleary, but unless Owen Dickerson has broken in and stolen something or you have evidence a crime has been committed, there's not much we can do besides run him for priors."

"Well, okay. But I'm going to keep my eye on him."

"On that limp Dick," Cass murmured, her gaze on Jed.

Like a champ, he coughed to cover his laughter. "Great. Well, you have a nice day, Mrs. Cleary."

"I will. Thank you."

They left in silence and were a minute down the road, continuing along patrol, when they both started laughing hysterically.

"Addicted to limp Dick." Jed guffawed. "Jesus."

"I'm using that at some point." Cass paused. "Just not around Newcastle."

"Good call." Jed wiped his eyes. "Mrs. Cleary is now my favorite stop. Hands down."

Cass snickered. "Mandy Cleary is addicted to weasel Dick. News at eleven."

Jed chuckled.

They moved on to a corner store robbery to take statements, then a motor vehicle accident, attended by EMTs from Station 44. Not spotting Revere, not that she'd been looking for him, Cass took a few witness statements and waited with Jed to get that Breathalyzer on the drunk driver of the Nissan.

The rest of the shift passed without incident, shockingly enough. By 04:30, she was ready to head home.

"Hey, Cass, hold on." Jed stopped her by her car.

"Yeah?"

"I really am sorry about Saturday night. I'll talk to Shannon." He paused. "Though it was pretty funny watching you deal with Handleman and Newcastle. You scared them, partner. I swear I heard Newcastle whimpering after you left."

She grinned. "Mean is how I roll."

They bumped fists.

"I think she's all over you about dating because she's afraid you're going to ditch her."

"What?"

He shrugged. "It's something she said last week. I could be wrong, but I think maybe she's worried you'll stop coming out with us because you think you're a third wheel."

"Ha. I'll stop coming out with you if you keep spending the night making out when I'm trying to have a conversation."

"That was her fault, not mine," he protested. "I'm weak."

"A weak dick," she said with a big grin.

He shook his head. "Mrs. Cleary has a potty mouth." He chuckled. "I can't wait to tell Shannon."

They left, and Cass arrived home at five. After entering and locking up behind her, she looked around her empty house. Jed would return home and snuggle with Shannon after checking in on the twins. He'd sleep in, then spend time with his wife before picking up his kids and bonding with the little demons—as he lovingly referred to them—until he went back on shift at 19:30.

Cass would sleep in until noon. Alone. Wake up. Alone. Spend her day at the gym or help at the local community center. Eat dinner. Alone. Then be back on shift with Jed.

What a boring life.

She frowned. That sounded suspiciously like her father in her head, his therapist hat on.

Which made her remember the missed call on her phone. She scrolled through her messages and heard her father's invitation to lunch. Since she hadn't seen her parents in over a week, she knew she was due for some family time. And though she didn't like lectures, she loved her parents, so she texted her father a yes and asked for details, then set her phone aside.

She needed some sleep. Dealing with her parents not at her best would be like going into a gunfight with a rubber chicken. Amusing until the bullets found their target.

Seven hours later, she'd rested, showered, and dressed. After putting everything in its place, her home neat as a pin and just the way she liked it, she met her parents at a popular downtown restaurant that served an amazing Italian-only lunch. They'd gotten lucky, as getting a place to sit was more a matter of timing than planning.

She spotted her mother gesticulating wildly, her normally stern face lit up as she said something to her husband. The pair looked like a matched set. Dr. Jenny Carmichael, cardiologist, had a firm yet pleasant bedside manner reflected in her light-brown eyes. Despite a pale complexion due to spending so much time in the hospital treating patients, Jenny appeared in good health. Slender, of average height, but brimming with vitality, Jenny Carmichael inspired confidence in others.

Just like her husband, Dr. Aaron Carmichael, a psychologist who specialized in child and family therapy. He was handsome and smart, a trim academic with a tall, lean build heading into his sixties. He always listened with intensity. When talking with him, a person felt as if no one and nothing existed but them in that moment. Cass got her looks from him but her drive from her mother. Thank God. Aaron Carmichael drove Cass crazy with his laid-back manner and easy smile. She loved him, but honestly, she had no idea how her mother could handle a man who smiled during a crisis.

Yet the pair fit.

Spotting her, her father must have said something to her mother because Jenny waved and smiled.

Cass gave each of her parents a kiss on the cheek before sitting down with them. The server arrived immediately with a menu, left to get her beverage, and returned posthaste to take her order.

Obviously schooled by her mother to hurry the hell up. Jenny only had so much time before she needed to be back at the hospital.

"Nice job, Mom. You already have our server scurrying to obey your commands."

Her mother huffed. "It's all about efficiency, my dear."

Cass grinned. "Exactly."

Her father sighed. "Honestly, you two. Sit back and relax. Jenny, you're going to give yourself an ulcer if you don't slow down."

The familiar banter soothed Cass, and she relaxed into her chair as they teased each other about working harder and working smarter. Then they turned to her.

"So, how are things at work? How's Jed?"

Her parents loved her partner, especially because he had a stable, loving homelife with Shannon and the twins. A high mark of praise from her father, considering a police officer's tough profession.

"Good. All good." She paused and, frowning, blurted, "Except Shannon tried setting me up with a new guy I work with. And that on top of matchmaking at a party they tricked me into going to. I mean, I work with the guy. No way I can date him and not have that blow back in my face." Not that she would.

Her mother nodded. "Exactly. Never muddy the drinking water, I say."

The word *mud* made Mack Revere's face pop into her mind's eye, and Cass fixated on him despite herself. She still considered that she'd gotten the best of him the other day and smiled. "But on a good note, we would have won our soccer game Saturday if those cheating firefighters hadn't gotten us all booted from the game. They started a mud fight."

Her parents laughed.

"I'm sorry we couldn't be there," her dad said. "Your mother was in surgery, and I had an emergency with a client. He's fine, but he needed my help right away."

She waved away his apology. "No biggie. You guys can come to the next one. If we have it. Looks like it's going to snow sooner than they keep predicting. I can taste it in the air."

"You know it." Her mother paused to smile up at their server, who delivered their food.

Cass blinked and waited until she left to say, "You must have promised one heck of a tip. I just ordered, and my food is already here."

"The server's mother is at Swedish, and I know her doctor. We chatted a bit before we sat down." Jenny was a top cardiologist at Swedish First Hill Campus, a premier hospital on Broadway downtown.

Aaron grinned. "Your mother gets stuff done. She's the queen of networking."

"No kidding."

Cass nibbled on the mouthwatering focaccia at the table, loving the flavorful bread she dipped in spiced olive oil. She did her best not to dive into her plate and smother herself in the delectable pappardelle Bolognese, her absolute favorite. Since she'd been raised to have manners, she forced herself to eat slowly.

At home she'd have stuffed her face full. Because there'd have been no one there to see.

Her mother winked at her. "You're just like me, honey. I see great things in your future."

Cass swallowed before saying, "Thanks."

They ate for a while, talking about the uptick in heart patients and anxiety in teens. She filled them in on Mrs. Cleary's recent visit, inciting laughter.

Her mother left to use the restroom.

And then, as expected, her father gave Cass a wide smile and said, "You look good. You sound like everything is going well." Pause. "But I worry about you."

She mentally groaned but said nothing, letting her silence do the talking.

"Honey, you have no social life outside work. That's not healthy."

"Dad, please. I'm fine."

"Jed's fine. Your sergeant is fine. Your captain is fine. They have healthy relationships outside work. Being a police officer is stressful. You need something to release all that tension or you'll have problems."

Alcohol, drugs, abusive relationships. She'd been told this time and time again by both her father and the many lectures the officers received from the station's positive reinforcement expert, a perky woman who insisted talking about problems would promote a stable and healthy homelife. The new statewide program was supposed to help first responders with an outreach, a place to go when they needed help.

But Cass preferred to keep her problems private. Something her oversharing father didn't understand.

"You are so like your mother," he said with a sigh when she continued to just stare at him.

"Dad, I'm not your patient. I'm your daughter." She'd had this conversation so many times she *should* need therapy. "I'm fine."

"What do you do for fun?"

"I go to the gym."

"Okay, you exercise your body. What about your mind?"

"I do crossword puzzles and word searches." *And I sound like I'm ninety, but I like word puzzles.*

Her dad coughed, and she mentally dared him to once again compare her to Great-Aunt Martha. Fortunately for him, he asked, "What about social interaction?"

"I hang out with Jed and Shannon. Sometimes Bob."

"Who's Bob?"

She flushed. "He's a janitor at the gym. He's a nice guy." And she hadn't seen him lately. Hmm. He might have moved, now that she thought about it.

"I'm just curious. How old is he? Someone you'd consider a potential boyfriend?"

"Dad."

Aaron just waited.

"Bob's sixty-nine. But he's in great shape. He's a retired Marine who still works out and does the janitorial stuff at the gym. He tells funny stories."

"So not a romantic connection then?"

"No way."

He sighed. "Do you realize your only social outlets are Jed, the man you see at work all day, and his wife?"

"And kids," she muttered.

"In addition to an older man at the gym, the only other consistent place you go when not on duty? I love you, Cass. But I see problems for you if you don't get out and let loose a little. It's not bad to be focused on your job. Not at all. But you need balance."

"Oh look, there's Mom."

Her mother finally returned to the table. She leaned down to kiss Aaron and picked up her purse. "Sorry, I have to get back. Cass, next time you're off, let's do dinner at the house. And don't forget to leave our server a big tip, Aaron." She waved goodbye and darted out the door.

Cass tried to get money out of her wallet stuffed in her backpack, but her father insisted on paying. She didn't mind, but she didn't want him to think she couldn't take care of herself. She made a decent paycheck and had little overhead thanks to an inheritance years ago from Great-Aunt Martha. She was successful, so why was her father so bent on making sure she had a life?

Maybe because you don't?

She shoved the thought away and waited for her father to take care of the bill. Once outside, she walked him to his car.

"What's on your agenda today?" he asked.

"I thought I'd see a movie, actually."

Her dad brightened. "That's great. Which one?"

She mentioned an action flick she'd been wanting to see. With the cold outside, she wouldn't mind being indoors. "Then after that, I'll probably hit the gym and grab a quick dinner. Then it's back to work. I'm off Friday and Saturday this week if you guys want to do dinner."

"I'll check with your mother, but I'm leaning toward Friday. We'll text you details. But if plans come up that interfere with dinner, you let me know."

"Plans?"

He grinned. "If some hunk of a man sweeps you off your feet into a date, we'll reschedule."

She rolled her eyes. "Sure, Dad. In fact, I do meet a lot of people. Maybe one of the hunks behind bars will sing me into a yes. Then you could have a felon for a son-in-law."

Her father ignored her sarcasm. "As long as he treats you right, I'll be happy to invite him to family get-togethers."

"*Argh*. Go scramble some kid's brain while I get back to work keeping the streets safe."

"I'm proud of you, honey. You do good work." He hugged her but had to get the last word in. "Now go do good work with someone you can bring home to your sad, sorry folks."

He raced away with a laugh, and she watched him go, wondering why she felt more depressed than uplifted after her favorite food with the people she loved.

Chapter Three

TUESDAY NIGHT, MACK SAT WITH THE GUYS AT REGGIE'S house in the dining room, poker night in full effect. It should have been manly and filled with laughter. But he was distracted, listening to the guys' girlfriends laughing and hanging out in the living room.

How the hell had guys' night turned into bring-your-lady-to-hang night? But if he complained, he'd look like the single loser he was turning out to be.

In a low voice, Reggie said to him, "You need to get laid."

The others nodded.

Brad and Tex said something between them that had them smirking and staring at him.

"What?" he snarled, annoyed he was down twenty bucks after only three games.

"You're always irritated anymore," Brad said and laid down his cards. "I'm flush. Read 'em and weep."

"Yeah?" Tex grinned. "Try these ladies. Four of a kind."

Reggie sighed. "Shoot. I had a straight."

"You're all losers." Gleeful, Mack tossed down his cards. "Straight flush. Bite me."

The guys frowned at him.

"You're still down," Tex said. "So it ain't all sunshine and roses."

"You got that right." Brad frowned and ran a hand through his sandy hair. Hell, in this light, he did look like a Ken doll—something the guys liked to razz him about. "When's the last time you went out with a real girl, Mack?"

A muddy, angry cop from the soccer game immediately came to mind. "First of all, it's *women*, Brad. I don't date *girls*."

Reggie chuckled.

"And second, I went out a few months ago with Carol."

Tex cocked a brow. "Isn't Carol the name of your dad's Shelby?"

Busted. "Well, maybe. But that mustang is classic."

Brad groaned. "You need therapy."

"Vella keeps me company," Mack tried to defend himself. Lame, but it was all he had. He hadn't dated in a while, and he didn't know why. It wasn't for lack of offers.

"Vella is your car," Reggie said slowly, as if to explain to an addled mind. "Cars aren't people, Mack."

"Oh, shove it. You guys are so damn chipper all the time. It's beyond annoying."

He glared at them, three men so different yet brothers all the same. They'd been in the military years ago. Brad and Tex had been Marines. Reggie had done time in the Navy, and Mack had served in the Air Force.

Of the four, Mack considered himself the best-looking. His light eyes and muscular build definitely put him paces in front of the rest, though the ladies seemed to like them all well enough.

Brad had sandy hair, skin that tanned surf-bum gold in the summer, a rugged build, and muscles that almost rivaled Reggie's. He might as well have had the words "Responsible and Reliable" tattooed on his forehead. Reggie, with medium-brown skin and a smile that killed at ten paces, gave off that strong but silent heroic vibe. One look at him and you knew he'd protect you from Godzilla. Tex, a good old Southern boy, had been quite the ladies' man before he'd settled down. A funny, smart guy who always had your back, he had dark hair, bronze skin, and a "tall, dark, and gorgeous thing"—his words, not Mack's—going on.

Mack's best friends had all coupled up. And he felt left out. Plain and simple. But he couldn't tell the guys that, or they'd try to set him up, which for some reason felt like cheating in the game of life. Was he so lame he needed help finding himself a girlfriend?

Reggie studied him, a dimple appearing. "Yep. I told you guys. Little fella needs a lady love."

"Up yours." Mack glared.

Brad nodded. "Avery has a few friends."

"Bree does too."

"See?" Mack shoved his chair back and grabbed a beer from the cooler in the corner of the room. "This is why I don't talk to you guys about stuff. You think I need your help. Hell, if I want a girlfriend, I'll find one."

"A boyfriend, maybe?" Brad said. When Mack scowled at him, he held up his hands. "Whoa. Not judging, Mack. Just here to be supportive."

Tex snickered. Reggie tried to muffle laughter.

Mack sat back down and sighed. "Shut up, Brad. If I wanted a guy, I'd have Alec hook me up. My brother acts like he knows everyone in the gay community in this town."

"Mr. Social Butterfly," Brad teased. "So why are all your brothers, us and the bio bros, all dating or engaged and you aren't?"

Mack pounced. "Hold on. You proposed to Avery? Reggie had the stones to ask Maggie to marry him, and Tex is barely holding on to Bree with both hands, so we all know that's too soon."

Tex frowned. "Hey."

"I mean, we know you guys are making a baby, but I didn't think you had it in you to actually propose," Mack finished, grinning at Brad.

Brad's face turned pink, and he leaned forward to whisper, "Not yet, asshole. At Christmas."

Suddenly conscious of the quiet from the living room, Mack raised his voice and said, "What? Avery isn't treating you right? She did what?"

The women appeared in the dining room in seconds with Avery wearing a big scowl aimed at Brad. "What lies are you telling, Bradford?"

Mack chuckled. "I knew you three were eavesdropping."

Bree shot him the finger. Tex's golden girl had an attitude to go with her model-gorgeous good looks. Mack liked her a lot. Just the way he liked shy but sweet Maggie and fierce Avery, reporter extraordinaire.

"Next time we need to have poker night at my place," Brad muttered.

To which Tex added, "No girls allowed."

Bree chuckled. "Mack's such a shit starter."

Avery agreed. "I love that about him. But Mack, we overheard enough. We'll find you a new friend."

"No, I—"

"In the meantime, you guys are boring." Avery kissed Brad on the lips, just long enough to put a deeper flush on Brad's cheeks. "We're heading out. We'll see you guys at home. Not mine, I mean, at our respective places."

Mack didn't act relieved to have his friends to himself, but he saw something in Avery's eyes he hadn't expected. Empathy and understanding. Which made him feel two inches tall.

"No, you guys should stay." *God, don't leave because of me. I'm not that much of a killjoy.*

"Nah." Bree shook her head. "We can't talk about stuff with you guys too close."

"Oh, girl secrets." Tex wiggled his brows.

Maggie grinned. "Yeah. Reggie has big ears. I can't say anything without having to pay for it later."

"You got that right." Reggie smiled at her. "I'll see you later, okay?"

She nodded. Her daughter was spending the night at her father's, so at least the kid's virgin ears would remain innocent away from game night.

Seeing how much his friends loved their girlfriends, Mack felt terrible for wanting them to leave. "You guys should stay."

"Nope. See you losers later." Avery laughed and left, ignoring Brad's scowl that turned into a grin.

"You'll pay later, woman."

Once they left, everyone turned to Mack.

Brad nodded. "Okay, now we can speak frankly."

Mack sighed. "You weren't doing that before, Brad?"

"This is a man-tervention."

Mack sighed again.

"In addition to the asthma you've suddenly picked up," Tex drawled, "we've noticed some concerning things."

"One, you don't talk as much in the truck," Reggie said. He and Mack typically partnered together when on medical duty, two EMTs per aid vehicle, as opposed to all four of them manning the engine when on engine duty.

"I thought you always said I talk too much," Mack said.

"You do," Brad agreed, "but that's part of your charm."

"Thanks so much."

Apparently not reading that as sarcasm, Tex nodded. "Exactly. You're not mouthing off as much, you're not dating, and you seem off."

"Off?"

Brad explained, "Not as wacky and laid-back. Which isn't like you. Are your parents and brothers giving you crap for something?"

As they typically did. "Not any more than normal."

"Is Alec's upcoming wedding stressing you?" Reggie asked. "Weddings stress everyone."

Mack noticed a look on his friend's face. "I think you're project-ing. You nervous about *your* wedding?"

Everyone turned to Reggie. Thank God.

"Nah." Reggie cleared his throat. "Well, maybe. I mean, I love Maggie and Emily."

"Hell, everyone loves Emily. That kid is six going on forty-five. She's so smart she's scary."

Reggie nodded. "She's one amazing little girl. But this is a big step."

"Your family loves them. You love them. What's the problem?"

"What if I screw it up? I'm really in love. I'm afraid she'll leave."

"Oh my God." Mack smacked his friend in the head.

Reggie rubbed his head and glared.

"Reg, Maggie isn't Amy. Your ex is a loser. Sorry to say it, but it's the truth. She used you. Maggie's not a user. She's good people. And Emily is too smart for her own good. She needs you to keep her in line."

Reggie lost his glare. "Well, that's true."

"And come on," Brad interjected. "Have you ever seen Maggie smile any wider than she does when she's looking at you?"

"Well, no." Reggie took a deep breath and let it out. "But I just don't want to make more mistakes. I mean, I'm engaged. That's a big fucking deal." He turned to Brad. "You'll see."

"When is the big day?" Mack asked Brad, surprised his friends could feel so off-kilter when they had women who clearly loved them. Apparently, being part of a couple didn't cure you of being an idiot after all. "You said Christmas?"

"No, that's when she'll be expecting it. I'm taking the week off between Christmas and New Year's. I'll ask her on the 27th."

"That's kind of specific," Tex said. "You sure she'll say yes?"

Mack laughed.

Reggie and Brad glared at him, and Brad said, "Not helping, Tex."

"Oh, come on. Avery loves ya. She's a sure thing."

Brad shrugged. "A sure thing doesn't mean I won't screw something up somehow. I've done it before."

"True." Mack recalled each of his friends having fits and starts with their girlfriends. "You know, you've all nearly screwed up your relationships. You really have no call to be lecturing me."

"You don't get it because you're not in a heavy relationship yet,"

Brad said. "Come to think of it, have you ever been so in love you thought about getting married?"

"No." Huh, how about that? "I mean, I've dated. Not anything too serious. I liked playing around."

"Liked?" Brad asked.

"Well, yeah. You guys acting all dopey is making me think I might want to find someone more permanent. I mean, not marrying-permanent. But girlfriend-permanent."

Reggie held up a hand. "For the record, we're talking about a real girl, right? I'm sorry, real *woman*. Not a blow-up doll or car? Nothing with wheels?"

Mack gave him the finger, which had the guys laughing.

"I happen to have my eye on someone, as a matter of fact."

Brad and Tex looked at each other before Tex held out his hand. Brad planted a five-dollar bill on it.

"What the hell?" Mack waited for an explanation. Considering the guys bet on everything, he should have known he'd be a hot topic at some point.

"It's the mean chick." Tex nodded, studying Mack. "The sexy cop who nailed you at the game."

"Oh, she's way out of your league, son," Reggie said with a wince. "Sorry, truth hurts."

"Excuse me?"

"Not looks-wise. You're even there. She's just more aggressive than you can ever be."

Brad agreed. "She's got a reputation on the Top Cops. She's a brawler. And she looks it."

"But a beautiful brawler," Mack stated. "Did you see her slide tackle? Soccer's not my favorite sport, but even I had to admit she nailed me with precision."

"That's true." Tex's eyes sparkled. "Took you down like a prize heifer. So if you like looking up at her, letting her lead the relationship, you'll probably do okay."

"Oh please. It's not like I'm weak or... Why are you all shaking your heads?"

"You're too nice when it comes to women," Brad said bluntly. "Not Reggie-nice. We all know he's a pushover."

Reggie scowled. "Thanks a lot, *Ken*."

Brad ignored him. "But gentlemanly nice. And that won't cut it with Officer Aggressive."

"I'm nice, but I'm sneaky," Mack said, defending himself. "I'll charm my way past her defenses. Then we'll see who's tackling who."

"I think you mean *whom*."

"Naw," Tex said. "It's *who*."

Reggie broke out a book on grammar—what a geek—and while the crew argued, Mack thought about what they'd said. Just how devious would he have to be to worm his way into Office Carmichael's good graces?

Oddly, just thinking about her put him in a great mood. He cleaned the guys out before they all left in huffs filled with threats and blind date suggestions.

"I'm not dating anything with hooves or antlers, Tex," Mack yelled before gunning down the street in his prized Chevelle.

Now with renewed purpose, he committed to trying to find a way to get Cassandra of the mighty soccer legs to go out on a date. And without asking her anywhere near his brother, Xavier, who worked in her precinct. That would be the real trick...

Thursday night, Mack and Reggie rolled up to a bar fight in Aid 45, which was essentially an ambulance that belonged to Station 44, not a hospital. As an EMT, Mack could do basic life support, handling minor injuries. He couldn't push drugs, but he could patch up scrapes, splint sprains or breaks, and assess for further medical assistance, where he'd take the patient to a hospital.

Tonight, they'd been turn and burn since after dinner. He could tell they had a full moon because the crazies were out in full force. Like at this bar, where a fight had broken out between five drunken idiots over who had the best drink.

Mack turned to the bartender as they waited for the bouncers to get the fighters separated. "So who won?"

"I did, but the winning group gave the title to her." The guy nodded to the woman still serving a crowd away from the mess. Broken tables, chairs, bottles, and glasses littered one side of the bar, near the back entrance, fortunately. "Personally, I make a killer Long Island iced tea. But the winner was a boilermaker." In a lower voice, he confided, "That whiskey is for shit, you ask me. Especially combined with a Budweiser. I mean, seriously?"

"Good to know." Reggie shook his head. "Me? I'd have gone with a classic. Whiskey sour or a mojito."

Mack sneered. "More like low class. I'd have gone Moscow mule."

"That's what I said!" one of the assailants slurred, overhearing Mack.

The woman next to her said, "Bitch. You have no idea what you're talking about."

The fight heated up again, but it quickly settled when the police arrived.

And low and behold, Mack watched sexy Officer Carmichael and her giant partner scowl their way into the bar from the back door. When Carmichael saw him, she blinked in surprise before pretending she hadn't recognized him.

Reggie leaned in to ask, "Isn't that—"

"Yep." Mack's grin went up in wattage; he could feel it.

While Carmichael and her partner took statements from the bartender and witnesses, Mack and Reggie started helping the injured. Mostly bruises, a few lacerations—one that might need stitches—and a sprained ankle the inebriated patient continued to blame on his friend, the boilermaker winner.

As Mack continued to apply bandages to the open cut on the drunk guy's head, Carmichael came over to talk to the miscreant.

"Your name is Buddy Echols?"

"Oh, a pretty cop. Nice." He gave her a thumbs-up.

Mack bit back a grin at Carmichael's sigh.

"Buddy. Echols. Yes?"

"Yep."

"License please?"

He managed, with Mack's help, to get his wallet out of his pants pocket.

After Carmichael verified his information, the man explained how astonished he'd been at the quality of his drink. Which had led to some friendly competition with his friends over who had the best order.

"And that devolved into you five beating the crap out of each other?"

"Betty started it!" Buddy pointed to a petite blond sitting in a dress covered in her own vomit. She had crazy curls half-plastered to her head and a swollen left eye that would grow darker with time. "She slugged me. See this?" He pointed to the blood crusting his ear.

Mack started attending to it, gloved up and loving the way this Thursday night was shaping up.

"She bit me," a petite brunette slurred.

Mack paused, exchanged a glance with Carmichael, then continued to bandage Buddy. It took another twenty minutes before he and Reggie had finished attending to everyone. While Reggie helped two of the more amicable patients needing care into their med unit, Carmichael's partner put three of the others into the back of their squad car.

Mack and Carmichael stood in the back lot between both vehicles, watching.

"Nice uniform," Mack said.

She turned to him with a glare. "Excuse me?"

"It's not dirty, like your soccer uniform was. This one looks nice and clean. You managed to steer clear of Betty's vomit. Nicely done."

Carmichael gave him a rare grin. "I noticed you got lucky too. Though your boots are pretty crusty."

"Yeah. I stepped right into a puddle of Bud and vermouth, apparently. Spiked with blood and saliva. Good stuff."

She looked Mack over. Lingering on his shoulders, perhaps?

"Offer's still open," Mack said, conscious of her partner and Reggie within hearing distance.

"Oh?"

"If you ever need help getting clean."

Her partner's head shot up, and he narrowed his sights on Mack.

Carmichael snorted. "You're still an idiot."

"Although maybe we should go out this weekend instead. To settle a bet."

"A bet?" Her eyes turned frosty, well, colder than the light snowfall of gray coming down.

"To see which drink is the best. Betty really has no idea what she's talking about."

Officer Carmichael blinked. "She doesn't?"

"Hell no. Moscow mule is the real winner. Or a White Russian if you're into Kahlua. Are you?"

Out of the corner of his eye, Mack noticed her partner smother a grin. Reggie poked his head out the back of the aid truck. "Hey, Mack, we need to go. Get your flirt on faster. You can drive. Buddy's telling me about a bet he made with Elvis concerning snakes, vodka, and a waffle iron." The back door closed behind him.

Carmichael's partner sighed and said, "Yeah, Cass. We need to get back and get out on the street again. Especially before one of these drunks in the back throws up in the car. It's a full moon all right."

Mack nodded at him. "Right? This one's worse than last month. The stories I could tell you..."

The cop narrowed his eyes. "You look familiar."

"Well, not only did I kick your partner's ass on the soccer field, but my brother works in your precinct. Xavier Revere. I'm Mack. The smarter, better-looking brother."

"Ah, right." The guy grinned. "Jed Karsten, Cass's amazing partner. Who's going to get his ass reamed when she puts them both behind. She'll have to talk to you later."

"She should, but she won't. She's scared of her feelings for me. And, well, we did kick your ass last week. So maybe she's scared that no matter what we play, she won't be able to keep up."

Cass gaped. "I—what?"

"Yeah, I'm a lot to handle for most women. I thought you might be able to deal with my competitive nature. But I guess not." Mack made a sad face. "Sorry, Cass. Maybe some other time."

"You wish." She fumed and turned on her heel.

Jed looked back at Cass and said, "Seriously? You're going to let a firedog make you run scared? Challenge him to pool or darts or something. Tomorrow night. I'll back you up."

Cass turned to look at Mack, not seeing the thumbs-up Jed shot him. "Fine. Bessie's Bar at seven Friday night. Try not to be late, Revere."

"Oh, I'll be there. But will you?"

"With bells on," she muttered.

"Anything else?"

"Huh?"

"Just bells? Or shoes and a hat? Pants, maybe?"

He heard her partner laugh before she slammed into the car, and they drove away.

"Mack, hurry up," Reggie yelled from inside the truck.

Mack scooted to the driver's-side door and let himself in. As he drove them to the hospital, he heard Reggie ask, "So then Elvis put the snake where? For real?"

Elvis danced with snakes. Cass Carmichael had said yes to seeing him again.

Talk about a crazy night.

Chapter Four

CASS COULDN'T BELIEVE HER PARTNER HAD TALKED HER INTO schmoozing—make that slumming—with Mack Revere. Jed knew her stance on interoffice dating. No peer dates. No peer-*association* dates either.

Yet Friday night, she found herself drinking a beer, nervous and not sure why, as she waited with Jed by a pool table.

She considered Bessie's Bar a go-to place to relax. The food and drinks weren't too expensive but still tasty. It wasn't a cop bar, college hangout, or hookup joint. Her feet didn't stick to the floor, and the funky music stayed quiet enough that she could talk without having to yell to be heard. Regular people who liked to relax, shoot pool, and watch sports filled booths and tables. Hardworking, blue-collar types mixed with the occasional corporate suit. It felt comfortable.

Normally.

She sipped from the longneck in her hand and worked to calm her jitters. "I can't believe I'm here."

"Don't knock it. I finally managed to find a way to get Shannon off our asses." Jed grinned, proud of himself.

"So this has nothing to do with me and everything to do with you and your wife."

"Yep. This way, Shannon sees you having a social life, so she'll stop trying to set you up. I don't hear crap from you or her. Win-win! And let's be real. Since you'd never want to go out with a firefighter—"

"It's not that he's a firefighter. It's just—"

"—you aren't really on a date since I'm here with you," Jed finished. "Technically, you should count this as a competition. You can handle a contest with some lowlife fireman. Hell, beat him at darts or pool to make up for that mess last Saturday. You can do that, can't you? You beat me at bar games all the time."

"But you suck."

Jed glared. "You're buying the next round."

She sighed. "Sorry, but it's true. It's not exactly a secret, you know."

Jed lined up a shot and ended up sinking the cue ball instead of his intended red. "I'm good. That was just bad luck."

"More like a bad shot," she muttered and pretended she didn't see him moving around the balls to find a better angle when he went again. Another perk to playing one of Jed's "practice rounds."

As they took turns sinking the balls, or, in Jed's case, missing them, Cass realized she enjoyed hanging with her friend, excited to challenge others. Her blood hummed, and her smile continued to upstage the normally flat expression she'd perfected long before joining the force. She'd always been a loner and more serious child despite what her parents thought.

Her father had always encouraged her to be herself, not a person others wanted her to be. So why did he keep nagging her to date? To socialize with anyone not Jed? Because here she was with Jed, having fun, and she felt good about it.

"Dad was practically dancing with joy when I told him I had plans tonight," she said to Jed.

He shook his head. "Still on your ass to get married and give him grandkids?"

"Yeah, only he never acts like that's what his nagging is all about. It's about me being healthier by having a life outside work and you."

Jed blinked. "Me? What do I have to do with you being a disappointment?"

"Ass." She quelled laughter at his smirk. "My dad thinks I'm sublimating a desire for intimacy by using you and your family as a substitute for familial affection."

"It's like you're channeling Dr. Aaron Carmichael right now." He took a step back. "For a second, you almost sounded smart there."

"This from a guy who can't stay away from one little white ball in a field of solids and stripes."

He frowned. "That's a matter of skill, not intelligence. Although a smarter man would know to steer clear of a game he's never been any good at."

"Well, I'm not going out to play tackle football with you in the parking lot."

Jed grunted. "Your loss."

"Did someone mention football?" Mack Revere asked as he approached their table. Dressed in jeans and a plain navy-blue sweater under an open jacket, he looked like sex on a stick. "Because I'd be into challenging the Top Cops to a *real* game instead of soccer-for-losers."

Jed blew out a breath. "Amen, brother. But the league is filled with a bunch of weak whiners who insist on keeping injuries to a minimum. It would have to be flag football instead of tackle. I've tried before."

Mack looked up at Jed and cocked his head. "Well, for those of us without all that beefed-up muscle, I have to admit I wouldn't want to be knocked over by you." He paused. "That's if your lumbering ass could catch me to hit me."

"Oh, I'd catch you." Jed pounded his fist into his hand.

As much as Cass enjoyed the testosterone-laden byplay, she'd been ignored long enough. She cleared her throat. "Why yes, Mackenzie Revere. You should be honored that I actually showed up. You're welcome."

Mack gave her a dazzling smile she had to work not react to, tamping down all that panting and staring and sighing. "Cassandra

'I'm a Hard Ass' Carmichael, as I live and breathe. You look lovely as usual."

The bastard got her cheeks flushing. She could feel them heating. "And your prettiness is beyond compare," she said back.

Jed guffawed.

Before Mack could respond, his friend joined him. She recognized the guy from the soccer field. The tall one with the Southern twang. "Hey, now, don't start without me." He wore a black Stetson, a Seahawks T-shirt that lovingly clung to his chest and arms, and jeans with biker boots. She'd rank him right up there with Jed but slightly less good-looking than Mack.

Mack made the introductions, and she learned Tex hailed from Texas. Small wonder.

She gave a subtle glance to the guys suddenly surrounding her, realizing she stood in a group of manly men who would totally make her the envy of many women she knew. Including Shannon.

She stood back and snapped a quick selfie, making sure to get them in the background.

Mack blinked. "What was that?"

"Proof of life before I take it away."

He frowned. "I have witnesses that heard you say that."

Jed chuckled. "Oh, she means that she'll be stealing your dignity. After she mops the floor with you at pool."

Tex tilted his hat back and grinned. "Yeah? You want to bet on that, big guy?"

Jed stood maybe an inch taller than Tex. So big *guys*—plural—made a better description. Mack had leaner muscle and stood a few inches shorter. Still over six foot but not a giant, which made her more comfortable around him. Heck, she'd be able to reach up to drag him close if she wanted to plant a kiss—

Put him in a headlock, she quickly corrected. *Jesus, Dad is right. I need a life if I'm even thinking of locking lips with stud muffin Revere.*

He quirked a brow at her. "Thoughts in that pretty little head?" He gave her a sly grin. "Scared?"

"Of making you cry, yeah."

He laughed.

Tex grinned. "I like her."

"She's not kidding. She's pretty good at pool," Jed warned.

Mack shrugged. "I'm not too shabby either."

"Okay, then, go ahead and rack 'em." Cass nodded at the pool table. "Ten bucks says I can take you in three games."

"Oh, you're on. Eight ball?"

She nodded.

He racked the balls on the pool table. "Yo, Tex. Grab me an ale and an order of nachos. Jed? Cass? You guys want something?"

She felt funny hearing him call her by her first name but ignored it. "I'm good, thanks."

"I could use something to eat," Jed said. "I'll head over to the bar with Tex. What do you think about the team this year?" He asked, nodding to the Seahawks logo on Tex's shirt. "Pretty damn good, yeah?"

She didn't hear what Tex said back, watching Mack size up the table. He looked comfortable as he positioned the balls correctly. A little *too* comfortable. She saw him eyeing up the play after he set the flat end of the rack parallel to the end rail of the table, making sure the top ball of the triangle centered on the table's foot spot.

"Are you planning to hustle me?"

He chalked his pool cue. "Me? Do I look like a hustler?"

"Yes."

He grinned. "Didn't need to think about your answer, huh?"

"You look tricky."

"I think the word you were looking for is 'skilled.' Or maybe 'spectacular.' 'Gorgeous.' 'Breathtaking.' Yeah, that's probably it."

She rolled her eyes.

"No, no, you meant 'superior.'"

She snorted. "'Superior'? You wish."

"Well, that remains to be seen." His devilishly handsome grin made it tough to focus anywhere else. "But I notice you didn't object to 'breathtaking.' And you wonder why it's so hard to be me. There's only so much of me to go around."

"Oh my God. Stop talking."

He chuckled.

She glanced at the bar to see Jed and Tex still chatting as they drank and waited on their order. Jed hadn't been lying about not considering this a real date because he'd clearly left her on her own with Mack. Typically, when they hung out, he hovered like a mother hen if a guy so much as twitched in her direction. Big brother to the extreme.

She took the pool stick Mack handed her and lined up to break. She hit and managed to sink the one ball—a solid.

"Nice break," Mack said. Then ruined the compliment with "Run with it while you can."

What an ego. His pride made her that much more determined to crush him. She did pretty well, sinking two more balls before the last one just missed hitting the corner pocket.

Mack looked serious as he concentrated on the game. He stretched his neck and shoulders before taking position behind the table. And then he managed to sink the rest of his balls, followed by the eight ball, which he called.

"Son of a bitch."

He blinked, all innocence. "Ready for our second game?"

"Fine. You break this time."

"A pleasure, Officer."

She wanted to smack him with her stick, not sure why she felt equal parts annoyance and amusement. Cass hated to lose at anything, but Mack clearly knew how to play the game. That she could respect.

"Want me to move slower so you can see what I'm doing? It might help you."

"Shut up, Revere. Just handle that stick like you mean it."

He didn't look at her as he muttered, "I always handle my stick like I mean it." Then he glanced up and smiled. "Watch." He stared at her while he broke, and the smack of the balls as they raced around the table drew her attention.

A striped ball went in.

"You got lucky," she groused, wondering what new and wonderful adjectives he'd use to describe his play.

Jed and Tex approached with a tray of food and pitcher of beer in time to overhear Mack boasting, "Lucky? More like freaking amazing. What a talent! That's what you're really thinking. It's okay. You can say it."

"Damn." Tex sighed. "Thought I'd missed most of his jaw-jackin' by hangin' at the bar."

Jed chuckled. "What game is this?"

"Our second," Cass said as she watched Mack study the table before sinking another ball. "And before the chatterbox runs at the mouth, I'll just let you know he won the first game."

"Annihilated her." Mack sank another.

She frowned. "You did not. You got a few nice shots in is all."

Fortunately, after putting the third ball in the side pocket, he managed to miss his fourth ball, so she got her turn. She sank all but the eight ball, taking her time with the last one and staring Mack in the eye for a few moments to try to psych him out.

Except he was grinning at her, not at all upset about maybe losing.

"I'm not sure what I'm seeing," Jed murmured to Tex. "Is my partner just about to whip his ass or what? Is this staring contest part of the bet?"

Shut up, Jed. This is crucial to my win.

Mack snorted. "She's just trying to get in my loop." Mack tapped his forehead. "Because if she misses, she knows I'm going to end her. Then our last game will be out of pity because I'll have already taken her money and made her cry."

Jed laughed. "Cry? Nothing makes Cass cry. Not even when she stepped on a LEGO tree and nearly broke her ankle tripping down the stairs."

She grinned. "Last time I babysat for you, wasn't it?"

He shook his head. "I don't blame you. Those fucking building blocks have even made me cry."

"I'm not gonna lie. That hurt like a mother."

Jed chuckled. "I know. But don't worry. Shannon got the kids in line. Ever since you nearly took that header, no playing on the stairs. Period." He said to Tex, "My wife doesn't mess around. The kids and I do what she says."

"I hear ya." Tex pushed back his hat. "My girlfriend looks sweet as pie, but she's a total ballbuster."

"She really is." Mack smirked at Cass. "Though I don't know if she's as mean—or sweet-looking—as Cassandra." He winked as he looked her over.

But she knew better. She ignored that smolder and said, "Eight ball, left corner pocket." She sunk it.

"Damn." Mack was still smiling. "Best out of three, I guess."

"That's right."

"I'll rack 'em."

She watched as he worked, liking his hands. Long, graceful fingers, large palms, and he had the dexterity to move with quick, concise speed.

Jed nudged her. "Beer?"

Since she'd been nursing her first that had probably gone flat, she put it on the bar table next to them, where Jed and Tex had been standing, and nodded. "Sure. Who bought the tower of onion rings? I thought you were getting nachos."

Jed shrugged. "Thought you could use some motivational calories."

She snorted. "Yeah, right. You bought them for yourself, but you'll tell Shannon later all the junk food was my fault."

"Well, yeah."

"Why not just tell her you didn't buy food that's bad for you?" Mack asked.

"Because," Cass answered for Jed, "one, Shannon can smell a lie from ten feet away."

Jed nodded.

"And two, Jed doesn't like lying to his wife. He did kind of buy it for me." She took an onion ring and groaned. "Oh man. I really hate you. You know how much I love these things."

Mack was looking at her in an odd way, so she wiped her mouth, hoping she didn't have ketchup smeared on her lips.

He glanced down at the table and cleared his throat. "You ready?"

"Bring it, Revere."

"I was born ready."

Tex shook his head. "Such a hack."

"Hey." Mack frowned at Tex then took aim and shot at the racked balls. This time nothing went in, so she got a chance to take the lead.

She was doing fine until she heard Mack laugh. She glanced up to see him grinning at her partner, and the clear joy on his face took her aback. Sure, she liked the look of him. Mack was handsome. No doubt. But laughing, smiling, he was absolutely gorgeous.

Cass put her head back in the game, but her hands hadn't gotten the memo, and she missed the next shot.

So *of course* Mack started sinking the balls one by one. He happened to look up as she was taking a sip of her beer, with Jed trying to give her advice on how to play.

"You can do it, Cass. Don't give up. We never give up when it comes to beating a firedoggy."

"That hurts," Tex said, laughter in his voice.

Mack shook his head. "Maybe she could beat me at boxing. I can see her having a mean right hook. And we know she could crush me at soccer. That slide tackle still burns. But at pool? No way."

Cass tried not to, but Mack made her laugh. "Show me what you got, chatterbox."

He gave her a look she couldn't read. "You sure? I don't want to embarrass you in front of your partner."

Jed snorted and muttered, "Dead man talking."

Tex just grinned.

Cass shrugged. "You're wasting my time. Either shoot or let me finish winning."

He seemed to come to some decision and turned back to the table, sinking two more balls before calling the eight with an impressive bank shot. Extraordinary playing, actually, attested by the small crowd gathered to watch his final shots. Once he won, the small gathering clapped and whistled.

Mack took a small bow before approaching Cass with his hand out. "That'll be ten dollars, Miss." He smiled though he held himself ramrod straight.

"That's Officer Carmichael to you." Cass did her best not to snarl. Or laugh. "But we're not done."

Mack raised a brow as he relaxed and leaned back against the table. "Oh? Double or nothing?"

"At darts." She nodded to the board currently occupied by a couple flirting with each other.

"Finally." Jed stretched. "Our turn, Tex. Let's play."

"You sure, bud? Because my guy just whooped your partner, and I'm gonna crush you with my skills. That'll put us two over on you lonely, sad little men and women in blue."

Jed straightened and gave Tex his cop glare. "Let's go. Ten bucks on best of three."

Mack chuckled. "Easy money."

"No kidding," Cass said, trying not to be too loud.

Unfortunately, Jed heard. He shook his head. "Where's the loyalty?"

"Jed, you said something earlier about being a smart man?"

"Ha," Tex removed his hat and slapped it against his thigh. "Smart man? This guy don't know a good running back from a good quarterback."

"I can make you eat this stick," Jed growled.

Tex didn't have the sense to laugh, though she could tell he was just yanking Jed's chain. "Please. You and what police force?"

Mack put his hand on the small of her back to nudge her away. "Come on. While my buddy is getting in your partner's head-space, we have a date at the dartboard. But my darling officer, I'm a wizard at darts as well. You really want to lose ten more dollars?"

"It's double or nothing, so that's twenty you'll owe me." Cass might have lost at pool, but they didn't call her Deadeye for nothing. She couldn't wait to show Mack just what she could do.

Chapter Five

MACK DIDN'T UNDERSTAND IT, BUT HE WAS LOSING TO CASS Carmichael. Badly. The king of pub games suddenly found himself down by…well, by a lot. Though he liked to win, losing to Cass didn't bother him at all.

The more Cass showed how good she was, how competitive, the more she turned him on. So weird. He'd never been into super-aggressive women, not that Cass was *that* bossy. But he'd swear she didn't have a passive bone in her. Not that he could tell, and he'd been subtly studying that fine body since he'd come upon her and her giant partner over an hour ago.

He watched her nail his coffin as she hit another bull's-eye.

"Damn, Cass. I'd say you have some anger issues the way you throw those darts," he said just to needle her.

But she only laughed and jotted down her winning score. "Sucker. Pay up."

They hadn't talked much as they'd played. She'd competed with intensity, dedicated to the game. He'd done his best as well, concentrating on the board when not watching her lean forward, emphasizing the power in her arms, the sleek contour of her lovely breasts, the amazing curve of her ass and those powerful legs encased by tight jeans.

Hell. He felt uncomfortable, hard and doing his best to rein in his desire. But who could blame him? She'd worn her hair down, the silky black mass curling over her shoulder to cover the top of one full breast. Cass was built like an athlete, compact, tight, and toned with muscle but having a woman's soft curves in all the right places.

"Ah, I'll be right back. Gotta hit the head," he said, meaning the bathroom.

Cass understood, cop talk and military talk too similar not to.

He hadn't been lying, having consumed a fair share of beer and some of the nachos Tex had ordered. But he'd left Cass to her onion rings, pleased enough to sit back and watch the pleasure on her face, imagining how he might get her to look that way. In his house, in his bedroom, without their clothes on.

After taking care of business and washing up, he left the restroom and started down the dim hallway back to the bar. And ran into Cass, leaning against the wall. Waiting for him?

"Is this a shakedown?" he asked.

She smirked. "Why? You going to cut out on me?"

"Maybe." He patted his pocket and realized he'd given his cash to Tex for his share of beer and food. "Um, I might have given your money away earlier. I bought the food with it. But I'm good for it, I swear."

She didn't look amused.

"Wait. Do you seriously think I won't pay you?" Had she really been waiting for him outside the bathroom? That was a little weird.

"I don't trust men who smile all the time."

He purposefully let his smile drop.

She didn't react.

"But—"

And then she *moved*. She slammed him up against the wall, her arm across his throat, not hard, but firmly keeping him in place. He let her, curious to see what she would do and more than happy with anything that eliminated the space between them.

So close he could smell the beer on her breath, and he felt thirsty for a sip.

She stared up at him, her eyes bright. "You think you can stiff me out of my win, eh?"

Stiff you? Oh, hell, yes. He blinked. "Er, ah, no. I'll pay you. I promise."

She looked from his eyes to his mouth and stayed there. "Well, how about a first installment?"

Before he could ask what the hell she was talking about, he felt her lips on his.

Mack froze, wondering if perhaps he was imagining what he'd been dreaming about for days. But, no, Cass Carmichael was kissing him, her eyes closed, her lips soft, waiting for him to respond. Apparently, she didn't like to wait because her tongue slipped between his lips, drawing him out of his haze.

Mack groaned and kissed her back, trying to get closer despite her forearm, which she finally moved to pull him closer, her hands behind his neck. Not close enough though. In seconds, he turned them around and had her back to the wall, pushing closer to plaster his mouth against hers, conscious not to press for the full body hug he wanted for fear of breaking the spell she'd cast.

The taste of her sent his entire body into a tailspin, his dick like steel, his ability to breathe caught up in inhaling the intoxicating perfume of Cass herself. Then she moved her hands to his waist and yanked, and his body met hers.

Heat licked from his mouth down to his balls, the feel of her breasts against his chest burning him from the inside out. And then she shifted, and his groin notched perfectly against hers, their heights more than compatible for what he had in mind.

Unfortunately, Cass shoved him back and stared, wide-eyed. "Whoa. You're lethal."

He wanted to grin and say something smart, but he just stared at her like a jackass, unable to put a thought together.

"Okay, Revere. That's a down payment on the interest you're accruing." She gave him a snotty look that had him aching to reach for her and give her what they both wanted. And, no, that wasn't him acting arrogant. The frustrating woman was staring at the fly of his jeans and smiling. "Well, the jury's still out on how amazing you really are. But I'll take that twenty when you have it."

The door behind her opened, and a woman walked out patting her hair. She smiled at Mack and Cass and walked away.

Cass entered the ladies' room, the snick of the lock loud in the otherwise-empty hallway.

Mack blinked. She'd been waiting in the hallway for the bathroom. Yeah. That made more sense than that she'd been waiting to accost him in the hallway for her money. Except he wanted desperately to pay her everything he owed. Twenty dollars and then some.

He walked back down the hall, not wanting her to see how badly she'd shaken him yet not ready to rejoin the guys now sitting at a table by the back, arguing about something. Holy fuck, but Cass had shaken him. He'd known they shared some chemistry. At least, *he'd* felt it. But after that kiss, there could be no doubt she'd felt it too.

Her nipples had turned to hard points against his chest, and he'd sworn he'd heard her sigh into his mouth. But to just push him away? She'd gone straight into the restroom. Like him, she'd consumed her fair share of beer. Oh hell. Had she been drunk?

He wasn't. A few beers spaced over a few hours were nothing to his weight and metabolism. But maybe Cass had been a little loopy. He'd have to wait and see how she acted when she rejoined them. Should he be with the others to make things easier for her? Would she be upset after realizing she'd kissed him? She didn't seem shy. Not that he knew too much about her. For all that they'd spent time together, their concentration had been on games, not on getting to know each other better.

The blasted woman had refused to talk to him while playing.

And then she'd kissed him in the hallway while waiting to use the restroom.

Mack groaned.

To his dismay, Cass found him leaning against the wall, staring at the middle of the bar but seeing nothing.

"Kissed you into oblivion, huh? Rocked your world, I bet." She gave him a superior look.

God, I want her. But he knew enough to understand that if he acted besotted, she'd probably toss him back into the pond with all the others who worshipped at her feet. Nope. Cass Carmichael liked a challenge. Best to pretend indifference before showing her how much *she* really wanted *him.*

He shrugged, playing it cool. "Just wanted to make sure your drunk ass got back to the table safely."

She scowled, her gray eyes like diamonds, glinting with anger. "Honey, my ass is far from drunk. And I can protect myself from any of the people in here just fine." She took a step closer and poked him in the chest. "Including you."

He ignored the ache between his legs. "Easy, killer. Just trying to be a decent guy. I mean, I was just mauled in the hallway. You never can tell who's dangerous around here."

Instead of looking abashed or giving him the upper hand, she laughed. "You make a good point." Then she linked her arm through his. "Let me help you back to your table, sweetie. It's okay. No one here is going to hurt you."

A few guys nearby heard her and laughed.

Mack didn't find her so amusing anymore. Though he couldn't argue her sex appeal. "You're kind of mean, aren't you?"

"Yep. What clued you in?"

They arrived at their table to see Jed and Tex staring at them, no doubt misconstruing how close they'd gotten.

Mack pulled away from her and leaned back. "Honestly, Cass. I'm not a toy for you to play with, you know. If you're so sex starved, find someone else." He moved his chair from next to hers and parked himself between the guys, forcing them to move over.

She just stared at him while Tex laughed his fool head off.

Jed, proving he had a sense of humor, shook his head. "Cass, how many times do we have to have this conversation? We do not grope strange men in public."

Mack smirked back at her.

She sighed. "I hate all of you." She pointed at Mack. "You especially." She paused, and her lips quirked. "You big loser. That's right, guys. I have restored my reputation. I trounced him at darts."

"True," Mack agreed. "She did trounce me. And then she threatened to break my arm if I didn't pay her." He rubbed his forearm, pretending it still hurt. "I'm filing a complaint."

"Get in line," Jed muttered.

"I heard that," Cass said. She and her partner shared a grin.

And Mack couldn't take his eyes off her.

Until Tex smacked him in the back of the head. "Ow."

In a low voice, Tex said, "Trust me. That dopey look won't do you any favors."

He replayed what Tex had told him earlier before they'd arrived. *You want the girl? Play it right. This one doesn't do nice and sweet. Show her you can meet her halfway. Remember that slide tackle, son. Carmichael plays for keeps.*

So Mack did as he'd been cautioned to and continued to tease Cass in between talk of football and working in the city, the highs and lows and dealing with crime.

And all the while he thought the *real* crime had been that he and Cass hadn't finished what she'd started in the hallway. But he knew to bide his time. He could be patient.

When she looked up at him, he winked. She blushed, then dragged a finger across her throat in warning.

He laughed, excited about how many ways she might think to punish him, starting with a kiss or two.

Cass didn't know what had come over her at the bar, but she'd had just about enough of Mack Revere and his alluring grins, hot blue-eyed stares, and *very* fit body. She couldn't blame her actions on alcohol. She didn't drink to excess, never willing to let go of herself in public to the extent she'd do something stupid.

Like kiss a forbidden, firefighting playboy.

As she pulled into her driveway and parked, she took out a napkin from her pocket and stared at the writing on it. She'd watched Mack tuck it into her jacket right before she'd left.

He'd left his number and a short message. *Let me know where to drop off your $20. Unless you prefer a wire transfer.*

Such a smartass. She felt herself smiling and flushed, recalling how he'd felt against her, how he'd tasted when she'd kissed him.

Cass groaned and leaned her head on the wheel. What had she been thinking to kiss Mack Revere? Unfortunately, he'd been as charming as she'd suspected he might be. Had she not pulled herself away from him earlier, she might have done a lot more with him in the *hallway of a public bar.*

"I'm such an idiot," she lamented as she dragged herself inside her small but charming home.

After locking up, she readied for bed and set the napkin on the kitchen counter. She needed space from thoughts of a man who'd made her react despite herself.

She should throw the napkin away. She didn't need twenty dollars that badly. Because, honestly, Mack Revere had trouble written all over him. Heck, they weren't even alike except for the fact they both played to win. She was serious. He joked around a lot. She was a cop. He fought fires for a living. She… Cass snuck a peek at the note again, not surprised he had bold, clearly legible handwriting. She'd bet his home was orderly, neat. They probably had that going for them. And Mack might like to have fun, but she'd seen him at work, where he had treated patients and been kind yet professional. Smart, flirty, but at heart, most likely decent.

Perhaps she should call him to tell him not to pay up. Let him know to forget about it.

No. She didn't need to hear his voice. But she could text him to let him off the hook. Yes, she'd do that.

They'd had fun, and now it was over. She'd end things that had no place beginning. Yet somehow she found herself texting him her address in addition to letting him know he could drop off her winnings tomorrow morning around nine if he wanted.

Seeing his thumbs-up emoji in response, she stared in horror at what she'd just done. Now, not only did Mack have her phone number, he had her address as well.

She set her phone aside and refused to look at it again before she did something even worse, like invite him to send some selfies she could drool over in bed.

Flushed and feeling stupid, Cass blamed her father for getting her so obsessed with dating. Then she blamed Jed for pushing her to go out with Mack—and Tex, not a date—in the first place. And because she wasn't being rational, she decided to blame Great-Aunt Martha too, for leaving her a house with an address she'd given Mack.

Feeling like a big dope, Cass settled into bed and tried not to think about Mack possibly swinging by in the morning.

But as the minutes passed and she remained wide awake, she started arguing with herself about why seeing Mack would necessarily be a bad thing and ignored the danger signal lighting up her brain.

Cass had always had a strong will. She and Mack obviously shared an attraction. She hadn't missed that bar in his pants when they'd been kissing. And she sure as heck liked him. He'd even tasted good. No bad breath, no forceful handling of her. Mack had been at first tentative, letting her lead, then naturally taking over the embrace. And, wow, could he kiss.

How bad would it really be if they hooked up? She was a grown woman with a grown woman's needs. Mack didn't work with her, and so what if he ever told Xavier they'd had sex? She and Xavier weren't partners. She'd be damned if she'd act the nun so her peers wouldn't think her a slut. Screw that. Women could have sex whenever they wanted with whomever they wanted. It sure didn't hurt the guys' reputations when they took home women they barely knew after a night on the town.

She continued to come up with valid reasons why she and Mack should have sex, from relieving stress to defying patriarchal stereotypes keeping women virginal pure. Until she finally tired herself out and fell asleep.

═══════

The next morning, Cass was in the middle of dusting when a knock came at the door. When nine o'clock had come and gone, she'd figured Mack wouldn't show up and swallowed any disappointment she might have felt. But she couldn't deny the butterflies in her stomach as she moved toward the front door and saw Mack's face through the upper door lite.

He smiled at her through the windows, and she gave him a half smile back, not sure she liked how happy she felt that he'd shown. Then he waved a twenty-dollar bill at her, and she had to laugh as she opened the door.

"Paid in full," he said as he handed her the bill.

"I see that." She looked at it carefully while subtly studying him from the corner of her eye. He wore jeans and an open coat showing a button-up flannel shirt he hadn't tucked in. A shadow of beard showed he hadn't shaved. His hair looked neat but a little mussed, as if he'd run his fingers through it. The unkempt Mack Revere, unfortunately, looked even more appealing than regular, cocky Mack Revere.

"What?" He narrowed his gaze on her.

"Just checking to make sure the twenty isn't counterfeit."

He huffed. "Please. I can afford to lose twenty bucks. I'm not poor." He smirked. "I'm not a cop."

"Hilarious." Out on the porch, she noted a small paper bag and coffee cups sitting on the table to the side of her front door. "What's that?"

"A bribe to get me in the front door."

A kiss would get you that, no problem. She cleared her throat. "What kind of coffee?"

"I didn't know if you were a coffee drinker, so I brought one coffee and one cocoa. And there are pastries from Sofa's in the bag. That's why I'm late. Huge line at the bakery."

"I don't think I've been to Sofa's."

He blinked. "Seriously? They're the go-to in Seattle for baked goods."

"Huh. I'll have to try them." She grabbed the bag and let him bring in the cups, belatedly feeling the cold. She shut the door behind him. It seriously felt like it should snow outside. "So where's Sofa's?"

"Green Lake, right off the lake, as a matter of fact."

"You went all the way to Green Lake for doughnuts?"

"Pastries. And don't judge until you've tried their apple fritters."

"I'm sensing you have a sweet tooth, Revere."

He followed her past the small, enclosed dining area into her galley kitchen, making no effort to hide his curiosity as he looked around. "Neat, compact, organized. Just like you." He turned that panty-melting grin her way.

To save her dignity, she took one of the cups he carried and took a cautious sip. "Cocoa. Yum."

He drank from the other one and made a face. "Do you have any creamer?"

"Lightweight." She grabbed him some hazelnut-flavored half-and-half. "This is all I have."

"It'll do." He stirred a healthy amount into his cup and took a sip. "Ah, much better. Do you have a plate for these?" He nodded to the bag.

She grabbed a plate and turned to see him staring at her butt. "Caught you."

"Staring at the amazing countertop." He nodded. "Is that ceramic?"

"Formica." He had been staring at her ass. Hadn't he? She handed him the plate and watched as he took out a lot more food than she'd thought the bag might contain. "So, do you live in Green Lake then?"

"Huh? Oh, no. I'm Hillman City. Just east of you." He grinned. "Neighbor."

"Ugh. I think I just felt my house value decrease."

He chuckled. "This place is cute. Are you into house projects?"

"I would be if I had the time. It's a constant work in progress." She settled with him in the dining room at her cozy table and set down their plates.

He took two pastries and put them both in front of her. "You have to try the apple fritter, then the danish."

"Pushy."

"I grew up with three older brothers. You don't push, you don't get respect."

"Huh. I'm an only child."

"I can tell."

She frowned at him.

He just waited.

She bit into the apple fritter first, and wonder exploded in her mouth and brain simultaneously. After chewing that bite and several more, she managed, "That's amazing."

"Told you." He was cute when smug and polished off his fritter and two pastries in the time it took her to finish savoring her apple fritter. He watched her, a curious expression on his face.

"What?" She swallowed down sugar with more sugar and

wondered when she might go into diabetic shock. Wow, the food was good, but geez, she'd fulfilled her quota of carbs for the day.

"Oh, ah, nothing." He sipped more coffee.

"Just say what's on your tiny mind."

"If I do, you'll slap me."

"Oh, now I have to know."

"You sure?" He leaned back, a smirk on his face. "Because I don't want you hitting me or calling me a pig. I can't help where my mind wanders when I look at you."

"Just say it."

He sighed. "Never mind. It's crass, and I'm trying to impress you."

"With sugar and caffeine?"

"Well, yeah. Is it working?"

She really wanted to know what he'd been thinking. "Tell me."

"What?"

She gritted her teeth. "Tell me what you were thinking. You had a weird look on your face."

"You have to promise not to hit me."

"I won't."

"Or be offended."

"I can't promise that." What the hell had he been thinking? "I have a thick skin, Revere. I won't bolt at the mention of something crude."

"Mack, not Revere. I don't want you confusing me for my annoying brother."

"Fine. Mack." She'd play along.

He sighed. "I was just thinking that you're beautiful, and that face you were making when eating… Well, I wondered if you make that same face when you orgasm."

She stared at him.

He stared back.

Then she decided to be bold and asked, "Would you like to see?"

Chapter Six

MACK STARED, WIDE-EYED, AND WONDERED IF HE'D HEARD what he thought he had. "Excuse me?"

Cass rounded the table and pulled him to his feet. "Do you want to see if I make that face when I come?"

His heart raced, and he swore he could hear his heart racing. "Is this a joke?" He waited for her to lull him with those bedroom eyes, then slug him.

"Look. We kissed last night, and it was pretty good."

"No, it was spectacular."

She smirked. "You and your words. Anyway, you wanted me then. I'm getting the impression you want me now."

"You would be correct." Funny, but for someone who had his libido racing like a freakin' greyhound, she sounded way too rational and robotic about a possible booty call.

"So let's do it."

"It?"

"Have sex. No expectations of anything but having fun right now. Yes or no?"

He wanted to joke about needing some time to think about it. Or phoning a friend for advice. But he in no way wanted to ruin his chances with the woman haunting his dreams. "Hell yeah. But I need to know what your rules are." A woman like Cass would have a ton of conditions. He could feel it.

She smiled, and he wanted to kneel at her feet and bask in her hard-assed beauty. "Good point. One, you wear a condom. I'm clean, but I don't know about you."

"I'm clean, but a condom works, yeah."

"Two, I'd appreciate if this stayed between us. I'm a little old for kiss and tell, but guys seem to want to brag."

"Not a problem. I never hit the bang-and-boast phase of puberty."

She laughed. "Good. And third, we don't get weird. You don't get possessive."

He was already feeling that. "Yeah, and you don't get clingy."

She seemed to consider that before agreeing. "Perfect. Just some good old-fashioned sex."

"I was going to say fucking, but okay."

She laughed. And Mack realized Cass hadn't been lying. She didn't seem bothered by coarse language, not as sensitive as other women he'd dated. But then they weren't dating. This would be a one-time-only deal, from what she made it sound like.

So he had to do better than his best to ensure he got another chance to impress her. "Anything you don't like?" he asked.

"Um, not really." She blushed then glared at him, as if holding him responsible. "Let's just get back to what we were doing last night and go from there."

"Okay." He took off his jacket and hung it on the chair behind him. Then he took off his boots and socks. "Do you want me here or over there?"

"Huh?"

"You know, for when you jack me up against the wall then take advantage of me?" he teased.

She turned a brighter red, which made him laugh.

"Smart ass." Cass crooked her finger, and he followed her through the small living room to a short hallway facing three doors, one in front of him and two on the side. In front lay a bathroom. Cass took him to the larger of the two bedrooms.

Bright sunlight streamed through opened blinds that she closed.

"No show for the neighbors," she murmured. She stopped in the middle of the room and waved her hand. "This is it. My bed. My bedroom."

The bed had been neatly made. No clothing on the floor, everything in its proper place.

"I see that."

"Well? Get naked."

He laughed, pleased when she frowned. She might have instigated this encounter, but no way was he going to let her lead the action. "Hold on, Officer Sexy. I want to see that O-face. We need to do things my way."

She rolled her eyes. "I don't need a seduction, Mack. I already want you. Let's get to it."

He found her straightforwardness delightful. "Cass, you take my breath away."

"You're a lot of talk."

"Oh ho. And a blow to my ego." He unbuttoned his shirt but left it on, pleased to see her eyes widen as she stared at his naked chest. "Before we get started, do you have any condoms?"

"You didn't bring any?"

He shrugged. "I honestly came over to pay off my debt and bring you a treat. Not that I don't consider my dick a treat, but I intended to feed you something else."

She barked a laugh. "Oh yeah, *you're* a treat. Especially if you think I'd be up for eating some of Mack Junior."

"I didn't think that. That's why I didn't bring a condom. I didn't come over to sex you up. Not that I'm complaining." Actually, he did have a condom or two in his car because a guy should always be prepared. But he didn't want to say he had any or she'd think he'd intended something he hadn't. Mack wanted her like crazy, but he also wanted to show her he was more than a one-trick dick. So to speak.

"Oh." She grabbed a packet from her nightstand and tossed it to him.

He walked past her to put it on the nightstand. Then he turned and backed her to the bed.

When she saw what he'd done, she scowled.

Before she could take charge, he kissed her. And like before, touching her lit up his entire body like the Fourth of July. She groaned and relaxed into his arms, her height perfect. Not too small, but not too tall. He didn't have to do more than lean close and angle his mouth over hers.

She tasted sweet, like cocoa, and he wanted badly to taste more. To taste all of her. Would she mind?

Her hands were rough. He liked them. A lot. She touched his chest and biceps and ran her hot hands down his abs to flick the top snap of his jeans open. Fuck, she made him hard.

Mack reached for the hem of her sweatshirt and lifted it off her, only to see her in nothing but a white lace bra and lounge pants. A wet dream of a woman if ever he'd seen one. Cass had a toned body with a flat stomach. On hell, he could see lines in her abs.

"Shit, woman. You're cut."

"I work out." She sounded defensive.

"Hell, yes, you do. Stop touching me or I'll come too soon." He just stared at her, in lust.

Apparently realizing he liked her looks, she relaxed and smiled. "Like what you see?"

He cupped himself. "You're kidding, right?" Then he wasted no more time and got Cass naked. Mack shimmied out of his jeans, unable to take his gaze from her body.

He left his boxer briefs on, needing something to slow him down. He hadn't been kidding. Being so close to a naked Cass had done as much to arouse him as touching her did. He drew her down on the bed, positioning her flat on her back underneath him.

The moment their bodies touched, from chest to groin, they both froze. Then she wrapped her arms around his neck and yanked him in for a kiss.

Mack wanted to slow down, but he couldn't stop as she devoured his mouth, grinding up against the hard ridge between his legs. He felt himself on the verge of coming, hearing her breathy moans and teasing her tongue as he felt her steal into his mouth, taking his prized control.

So he forced himself back and turned her onto her belly.

She froze. "Mack?"

"We need to slow down," he told her, trying not to sound so out of breath. "Unless you want me coming in my underwear."

She snickered. "No staying power, eh?"

"Laugh it up." He knelt over her, giving himself some respite from the pressure on his cock, and kissed her shoulders, her back, down to her ass. He rubbed her muscles, learning her body as he eased the tension out of her frame one stroke at a time.

While doing so, he eased out of his underwear, not surprised to find himself slick with need. Then he rolled Cass back over, pleased to see her eyes half-closed. He leaned over her to grab the condom. Only to freeze when he felt her hands around him.

"You're pretty big." She sounded surprised. "I mean, wow."

"I think I should feel insulted you thought me small," he said, breathing hard. "But I don't care right now."

She chuckled as she stroked him, her hands firm and torturous, pumping him. Then she stopped and cupped his balls, and he couldn't help pushing into her touch.

"*Fuck.*"

"So pretty. Just like the man himself." She licked her lips, and he swore it took all he had inside him to stop from begging her to scoot down and suck him dry.

Instead, Mack shakily donned the condom then pulled himself away from her.

He needed her out of control so he wasn't the only one lost in lust. He refused to let her take charge again. Mack kissed his way to her shoulders, then to the slopes of her breasts while he caressed the firm globes.

"Oh, yes," she moaned as he finally reached her nipples, sucking one bud into a taut peak. He nipped with his teeth, and she arched up into him with a cry. So he continued to tongue and teethe her while she whimpered. His dick ached, so hard he feared exploding.

But Mack needed more. "I want to taste you," he growled, groaning when her fingers sank into his hair, gripping him to hold him in place.

"T-taste me?"

He glanced at her face and saw the passion there, the same pleasured expression she'd had earlier. He smiled. "I bet you're even sweeter than Sofa's."

She blinked and flushed. "Um, okay."

He kissed his way down her belly, gently spreading her thighs wider. A thin strip of hair guarded her sex, and he closed his eyes as he kissed his way to what he wanted most.

"Oh, God. *Mack*." She keened as he sucked and licked her to a massive orgasm.

And as she came, he slid up her frame and entered her in one swift push. He saw stars as she gloved him tight like a fist, letting him feel so damn much. He pushed deeper into her, thrusting faster, harder, as her body clamped down on him. Mack couldn't stop as he took her, the pleasure so extreme he was aware of nothing but Cass as he found his release.

He groaned her name as he poured into her, the ecstasy all-consuming.

When he finally regained his senses, he felt her shivering beneath him, still caught in the aftershocks of passion.

"God, Mack," she rasped.

He had to catch his breath before responding, "Yes, I am a god."

She tried to laugh, but the chuckle caught in her throat and turned to a sigh. "I feel so good."

"You do. You really do." He leaned up and rotated his hips, feeling another jolt as he spurted into the condom. "Cass." He had to kiss her again.

She kissed him back, but not with the urgency she'd earlier shown. Her kisses were tender, calming him down, until he pulled back to look down at her. They remained joined, and he was half-hard. Hell, he'd be ready to go again if she gave him a little time.

But a flash of caution appeared in her eyes, and he knew to be ultra-careful with her.

"I think you broke me," he teased, though part of him spoke the truth. The sex with Cass had been phenomenal and woke up the rest of him needing more. To know her as a person. To spend time with her, to make her fall in love with him.

The thought should have scared him straight.

It didn't. Which he found interesting. And that might be a problem because he had a feeling he'd gone about this all backward. They should have gotten to know each other *before* having sex. Then they could call it making love and ease into the emotion. But a guarded Cass had already given him her body. He knew he'd have to be smart and extremely lucky to get her to bare her soul.

Mack centered himself in the now. With one more kiss, he pulled out and hastened to the bathroom to dispose of the condom. He returned to find her lying stark naked on the bed. "Damn, girl. Just…damn."

She grinned at him, not bashful or tense as he'd figured she might be. "That's how to spend your Saturday morning."

"Not doing chores?" He watched sadly as she dressed, forcing him to do the same.

"No, doing Mack Revere." She winked at him.

She smiled. She teased. But he sensed a distance that hadn't been there before.

"So, Cass…" He paused, determined to keep things light and lift the sudden tension in the room. "If I say something about having just paid off my debt in full or that I can technically count myself as prize winnings, are you going to lock me up?"

She tried to glare at him, but a smile stole her thunder. "Very funny, Revere."

"*Mack.* Like I told you, I wouldn't want you to confuse me with my much less handsome brother, Xavier."

"Trust me. I'd never confuse you two. Ever."

He grinned. "I hope not."

She snorted. "No way I'd ever sleep with Xavier. He's a dog."

"Right?" He followed her out in search of his socks and shoes. "I know you didn't ask, but I haven't been with anyone in about four months. I wore a condom then too."

"Good." There. She turned pink again. Cass was shy when it came to talking about sex? How sweet…and unexpected.

He finished putting on his boots and stood. "What about you?"

"Me?" she squeaked and tried to hide it with a cough.

He forced himself to keep a straight face. "Well, health is something we both take seriously. It's a legit question."

"True. I haven't been with anyone in a while."

"A while?"

She frowned, which oddly amused him. "A year and a half, okay?"

He stared. "But why?"

"Why?"

"Yes, why? You're hot as fuck," he said bluntly and thought she might have liked that because her expression turned shyly pleased. "And you're funny."

"You think I'm funny?" She looked flabbergasted.

"Yeah. And you like sports. You have the trifecta of woman gold. I'm surprised you're not married with five kids already, to be honest."

"You and my dad," she muttered before clearing her throat. "I love being a cop. Work comes before relationships, and a lot of guys can't handle that."

"I hear ya." He sighed. "Work is my everything right now. When I'm not working, I like hanging with the guys."

"Not your family?"

"Well, no. I love them, but we're all very different people. I'm a fireman. They're all cops. I mean, *all*. My mom still works in admin, my dad's retired, and my three brothers are still active."

"I know what you mean. Both my parents are healthcare workers, and I'm in law enforcement."

"But you care for people."

"I do, but it's not the same."

They looked at each other. She blushed again, though he wasn't sure why.

Seeing her so open, so beautiful, he wanted her even more now, something strange gathering in his chest as he watched her. But before he could figure it out, she was literally pushing him toward the door and shoving his jacket at him.

He laughed as he resisted, making her work harder. "I take it this means I'm not invited to move in? No short engagement?"

"Shut up." She chuckled. "And stop pushing back against me. If I let go, you'll fall."

"Nah. You're strong. You'll catch me." But he did straighten and walk to the door. Before he opened it, he turned and gathered her in his arms. "One last kiss before I go? And Cass, you don't need to worry about me kissing and telling. This was just for us, okay?"

She seemed to believe him because he could see the smile in her eyes. "Okay."

He kissed her, and like before, fireworks blazed between them. But Mack understood what she wouldn't say—that today had been more than she'd expected. It had been a lot more than he'd expected, at any rate. And he needed to figure out his next move.

Mack pulled back, gratified by her shortness of breath. "Okay, Officer Carmichael. I expect you to put me in your little black book. You know my number now." Then he added what she'd find hard to forget. "I just want to be clear—I'm now ahead by one."

He smirked, left the house, and had started his car when she knocked on his window. He rolled it down. "Yes?"

"Nice car, by the way," she said, studying his classic Chevelle. Another point in her favor—she knew class when she saw it.

"Thanks. You needed something?"

The wind blew, and Cass tossed her hair back and scowled.

Mack refused to believe he could fall in love on the spot, but damn, he pretty much came close. What was it about this cantankerous woman that enthralled him so much?

"What the hell do you mean you're ahead by one? You stopped by to pay me twenty bucks, remember?"

"Yeah, I paid you back. But after what we just shared, I think we both know I came out ahead."

She looked puzzled, and he deliberately remained silent, adding to the confusion. "Hold on. Are you saying I somehow lost at sex?" She frowned. "Sex isn't a sport."

"It is if you do it right. And we were both pretty damn amazing just minutes ago."

"We were." She paused. "Wait, wait. How are you ahead by one?"

He grinned and revved his engine. "Think about it. I'm sure it'll *come* to you." With a chuckle, he rolled up his window and backed out of her driveway. He waved as he left.

But in the rearview, he saw her standing there, watching until he rounded a corner and drove away.

Operation Bait Cass Carmichael was in play.

Mack spent the remainder of his morning thinking about Cass and the amazing sex they'd had before putting his mind right and joining Reggie and his ladies for lunch and game day.

Cass stared after Mack as he left in a vintage muscle car that fit him. Stylish, sleek, and all muscle. She still had a tough time getting her feet back under her after that bone-melting orgasm. Mack Revere had earned every single compliment he'd ever gotten about sex. Then again, she'd almost made *him* lose control. If they had been playing some sort of sex game—which they hadn't—then wouldn't she be the winner?

His comments about winning bothered her for the rest of the day and on the drive to her parents' for dinner.

She hadn't had sex for a long time, at first too busy to bother with a man, then worried she'd never find one who could keep up with her or let her lead the way.

Yet with Mack, she'd been content to step back once he'd taken charge. Huh. She wondered why she'd let him. She hadn't thought too much about their dynamic. Typically, Cass set the pace. She'd been the one making the rules, taking charge. And Mack had gone with all of it…right up until they'd had sex.

Who knew the laid-back guy had it in him? She surely hadn't. And she hadn't been kidding when she'd been surprised about his size. Not only a looker, but he knew what to do with what he'd been given. She still tingled, remembering how he'd brought her to that massive climax.

Part of her had wanted to keep him in her bed and try it again to make sure they hadn't been a fluke. She hadn't had sex in a while. An orgasm might happen from desperation, right? She didn't have a ton of exes, but she knew when a man fit. Mack fit her. Physically, at least.

Now she'd have to see if he'd agree to their terms. No possessiveness. No clinginess. Just that one instance of rip-roaring ecstasy for them both. Nothing more. Right?

Her father called her name again. "Cass? Honey, are you all right? You seem out of it tonight." He heaped another helping of beef stroganoff onto her plate.

"Oh, sorry." She felt ridiculous, still musing over Mack Revere and his gorgeous eyes, perfect body, and big dick.

Her dad frowned at her. "What's wrong?"

Oh my God, no more thinking about body parts in front of the parents!

"I lost at pool last night."

He seemed to lose a little steam. "Oh. I thought you might have had a date."

Once again, she had let down her parents. But this time, Cass knew she hadn't. Because she and Mack had connected, if only on a physical level. That qualified as a social bond, didn't it?

"Well, it was kind of a date."

Her mother reentered the dining room with a pitcher of water and froze. "Wait. You had *a date*?"

Great. Now Cass would have to run with her date-that-wasn't-a-date. Her mother grinned like a loon, and her father looked ecstatic.

Cass cleared her throat. "Well, I met a guy at Bessie's. You've been there. It's not a dive bar or anything. I hang out there with friends a lot."

"With Jed or Shannon, you mean," her father said, and she could hear the tinge of disappointment in his voice.

"Right." Her mom frowned at her father and poured her a glass of water. "So, you liked him?"

"We hit it off. He beat me at pool, then I beat him at darts. And he wasn't a sore loser." Mack had been pretty decent about it all. Even about the kiss she'd stolen in that darkened hallway. "He's nice. We might go out again." Huh. How about that? Not a lie. Even after all his nonsense about beating her at sex—*please*—she honestly wouldn't mind seeing him again. *Wait. Does this mean I'm becoming clingy?*

"What does he do for a living? Where does he live? How—"

"Aaron," Jennifer said loudly, then said to Cass, "Your dad is just happy you met someone. Aren't you, dear?"

Her father started and with a nod apologized. "Sorry. I think it's great you met someone. Even if you don't go out again, making new friends is healthy. Even better if the man you met is unattached. Maybe financially independent. That never hurts. I'm just saying," he added when Jennifer gave him another look.

Cass bit her lip not to laugh at how hard he was trying to keep his questions to a minimum. Her mother met her glance and rolled her eyes.

"Oh, stop," Aaron grumbled. "You know I can't help myself when I get on a dating kick. Go ahead and laugh. I know you both want to."

Her mom coughed into her hand, unsuccessfully hiding her amusement. "Honey, give her a break. You complain because she never goes out. She's going out and having fun. We're not so old we'll die before we get grandchildren. I mean, I'm fifty-six years young."

"And don't look a day over forty."

"Flatterer."

Cass could deal with their flirting if it meant they left her alone.

"I will admit I'm a little curious," Jennifer said to Cass. "Will you go out with your new friend again? I'm not pushing, just asking."

Passively pushing, more like. Cass forced herself to sound casual when her thoughts about Mack were anything but. "I'm not sure. He was nice." And smokin' hot in bed. "He's funny. I'm not committing to anything. But maybe."

Her parents exchanged a glance she ignored.

"Anyway, just a reminder, but I go back to work tomorrow. I'm not off again until Thursday."

"Your father and I have a fancy dinner to attend this coming week. But if we can't meet up, we'll definitely meet you the following week. And then of course for Thanksgiving."

"I'm working the twenty-eighth. But we can celebrate the Wednesday before, if you want."

"That works." Her mom left to make a note on the wall calendar she kept in the kitchen. For someone who worked with the latest technology, she was surprisingly low-tech at home.

Relieved her parents weren't going to guilt her for working the holiday, she spent the remainder of her evening enjoying being with family, trying not to think about how happy they seemed because she'd gone on a simple date.

Or that maybe the festive mood had more to do with *her* bright happiness. Which had nothing to do with her morning. No. Nothing at all.

Chapter Seven

SUNDAY AFTERNOON, MACK SPENT A FEW HOURS WITH THE guys. They exercised at the station gym, where they normally spent much of their off time. Though Mack enjoyed being away from work, he genuinely loved his job and *most* of the people he worked with. Since the fire station had a decked-out gym, he and the guys willingly spent their fitness time there.

He'd just finished a set of triceps curls when an unfamiliar face tried to start a heated argument with Reggie. Not wise. The old Reggie would have handed the guy his liver on a platter. The new, fun-loving and chill Reggie—since he'd fallen for an amazing lady—stood like a statue, his massive hands planted on his hips, likely so as not to strangle the guy.

"I was waiting on the bench," new guy growled. He stood maybe an inch taller than Reggie and in a tank top and shorts showcased serious muscle. Odd, but Mack couldn't place him, and he knew everyone in the station. Maybe he was training with Station 44 for some reason? In any case, he was acting like a major dick.

"Roid rage?" Mack offered and received a few laughs.

"Good one, Revere," one of the crew on D shift said.

The guy turned from Reggie, his beady eyes narrowed. "Revere?" He sneered. "Who the fuck is talking to you?"

"Did I ask?"

"What?"

Brad snorted. "Mack, leave him alone. Let Reggie handle him."

Annoyed no one seemed to be taking him seriously since Reggie had turned to lie down on the bench and started pumping with one of the A shift guys spotting him, the rager instead focused on Mack. "Hey, little guy, I'm talking to you."

Mack turned back to Brad. "Brad, he says he wants you."

Of the two of them, Brad had more height and brawn, and Mack's comment brought more amusement from the crowd now focused on the new guy.

Who seemed to grow even angrier at being the butt of the joke. He took two steps in Mack's direction, stopping directly in front of him. "Do you know who I am, shithead?"

Silence claimed the gym. And that took talent because getting a dozen firefighters to do anything at once, even quiet down, wasn't easy.

Reggie sat up on the bench and cocked a brow. His approximation of *Need help?*

Mack answered with a subtle shake of his head.

Brad crossed his arms, looking less than pleased that some jackass was messing with *his* crew. *As if we all belong to him,* Mack thought with amusement, conscious that, like the rest of his friends, he let Brad lead because the guy was naturally good at it.

Tex ambled next to Brad and watched. "I was telling Nat the funniest thing, and we got distracted." Behind him, Nat chomped on her gum and grinned at Mack. "What's goin' on?" Tex glared at the angry guy. "For fuck's sake, Templeton. Ease up. You just got here."

"No one's talking to you, redneck."

"Who *is* this guy?" Mack asked, still ignoring him as he directed his question to Tex.

Tex answered with a sigh. "Ben Templeton. He's just training with us for a while." In a lower voice, he added, "Governor's nephew, I think." But not related to his lieutenant or chief.

Good. When Mack wiped the floor with the dickbag, he wouldn't get in as much trouble.

"Ease up, Templeton," Tex said. "Connections don't mean shit in Station 44."

A collective groan went up, and Templeton's face turned bright red. Before he could turn that aggression on Tex, who would return it tenfold, Mack intervened. "Look, man. We all get along here. Even no-neck Washkowski."

Wash scowled. "Hey."

Nat grinned. "He called it…No-Neck."

Others laughed and teased Wash while Templeton grew even more livid, obviously aware he didn't belong and wouldn't with his attitude.

"I'll cut you a break." Mack felt for the guy. "Around here, bigger isn't better."

"You would know, Mack," Nat taunted.

Wash laughed at that.

A good one, but Mack was trying to make a point. He cleared his throat and had to look up at the red-faced monster glaring at him. *Ready to coldcock me if I'm not careful.* "We're off duty and chilling out. Save all that testosterone for the job. And try to be more gracious. We're a family here."

"And every family has its black sheep," Templeton said as he telegraphed his next move, shifting his weight.

Standing in the middle of the gym and trying to start a fight was beyond stupid. Even if the guy landed a punch, he might trip over a bar or stack of weights. Or worse, bump into someone who would then hurt themselves in the middle of a rep. The guy reached out.

Mack simultaneously stepped aside and caught the guy's fist, using Templeton's momentum to take him down and try not to hurt anyone. He had Templeton flat on his stomach and muscled the man's arm behind his back, his control of Templeton's shoulder and elbow keeping the man in place. The whole move took maybe four seconds. Fortunately for Templeton, he narrowly missed a face-plant into a thirty-five-pound plate.

"Like roping a baby calf," Tex exclaimed. "I'm makin' you a quarter Texan for that, Mack."

"You lose, Mack," Wash taunted. "Who the hell wants to be from Texas?"

The rest of the gym was busy making fun of Tex as well as Templeton.

"What the fuck?" Templeton said, muffled against the floor. "I was reaching for the bar by your head, asshole."

Mack leaned down to murmur in a low voice, "We both know you were reaching for my head. You lost. Now, are you done playing I'm bigger and badder?" He shifted Templeton's wrist higher on his back, causing painful tension in the elbow and shoulder joints.

Templeton moaned and nodded, his cheek kissing the floor-mat. "Yeah, yeah. Sorry."

Mack moved back to let him up and jumped to his feet. "I may be small, Nat, but I'm spry."

"To me, you're all giants," she said with a frown, saving a wink for him.

They stepped away, the guys congratulating Mack on his take-down when another sudden silence settled over the gym. And not a good one.

Mack turned to see B and D shift's lieutenant, Sue Arthur, along with their battalion chief standing in the doorway.

Crap.

Sue scowled. "Revere, McGovern, with me."

"What the hell did I do?" Tex muttered and shuffled behind Mack as they joined Sue and the battalion chief—who happened to be the father of Tex's girlfriend—into Sue's office.

Typically a sweetheart with balls of steel, Sue was a petite yet strong woman who managed two shifts of firefighters with ease. She had short brown hair and a cute face, and everyone respected and loved her. So much so, they included her in their many station pranks. Thus the plethora of Dora the Explorer stickers all over her notebooks and papers, since she resembled the titular charac-ter a little too well.

Mack spied one on her notebook by the phone and quickly looked away, catching the battalion chief's eye. The older man bit back a grin, and Mack figured he wasn't in too much trouble.

Instead of lighting into him, Sue grinned. "That was a beautiful takedown."

Tex's future father-in-law smiled as well. "I have to say I enjoyed that. Ben Templeton's a real thorn in my side, but I'm doing a favor by giving him a shot here. Mack, nice job."

Mack didn't know if he liked the battalion chief remembering his name.

Tex sighed. "I told you Templeton wouldn't fit in here. We're gold. He's a piece of shi—"

"*Tex*." Sue shook her head. "I think he just needs help finding his feet."

"You mean the ones I took out of his mouth?" Mack asked with a high five from Tex. Too bad Sue didn't find the humor in that.

"You're lucky he didn't brain himself on the equipment."

"Hey, come on, LT. Mack didn't start it," Tex said, defending him.

And that, right there, was why Mack loved his job. He had real brothers who backed him up.

The chief sighed. "He's got a point, Sue. Look, Templeton's not going to last here. I think we all know it. But no one can say it's because we stuck him in the worst department in the city."

Mack agreed. Hands down, Station 44 did the job and did it well.

"I really appreciate you taking him on for me, Sue."

The lieutenant groaned. "For how much longer?"

"Give it another two weeks. Why don't you tack him onto C shift and make him Ed's problem?" Lieutenant Ed O'Brien commanded both A and C shifts—of which Mack's crew was a part. "In fact, I insist." The chief grinned at Tex, who swore under his breath. "Let Tex help him adjust."

"Aw, man. This is about bowling last weekend, isn't it?"

"Is it?" The chief slung an arm around Tex and walked him out of the office. "Let's have a chat about that, son."

Mack wanted to laugh at his friend's discomfort.

Sue did it for him. "I swear. Tex dating the chief's daughter is like a gift from heaven. Ed and I thought it would be a nightmare, but it's turned into so much fun. For me." She laughed again.

"Me too." Mack waited until Sue's laughter died before he added, "I'm sorry about Templeton. I wouldn't have touched him at all except he threw a punch."

"And once again, you're my problem and I'm not even your lieutenant." Sue sighed.

"We all know how crowded and unsafe a fight would be in the gym. I'm really sorry, Sue."

"But that hit had to be satisfying, right?" She grinned. "I've been wanting to deck that prick since he got here last week. Not that I'm telling you that."

"Not that I'm hearing anything you say. I never listen."

"Yeah, that's what Ed says about you." Sue shook her head. "Say, that reminds me. Make sure you get with Ed when you're back on duty. We've been checking schedules since the holidays are nearly here. I don't think your crew has had any vacations in a while. Not that you'd get one this close to the end of the year, but still. Time off helps. Take it."

"Nah, I'm good. Besides, we don't work Thanksgiving or New Year's."

"Lucky bastard."

"Yep." Mack grinned, talked a bit more with Sue about his car, of which she was a huge fan, then left for the gym once more.

The great thing about working with his team in their fire station was the people. He wasn't lying to himself when he admitted to loving his job because of his crew. But it went deeper than that. Mack enjoyed his peers and his bosses. As much as their four-man crew teased the other crew in C shift, he would go into a fire with any of them at his back.

But he knew how badly one bad apple could spoil the barrel. It had happened often enough back in his Air Force days. A great platoon with an awesome lieutenant and terrific staff NCOs. Then a new sergeant would come in and ruin everything. They'd need to make sure nothing hampered the team with Templeton on board.

Especially since it seemed Tex would have to monitor the guy.

"Get your ass chewed?" Reggie asked.

Brad joined him, cornering Mack by the pull-up bar.

"Nah." In a low voice, Mack said, "Sue laughed, and the chief cheered us on." Not everyone needed to know about the hate on Templeton, not if the guy had a passing chance of turning good. "Then the chief said Tex could babysit the guy and walked him out of the office for some 'father-son' time."

Brad laughed, and Reggie slugged Mack on the shoulder.

"I love it so much that Tex is dating Bree," Reggie said. It hadn't always been that way, but with Bree such a terrific match for Tex and Reggie softening his views on dating thanks to his recent engagement, love was in the air.

Perpetually.

Probably why Mack kept thinking about Cass and what *she'd* think of his takedown. She'd be into it, for sure. Probably give him pointers on how to be more effective when dealing with an unruly perp. He grinned.

As a former Security Forces specialist for the Air Force, or what the other services referred to as military police, Mack knew how to handle physical conflict. In his job as a firefighter and EMT especially, that knowledge came in handy.

He wondered how much in-depth knowledge Cass had about hand-to-hand combat. She'd jacked him up nicely at the bar, but he hadn't put up any resistance.

"What are you thinking so hard about?" Brad asked, staring at him.

"Huh?"

"You have a dopey look on your face." He looked at Reggie, then they both looked at him and said at the same time, "It's a woman."

"Ha. Whatever." Normally, Mack shared everything with the guys. They knew how much he loved classic cars, that he didn't care too much about dating since women had always come easily to him, and that he would never, *ever*, indulge in peppermint schnapps and mint Oreos ever again. But getting real about Cass was different. He'd never been so lovestruck before, and it confused him.

Tex entered the gym with an annoyed expression. "Talk about a shitty day."

"Maybe for you." Reggie smiled wide. "Mack's got a new girlfriend."

"Oh?" Tex turned to him with surprise. "Didn't realize you and the sexy cop hit it off."

Brad and Reggie stared. Brad said, "Wait. The mean one from the soccer game? That one?"

"You say *mean* like it's a bad thing," Reggie said. "She was aggressive for sure. A terrific soccer player. And really, really pretty."

"I don't know I'd call her pretty." Words had importance to Mack. "Beautiful, sexy, sure. Mean in a cruel, stiletto-to-the-crotch-and-handcuffs kind of way."

"Oh, that's nice." Tex grinned. "So after you beat her at pool and she kicked your ass at darts, you two made up proper?"

"Wait, wait." Brad frowned. "What's this about pool and darts?"

"And why weren't we invited?" Reggie wanted to know.

Mack wrangled them out of the gym, not wanting to entertain Wash, Nat, and the half dozen other nosy types lingering on their every word. "Mind your business," he growled at them.

Nat and Wash whispered to each other before laughing in Mack's face. The others flipped him off or told him what to do with his "business." Just another day at the gym.

Mack smirked at the others and said to his friends, "I'll tell you at Swirlie's."

"So you're treating, then?" Reggie asked.

"Yes, you cheap bastard. I'm treating. Save all your questions for Swirlie's."

Brad and Tex congratulated Reggie on getting Mack to pay. Then they drove the few blocks to the popular smoothie and snack shop.

Mack would have walked, but the cold was killing him. Wearing shorts and a T-shirt in low-digit weather didn't help. He shrugged into a sweatshirt before joining the guys inside. Then, after paying half his monthly salary on food and drinks, they sat at a table in the back.

"Cold as a witch's ti—I mean, a witch's britches out there," Tex amended after glancing at the little kids sitting a table over from them.

The mom sniffed and turned back to her kids, then did a double take at all four of them in workout gear. Her eyes widened, and she smiled before turning back to her clamoring children.

"It's the thighs," Tex said in a low voice. "Gets 'em every time."

"More like my arms," Reggie argued, his voice low as well. "You weak ex-military types know nothing about true muscle." He eyeballed Brad. "Well, maybe not you, Brad. You lift. But the runners in the group could use a little help."

Mack loved how Reggie sneered the word "runners," likely because he had yet to beat Tex or Mack in a footrace. "I'm all about stealth and subtlety, slowpoke."

"Yeah, sure." Reggie snorted.

They all paused while two teenagers brought trays of smoothies, sandwiches, and veggie sticks.

"I'm going to have to work overtime to afford this," Mack muttered and sucked down his pineapple-mango smoothie.

"Tell us about Friday night, Tex," Brad insisted, his grin slightly demented.

"I'll tell you," Mack insisted, knowing Tex would exaggerate. "Otherwise Tex will 'spin a yarn.'"

"It was a cold winter's night." Tex intentionally exaggerated his Southern drawl, which Reggie and Brad found hilarious.

Mack shoved his face into his food.

"Friday night, while you two were schmoozing your women, I went out with Mack to Bessie's. He'd been challenged by some cops to a game of pool. Our boy here piled on the charm, but Officer Carmichael wasn't having it. I did my best to clear the way. Took her yeti of a partner with me to the bar and kept him occupied with football talk. Nice guy, but he should stick to the Seahawks. He's got no sense when it comes to the Cowboys. I mean, Coach McCarthy is gold, son. Don't think a guy can dispute that and have a brain, know what I mean?"

Brad rolled his eyes. "I wish I cared. Get back to Mack."

Before Tex could get all pissy, Reggie slapped him on the shoulder and made *there, there* sounds.

Mack did his best to hide a grin. Tex was a such a doofus.

"Fine, you heathen." Tex glared at Brad a moment, saw Brad simply stare back at him, then sighed. "Where was I?"

"It was a dark and stormy night," Reggie said.

Tex smirked. "*Raaght.*" Twang for "right." "Then our golden child, Mackenzie Revere, stepped up the plate. He whooped the woman at pool, holding back some, I could tell."

"I won fair and square," Mack protested. Sure, he could have made some trick shots, but he hadn't wanted to rub the win in her face too badly.

"But then she took him aside and crushed him at darts. That's one fine-shootin' gal, I tell you."

Brad listened with enthusiasm as he stuffed his face with carrot sticks and ranch dip. "Then what happened?"

"Well, as I was schoolin' the yeti on the proper way to talk about my Cowboys, Mack disappeared. The little lady followed him. Next time we spotted them, they were strolling back to the table, arm in arm. Then Mack told her to stop treating him like a toy because he's a real man, so he says."

Mack would not laugh at Tex's animated face or Reggie's big thumbs-up.

"Yeah, little man won her precious heart, I'm thinking."

"Thinking? Is that a new pastime?" Mack asked. "And I'm six-two, dumbass, not that little."

"Oh, you bruised his tiny pride," Brad said, which had Mack laughing despite himself.

"You're all ass…wacket knobs," he said, catching himself when one the kids next to them grinned at them, showing a missing tooth.

"Mom, what's an asswacket?" the little girl asked.

Her mother sighed. "We'll talk about it at home, honey."

"Sorry. I tried to cover my slip," Mack apologized to the mother of four. He turned back to the guys, secretly relieved when she bundled her children up and vacated the spot next to them. "Look, I like Lady Law. And yeah, she's real," he said before Reggie could ask. "She's smart and has a job."

"But she's a cop," Reggie just had to point out. "You screw her over, she'll make your life a living hell."

"Screw her over? How's that?" Mack wanted to know. Unlike Tex, he was no playboy. He'd never had a problem finding a date. He'd also never had a problem moving on. When he broke up, he did so nicely and typically remained friendly with his exes.

"I'm not implying you'd cheat on her. You're not that kind of guy."

Mack accepted Reggie's apology that wasn't quite an apology.

"But you're oblivious to long-term feelings," Brad said. "You love your job, your car, your family. You never seem to have room for much else. Your last girlfriend was how long ago?"

"A few months."

"Four months," Tex corrected. "Hey, I pay attention. Mack, you love you more than you love love. That's all I'm sayin.'"

What? That I'm a selfish asshole?

"What Tex said," Brad agreed. "Which isn't a bad thing at all. You're happy with yourself, which is why you live with little drama."

"Always a plus," Reggie said, having been through his fair share not long ago.

Brad nodded. "That's not a bad thing at all. But you being interested in a woman is great."

"You're growing up, little fella," Tex said with a grin.

"Oh please." Mack turned to each of them. He pointed at Brad first. "It wasn't that long ago you were miserable because your inability to stop controlling everything almost lost you the girl."

"Not exactly."

He turned to Tex. "You got involved with the chief's daughter after ruining how many dates with her first?"

"Not my fault. It was bad circumstances," Tex muttered, his cheeks red.

Mack turned to Reggie, who held up his hands in surrender and said, "I plead the fifth."

"Too late." Mack grinned. "You, who can't help helping, even if it's an old girlfriend who would grind you into yesterday, nearly lost Maggie when you let your ex stay with you. It's like you have STUPID stamped to your forehead."

"It was a mistake," Reggie said through his teeth. "And I learned from it."

"So how any of you think you can counsel me in matters of the heart, I just don't know."

They all stared at him before bursting into laughter.

"Matters of the heart?" Tex sputtered. "What are you? A Lifetime movie?"

"You mean Hallmark," Reggie added, still laughing.

Mack glared. "I'm *so* telling your sisters you said disparaging things about Hallmark."

Reggie paused. "Erm, no. Nadia and Lisa are being nice since I'm engaged to someone they like. I apologize, Mack."

"Ha. That's what I like to hear."

Brad punched him in the arm.

"Ow."

Brad lowered his voice. "Oh, stop being a pussy. You know we care about you. If you like this tough-as-nails cop, she must be pretty great. Because she was seriously on your ass at the soccer game. Good luck charming her. I don't think she's the naive type."

"She's not." Mack thought about her. "She's tough, generous, and funny. It's a dark humor, and she's vicious, but I'm finding that I like that about her."

"See? I told y'all. He's gone on her."

Mack blinked at Tex. "What?"

"Yeah, there it is. That same stupid look on your face when you talk about her."

Brad nodded. "I see it."

"Me too," Reggie said. "Mack, I'm betting ten bucks you seal the deal. A girlfriend by Christmas."

"I'm in," Tex said. "But I've met this woman. Twenty says he screws it up."

Mack frowned. "Thanks a lot."

"I call 'em like I see 'em." Tex tipped an imaginary hat. "But I think you'll eventually find a keeper. I believe in you."

"Asshole."

"Hey now." Brad shook his head at Tex. "Mack's better than that. He'll ruin things by Thanksgiving but make it up to her by Christmas."

"You guys are hilarious." Mack gave them a snide grin, followed by the magic finger for their eyes only.

They laughed.

Despite the jokes at his expense, he accepted the taunts. He'd done his own share of tormenting the guys when they'd been having troubles with the women in their lives.

Oh wow. Is that what Cass is? Is she the woman in my life? He'd never had one of those before. He didn't know if he should feel excited or unnerved at the prospect.

Well, she might not be his yet, but soon. "I mean, come on, guys. Cass has met me. Of course she'll be falling for me in no time. I showed her my devastating peepers." He batted his eyelashes.

"Jesus, you need help." Reggie slapped him on the back and nearly broke him.

Mack gasped and collapsed to the table. "Help…me…"

The guys laughed, Reggie especially. They thought him funny. Charming. A great guy. Oh yeah. Cass would be his sweetheart in no time. He could feel it.

Chapter Eight

Tuesday evening, Mack felt annoyed, angry, frustrated, and a host of other negative emotions in regard to a certain wolf-eyed cop too busy to pick up the damn phone. It had been almost three days since their last encounter. Cass had yet to call, text, or shout his way. He'd thought for sure that orgasm, on top of all his charm, would have convinced her to give him another shot. And, yeah, three days wasn't a lot. Except it was when he could think of nothing but the sexy, stubborn woman.

Mack growled under his breath as he patched up a distracted teenager who'd been more interested in groping his date than keeping his eyes on the icy roads. Mack fixed the gash over his eye with a bandage, while Brad, his partner for the day in the aid vehicle, saw to the boy's poor date, who looked as if she'd either sprained or broken her wrist.

"I'm so sorry, Janna. Man. My parents are gonna kill me for this," the boy kept moaning.

Mack felt for the kid, but it could have been a lot worse. This was the third accident they'd been called to, and it had only been snowing for two hours, barely six o'clock. Way too early to think they might get an easy night.

After checking over the rest of the teen, he loaded him and the girl into the back of the vehicle. Brad insisted on driving, which didn't bother Mack at all.

They took the pair to the hospital but had to wait for a nurse to check them in.

"Holy cow, it's crowded." Brad sidestepped so he didn't get run down by a pair of attendants racing after a patient being wheeled toward an OR.

"And it's not even a full moon."

"It's all the ice on the roads," another nurse said as she took the intake form Mack handed her. "Okay, you two. Come with me."

She left with the teens, and Mack and Brad set out again, driving carefully as the snow started to really come down, from pretty, soft flakes into a downpour of white that covered everything.

"Shoot. It's gonna stick," Mack said, staring around them. "It's pretty, but tonight is gonna suck."

And suck it did. They helped a man who had fallen off his roof while putting up decorations, trying to beat the rest of his block. Mack thought him a nut. Who put up Christmas lights in mid-November?

"You sure you don't want to go to the hospital?" Brad was asking.

The man hadn't broken anything, that they could tell. But he clearly had pain and flinched when he shifted wrong. He stood, pretending to be just fine in front of his children, both of whom were old enough to know that standing on an icy roof with snow coming down was not a smart move.

Mack pulled the man's wife aside. "I know he said he doesn't want an ambulance. We can't make him go. But it never hurts to do a thorough check. He hit hard, and I'm sure he's got muscle strain making him sore. But it could be something else. Watch him closely to make sure he's not concussed, and do your best to talk him into going to the hospital. We can't see what might be wrong with him internally. Better a doctor bill than losing someone you love during the holidays."

Mack didn't want to scare her, but the husband didn't look right. Beyond hurting his back when he fell, he just gave Mack the impression something worse awaited him if he didn't get checked out.

"I have an intuition about these things," he told her, all seriousness. "And something's off with your husband."

The woman looked from her husband to Mack. She studied him, a no-nonsense woman wrangling three children from ten to sixteen in addition to a dunderhead for a husband. She nodded. "Mitch, grab your wallet. We're heading to the emergency room."

"Damn it, Sheila. Fine. But no ambulance! We can barely afford our health insurance as it is."

Mack had him sign the paperwork confirming his refusal, and nodded to the wife. "Best of luck, ma'am." With *all* your kids, he wanted to say but didn't.

He joined Brad in the truck again, and as they drove back toward the station, the snow tapered to dusty flakes, the city almost still. Then another call came in. This one sounded more chaotic than dangerous.

They pulled up on Beacon Avenue South to see a herd of cars parked alongside an elementary school and what looked like a brawl taking place on the snowy, grassy area in front of the school, well lit by moonlight and a few overhead lights.

Brad barked a laugh. "What the fuck? Are they wearing flag football belts? Is this a football game gone wrong?"

"Between adults, no less." Mack sighed. "And to think Jed called the township wimpy for not wanting to play tackle. I bet if they played flag football like this, the Top Cops would be all in. Those monsters." He grinned, imagining tackling Cass. Then he frowned because knowing her, she'd miss the game due to something more important. Like avoiding Mack.

"Here we go again." Brad sighed as he pulled up behind two cop cars.

Mack's heart raced, though he knew the folly of expecting Cass to be in attendance. Every time he saw flashing lights lately, he prayed she'd show up.

What looked like two dozen people milled around, half of them fighting while the other half moved to opposite sides of a marked field, bordered by orange cones.

The snow picked up again, and he shivered in his coat, bag in hand, as he looked where to best help. Another vehicle arrived, and two more officers joined the four already there, working on the rowdy half of the group, settling them into sections while taking statements.

And there, *finally*. He saw Cass next to Jed. Jed kept trying to push the three largest combatants aside, keeping them from hitting each other, while Cass dealt with the bloodied ones standing against the brick wall of the school. One large man appeared to be cupping snow to his eye. Another held snow to his nose, while a third stood against the wall, swearing and spitting out blood.

"Stupid bitch. This isn't your business." The idiot seemed to be directing his comments to Cass.

Mack swapped a look with Brad, both of them wondering if the man had a death wish.

Cass opened her mouth to say something and must have noticed Mack and Brad standing there because she closed her mouth and jerked her head at the bloodied trio before her. "A little help here."

"Don't need no help." The argumentative ass she was dealing with, a man twice her weight and easily Brad's height, tried to push her away as he left the wall.

"Mistake," Mack muttered.

"Oh boy," Brad said as they watched her yank him by the arm, moving him in front of her, so she could then angle his arm behind his back and take him to the ground, much as Mack had done to Templeton the other day.

She cuffed him, and he became as docile as a sleeping kitten.

Mack watched with real appreciation. "That was beautiful." Would she be offended if he clapped?

Not police officers, Mack and Brad had no business getting in the middle of an altercation. They had to let the police do their jobs and wait to be asked into a stable situation. Firefighters had no right getting in the way of the police—as he'd heard his family insist time and time again.

So Mack waited with Brad while Cass, Jed, and the other officers got everyone calm.

But one dense—or maybe drunk—man didn't seem to want to obey the order he'd gotten to stand down away from the men he'd been fighting with. He slipped by Jed and headed for Cass, shaking his finger at the man she'd taken down, now sitting with the other injured against the wall.

"Cass, incoming," Jed called before slapping cuffs on the two women who refused to stop slapping at each other.

Before Mack could intervene, Cass said something to the bloodied crew against the wall, which had them all sitting still and quiet, more so than they'd already been. The man wagging his finger and fast approaching got one step closer, nearly touching her before she shut that down.

She had him on his knees, his arm behind his back, contained. "Now, sir, I don't think you were going to assault me. But I can't be sure, so we're going to wait right here until you sober the hell up. Understand?"

He was crying and trying to obey, but her hold wasn't making it easy.

"We should help," Mack said.

"We should *not* help," Brad argued. "This isn't our job. Keep it in your pants and let the officers do their jobs."

"Fine. But if he even looks like he's thinking about trying to hit her again, I'm going in."

"Sure thing, Romeo." Brad put a friendly hand on Mack's shoulder that felt like the grip of death.

Cass waited for the angry man to settle before letting him go. She ordered him to join the others against the wall, and he obeyed with a subdued "Sorry. Yes, ma'am."

She nodded to Brad. "You guys can come over. Looks like a broken nose, broken tooth, and maybe a sprained ankle."

"Don't you mean sprained wrist, Officer Deadly?" Mack murmured as he looked down at the latest man she'd cowed, now sitting with his buddies against the wall.

"I'm sorry. What did you say?" She turned on him like a rabid wolf.

God, she made him want.

"You said a sprained ankle?" Mack said politely.

She glared at him. "Jed's got him over there."

"I got it." Brad jogged to Jed and the miscreants now lined up against the far building.

"What the hell happened?" Mack asked as he moved around Cass to check on the mouth bleeder. Yep, two broken teeth. Ouch. He set his bag down, donned his gloves, and got out the gauze, some tape, and bandages.

While working on cleaning up the guy with broken teeth and after checking the man's vitals and pupils—no head wound—he listened as the one with the swelling eye ran down the events.

"So Team Ryder was beating Team Wilson. It's a family reunion, and we usually come together for a friendly game of flag football. Except Gary Ryder is a huge douche who always takes it too far. We normally don't let him play."

The man with the broken nose nodded. "Broke my nose," he said in a nasal, muffled agreement.

"But this year we wanted to be fair, since one of our uncles left some of the Wilsons a lot of money. It was Gary's dad, actually, and Gary's sad about his dad dying and angry he got nothing. Well, the jackass took his anger out on the field. Nearly crushed my brother's foot, broke Nelson's nose, and knocked out my dad's teeth."

"Shithead!" someone yelled at the man sitting quietly near them, saying nothing, especially since Cass seemed to have her eye on him.

"Not to take his side," the well of information continued, "but I think he might have given himself a concussion earlier. He's not so stupid he'd intentionally come at a cop."

"Great." Mack sighed. "I'm going to give you this to put pressure on your bleeding gums. Let me take a look at the concussed shithead. In the meantime, please put this on your nose," he said to the man's father. "You're okay breathing?"

Broken Nose nodded. "Just hurts."

"Yeah, that'll happen." Mack glanced at the man with the swollen eye. "That needs to get looked at too."

"Just a punch that hit my cheekbone. I've been in fights before. Trust me. This is nothing."

Cass shook her head.

Mack reminded himself to look the guy over after checking on the potential concussion. "Cass, help him sit up, would you?" Gary, apparently, had tipped forward. He sat cross-legged, his elbows on his knees, resting his head in his hands.

She sighed but helped get the man to sit up straight, letting him lean on her for support while he braced himself against the wall behind him.

"How many fingers?" Mack asked.

"I don't care," the grown man wailed.

So much for keeping quiet. Mack shook his head. "Great. What's your name?"

"Gerald Ryder," Cass answered for him.

Mack shot her a look, managing not to laugh when she blushed. "Sorry."

"Sir?" Mack looked him over again. "What's your name?"

"I go by Gary Ryder."

"How old are you?"

"Dunno."

Someone against the wall near Jed yelled, "You're forty-five, Gary. Not fourteen! Why start a fight, you idiot?"

"Because the Wilsons are crooks!"

"I bet that's Gary's sister," Mack said.

"Cousin," Cass corrected. "His sister and mother are over there." She nodded to the women who'd been pulling each other's hair.

"Great."

Mack worked with Brad and the officers to gather those needing a trip to the hospital. Gary definitely had a concussion. And the bloody mouth and sprained wrist candidates got a ride as well after Mack called in for help.

Before they left, he yelled out to Cass, in front of her friends because he couldn't help himself, "Hey, Carmichael. No hard feelings. I know it's intimidating to try to go for a second round."

He saw Jed give her a look. "What the hell's he talking about?"

"I don't know." The glare she shot Mack told him she knew exactly what he was talking about. Their Saturday morning.

He'd rather have just asked her on a date, but then she'd call him possessive. So he resorted to antagonizing her. Whatever worked.

He smiled easily. "Hey, you tried hard, I'll give you that. But it's okay. I still haven't found anyone who can keep up with me. But you were better than most." That was pushing it, but Cass would have to come back to him now. If only to punch his lights out.

Her eyes narrowed, and he could almost feel the laser beam slicing him from neck to groin.

"Great job tonight." He waved and hurried into the truck before she could respond.

Brad drove them away, shooting Mack a questioning look in the rearview. He said over his shoulder, "What was that about?"

"That was to remind Cass that I'm not about to let her run scared. If she wants to win this fight, she needs to meet me head-on." He gave the broken ankle patient more ice and shone a light at the potentially concussed man's eyes. Yep. Pupils were definitely of unequal sizes.

Brad snorted. "I have no idea what you're talking about, but she looked beyond annoyed. Watch out that she doesn't swing by the station and clock you in front of everyone. Because if she puts you on your ass, you will never hear the end of it."

Mack laughed. "I bet she could do it too."

"You need help."

"Yes, police help. I need a sexy officer to show me the error of my wicked ways."

"Professional help," Brad muttered. "Of the psychological kind."

"I wonder how many pairs of cuffs she owns…"

—————————

Cass watched the mouthwateringly handsome Mack Revere take off in an ambulance with several men pending assault charges. But she couldn't think past the fact he'd challenged her in front of people she knew. In front of Jed.

Should she confront him after her shift ended or just continue to ignore him? He hadn't exactly hinted that they'd had sex. But he'd deliberately needled her about it in public, forcing her to hear him.

Tricky, manipulating son of a bitch.

She hated that she kind of liked that about him.

"What the hell was that about?" Jed asked later as they rode back from the precinct, having delivered several men for processing. "I thought you came out ahead Friday night. You beat Revere at darts, didn't you?"

She fought a blush. Since Saturday morning, she hadn't been able to stop thinking about Mack and how amazing he'd been in bed. It bothered her more than she could say that she still had no idea what he'd meant about being "one up" on her. Especially because that orgasm had rung her bell, and she honestly didn't care who might have won some imaginary contest. To her way of thinking, they'd both been winners.

Her indecision on how to approach him had dragged, and several days had passed. What were the odds she'd find him out in the snow, taking care of the drunk and disorderlies she'd been calming down?

"Hello? Space cadet? What was he talking about? I thought you won the big money. You lost at pool but nailed him at darts." Jed paused with a grin. "See what I did there? You *nailed* him at darts?"

"Yeah, well, apparently he's holding on to that win at pool."

"You should make him eat those words. Challenge him to something else."

"Why the interest, Jed?" She almost said *Why the interest in my love life?* but fortunately censored herself. Dating a firefighter? She'd never hear the end of it.

"Because no man I know can best Cassandra Carmichael. And no firefighter—no matter how connected he is through his brothers—deserves the Princess of Pain. You're meant for bigger and brighter things, in my opinion."

"Aw, Jed, you say the nicest things." Princess of Pain? Ha. She'd have to jot that one down.

"Well, actually, there's a reason you shouldn't let his challenge go."

"Oh lord. What now?"

"Did I tell you how excited Shannon was that you went out last Friday? She's now saying that she's responsible for it all."

"How's that?"

"She thinks she scared you so much by inviting Handleman and Newcastle to the party that you finally found a man of your own." He shrugged. "Your personal life is your business. Frankly, Shannon's obsession with your lack of a love life is a little alarming."

She snorted. "A little?"

"But I know it's not because of any jealousy about you or me.

She misses her sisters, and she thinks of you as a stand-in for Jessica."

Cass had met Jessica once and liked her. She had a mouth on her and didn't take any of Shannon's crap.

"It was Jessica's birthday last week, so Shannon is really missing family. I think she's shoving all that sister love on you." He nodded. "I listen when you talk, and it fits. Your dad would agree."

"He probably would." Cass sighed. "So what do you want me to do?"

"Invite Mack over for dinner at our place. You and he schmooze it up. Act like you like each other. Shannon will feel like she's—indirectly—made a love connection, you get a break from the matchmaker from hell, and she'll be so thrilled to share love that I'll get lucky when the kids are asleep later that night."

Cass shook her head. "Why is the entire world so invested in who I date or don't date?"

"I have no idea. But Newcastle was asking about you a few days ago. I kind of told him you had a boyfriend."

"Why lie?"

"Because he's not the only one interested. I hate to say it, but the guys at the station want in your pants." He grimaced. "And the more you act like you hate all of them, the more they're interested. You want to put it to bed? Become unavailable."

"That's stupid."

"It is. But I did the same thing when Shannon's friend was after me."

"What?" Cass couldn't see Shannon taking that well.

"It was back when we first met. I tried nicely telling this woman I wasn't interested, but it never registered. It was only when the chick realized I was into Shannon that she left me alone. And, well, Shannon threatened to cut her tits off. But you've met my wife. This shouldn't surprise you."

Cass grinned. "It does not, in fact." She mulled over what he'd said. "You really think it would settle down the interest in my personal life? I don't like people talking or thinking about me much." Too much notice felt intrusive.

"Yeah, I feel you. I know you just want to do your job and be left alone. Being a female cop is headache enough. Now, I'm not saying anyone's talking behind your back or anything. No one's making a play for you at work, are they?" came out in a growl.

Cass relaxed. Jed would never let anyone harass her, physically or verbally. Of course, he'd only get to trounce her harasser *after* Cass finished ripping the guy's arms off.

"Nope. No one has said a word wrong, which is why your comments about dating are freaking me out."

He sighed. "I didn't mean to. I'm probably making too much of it. But Shannon's got me thinking."

"Not a good look for you."

"Jackass. I'm just saying, get everyone off your case. Pretend to mess around with Mack. I liked him. He's not a cop, and from what I gather, he's kind of on the outs with his family. Xavier never talks about him much. Not like he talks about his other brothers."

Cass wondered about that. Did Mack not get along with his family? Or was it as he'd said, that he'd never really fit in?

"Look, Cass, I don't want to sound like I'm pressuring you. If you don't want to see Mack, don't. It's no one's business what you do with your time. And God knows I'm not one to talk feelings." Jed shuddered. "But it would make Shannon happy, weird as that sounds."

She sighed. "Your wife is weird."

"She is."

"And bossy."

"Totally."

"She scares me a little," Cass admitted on a groan.

"She scares me a lot."

"Fine. I'll see if I can't get Mack to a dinner date with you two.

This Thursday or Friday?" At his nod, she added, "I'll have to see when he has off."

"Do it. I'll owe you one."

"Please. I'm adding that one to your list of many."

———————

Jed waited in the car while Cass took a quick pit stop at a gas station. The place was empty, most folks smart enough to realize that driving under the hazardous conditions outside made no sense.

He called home, keeping an eye on the front of the store.

"Jed?"

He smiled. "Hey, Shan. The kids okay?"

"In bed, finally." Shannon let out a breath. "I swear, I blame you for the demon twins every day."

"Yeah, I love them too."

They both laughed.

"So, did she fall for it?" Shannon asked.

"Like a fat trout sucking down some plump night crawlers."

"That's disgusting." Shannon sniffed. "But for our best friend, fine. I'll be the bad guy." She paused. "You're sure this fireman is okay?"

"He's perfect. He doesn't mind Cass's control issues and is just as competitive as she is. I checked into him, and he's a genuinely nice guy. Plus, his partner told me that Mack's got a thing for Cass. Even better, Mack gets the lifestyle. He's a firefighter with Station 44. You know those posters you were drooling over about the new station?"

"Wait. That's him?" Shannon sounded giddy.

He frowned. "Yeah, that's him."

She cleared her throat. "Oh, well. Good. He sounds like someone she'd do well with. And you did say you saw them kissing at the bar."

"I said I saw them sucking face. More like she was devouring him. Kind of like a great white going in for the kill, if you want the truth."

Shannon laughed. "Stop, please. And what's with all the fish references?"

"My brother called again. He's making plans for next summer. A week at the cabin on the lake. And fishing! Please, Shannon? I'll even take the twins so you can go glam up at the spa in town. They apparently have seaweed wraps now." Sounded disgusting, but his brother's wife loved them.

"You sweet talker. Fine, we'll go, and you'll give me a spa day. But at some point you'll have to tell Cass I wasn't the wacko so invested in her dating life. You're Mr. Matchmaker. You weirdo."

"I'm weird. You're weird. That's why I love you."

"Huh?"

"Gotta go. She's back." He quickly disconnected and pocketed his cell.

Cass entered the car and tossed a pack of gummy candy at him. "Tropical fruit. They didn't have berry." She buckled up and looked at him. "What?"

Cass wouldn't want to hear that he worried about her. Or that he loved her like his own sister. So much so, he knew if he didn't at least try to help her, she might one day regret the path her life had taken. He knew all about regrets, and if his own brother hadn't helped him, he might not have Shannon today.

Jed knew what he'd seen watching her with Mack Revere. A spark of joy, laughter, and real connection he'd never seen her share with anyone else. Something all too rare in life and something she deserved.

"Ah, nothing. Just wondering if you actually looked for the berry gummies or decided to save time by grabbing whatever was on the nearest rack."

She frowned. "Give them back."

"No. You don't need the sugar. It makes you more angry."

"Angrier."

"See what I mean?" They argued on their way to their next stop—a pregnant woman stuck five miles from the hospital and crowning all alone in her back seat.

Thank God he and Shannon were done having kids. And that he'd made it to the hospital with her *before* she gave birth.

Chapter Nine

WEDNESDAY MORNING, MACK PUT HIS HANDS BEHIND HIS head and stretched, warm and comfortable in bed. He had the day to do whatever he wanted. Well, after he met his brother for lunch. Apparently, Alec had wedding stuff he wanted to talk about, and for some reason he thought Mack would be the best person in the family to bounce ideas off.

Mack loved Alec's fiancé. He hadn't liked his brother's last girlfriend at all. Then Alec had brought home Dean, a man with a sense of humor and a confidence that meshed well with Alec's ability to charm anything that breathed.

Alec, a bisexual cop and member of SWAT, was so good at his job, so dependable, and such a dead-on shot that he took a lot less flak than anyone might have guessed when entering the elite unit.

And so, for the most part, Alec's lifestyle became nothing more interesting than his fellow officers' fixation on *Hamilton*, his sergeant's obsession with sudoku, or the team commander's fourth attempt at marriage. Alec's pending marriage was what it was.

All that made Mack very happy. Having to talk about wedding planning over lunch? Not so much.

He sighed. Life would be bearable if Cassandra Carmichael would put him out of his misery and freaking *call him*.

He'd taken a chance by provoking her last night. He'd been vague enough that no one would know anything about them being lovers. But he'd still talked down to a cop among her peers, hoping for a reaction.

And what had he gotten for taking such a risk? Nada.

He groaned and turned onto his stomach, burying his face in his pillow. He should have just asked her out on a date. Gone for the tried and true, keeping it simple. Yet some part of him still insisted he wouldn't have had a chance if he treated her with gentle teasing and kindness. Bah. She'd eat that up and spit it out.

Hell, he couldn't go a few minutes without thinking about her. About how she smiled, how angry she seemed to get over little things, how hard she concentrated when competing.

And, of course, how good she'd felt when he'd been buried balls deep inside her.

He turned over and stared at the ceiling. "This sucks." *Stop thinking about her, moron.*

He washed up, taking his time since he had nothing planned except lunch with his brother. Other than that, he'd be bumming around for the day, something he hadn't done in ages.

Once dressed in jeans and a "Chevy Does It Better" sweatshirt, he stared out the front window of his house and sipped hot chocolate with mini marshmallows. The snow kept coming down, and he could only be glad he'd put his snow tires on at the beginning of the month.

The whole family had stopped by Mom and Dad's to utilize their garage after Halloween. Mack could have changed his tires at home in his own decked-out garage. But he'd subjected himself to a family brunch after helping his mechanically challenged brothers work on their cars. It hadn't gone as badly as most of their family get-togethers had. They never teased him about his knowledge when it came to cars.

Born with a wrench in hand, his dad liked to say, Mack knew automobiles. He loved everything about them, even the new technology that made it difficult to diagnose problems without system schematics and the right electronic gizmos.

Still, he remained partial to the old muscle cars and trucks that needed no more than simple tools, mechanical know-how, and a paper manual to fix most problems. For a while growing up, he'd wondered if he might become a mechanic, but he loved cars too much to make them a job.

The Air Force had been a great start out of high school. Though it hadn't been the Army, it had been close enough to eventually satisfy his parents. Especially because he'd become a military cop. Until he'd been done. Needing something more, something else.

To say he'd disappointed his parents would be putting it mildly. Though he knew his family loved him regardless, they just loved their sons who toed the line a little more.

Mack sighed.

He kept feeling anxious about Alec's wedding and didn't know why. Or he did but didn't want to face the truth.

James, the oldest at thirty-six, had married a woman content to be a cop's wife. Mack liked her a lot. She was sweet and kind and had always treated everyone as real family.

Alec, the second oldest at thirty-four, had finally gotten engaged to be married. Man or woman, his parents didn't care so long as he started on a family.

Xavier, that tool, was only older than Mack by two years and dating the woman who would surely become his wife. A smartass like Xavier and sexy as all get-out, she fit his brother to a T.

Then there was Mack, the odd duckling without a woman on the horizon. He cared more about cars, exercise, and fires than entering a relationship, and he spent more time with his firefighting brothers than he did his own family. The shame...

God, I sound so dramatic. Cass would totally laugh at him for that.

He smirked and drank his cocoa, thinking instead about the men he loved like real family, brothers at heart, men who had his back regardless of anything that might be going on in their lives.

Which was what had initially made him so nervous about his crew entering relationships. But Brad's girlfriend always made sure to include him, same with Tex's and Reggie's ladies. Heck, the girls had left during a game night, sensing his need to have more guy time. They cared about what he thought and felt.

Though he knew his family loved him, he didn't think they cared about him as much as they wanted him to fit into their expectations.

Mack sighed. *This is why I like to be busy. I don't think so much.*

Sadly, he knew if Cass were to call, his crappy mood would vanish as if it had never been despite nothing changing with his family.

After doing some much-needed laundry and entertaining himself with his secret indulgence in *The Golden Girls*, an '80s sitcom about four older women living in Florida—and who *didn't* love Betty White?—he finished folding his last load of whites, wondering where the hell half his socks had gone.

His cell phone rang. He glanced at the number, intending to ignore it, and froze at the sight of Cass Carmichael's name. His heart raced, and he forced himself to be calm as he answered.

"Hello?"

"First off, I'm not afraid of you."

"Who is this?" He heard a small growl and grinned.

"Nice try. I know you have my contact info, buddy."

"I'm sorry. My name is Mack, not 'Buddy.' Are you sure you dialed the right number?"

When she swore, he had to stifle laughter.

"What the hell were you talking about last night? And why call me out in front of everyone?" She didn't sound annoyed, just curious. Huh. He'd have expected anger.

Mack needed to put one fear to rest. "Look, what happened between us Saturday stays between us. I told you I wouldn't say anything about it, and I didn't."

"I realize that, but—"

"I think I know why you're avoiding me." He deliberately gentled his tone. "And I wanted you to know it's okay. I get it."

"Get what, exactly?" Ah, now she sounded annoyed.

"That Saturday was so good you're afraid it wasn't real. We

share some amazing chemistry. I think you know that, and it scares you."

She snorted. "You don't scare me, sweetcakes."

"See? You're making jokes over the phone, but you're too afraid to come say all this to my face."

A pause. "Fine. You want to talk face-to-face? Give me your address."

"Oh please. Like you don't know it already."

"What?"

"You mean you didn't already look me up in your cop database?"

"Um, no. You're not an official suspect in any crime—not yet, at least—and we don't do things like that."

"*Sure* you don't."

"Mack, do you want me to come over to talk this out or not?" she growled.

He rattled off his address. "I'm just folding clothes and watching TV."

"Fine. I'll be there in ten."

He hurriedly turned the TV to something sophisticated. *The Punisher* seemed like something she'd like. While he watched the start of the second season for the fifth time, he kicked back on the couch and shoved his clothes basket aside.

Ten minutes after he'd ended the call, a knock came at his door.

"Damn, you're punctual," he said as he opened it.

She looked better than good with rosy cheeks, her eyes sparkling, and her dark hair pulled back in a ponytail. She had her jacket all buttoned up and a scarf around her neck. He wanted to tug her in with it but feared she'd put him on his ass, so he stepped back and allowed her to enter.

Cass glanced around. "It's nice and warm in here at least. Makes up for all the trouble you're turning out to be."

He gave her his best smile.

She sighed and glanced at his lit fireplace. "Gas?"

"Oh yeah. Wood is way too much work."

She nodded and turned to him, slipping out of her boots.

He had her stripped out of her coat and scarf before she could blink.

She frowned at him. "Thanks."

"Sure. Coffee?"

Cass brightened. "Okay."

He led her into the kitchen, proud of his home as she looked around her, and fixed her a K-Cup.

The charming two-story home had three bedrooms and two baths, hardwood floors, and a completely remodeled kitchen. Instead of the old, dark cabinetry, he'd upgraded to white cabinets, navy-blue walls, and an awesome butcher-block island with a ton of cabinet and drawer space. Mack didn't need anything fancy, but when he'd bought the place, the kitchen had been standing on its last legs.

"Creamer or sugar?" he asked.

"Nah. This is surprisingly cute." She accepted the coffee he handed her with thanks.

"I know."

She grudgingly laughed. "Okay, Mr. Ego. I'm here. I'm not scared. And I have no idea what you think you won the last time we were together."

He stared at her until she blushed and barked, "What?"

"You're just so beautiful."

Her blush deepened.

He grinned. "For the record, what I said on the phone is true. I do think you're scared of what we might have together."

She sipped and watched him, like a wolf analyzing the best way to take down weak prey. "You're serious? We fucked once, and now you think I'm scared of you?" She laughed.

But he saw that flash of vulnerability in her eyes and smiled. "Yep."

She sputtered, and he knew he had her. "That's ridiculous."

"Maybe."

"I..." She took a deep breath and let it out. "I need your help, so I'm not going to storm out of here and show you how much I think you're full of crap."

"Ask and you shall receive." He made a short bow, conscious of her biting her lip to keep from smiling. Oh yeah. The Revere charm was in full effect if she hadn't yet gone for his throat.

"My partner's wife is obsessed with my dating life. And I don't date much, like I told you. I'm too busy with work and stuff."

"Yeah, me too."

"Right." She cleared her throat. "So Jed, my partner—"

"I remember."

"—mentioned me beating your ass at darts last week."

"I don't know I'd say 'beating my ass.' I mean, you won, but that's after I crushed you at pool."

Her eyes glinted with anger, and Mack forced himself not to look so captivated.

"Can you shut up for two seconds so I can explain myself?"

"About that *favor* you need?"

She gritted her teeth and set her coffee cup on the counter. Likely so she didn't throw it at his head.

He grinned and zipped his lips with his fingers.

Cass let out breath and pinched the bridge of her nose. "Right. So anyway, Shannon is convinced that you and I are somehow made for each other, and she wants to invite us over for dinner this Friday."

"I'm working Friday, but I'm off next Thursday and Friday, if that helps." He checked his phone for his schedule and nodded. "Yeah, either of those days."

"Hold on." She texted Shannon. "Next Thursday works. You and I will act friendly. Then Shannon's happy and not trying to set me up with any more jackholes, and my partner's happy because his wife is happy."

"What about me?" Mack asked, loving how steamed Cass seemed to get whenever he asked a simple question. "Do I get to be happy?"

"Look, Revere. It's a free meal. Shannon is an amazing cook. And you get to spend time in my stellar company."

"Ah, I see." He watched her, waiting to see how long she could go without exploding.

Five seconds, apparently.

"*Well?*"

"Well what? I'm still waiting to hear how this date will make me happy."

"Are you serious? You just told me we share all this 'amazing chemistry.' You obviously want us to hang out more."

"Are you sneering?"

She sneered. "No."

He had to laugh. "Right. So you're begging me for a favor by growling and snarling at me. But not sneering."

Her lips twitched. "Maybe."

He stepped closer, taking a chance with his health. "Because you think I want to be with you again."

"Well, yeah. I'm a ball of joy."

Mack rested a hand on her shoulder and slid it to the back of her soft neck. "Oh, right. So much joy."

Her breath hitched, though she tried to keep a straight face. "I told you before not to get possessive."

"And you won't be clingy," he reminded her.

"Not clingy." She moistened her lips.

Mack was only human. He leaned in for a kiss meant to be quick but that lingered instead. He threaded his hand through her hair, keeping her in place while he kissed her with a warm thoroughness that had him hard and aching and had Cass gripping his waist.

"Wow," she whispered when he pulled back. "You're really good at kissing."

The innocence in her eyes, at odds with the heat from their embrace and passion from her kiss, did him in. Mack wanted to fuck her and take care of her. An odd feeling of protectiveness battled his lust. Cass Carmichael had the strangest effect on his senses.

"So are you," he said as an afterthought, content to just look at her.

"Huh?" Her hands crept to the skin under his waistband, her touch lighting him up all over.

"Good at kissing," he said, his voice low, gravelly.

She unsnapped his jeans, which sounded incredibly loud despite the gunfire on television. "About this favor…"

He couldn't help the laugh that escaped. "Are you trying to sex me up to get me to go on a date with you?"

She paused.

He fitted his hand over hers to get her moving again. "No, no. It's working. I just wanted to be clear."

She grinned and unzipped his fly slowly.

"Cass, I'll go to dinner with you."

She parted his jeans and reached inside, down past his underwear. "You're not supposed to agree until after you come."

He'd swear his eyes rolled back into his head when she gripped him with her hot hand.

She chuckled. "Let's take a look at your bedroom this time, shall we?"

"Is this where you say you're leading me around by my dick? Because you really are."

She pulled free from him only to shriek with laughter when he lifted her in his arms and booked it down the hall to his bedroom.

He kissed her before she could say a word and continued kissing her before he tossed her down onto the bed and followed, quickly getting naked while she did the same.

The fun left as frantic need engulfed them both. Writhing

together, touching, kissing, licking, they rolled around his neatly made bed like two combatants struggling to victory.

"In me," she breathed as she pumped him, her clever hand stealing his ability to reason.

"Yeah." He reached blindly into his nightstand and found a condom, thank God. "Put it on me."

She hurried to do so, but before she could move back beneath him, he turned so that she straddled him instead. Mack wanted to watch her, committing this to memory.

She met his gaze as she positioned herself over him and slid down, one glorious inch at a time. Seated fully inside her, he gripped her hips as she began to move, up and down, riding him faster and harder.

He reached for her breasts, in lust with her curves, and palmed them, tweaking her nipples as she threw back her head and moaned his name.

Finding the sensitive spot between her legs, he rubbed, feeling her excitement build as she slammed harder onto him. Mack wanted to last, but watching her incredible body and feeling it at the same time, he simply couldn't.

"I'm coming, Cass," he warned, his body one giant supernova waiting to happen.

"Me too. Oh God, Mack," she cried as she slammed down one final time and shivered.

He jetted into the condom, light-headed and thoroughly done in by one very sexy cop. He did his best to catch his breath while she did the same, leaning over him.

They remained joined, and he didn't want her to move ever again.

The feel of her body against his just felt *right*. He couldn't explain why, even to himself, but Cass fit as no one ever had. And now he had a second sexual memory to torment him into eternity. The sight of Cass, naked and grinding on top of him, was better than anything he'd ever had. Seriously, *ever*.

He pulled her in for another kiss that turned hot from one breath to the next.

"Do you ever turn off?" she asked, kissing her way to his ear, where she whispered, "Does that big cock inside me ever go down?"

He groaned and palmed her ass, rotating his hips and making her moan as well. "Do you want it to go down?"

"Um, not yet." She nibbled his ear, and he moved a little more.

"I should probably get a new condom."

"You probably should." She pulled back and sat up straight, shoving him deeper inside her. She closed her eyes and sighed. "Hurry."

She lifted off him, and he replaced the used one with a new one in seconds. But this time he had plans not to be rushed. He forced her onto her back and smiled down at her, wearing a wicked grin he'd perfected long ago.

"I don't trust that smile." She narrowed her eyes.

"Smart woman."

"It's the cop in me."

"No, honey, it's the firefighter in you." He entered her in a swift push, his cock hard and getting harder. "One that needs just a little time to work up to a flash fire."

"Seriously? More fire puns? I'd arrest you if you weren't so good with your hose."

"Good one." He was relieved to be in control of himself again. With Cass, his body seemed to turn on and off at will—her will. "Now lie back and enjoy."

"If you insist."

"I do." He took his time insisting, and one sweaty hour later, he'd say his efforts had been well worth it.

Chapter Ten

CASS HAD A HARD TIME BREATHING, HER ENTIRE BODY ONE giant nerve. How the heck had Mack Revere played her so well? He'd roamed her body, lingering on sensitive spots she hadn't even realized she'd had. He'd left her breathless one minute, had her begging the next, then screaming out his name as she orgasmed. It would have been embarrassing except she just didn't care, too caught up in endorphins to do more than exist.

"I bet we could do better against the wall," he teased, his breathing having settled.

"You touch me again and I'll break your arm." She drew in a deep breath and let it out slowly. "I mean, when I can move again."

"I told you." Didn't he sound smug. "We share some amazing chemistry."

"Yeah, yeah." Cass couldn't complain. At all. "I agree. But we're still not moving in together."

He didn't miss a beat, not put off by her teasing. "Not yet, at least. I have to meet your partner and his wife first."

Someone rang the doorbell.

They both tensed.

Then Mack swore. "Oh shit. You know that favor I'm doing for you next week? I need one from you first."

"Who is at the door?"

"My brother."

She cringed. "Xavier?"

"Alec. We're supposed to meet for lunch at"—he glanced at the clock on the table next to the bed and groaned—"a half hour ago. Shoot. Look, get cleaned up and meet me in the living room. I'll make up some excuse for you being back here."

"It's okay."

He paused. "What?"

"I don't care if your brother knows we hooked up." *Wait. I don't?*

"You don't?"

"I don't like people in my business, which is why I don't date the people I work with or their brothers." She gave him a look. "But we're not actually dating. Just having sex."

He looked at her. "Really?"

"What do you mean?"

The doorbell rang again.

"Hold on, Alec," Mack yelled.

"You don't even know it's him."

"It's him."

"Hurry up!" a man yelled. "I'm freezing my balls off!"

"Yeah, it's Alec."

"Wait. What do you mean by 'really'? This thing between us is just sexual."

"It's okay." His expression softened, which unnerved her. The guy was hot as hell, but when he looked at her that way, as if she mattered and nothing else existed, she felt…special. Girly and vulnerable. And emotional, which Cass didn't much like.

"What's okay?" she asked, her voice gritty.

"These feelings." He stroked her cheek, and she let him for all of five seconds before slapping his hand away.

"Clingy!"

He grinned. "Aw, now you're feeling possessive. That's great."

"What? I am not."

"Look, I owe you a dinner date? You owe me a brother date. Come with me to lunch with Alec. I need a buffer. He wants to talk about his wedding."

"I'm the girl, so I have to talk wedding plans with your brother?"

"No." Mack sighed. "I want you to be my plus-one for a change.

To show my brother that for once, *I'm* the one with the date and he's the lone guy tagging along."

"But didn't you guys agree to go to lunch?"

"Just work with me on this, hard-ass."

She knew exactly what he was talking about, often feeling the same way with Jed and Shannon or her parents. "Well, okay."

He kissed her. "Plus, you owe me for all the orgasms." He rushed to the bathroom and returned to dress in record time.

"You mean, all the orgasms *I* gave *you*."

"Yes, you're a big ball of joy. I remember." He winked and left the bedroom, shutting the door behind him. She heard the front door open, then, "Oh, hey, Alec. Sorry. I could have sworn we were supposed to meet at one-thirty, not one."

Cass couldn't believe she'd been playing with Mack for over an hour. What had happened to her stern resolution to remain friendly but distant? She admittedly liked Mack, what little she knew about him. But she didn't need the complications of a relationship again. Her last boyfriend, a year and a half ago, had been enough to warn her off needy men for a long while.

She went into the bathroom with her clothes to clean up and dress. And as she did, she wondered about this new dynamic with a man she had a real problem resisting.

How the heck had she gone from wanting a small favor to rolling around in bed with the studly fireman? She had to grin at that because, damn, but Mack was a shower and a grower. Handsome as sin and amazing in the sack. Yet still single. Hmm. Why was that? Because he had some serious personality flaws? Issues with commitment? Was he a closet serial cheater?

It sure couldn't be because he was a slob. The bathroom was surprisingly clean, smelled nice, and looked professionally designed. Same with his bedroom. The walls were a slate gray with white molding around the windows and baseboards. His bed had been made with tight corners, the pillows fluffed and in place.

Huh. He had a thing about neatness she could appreciate. His living and dining rooms had been the same. So Mack liked order. Cass liked order. What else did they have in common? Family pressure. A dedication to serving the public. Smart-ass friends…

Curious, she left the bathroom and joined him and his brother in the living room. She decided it wouldn't hurt to get to know Mack better, especially because they'd be helping each other out with family. And Jed and Shannon were part of her family, no matter how she felt about Shannon being a busybody. Which led her to think about her parents and how pleased they'd be if she brought a man home to dinner.

Wouldn't that be great, to show them she was mentally and socially healthy as a horse?

Mack smiled at her, and she moved to stand next to him, surprisingly not bothered when he put an arm around her shoulders. The action didn't seem motivated by any chest-thumping either, but by sincere affection. Or maybe she was still riding that pleasure wave off her last climax and couldn't see the real truth, basking in the afterglow.

"Alec, this is my friend, Cass. Cass, my brother Alec."

Alec narrowed his eyes, studying her as he held out a hand. "I know you. I think I've seen you when I've been at the South Precinct checking on my little brother, Xavier."

She shook his hand. "You Reveres all look alike. But you definitely look older than Xavier and Mack."

Alec snorted. "Oh, and aren't you a charmer?"

She smirked. "Truth hurts."

"Nice." Mack guffawed.

She hadn't been kidding. All the Revere men she'd met, and she hadn't yet run into Mack's dad, had dark hair and light-colored eyes, the combination striking against chiseled features and muscular frames.

Alec stood a little taller than Mack, was a little broader in the chest, but she found Mack to be the best-looking of the bunch. Perhaps because amusement at the world seemed to brighten his eyes. Or because he seemed sincere whereas Alec looked suspicious and Xavier could be over-the-top arrogant.

"I bet your parents had a tough time with you guys growing up."

Alec huffed. "It's like you've already been talking with my mom. She swears she's going to heaven just for having raised a bunch of hooligans."

"And that was before I was born," Mack said.

Alec added, "James was the worst. But it was really after she had Xavier that the glorious road to parenthood went steadily downhill." He sneered at his brother.

Mack ignored him and said to Cass, "He's just mad because he's not the prettiest Revere in the room."

"Yeah, that's it." Alec gave Cass a head-to-toe inspection, then surprised her by smiling. "So, little brother found a keeper, eh?"

"Well, I don't know about 'keeper,'" Mack said. "But she's definitely someone I'd think twice about throwing back in the pond."

"Please, Mack, all that flattery is making it hard to think." She elbowed him in the side, pleased when he let out an *oomph*. "Let's be honest. Mack is lucky I'm letting him breathe my same air. But I'm not so sure you'll make the cut." She gave Alec his own once-over. "So watch it, pretty boy. Or your soon-to-be husband is going to be sad when you go home missing your teeth."

Alec laughed. "Oh, I like you." He took her from Mack and helped her into her jacket, handing her the scarf. "Now let's head off to lunch and talk about my brother. I'll tell you anything you want to know."

He had her out the door while Mack yelled at him to wait.

She let Alec settle her into the front seat of his SUV, pleased to have noted his snow tires. With the roads being slick and the snow still coming down, every little bit helped. "Nice truck."

Alec buckled in, and they watched Mack hurry to lock the door before joining them, sliding into the back seat. Alec said, "It's especially good in this God-awful weather, but nothing counters black ice. We'll drive slowly."

"Where are we going?" she asked, enjoying herself, which was so unlike her. She hadn't planned this trip. Heck, she hadn't planned having sex with Mack either, but so far, rolling with life seemed to be going in her favor. Why not go two for two?

"Super Six. Have you been?"

"It's been a while." Her father raved about the place, and she'd liked it enough the one time she'd gone. But somehow it hadn't worked its way back into her routine. "It's Korean-Hawaiian food, right? Not too fancy."

"Not fancy, no. But delicious," Alec said. "The char siu burger is killer good."

"I like the pork katsu sandwich." Mack smacked his lips. "That's what I want. And Alec is treating, Cass, so feel free to get whatever you want."

She shot a glance at Alec and saw him scowl at his brother in the rearview.

"Hey, I'm doing you a favor by going out with you on my day off."

Cass shrugged. "And I'm working later. Consider this my good-will move of the day."

"Oh? I would have thought that would be slumming around with my brother," Alec taunted.

She laughed and turned to see Mack glaring at the back of his brother's seat. "You have a point."

"Don't agree with him," Mack said.

"But he's so pretty. How can I not agree with him?"

Alec patted her on the knee. "And so smart. What are you doing with Mackenzie?"

Mack sighed. Loudly. "Are we there yet?"

Surprised to find an open table, they snagged it and were soon eating and listening to Alec talk. Mack had been kidding earlier. He didn't mind spending time with his brothers one-on-one. Without the others egging each other on, they'd forget to gang up on him and enjoy a shared camaraderie. Alec especially had always been fun to be with.

Mack watched his brother make Cass laugh.

Enjoying himself, Mack ate and smiled, chiming in here and there, mostly watching Alec talk Cass's ear off about Dean and the coming wedding. Mack listened, noting things Cass probably didn't realize she revealed.

Like that as gruff as she could be, she had definite attitudes about dress length, heels, and makeup. "Alec, do not make any bridesmaids wear dresses with puffy sleeves or sashes. Please."

"I'm kidding. That was a joke." He winked at Mack. "Only my groomsmen have to wear obnoxious fluffy pink sashes."

"Funny." Mack shook his head and downed more soda. He said to Cass, "At your wedding, what will your bridesmaids be wearing?"

She didn't pause in her answer, so she'd obviously given it some thought. "The same color dress but different styles. And I won't force them to buy superexpensive dresses. I've even thought about doing a destination wedding or eloping. Though my parents would have a hissy if I did that. They're all about my life progressing according to their plans."

"I hear you." Alec clinked his glass against hers. "My mom and dad expect me to do a repeat performance of James's wedding. Now, just because I helped Ashley plan it does not mean I want to make mine the exact same way."

"You helped your sister-in-law plan her wedding?"

Mack nodded. "Alec is the most organized person I know. Ashley asked him to help, and her mother seconded that."

"Huh."

"Dean expects me to plan ours too," Alec said with a huff. "But I'm not a big flowers guy, so I told him he has to figure those and the cake. I can do all the other logistical stuff. In fact, I thrive on it."

Mack explained, "He was in logistics in the Army. You can tell."

Cass nodded, looking from Alec to Mack. "Didn't you say you'd been in the Air Force?" she asked him.

"Yep."

"Have all your brothers been in the service before serving in the police department?"

Alec sighed. "We're a family long on tradition, which is both good and bad." He shot Mack a look. "All my grandparents have served as cops or soldiers. My dad was Army before he settled down and married my mom—who was also Army. Then they both worked for the Seattle PD, Dad as a cop, Mom as an administrator who's still administrating. James and I joined the Army before the Seattle PD. But Xavier took the direct road and majored in criminal justice before joining the force."

"He also took a sabbatical to join the Army Reserves before coming back to the police department," Mack explained, "which is why he's not a higher rank in the department."

"Plus he loves what he does," Alec said.

"He's loud enough about it," Cass said, amusing Mack and his brother, "but he's a good cop."

High praise coming from Cass.

Alec nodded. "So how did you and Mack meet anyway?"

"Well, first she lost to the Burning Embers at a baseball game. Then she gave me a ticket for speeding," Mack said, amused to see Cass flush.

"It was a warning, Mack. And it was your own fault for doing forty-five in a thirty-five."

"More like fifty." He saw her eyes narrow and coughed. "Yep, you're right. I was too fast."

Alec shook his head. "He's obsessed with Vella."

"Vella?" Cass lifted a brow Mack's way.

"My 1970 Chevelle. A classic tuxedo black with white super-sport stripes." He sighed, still in love.

Cass smirked. "A car has all that devotion. Should I be jealous?"

Mack winked at her. "She's got nothing on your lines, baby."

Alec and Cass at the same time said, "Baby?"

"The looks on your faces." Mack chuckled. "I'm kidding. Not about the car, who is amazing."

"That. Cars aren't 'who.' Cars are 'that.'"

Mack cringed. "And still grammatically *way* incorrect. Anyway, my dad gave me that car. I helped rebuild the engine with him."

"It—"

"She," Mack corrected, in love with the car and for so many more reasons than Alec realized. Working with his dad on the Chevelle had given them something in common. They still talked about cars to this day. Not Station 44, not Mack's past service in the Air Force. Cars.

Alec rolled his eyes. "*She* was Dad's pride and joy until he bought the Shelby," Alec informed Cass. "I think my mom was relieved when he handed it down to our car monkey. Mack's obsessed with anything that has wheels."

"That's why I like Cass so much. She has wheels. She's *fast*. Like a cheetah on the soccer field. That's where I ran into her the third time."

Alec brightened. "Oh. So this is the cop who took you down. Nice, Cass."

She nodded. "It was a beautiful slide tackle, if I say so myself."

Mack watched her chat with his brother, enamored with this comfortable, tough-talking beauty. She seemed so confident in herself, having fun. She didn't flirt or pretend to be any less than she was—a powerful woman who knew her own worth. Cass didn't need him to do anything for her. If she wanted something, she'd ask. He didn't sense in her a woman who played games.

Was it any wonder he thought about her all the time? Missed her when she wasn't with him?

"Enchanting in a kick-your-ass kind of way," he said aloud, aware his brother and Cass were watching him moon over her.

"Oh boy. Baby brother is enamored." Alec snickered. "Wait until I tell Mom."

Cass's cheeks turned pink, and she glared at Mack. "Cut it out."

He smiled. "Sorry. I can't help myself." Before she could kick him under the table, he turned to his brother and said, "So what about the wedding did you need help with?"

"Nothing really. Just an excuse to see you."

Mack frowned. "You see me all the time."

"Yes, but not without everyone else in the way. You're a lot more relaxed when just you and I hang out together. I'm sorry I missed your last few phone calls. Dean and I have been busy planning."

"As you should be," Mack said, now feeling a little nervous at the way Cass looked at him. Mentally dissecting him. He felt like the proverbial butterfly pinned to a specimen board for further study. "Don't listen to Alec. I'm always relaxed."

"Yeah, when James and Xavier aren't picking on you." Alec snorted.

"Please. You're all just jealous of my ability to live outside Mom and Dad's shadow."

Alec frowned. "What does that mean?"

"Nothing." Mistake to bring that up. "So have you guys set a date yet? I know you have two or three you've been deciding between."

Alec seemed to want to talk about Mack's previous comment but saw Cass watching and forced a smile. "Either April 30th, when we first met, or August 28th, when Dean proposed."

"Dean proposed?" Cass asked. "How? Did he get on one knee? Did you expect it?"

She seemed genuinely lost in her enthusiasm over the romance. Another twist to her character he hadn't seen coming.

Alec smiled, his love clear to see. "I was surprised. I'd been planning to pop the question myself. We'd been together for a year, after a long relationship I'd been in that just fizzled. We took a day trip to hike out at Mt. Rainier. The sky was clear and blue, the weather not too cold or too warm, and surprisingly, there weren't too many people out. Dean stopped at a point on the trail with a little vantage of wildflowers behind us and proposed. It was a perfect moment I'll never forget."

"Wow." Cass blinked. "That's beautiful."

Mack expected her to gush some more, but she turned to poke Mack in the chest. "That's how you do it."

He blinked. "Ah, should I be taking notes? Is that what you want?"

"Me?" She laughed. "I meant for whatever poor woman you sucker into saying 'yes.' Women like romance."

"All women?"

"Well, most. I would, and I consider myself pretty low-key when it comes to the hearts and flowers stuff. I think it's more about intent and what you really feel than a big ring or perfect setting." She turned to Alec. "Although your proposal really does sound perfect. I mean, if you were into hiking and mountains."

"You aren't?" Alec asked.

"Not so much. I love sports and running—in a gym or a trail in the city. Not in the mountains so much."

"Good to know." His brother smiled. "Now let's talk about something that's extremely important to me right now."

"What?" Mack asked, cautious. He didn't like the glint in his brother's eyes.

"How much dessert do we want, and if we can't eat it now, how much do we take home with us?"

Relieved, they ordered doughnuts to go and had just left the place when Mack swore he heard a meow.

"Did you hear that?" Cass asked.

Alec had gone to warm up the SUV, so the two of them hunted down the pathetic crying behind the building. In a wet cardboard box, Mack found a pair of gray tabbies that couldn't have been more than eight weeks old, crying their little hearts out.

Cass's eyes grew huge as she stared at them. "They're so small."

"And all alone in freezing weather." He glared down at the box. "I hate when people do this."

"What?"

"Abandon animals." He reached down and plucked both kittens out of the box. "Can you see if they have any brothers or sisters around? Their mom?"

She looked but found nothing. "Nope."

Mack glanced down at the mewling fluffballs. "Okay, guys. You're coming with me." His crew in particular had been working with Pets Fur Life, a charity that helped home stray animals, for a little over a year. The only thing Mack loved more than cars was helping innocent creatures find homes. He especially had a thing for cats, yet another difference from his family of dog lovers.

He kept the trembling kittens close to his body heat, pleased when they stopped squirming so much. He felt Cass staring at him and glanced up. "What's wrong?" At her frown, directed at his bulging jacket, he said, "Oh, don't worry. We help out with strays all the time. I'll take care of these guys."

"We?"

"My crew. Tex and the guys," he clarified. "Station 44 has helped a lot with Pets Fur Life too. I don't know if you ever saw it, but Brad was on *Searching the Needle Weekly* for a while, promoting adoptions. Tex has been on once too." And they'd all done a beefcake calendar for the charity that Mack didn't think she needed to know about.

"Huh." Cass didn't say much more, but he didn't think she seemed all that bothered by the cats.

He continued to pet and care for them on the drive back to his place.

Alec said, "Let me know if you have a problem homing them." He shook his head. "Between you and Dean, I swear. Just warning you, Cass. My brother is a sucker when it comes to animals."

"I'm not a sucker, Alec. I'm a helpful kind of guy." Mack grinned, knowing Alec to be an even bigger sucker when it came to fostering strays. He still had an older Lab living with him until they could find the guy a home.

"Helpful?" Alec snorted. "Yeah right."

"Thanks for lunch, Alec," Cass said, "and good luck with your wedding."

"Thanks. I hope to see you again soon." He gave Mack a significant look. He waved and waited until they had made it to the front door before leaving.

"You coming in?" Mack asked, wondering how amenable Cass would be to getting naked again.

She studied him and the kittens, now trying to hop out of his jacket. "I have some things to do at home." She sounded a little distracted, still staring at the cats. "Still on for next Thursday, right?"

"Um, yeah. Just text me the time and address." They hadn't talked about their relationship, such as it was, with the exception of helping each other out with first Alec then her partner. "So, Cass, about us... I—"

"I'll talk to you later. Bye." She left in the blink of an eye, leaving Mack with two curious felines and the dread that he'd somehow done something very wrong.

Chapter Eleven

THE FOLLOWING THURSDAY ARRIVED BEFORE SHE KNEW IT, and Cass finally stopped being a coward and texted Mack the time and directions for dinner.

He'd texted her a few times since lunch with his brother last week, even left two messages on her phone. For the life of her, she hadn't been able to reply except for an *I'll get back to you on that* and a *Not sure yet.* To her defense, she'd had a doctor's and dentist's appointment she hadn't been able to delay as well as a bunch of community outreach to do. Stuff she could have invited Mack to...had she not been so freaked out after last Wednesday.

It was so odd. Being with him in bed was a no-brainer. The guy had game.

Hanging with his brother? Weird, but not so bad. She liked Alec, especially that he didn't seem to need to impress her. He was himself, and she liked how open and proud he was of his fiancé. She'd gotten her fair share of crap for being a woman in the department that she'd had to put a stop to. But it was easier than the hostility aimed at the lesbian and gay cops in the department. Fortunately, the captain had shot all that shit down. Hard.

Alec worked in a different precinct, and she could only imagine how tough it could be to work against the mainstream. Yet another point in Mack's favor, how much he loved his brother and celebrated his differences.

It had been those blasted kittens that had thrown her for a serious loop.

She didn't know why. She wasn't a pet person. Not that she had anything against animals, but Cass had never been home long enough to take care of one. It should have been no big deal to see that Mack wanted to care for the cute little things. He'd said he helped out with Pets Fur Life.

But for some reason, seeing him be so sweet and gentle with the cats struck her. It turned all that lust and maybe-like she had for him into this blazing mass of emotional need. God, she'd even thought of him holding a baby for a split second. *Her* baby!

It made no sense, and Cass didn't like what confused her. So, she tabled her emotions to deal with later. And after one day passed, then another, and another, in addition to her partner's questions about what she wanted to bring to the dinner, she realized she should probably call Mack and confirm their evening.

Except he didn't pick up the phone. Part of her couldn't blame him. Then she remembered how she'd told him not to get possessive. Just because they'd fucked didn't mean she owed him anything.

Right. *I'm such a liar.*

An angry Mack—and she didn't have to see him to know he had every right to be annoyed with her—texted back for Cass to get your ass over to my place and tell me why you're ignoring me or I'm not going.

Annoyed and embarrassed because she seemed, once again, like she was scared of communicating when she'd really just been puzzled at her motivations and feelings, she left her spotless house, grocery list in her purse, and drove over to Mack's, trying to get her story straight.

Not that it was a story, but she needed some excuse better than "I look at you and want babies," which sounded crazy no matter how she spun it. Because one, Cass did *not* want babies, not now, and two, she didn't want them with a man she'd just started to get to know. No matter how handsome, great in bed, kind, or organized he might be.

She knocked on his door, heard his "Come in but be careful of the kittens," and bit the bullet.

Cass entered, conscious she wore only a pair of grungy jeans and her favorite sweatshirt that read *Just Do It* and had a small hole in the bottom. She had showered earlier that morning but hadn't left the house in makeup or made a concerted effort with her hair, which she'd left down and finger-combed.

Staring at Mack, who looked completely put together in a long-sleeved tee and jeans, his hair perfectly styled and his face cleanly shaven, had her rethinking her effort to not impress. God, he was so handsome. And mad. Oh boy.

Mack glared at her. "Shocker seeing you again."

Yep. The snark was out in full effect.

"Uh, hi." She slowly toed off her snowy boots and set them by the door.

"That's it? Just 'hi'?" He held one of the kittens, stroking the little bugger who tried to cling to his shirt. "No, Copo. You need to stop climbing me. You keep getting nowhere." He chuckled as the other kitten meowed and pawed at him from the ground. "See? Impala knows." Then he gently set both kittens inside a toddler-sized pen near the dining area.

The little things mewed and darted around, playing with a fuzzy ball and stuffed mouse and climbing past the mound of blanket that served as a bed.

"Are you keeping them?" She swallowed, wishing she didn't feel so damn much around him.

"I'm just getting them ready for adoption. The vet said they were perfectly healthy, so I'm only helping to feed them."

Huh. He sounded defensive. "Really? Because they seem to have names." And a bunch of cat toys in a cat pen.

Seeing his flush made her feel better. It was nice to see the man looking off his game for once. Hell, she'd been off since she'd first met the guy.

She cocked a brow. "Copo and Impala? I know an Impala's a car, but a copo?"

He gave an exaggerated sigh. "COPO stands for Central Office Production Order. In 1969, Chevrolet rolled out the Chevy Chevelle COPO 9562. It had little in the way of extras, but its performance options were incredible. Heavy-duty suspension and radiator, 12-bolt rear limited slip differential, and an L72 engine."

She blinked. "Huh?"

"Then you have the 1968 Chevy Impala SS427 L72, which was also a queen. Not the 1967 version, I'm talking 1968."

She crossed her arms over her chest, amused. "Oh, sure. Everyone knows that."

"The '68 version is cherry. Chevrolet dropped a 425-hp, solid-lifter, iron-block L72 427 in the car, the same engine that powered the '66 Corvette and the COPO Camaro in '69. You could get the Impala with the Turbo-Hydramatic 400 three-speed automatic or Muncie four-speed. And don't get me started on the 1968 hard-top." He patted his heart. "Hubba-hubba."

"You have issues."

"Yes, I do." His good humor left as he glared at her. "The biggest of which is why you won't take my calls or answer my texts. Look, Cass, if you don't want to go out again, fine. But have the balls to tell me so."

"We're not exactly going out." She hated that he was right. Or that she was blushing. Or that she found his righteous anger and confidence to confront her such a turn-on.

"That's a bullshit answer, and you know it. Just be honest with me."

She felt like crap because he did deserve better. They both knew it.

Cass shrugged out of her jacket and tossed it on the floor. Then she pushed up her sleeves and approached him. She must have looked as aggressive as she felt because he backed up until he met the wall, his expression leery.

"Now hold on. You hit me, I'll defend myself." He paused. "I mean, well, I won't hit you back, but I'll take you down, Cass. I'm not kidding."

"I know." She stopped before him, leaving maybe two inches between them.

Then she kissed him.

He tasted delicious. A full-on combination of man, sex, and chocolate. The trinity of all that was good and addictive.

He got over his surprise fast, his participation in the kiss there then gone. He grabbed her wrists in his large hands and pushed her back a step. "Wh-what the hell?" He swallowed hard, and she didn't have to look down to feel his arousal. "You ghost me for a week, and now you want to use me like a dime-store rent boy?"

She just looked at him. "Like a what?"

"Isn't that what they call male prostitutes on *Law & Order*?"

She wanted to laugh. "I don't think so."

"Well, you know what I mean." His fingers gripping her wrists weren't tight, and she lowered one hand to his fly while staring into his eyes. The light blue had definitely darkened, his pupils wide. "What are you doing?"

"I'm trying to apologize."

"You, uh…" He stopped talking and let her go, his eyes wide as she slowly lowered to her knees. "You can't… You can't just expect…"

She unsnapped his jeans and unzipped him before tugging his jeans down to mid-thigh.

"I need you to…"

She pulled down his underwear and gripped his thick erection.

"I… I… You should, um, respect…"

She drew his cock to her parted lips and breathed over him.

He groaned and closed his eyes for a second before opening them to glare down at her. "You can't just… Oh fuck. *Do it.*"

She took him between her lips, working to get around his thick girth. Mack was huge and growing as she started to bob over him.

She closed her eyes, intent on how sexy she found the act, dominating Mack while giving him pleasure. Hearing his moans and pleas for more, feeling his hands cradle her skull, his fingers tangle in her hair to guide her, all increased her own arousal.

Had it been a week and a day since they'd been together? What had she been waiting for?

"Yeah, oh, Cass, yes." Mack pushed deeper into her mouth, his cock hitting the back of her throat, but she just kept going.

Cass gripped his hips, taking back control as she licked and sucked him toward orgasm. When she cupped his balls and caressed him, he threatened to come.

So she sucked harder.

"Cass, I'm not kidding," he rasped, still pumping. He tried to pull back, but she gripped his ass and pulled him closer.

He thrust once more, groaned her name, and jetted down her throat.

Mack came hard, much to her pleasure. She finished him off, swallowing the last bit down, then tucked him back into his clothes and stood.

He just leaned back against the wall, shell-shocked and breathing hard as he stared down at her.

She wiped her lips, left him for some water to drink, then returned with a mug of cocoa instead. "I made myself a mug. Hope you don't mind." She'd ladled out some of the good stuff from a pot on the stove.

He nodded, still wild-eyed. "You... I mean, you sucked me off."

"The term you're looking for is 'blow job.'"

"I know what it's called," he snapped, took a deep breath, then let it out. "Damn, woman. You ignore me for a week then you fucking blow me without warning. I came so hard I can't think."

She sipped her cocoa and smiled. "You're welcome."

He managed to drag himself to his sofa and flopped onto it, putting an arm over his face. "Why?"

"I felt like it."

He lowered his arm and glared at her, and his frustration aroused her. *Because, yes, I'm a wacko turned on by an angry Mack Revere.* "I'm not upset about the blow job, but do you think we could have an actual conversation that doesn't involve my dick?"

"Well, if you insist."

He didn't laugh.

She sighed. "Look, I'm sorry. I meant to talk to you before today, but I was busy. I had appointments, community events, and some crazy days on the job."

"I know you're busy, Cass. But you could have texted me back anytime before today. A simple 'forget it' would have worked."

"No." She didn't want that at all. At his raised brow, she said, "I want you to come to dinner tonight."

"You sure? Or do you mean you want me to come again?" He smirked. "Because you give me a little time, I can. Easily." His humor faded. "Is that why I got the little demonstration against the wall? To remind me we're only hanging for sex?"

"No." She flushed. "Look, I came over to apologize. I'm really sorry for acting all weird. I didn't mean to blow you."

"Sure. You just fell, open-mouthed, onto my dick."

She coughed to hide the laughter burbling inside. "No, I, um, no." He didn't appear to be amused, so she cleared her throat and explained, "I do want you to come to dinner with me tonight. And I'm sorry if the blow job was out of place."

"Out of place?" His voice rose embarrassingly high. He scrubbed his eyes, sat up straight, and stared at her. "I came so hard I almost blacked out. That was fine. I mean, an explanation or warning beforehand would have been nice is all. You can always use me for sex. But I'd like it if we sometimes talked too," he said sarcastically.

She nodded. "I know. I just... You're odd."

"Sorry?"

"You make it weird."

He watched her. "Weird how?"

"I don't know." She frowned. "But I'm not sure I like it. You're different. I like you. I don't know." She made little sense.

He seemed to understand though. He nodded. "I am different." Instead of asking for more explanations, he smiled. "Do you like the cocoa? It's got a peppermint taste I love."

"It's actually pretty good."

He had a goofy look on his face as he watched her sip some more.

She frowned. "What?"

"Nothing." He sat back and kicked his feet up on the coffee table, suddenly no longer angry. In fact, he looked pretty satisfied with himself. "Do you want to clue me into what to expect tonight? Are we pretending to be dating or what? Or are you just showing me off to your friends?"

"Showing you off? Please." She chuckled. "Like I told you before, you coming as my date keeps my friend Shannon off my butt."

"I thought she was Jed's wife."

"She can't be my friend too?"

"Well, sure. But you seem like the type to…"

"The type to what?"

He groaned. "Forget it. You'll just get mad at me again."

"Say it, Revere."

"Fine." He sighed. "You're hot. Sexy. A lot of women are threatened by that. I know Nat and Lori get pushback from some of the guys' wives. Or at least Nat used to, but she's married now, so it settled down. But Lori still gets some grief at barbecues from some of the wives and girlfriends. It's not fair, but it's a reality for women working in a male-dominated field."

She blinked. "You're pretty observant."

"I have a lot of friends who are women. Just *friends*," he

emphasized. "When I was in the Air Force, it was the same thing. I understand it because in the Air Force, a lot of my friends' boyfriends and husbands would be jealous of *me*. At least until I met them and showed them I respect the ring. I don't care how unhappy a woman might be. If she's married, she's off limits."

"Good. Remember that. Shannon's cute, and Jed's protective. Try not to flirt too much."

"Right. The rules. Go ahead. I'm listening."

He sure seemed to be understanding and easy with whatever she wanted. *I guess that blow job did the trick.* "Right. The rules."

"But I'm having a tough time hearing you. Could you sit next to me on the couch?" He patted the spot next to him. "Right here."

"You're going to be difficult about this, aren't you?" She sighed.

"Right. Difficult. But not hard." He glanced down at his crotch. "You took care of that."

She blushed. "Would you let it go already?"

"Not on your life, Cassandra." He smiled. "Now lay it on me."

━━━━━━━━

Mack watched her debate with herself before sitting next to him on the couch. He had a tough time getting his brain back online again. The woman had come into his home, stalked him like a hungry tiger, then dropped to her knees and blown him.

A fucking blow job out of nowhere.

Who did that? And how could he get her to do that again?

He watched her mouth move, taken with her soft lips. She'd hugged him with that mouth. Stroked him with that tongue. And those firm, capable hands had cupped him and taken him to heaven without even trying.

God, I'm easy.

But it was her acknowledgment that soothed him after all. He was different. He meant something to her, and she didn't know how to handle her feelings. Strong, confident, capable Cass had avoided talking to him because she'd been scared of how much she liked him.

Finally. The woman saw him as more than just a body to ride.

"Are you paying attention?"

"Yep." He focused on her words, or at least he tried to. "Shannon is fierce, gorgeous, and proudly half-Korean with roots in San Francisco, so I can't insult the city in any way, shape, or form. Jed met her while he was stationed there when in the Navy. They have twins who are precocious, and, yes, I do know what that means."

"Right. Shannon might look sweet, but don't mess with her family or her city."

"Seattle?"

"Hello. San Francisco."

He rolled his eyes. "Right. So even though she's even shorter than you are, you're saying I should be cautious of her iron fists?"

"Yes. And I'm not that small."

Ha. Someone thought she was tall, though technically she only stood a few inches smaller than Mack. "Will she hit me if I don't like her pot roast?"

"No, but I might."

He grinned. "Fine. I won't bad-mouth San Francisco, though I wouldn't have even without your weird warnings. And I'll love whatever she makes. I like food, and I'm a perfect guest. I'm polite to my hosts and know when to leave."

"Well, you'll be arriving and leaving when I do. Don't be late."

"Oh, so you want to go together?"

"No, I meant—"

"Great. We can take your car."

She frowned. "Why not your car?"

He gasped. "It's miserable outside. I don't take Vella out in this kind of weather." He'd been driving his ten-year-old SUV and would continue to do so until the weather warmed up.

She rolled her eyes. "Right. Fine. I'll pick you up at five-thirty. We're supposed to bring the wine."

"I'm guessing you're a Boone's Farm kind of gal. *I'll* bring the wine."

She scowled. "I know wine."

"Really?"

She looked like she meant to say something, then changed her mind. "I know red is refrigerated and white isn't."

"Not quite." He sighed. "What are we having for dinner?"

"For real, pot roast with potatoes and carrots. Regular food I like." She narrowed her eyes. "With gravy."

He considered that. "Like, a wine sauce or a heavier gravy?"

"Regular gravy. It's brown and tastes good over the meat."

"Okay. I'll bring a Bordeaux then. Beer too. Hmm. I'll grab an ale or a porter. That would go well with a roast."

"Whatever."

Mack did his best not to smile at her grumpiness. "Is it a problem if I bring the alcohol?"

"No. I was going to hit the grocery store after I finished soothing your wounded ego, you know, because I didn't jump on your text right away." Yet her blush said she knew she'd been wrong.

"Oh, I'm sorry." She wanted to go there, did she? "Let me ask you a question. If you called Jed and he didn't answer for a week, or you texted him and he couldn't find the time to text you back for *eight days*, would that be okay?"

"Well, no. But—"

"What kind of relationships have you had? And I don't mean your friendship with Jed or Shannon. I'm talking real, man-woman-type relationships?"

"What's that supposed to mean?" She turned her entire body on the couch to face him.

"I *mean,* when you've been dating, do you have some sort of system for communicating?"

She frowned. "You're making this into a big deal that it's not."

"Explain it to me."

Her pink cheeks said what she couldn't. She didn't know how to handle him, so she'd run scared. "Look, I apologize. I know it was wrong, and I have no excuse."

"Much better."

She glared so hard it was a wonder his face didn't melt under the glow. "I won't blow you off again."

"Blow me...off. Right. But you can still blow me."

"You wish," she muttered, her anger having faded.

"I do." He grinned. "Now, so I'm tracking about tonight... I show up with you. I'm polite. I don't look too hard at Shannon or think bad thoughts about San Francisco. I laugh at all Jed's jokes, and I tell them what wonderful children they have."

"Well, the kids are little hooligans, and Jed's not that funny, but yeah."

"Got it." He paused. "What about you?"

"What about me?"

"Well, should I know any important facts?"

"You know me."

"Do I?" He liked that she seemed uncomfortable. The fact that he'd gotten under her guard was a good thing. "What's your favorite color? Number? Animal? Do you prefer dogs or cats? Do you like movies? If so, what kind? Do you read? What's your favorite sport? I don't know any of that. But if we're in a relationship, I probably should."

She slumped. "You're going to be difficult about this, aren't you?"

"Not at all."

She sighed and sagged back against the armrest, half lying on the couch. "Yeah, you are. I knew you would be."

Chapter Twelve

MACK GRINNED. "HUMOR ME."

"Fine. I like the color red."

"For blood, I'll bet," he murmured.

She smirked at him. "Yeah, for all that blood you're gonna shed the next time the Top Cops smash you at soccer."

"Ha. If you can catch me."

She frowned and continued, "I don't have a favorite number. That's stupid. And do not tell me that yours is sixty-nine. How old are you? Thirteen?"

"Thirty, but close enough." He grinned.

She smothered the laugh he could see coming. "Um, I like animals, I guess. The cats are cute. I've never had a pet."

"Never?"

"Nope. My parents have always worked hard, and I knew if we got a pet, I'd have to take care of it. I didn't want the responsibility. I've always been busy with other things." She glanced at the kittens now snoozing together on the blanket. "Copo and Impala are sweet."

She remembered their names. A plus for her. "What else? Movies or books? Beach or mountains?"

"I like books *and* movies. I watch TV a lot, I guess. Mostly sitcoms. I like to laugh."

"Could have fooled me."

She glared at him, and he chuckled, which had her laughing as well. "You're an ass."

"So they say."

"I do like movies. Mostly action or superhero ones. Books, well, I read some."

Her blush intrigued him. What embarrassed her about reading books?

She quickly continued, "My favorite sport is soccer, followed by volleyball and track."

"Track isn't a sport. It's just a lot of running," he said to annoy her.

"Up yours."

"I'm kidding. I ran track in high school and college."

"You went to college?" She stared at him from a position that had to be uncomfortable. She sat on her butt cross-legged but leaned back to rest her head on the arm of the couch. Talk about limber.

He swallowed hard. "Yeah, who would have guessed? Seven years in the Air Force, then an associate's degree in fire science while I became an EMT before getting on with the Seattle Fire Department."

"Huh. I did four years at the University of Washington for criminal justice. Entered the police academy after and have been a patrol officer ever since. I was thinking about maybe becoming a detective at some point. I don't know. I love working with Jed."

"Why?"

"We help people. Real people with real problems. And Jed's cool. He's not a bigot, doesn't hate women, and loves helping people who need it. He's kind underneath the Terminator image."

"Like you. A protector, right?"

"I guess."

He launched himself over her before she could move, pinning her down into the couch with his lower body. "But you're not so great at protecting yourself."

She snorted with laughter. "Get off, you oaf."

"Pretend I'm a perp. How would you handle me?"

"I handled you just fine earlier." She tried to move him but couldn't. He had her hands pinned above her head, his weight and her crossed legs keeping her in place.

"You're saying you'd just blow the bad guys? Is that legal?"

"You're such an idiot."

He truly was because he had to kiss her or die. So he kissed her, and all the warmth in his body centered in his lips. He made love to her mouth, fascinated by this hard-nosed woman who had such confusing moments of vulnerability and kindness so at odds with the tough image she projected.

He put both of her wrists in one of his hands while using the other to cup her breast.

She moaned his name and kissed him back.

He continued to plunder her mouth, fitting his hand under her sweatshirt to play with her breasts through her bra. Needing more, he angled his hand down her belly, past her underwear into the hot, wet heat of her.

Mack pulled back to look into her beautiful face, her eyes slumberous. "What do we tell your friends about our relationship?"

"Mack," she breathed.

God, she got to him. He started moving his fingers. "Do we tell them you make me hard? Or that you're so good with that mouth that I nearly blacked out when I came?" He leaned in to kiss her, pumping his fingers faster, loving the way she ground up against him.

"Mack, stop."

He paused.

"No." She wiggled against his hand. "Keep going. I say, 'Mack stop' because you're too strong for me. And I can't stop you. And it gets me hot."

She liked to play. He was in love.

"Yeah, you're mine to do whatever I want with." He kissed her again, moving his mouth to her ear to whisper, "I want to feel you get my hand all slick. Come for me, and later, I'll take you from behind. Fuck you until you can't see straight. Holding you down while I drill you, and you'll be so helpless while I force you to come…"

She cried out, her body clamping down on his fingers like a vise.

"Office Carmichael, you got me all wet." Mack shifted his fingers, and she groaned. He kissed her again. "But you know, we really need to stop meeting like this. You taking advantage of me in my own home, no less. In front of the children!" He glanced over at the still-sleeping kittens.

She gave him a slow smile. "You're such an asshole."

"Yeah." He sighed and eased off her, wiping his fingers on his shirt. "Now go home before I finish what you started." No surprise he was hard again. "Pick me up no later than five-thirty. I don't want to be late and make a bad impression on your friends."

"Don't worry, Studly. I'm sure they'll like you."

"Of course they'll like me. It's you I'm worried about. When they see how in love with me you are, they'll grow concerned. I'll have to spend most of the night letting them know I'll be gentle with you."

———————

Cass didn't know whether to cry because she feared he might be right or slug him for being so incredibly conceited. Mack made her laugh regardless. "Jesus. It's getting deep in here."

"Deep?"

"With all the bullshit you're slinging around."

He laughed. "Yep."

"Dress nice. Do not embarrass me," she warned, as if the man knew how to not be charming and alarmingly sexy.

"I won't. Unless you throw me up against the wall at their place and blow me. Then I won't be able to keep my voice down. I'm a screamer, in case you haven't noticed."

He was not. She flushed and had to work not to stagger to the door, embarrassingly weak at the knees. "Whatever. Just be ready to go, Romeo."

"Of course, Juliet." He gave a showman's bow.

She put her boots on, grabbed her coat, and stormed outside.

Into a storm. Without having taken the time to first put her coat on.

I'm an idiot.

———————

At five-thirty on the dot, Cass pulled in front of Mack's house, noting the shoveled walkway to his door. The snow had eased into a dusting of light flurries, and thank goodness the forecast called for warmer temperatures to melt it all by next week.

Before she could text him to come outside, his door opened. He locked up and soon joined her in the car, bags in hand.

He looked damn good and smelled divine. She leaned closer and sniffed. "What are you wearing?"

"It's my natural scent of Eau de Mack." He winked. "Wanna jump me?"

Yes. She gave him a look of indifference, which wasn't easy. "You have the booze?"

"I do." He glanced at the two paper bags at his feet.

"Geez, Mack. It's one dinner. How much did you buy?"

He grinned. "Well, I brought a bottle of wine for the adults. And some beer for us and the kids."

"*What?*"

"Relax. I brought a bottle of nice wine for the adults. The apple juice—in cans—is for the kids. I couldn't decide between the ale and porter, so I got a few bottles of both for those adults who want beer."

"Oh, nice. How much do I owe you?"

He glared at her. "Are you insulting me?"

"What?"

"I was invited to a nice dinner. Your job is to make me happy. Mine is to supply alcohol to enhance our evening."

"Thank you." Then she had to add, "I hadn't realized what a big booze snob you were. I'd have been fine bringing along some Bud Light."

He slapped his forehead. "How can you be so talented with that mouth yet can't tell a quality beer from piss water?"

"That's disgusting."

"So's Bud Light!"

They argued all the way to Jed and Shannon's, and though Cass hated to admit it to herself, she loved debating with Mack. Her last boyfriend hadn't realized that discussing topics and not agreeing on everything was okay. It didn't mean she'd liked him any less. Though the fact he thought she had to like everything he said and did had caused her to sour faster on the relationship.

Mack, though, gave as good as he got. She didn't worry she'd offend him if she hated what he thought. Or if she blatantly argued just to argue.

"You're so wrong about so much," he said cheerily as she parked. "It's a good thing you're pretty."

"Screw you."

"Yes, such a way with words."

She laughed after giving him a light sock on the arm. Before she could get out of the car, he yanked her to him and kissed the breath out of her.

"There. I win." He sprung from the car like he'd been sitting on coils. "Grab the drinks, would you?"

She joined him at the door, fuming. "That was cheap." And way too good. She hadn't wanted that kiss to end.

"Cheap but effective."

She glared.

"You're just mad you didn't get the last word. And you wouldn't want to anyway."

"Why not?"

"Because you were wrong. Have you ever been to Germany, woman?"

"Woman?"

"They make real beer there. Lagers and weizens—wheat beers—and ales. The stuff of champions!" He lifted his fist in the air. "Champions, I say!"

Jed opened the door, stared from Mack to Cass and back again, and rolled his eyes. "I can tell it's gonna be that kind of night." He grabbed the bags from Cass and yelled over his shoulder, "Shannon, they're here."

Behind Jed, the twins stood staring at her and Mack.

Cass greeted them with a smile. "Hey Lucifer. Azazel."

Mack blinked.

Jed glared at Cass and said to Mack, "My kids, Mike and Sam."

Both dark-haired and dark-eyed, eight-year-old Michael and Samantha looked and acted a lot like Shannon. Beautiful children hiding imps inside.

"Hi." Sam smiled shyly at Mack. "I'm older than Mike."

Mike turned to her with a frown. "We're twins. She just came out of Mom's vagina first."

"Mike!" Cass tried not to laugh.

Jed nudged them back. "Go bug your mom, you two."

Mack coughed, hiding a grin from Jed, but Cass saw it.

Jed sighed. "Well, you've met the twins. My wife's in the kitchen."

"Barefoot and pregnant?" Cass asked with a perky smile.

"And fuck you too," Jed said under his breath, to which Mack did laugh. Loudly.

"We're done having kids," Jed said. "The twins scared us straight. I mean, we love them so much we can't imagine having anything to take our attention from our heavenly little angels."

Mack shut the door behind them and followed Cass and Jed into the kitchen. "How old are they?"

"Eight going on forty," Cass answered as the twins darted away and disappeared somewhere in the house. "Sam was my favorite last time I was over, but Mike whipping out 'vagina' in front of company? He's my new little darling."

"I hope you brought alcohol," Jed muttered. He looked inside the bags and smiled. "Oh, nice. Thanks, Mack."

Cass frowned. "Maybe I brought them."

Jed raised a brow. "The wine isn't sparkling or flavored with wild strawberry. And the beer is…" He peered inside the bag with the beer and smiled. "Sweet."

Mack shook his head. "She wanted to bring Bud Light."

"Oh, Cass."

Shannon joined them, the petite beauty beaming. "You must be Mack. Jed has told me all about you."

Mack shot Jed a look but smiled. "A pleasure to meet you. You're so much prettier and nicer than Cass said you'd be."

Shannon shot Cass her infamous death glare. Jed snickered. Shannon cleared her throat and said, "Mack. You're just as handsome in person as you are on all those posters."

Ha. That wiped the smile off Jed's face.

Mack ignored him, took Shannon's hand, and kissed the back of it. "Ah, a woman with taste." He gave Jed a once-over. "I take it you were drunk when you married him?"

She laughed while Jed stood to his full height and glowered.

Mack snorted, clearly amused. "Oh, relax, big guy. I'm just messing with you. I thought you'd have a sense of humor. I mean, Cass *is* your partner, isn't she?"

Cass gave him a look. "Such a dick."

"Who's a dick?" Sam said, appearing out of nowhere.

"Cass," Shannon snapped.

Mack hurriedly added, "I brought you and your brother beer too, Sam."

Mike suddenly stood by Mack's elbow. "You brought us *beer*?" His eyes were huge.

Jed looked to be trying to hide a smile. "I don't know, Shannon. I mean, Mack is company, but should we really give our children kid beer?"

Shannon saw the six-pack Jed held and sighed. "I guess they need to start sometime."

Mike took a can from his dad and frowned. "This says apple juice."

"Yeah, but I got it at the liquor store," Mack said and leaned closer to whisper loudly, "You know wine comes from grapes. You can get alcohol from apples too. Yours has a certain percent by volume alcohol even though it says it's juice."

Cass shook her head. Yeah, *zero* percent by volume alcohol.

Mike's eyes grew wide. "Oh, okay."

Sam took the can and looked at Mack as if he was her new hero. Cass didn't know whether to be offended or amused that she'd been so easily replaced.

"Thanks, Mack." Sam popped the top and took a long sip. "Ah. That's good stuff." Then she scampered after her brother, heading upstairs.

Shannon laughed. "Smooth. Are you a dad or an uncle, by chance?"

Mack smiled. "Uncle in another five months. My oldest brother just announced they're expecting."

"It's a joy." Shannon smiled.

Jed coughed.

"Oh stop. You know it is."

Her husband smiled back at her, and Cass loved seeing the happiness that flowed between them. She might not be great at dating, reading a guy's interest, or relationships in general, but that didn't mean she didn't love romance. Jed and Shannon had it for sure.

Mack glanced at her. "What do you say, Cass? Should we try for our own twins? What do you want? A boy and a girl? Should we try for a basketball team? Stop at five or keep going?"

Jed and Shannon just stared at them.

Cass had to laugh.

Mack snickered. "They're so easy."

"I know." She grabbed one of the beers Mack had brought and handed him one as well. "Shannon, I was telling Mack what a great cook you are. Tell him what we're having."

She did, pulling Mack into a discussion about food. He apparently wasn't a bad cook himself, and he had definite ideas about what drink paired well with what dish.

Jed pulled Cass aside, out of his wife's hearing. "What the hell was that?"

"What?"

"Are you guys talking about having kids already?"

"Are you high?" She stared up into his pupils.

He put a hand to her forehead and pushed her back. "Don't be a dumbass." He studied her. "You like this guy."

"You told me to bring him, as a date, and get Shannon to fall for it. I am. What's your problem?"

"Nothing. But when you used to bring Sean around, if he ever mentioned a kid, you got this sick look on your face. You're not even dating Mack."

"He was just kidding. Relax."

Jed gave her a sly grin. "*Oh.* I see."

She doubted he saw anything. "What's with making fun of my taste in booze?"

"You think wine coolers are hard liquor."

She flushed. "I do not. Unless you mix them with vodka and juice in a cup."

"I rest my case."

"Look, I'm here doing my part."

Jed sighed. "I know. Mack did bring some good stuff. Did you tell him to include the kids?"

"No, he did that on his own."

"He's a nice guy," Jed said, sounding satisfied. Odd.

"So?"

He looked at her. "So nothing. That was a compliment, Cass. For your date. Who'd better not be flirting with my wife," he added in a grumble.

Cass sighed. "Just play your part and we'll play ours. Dinner will be easy."

And it was.

While the kids took their meal in the playroom upstairs, treated to "kid beer" and some superhero movie she wouldn't have minded watching with them, Mack acted perfectly charming. He had Jed and Shannon laughing. He asked real questions of Jed and Cass about being on the job, relating the discussion to his siblings. He seemed genuinely interested in Shannon's career; she worked from home doing medical transcriptions. He spoke about the horror of what being on the posters for the new station had been like.

"Yeah, so these older women kept coming up to me and asking me out. It was weird."

"When you say older, you mean…?" Shannon asked.

"Like, thirty-four or thirty-five." At her glare, he laughingly amended, "Eighty or ninety, at least. On walkers. And they're hitting on me, and my friends are there. It was a nightmare. We play a lot of pranks on each other at the station. For a while, I was that old guy from that cartoon movie *Up*. And I had granny dolls doing bad, bad things to me all over the place."

Cass hadn't been able to stop laughing.

He'd complimented Shannon over every dish, though Cass had to admit her friend had done herself proud. Cass had never had a better meal.

"Geez, Shannon. How come you never cook like this when it's just me over?"

Jed frowned. "How do you think I feel? I live with her and never get this kind of service."

"I'll give you some service," Shannon told her husband while smiling sweetly at Mack. "Maybe it's the appreciative company."

"Nah." Mack shook his head. "It's the wine. It pairs incredibly well with a roast cooked to perfection."

Shannon sighed with pleasure, and Cass smothered a chuckle seeing Jed roll his eyes once more at something Mack said.

She pretended to be jealous. "Hey, Mack, you're here with me, remember."

"Of course I am, darling." He kissed her cheek, which had Shannon smiling openly at the pair. "But you don't cook for me like Shannon does."

Shannon tittered.

"But on another note, Jed, what exactly did you say to my buddy, Tex? Because he was complaining a ton about you and your ideas about the Cowboys."

Which had Jed going off about the loathsome team, with Mack interjecting here and there about his thoughts.

Dinner wound down. The kids brought their empty plates down and grabbed a second helping of kid beer then left for a second movie. The guys continued to bandy attitude about their favorite football teams, and Cass and Shannon headed to the living room to relax while the men cleared the table.

Shannon glanced around and, seeing them alone, whispered, "Oh my gosh, Cass, he's *amazing.*"

Cass flushed, having thought the same thing despite being annoyed at how over-the-top complimentary Mack had been to Shannon all night. She'd told him to be nice, but maybe not *that* nice. "He's okay."

"He's hot as hell, those eyes are killing me, and he's so polite and charming. How do you stand it?"

"It's tough, but I make do." She gave a put-upon sigh. "The sad part is that he's so big and lasts forever. I mean, I like sex, but come on. Three times a day? I need sleep, you know."

Shannon just stared, her mouth open wide.

So satisfying. Cass wanted badly to laugh.

Before Shannon could say anything, the guys returned.

"I brought Pictionary," Jed said with a grim smile. "No crying when you weak asses lose."

Mack guffawed, looking from Jed to Cass. "No wonder you two make such great partners. You're both competitors."

"Hey, I saw you at the bar." Jed sat next to Shannon. "You're no lightweight. I mean, you were at soccer, but you weren't half bad at the pool table."

Mack sneered. "Maybe if *Cass-an-dra*"—he just had to draw out her name —"hadn't tried to cut my knees out from under me, you'd have seen a lot more of me on the field."

Cass stood in a huff. "Who are you calling Cassandra?" Had she told him she hated being called by her full name? Because she usually did… Except when he said it, she got all hot and bothered.

"You, dumbass." Mack opened his mouth to add to that stellar comment when he suddenly stopped.

Cass turned to spy Samantha and Mike in the archway, watching and sipping from their cans.

Mack cleared his throat. "Er, you, funny lady."

Mike and Sam were pointing at Cass and laughing their little heads off. Mike said between giggles, "Ha. You're a dumbass, Aunt Cass! See, Dad? That's not a bad word."

Cass frowned at her partner. "Wonder where they heard that before."

"Jed, do something about that." Shannon waved at the twins. "Potty mouths don't get dessert."

"But we're drunk on beer, Mom," Sam said, deliberately slurring her words.

"It *is* zero percent alcohol, Shannon," Jed said, doing his best not to smile.

"Well, maybe I'll be lenient. This time. But you have to apologize to your dumbass aunt first."

"Shannon," Cass growled.

The kids giggled some more.

"Cass, be nice," Mack said. "Or no kisses for you in the car."

She blushed, especially when the kids started making kissy faces. And then their father did it.

Shannon chuckled. Mack smirked, and Cass called them all dumbasses before grabbing and tickling the demon twins to make them recant.

But what really made the night perfect—she and Mack crushed Jed and Shannon, becoming the new Pictionary champions of the Karsten household. First time ever. And wouldn't she hold that against her *dumbass* partner for the months to come.

Chapter Thirteen

MACK HADN'T EXPECTED TO HAVE SO MUCH FUN. WATCHING Cass let her hair down—and, damn, but she was amazing looking with it soft and long around her shoulders—metaphorically speaking, had been eye-opening.

She wasn't guarded around her friends. She still teased, still wanted to win at all costs, and had been downright rude rubbing their noses in it, but she softened into a funny, fun partner.

He wanted her something fierce but made sure to act light-hearted and casual despite feeling a lot more than like for this warm, edgy woman.

Shannon cornered him in the kitchen while Jed and Cass argued about who had to put the game away. "She's a keeper, you know."

"Cass? Of course I know. But she's skittish. I'm going in easy."

"Good plan. I don't think I've ever seen her laugh so much with anyone outside Jed and me. She takes herself too seriously. The girl just needs to relax." She paused. "Just make sure to always be honest with her. Cass hates liars."

"Yeah, me too." They shared a smile, and Mack said, "I can tell Jed's a good partner. Seems to always have her back. Cass is lucky."

"Sounds like you are too. Your friends sound great. Jed told me about Tex. He sounds like a funny guy."

"He's Texan. They're all a little funny." He made the crazy sign by his ear, which had her laughing. "But seriously, thank you so much for having me for dinner. I had a great time."

"That's sweet. I know it wasn't fancy. Just pot roast, but—"

"*Just* pot roast? Are you kidding? That roast is right up there with my mom's lasagna. But never tell her I said that."

Jed and Cass came in, saw Mack standing so close to Shannon, and froze.

Mack rolled his eyes at them both. "Really? Do you think I'd make a move where Cass might see me? Honestly, Jed. I'm not an idiot."

Jed lost his menacing glared and laughed. "Another person who clearly knows she's meaner than I am. Nice."

Shannon shook her head. "Men are idiots."

"Amen." Cass sniffed. "Shannon, I just wanted to say thanks for dinner. And thank you for keeping the twins upstairs."

Mack couldn't believe she'd said that. "Cass. The twins are adorable."

Jed blinked. "Ah, yeah. Maybe you can babysit them some time."

"No thanks. Kittens are one thing. Kids another."

"Kittens?" Shannon said.

The kids had a magical ability to appear out of nowhere. They emerged from the shadows and started interrogating him about the kittens.

"Mack rescued them," Cass told them. "He helps with Pets Fur Life, a charity that helps home stray animals. He found the kittens."

"*We* found them."

"Yes, *we* found them behind a restaurant last week. He's helping them grow big and strong so they can be adopted."

"Damn it, Cass," Jed growled under his breath.

"Kittens!" Sam looked to her mom. "Please, can we get one?"

Mike added, "Yes, Mom. Please? Please? Please?"

"Ah, well, they already have a promised home," Mack said quickly, seeing the trouble brewing. "But if more come in, I'll be sure to let your aunt know."

Jed clapped an arm around his shoulders. "You're a good man."

"Thank you," Shannon gushed. Her children's eyes narrowed, so she tacked on, "For helping those poor little kittens, thank you so much."

Her kids seemed satisfied and told Mack goodnight. Sam hugged his leg before darting away with her brother upstairs for bed.

"I guess I'd better go too," Mack said. "My ride looks annoyed with me."

Cass snorted. "Hey, you have nothing to do tomorrow, but Jed and I have to work."

"And I have the weekend free." Shannon gave her husband a smug smile.

"No, you don't."

"I don't?"

Jed drew his wife in for a kiss and whispered something in her ear.

She blushed and drew back. After clearing her throat, she said, "I guess I do have some work to do. I better be getting paid by the hour."

"Ouch. That sounds like a tough gig." Mack cringed at the sight of Jed's broad grin. "Come on, Cass. Before I start putting two and two together. I don't want any lingering images."

She snickered. "Get a room, you two." Then she hugged her partner and his wife and tugged Mack out the door by the hand.

Once at the car, he pinned her to the driver's side and kissed her. She was soft and warm, so sexy. He wanted to sink into her and never leave. "Ah. Been waiting to do that forever."

―――――――

Cass, out of breath, prayed no one had seen that. *Crap.* A curtain twitched. "Argh. Get in the car."

Once inside, he grinned and stared at her while she drove them back to his place. "Your friends are great."

She sighed. "They really are. And they liked you."

"Everyone likes me." At her huff, he added, "Especially you."

"You wish."

"I do wish."

They listened to music on the way home, arguing when he tried changing the station to classic rock. Cass preferred contemporary pop. He paused when an oldie by George Michael came on a different station. Of course, it had to be "I Want Your Sex."

Mack guffawed. "I do. I really do." Just as she pulled up to his house, he said, "Say, you want to come inside and play with my... kittens?"

"Oh stop. That was terrible. What the heck is 'kittens' a euphemism for anyway?"

"I'm not kidding. I'm in the mood for some pussy...cats."

"Mack." Her lips twitched, and she tried not to humor him. "I'd better get home."

"But it's cold out. Come on. I swear, I won't make a move on you."

Too bad.

"Cass, you can at least make sure I get inside all right. What if I'm mugged? What if I slip and fall and can't get up?"

"Stop."

"What if I get lost? It's dark out."

"Oh my God. Okay."

He waited for her to turn off the car before exiting. Then he opened her door and helped her out.

"I'm not so old I can't get out of my own car."

"Shut up." He put her hand in the crook of his elbow, like a perfect gentleman, and walked her to his door.

Cass didn't know why, but his treatment warmed her all over, and she could feel her heartbeat racing.

Mack let them both inside and hung up their coats. They set their shoes aside, and he immediately turned on the fire.

The kittens woke and started crying to be let out of their pen.

"Oh, hey guys." Mack smiled.

His expression looked so tender, she had to look away. *Huh. How about that fire? It sure feels, um, hot.*

"Want something to drink?"

She looked up to see him holding both kittens. *Ah-dor-ah-ble.*

Cass cleared her throat. "A cocoa would be nice. With marsh-mallows, if you have them."

"What, am I a heathen? Of course I'll serve them with marsh-mallows." He put the cats down and walked into the kitchen, mut-tering, "Does she really think so little of me?"

Cass sank to the floor and had kittens climbing on her. "Oh wow. You guys are definitely trouble. Cute and furry and so soft."

She let them crawl all over her and had fun playing with them. Their tiny teeth and claws no more than pinpricks against her skin.

"Be right back," Mack called from the kitchen.

"Take your time." She sat on the floor near the fire, laughing as they kept trying to pounce before falling over each other.

When Mack returned, he carried two mugs and had changed into lounge pants and a sweatshirt. But he still smelled amazing, that cologne of his wafting over her as he neared.

"Thanks." She noted the bobbing marshmallows and saw iden-tical ones in his mug. "I see you like your sugar too." She sipped hers and sighed. "Okay, this is amazing. But how much hot choco-late do you have? Every time I'm here you're drinking it."

"I like hot chocolate." He shrugged. "More than coffee, actu-ally. During the winter, it's my go-to drink."

"Not beer, Mr. Snooty?"

He smirked. "Only the good kind." He sat near her on the floor, his back against the couch, his long legs stretched out and crossed at the ankle, showing off dark-blue socks without holes. "So, how did I do at your friends? I'd give myself an A."

"A minus for flirting."

"With Jed? I was a perfect gentleman." He winked. "Come on, it's obvious how much those two dote on each other. And that Jed could break anyone in half with ease. I'm a smart guy. If I were going to flirt, one, I wouldn't do it in front of him. And two, I damn well wouldn't do it front of you." He snorted. "And three, she's married. Not my type."

She knew that, but she still felt relief. And that bothered her. "What did I tell you about her being so sweet and nice yet scary underneath?"

He shivered. "Yeah, she's tough. I swear she almost stabbed Jed in the hand when he tried to get more roast without asking. And she got those twins in line, fast. That was impressive."

Cass chuckled. "I love the whole family. I first met Jed nearly four years ago. I was new to the station and worked with someone else before being partnered with him. All I saw was this huge, muscular guy who barely talks and looks like he's thinking about the best way to either dismember people or hide bodies. Then we got partnered together, and I realized that tough, quiet guy is really sweet. He's kind and hates injustice. He's an awesome dad and great friend who's married to an amazing person. He's pretty much my brother."

Mack nodded. "I sensed that. Shannon warned me not to mess around with you."

"She warned you off me?" Odd since Shannon had seemed to like Mack and Cass as a couple.

"No, she told me not to lie to you. No messing around in a bad way. Like I'd do that." He shook his head and sipped from his mug. "I haven't been a perfect guy my whole life. I know that's a shock, but it's true."

"Here we go."

"No, seriously. I've dated a good bit, but I never cheated. I just never found someone I wanted to be with for more than a few dates. I never lied or made a woman cry, that I know of. I might have disappointed a few by not wanting to continue a relationship, but I could usually get them to smile about us being over. I'm charming."

"And so humble."

"I prefer the term 'remarkable.'" He sipped more cocoa and left a small chocolate mustache over his lip. She wanted so badly to lick that off that she forced herself to focus on the kittens.

"What's your point, Mack?"

"My point is I don't hide things. I am what you see. A firefighter who helps stray animals. I have my own house, my own car, my own parents and idiot brothers. My job and my friends are more important to me than anything. Though I do really like cars."

"Okay, I get it." *And I've been put in my place. He isn't out for a relationship. Fine. No need to be a dick about it, Revere.*

"But I also really like you."

Her head whipped up, and she stared at him. "What?"

He smiled at her and licked off his chocolate mustache. "I've decided to make room for you in my life. I like you, Cass. You're pretty much a what-you-see-is-what-you-get kind of person. You're smart, and you're strong. You say what you feel, and you don't sugarcoat it. Even better, you play to win. I really respect that."

Wow. She didn't know what to say. That might have been the nicest compliment she'd ever received.

"Plus, you're hot as fuck and know how to give one hell of a blow job."

"Jesus, Mack." Yet she couldn't help laughing, so pleased he liked her for her and not because he wanted her to be something she wasn't. "I mean, why play if it's not to win?"

"Exactly." He nodded. "I know we're helping each other out with some plus-one dating stuff, but wouldn't it be nice if we could actually be friends?"

"Yeah." She frowned. "But you already have a bunch of friends."

"I know. They're all great." Mack looked down at his mug for a moment before he looked back at her. His eyes were just so *blue*. "Over the past year, my best friends have all fallen in love. I'm really happy for all of them. It's great."

She nodded.

"But sometimes I get the feeling the guys hang out with me out of pity. Like they'd rather be with their girlfriends, but because I'm single, they feel like if they don't spend time with me, I won't know what to do with myself." His cheeks were red. "Sounds stupid, I know."

"God, I feel the same way with Jed and Shannon. I love them to death, but they have their own family. They have kids! They don't need me always hanging around, no matter how much they say they do."

"Exactly. We're awesome people with awesome friends, but those friends have their own lives going on. Not that you and I don't have our own interests."

"Right. We do." She agreed. "I, ah... Well, I guess I don't really have that much going on. I work. I exercise. I help out with community outreach projects. That's pretty much it."

He let out a breath. "Me too. I work. I go to the gym. I help with Pets Fur Life. Sounds lame."

They stared at each other and sipped their cocoas. Watching Mack while he watched her, she heard what they'd both been saying without actually saying it. They were lonely but felt pathetic about admitting it. Having someone understand her without judging, she felt oddly shy.

"So what are we then?" she asked, trying to rid herself of the cringey feeling. "Friends? Friends with benefits? Fuck buddies or just platonic pals? What?"

He seemed to consider that before answering, "I think the sex should be a separate thing. Why not just call us friends? That's what we are, right?"

"Okay." She hated that she blushed.

"The sex part always gets complicated. We should only have sex when we both want to and not make a big deal of it at this point."

Wait. Sex wasn't a big deal?

"I mean, obviously when it comes to safety and our health, we have to be open and honest with each other. But if the sex makes it difficult for us to be friends, maybe we handle that differently. I've never liked the title 'friends with benefits' anyway. Friends always have benefits. Fuck buddies is more honest."

"I agree." She did. But she had no freakin' clue what he was talking about. Did he want more sex or not? Did she?

Yes, yes, she did.

"Look, from what you said before, you're not looking for a boyfriend." He raised a brow in question.

"Right." *Though if I were, it would totally be someone exactly like you.*

"I'm not dating or planning on dating anyone," he said. "You said you're not."

"Nope."

"Then we have sex when we want to. But our friendship is a solid thing that sex can't touch."

"It sounds so easy." She snorted. "Sex always confuses everything."

"It does. Which is why I'm compartmentalizing. I'm a guy. This is what we do. Friendship first. Sex second. If I'm horny and you're not in the mood, we just play board games or hang out and I don't get to be an asshole. If you're horny and I'm not in the mood… Yeah, no. I'm always in the mood. We have sex."

She grinned. "So easy."

"Yep."

Yet because he'd put it in such simple terms, Cass, who had never had a sexual relationship with a man not turn awkward, somehow found herself agreeing to be friends with the possibility of sex as a complete aside. Weird, but it somehow took the pressure off her strange new relationship with Mack.

"Okay, friend." She shook his hand, refusing to feel disappointed when he let go. "In the spirit of having defined our friendship, I have to be honest with you."

"Go ahead."

"We only won at Pictionary because of my drawing and intuitive skills. You need help."

A kitten crawled into his lap and balled up, closing its eyes.

Mack glared back at her but, after a glance at the furball in his lap, said in a harsh whisper, "You're totally full of shit. I owned that game and dragged you along for the victory. Go get the pad of paper from the junk drawer in the kitchen. Bring two pencils. And be prepared to eat your words."

An hour later, after arguing, waking the kittens, then putting them back in their pen, Cass had to concede that she and Mack had tied. Surprisingly, he could doodle with the best of them. But she was the better guesser, so they evened out.

She yawned, toasty thanks to the hot chocolate and heat of the fire. "I guess I should get going."

"You need to work tomorrow, I know. I'll be hitting the gym and tinkering on my car. I think I'm supposed to meet the guys for lunch at Reggie's, too. Or maybe Tex's place. I can't remember." His cell phone rang from somewhere in the house. "Shoot. Wait here. I'll answer quick and be right back."

She waited, and while she waited, she tugged on the throw from the back of the couch and snuggled in it, watching the fire. She let herself bask in the warm glow, happier than she'd been in a long time, and cuddled into the blanket that smelled of Mack's cologne. And fell asleep.

Chapter Fourteen

MACK HADN'T INTENDED TO GET IN A LONG CONVERSATION with his mother at ten-thirty on a Thursday night, but she insisted on asking him a ton of questions about Alec and Dean, which she should have just asked Alec about.

Ten minutes later, he hurried downstairs from the study, where he'd found his cell. He wanted to apologize for being gone so long when he saw Cass asleep in front of the fire.

He stared at the shine of black hair splayed over the blanket and the floor, her flushed cheeks and parted lips so sweet yet surprisingly sexy. In sleep, Cass looked soft, touchable. That she'd hate him seeing her unguarded made him fall a little harder for the woman he wanted like crazy.

He'd been hoping against hope that asking if she wanted a boyfriend would get him a different answer. But she'd said no. He could respect that. He could also work to change her mind without pressuring her in any way. Let Cass make all the moves. Let her see what an incredible boyfriend he'd make, what a handsome fiancé he'd one day be.

He should have been more freaked out that his mind was going toward a place of permanence with Cass. Was it being around so many couples he respected? His friends, his family, heck, Jed and Shannon?

No, because the guys had been gravitating toward love and marriage for a while now, and none of those relationships had pushed him to find one of his own. Although, with even Reggie engaged and playing dad, Mack had been thinking more about what the future might hold for him.

He and Cass just had so much in common. Unfortunately, he

could see how that might also freak her out. When you weren't looking for love and you found the perfect man, how scary would that be? Finding Mack had to have shaken her, even if she couldn't see it yet. And, yeah, he realized how conceited that sounded, but he was still right. They fit on every level.

It had shaken him too…at first. But the more time he spent with Cass, the more time he wanted to spend with her. Even more than he wanted to work on his cars or go for a run, he wanted to chill with Cass, doing anything or, hell, doing nothing.

That wasn't to say he'd discount sex. Mack wanted her. Period. In his bed, in his life, wherever. All his rambling about being friends with sex a secondary thought? Talk about wading in his own bullshit.

For Mack, sex and love went hand in hand. But Cass had been different from the first. He hadn't charmed her at all, and she hadn't seemed to like him very much. They'd gone from unlike to lust to like to…something much more. But what, exactly? He couldn't really be in love with her. Not so soon. Could he?

He did know he was crushing on her. *Hard.* She made him feel happy, excited, aroused, and just from being herself.

He stroked her hair, her cheek. "Hey Cass, honey, you want to sleep here?"

"Hmm."

Not a yes, but not a no either.

He gently scooped her into his arms and walked them down the hall to his bedroom. After he tucked her into his bed and watched her curl up with his pillow, he sighed and turned to leave. As much as he wanted to scoot in with her, he didn't want her freaking out that he'd somehow taken advantage.

"No, stay," she murmured.

He smiled. An invitation he couldn't refuse. "Be right back."

He hurried to lock up and brought the kittens with him, placing them into the pen he had tucked into the corner of his bedroom, and joined Cass in bed, where he belonged.

When he woke the next morning, he was alone except for Copo and Impala making noise with their toys. Too bad. He'd have liked seeing Cass first thing in the morning, bedhead, morning breath, and all.

He grinned and stretched, in an amazingly good mood. A glance out the window showed the sun shining, hopefully melting all the snow so he could get back outside to run. He didn't enjoy the treadmill at the gym, but he refused to break a leg on an icy street or sidewalk.

After taking the kittens back into the living room and letting them roam at will, he fixed himself some breakfast. As he sat down to eat, he saw a note near the coffeepot he rarely used, one currently half-filled with hot coffee.

Had to get home. You're cute when you snore. Thanks for not kicking me out last night. Oh, and you owe me for not taking advantage of you when I could have. PS Call me later, Rent Boy.

He laughed as he ate his eggs and managed a cup of coffee with flavored creamer to go with it. Mack spent an enjoyable morning with the kittens while cleaning the house. After allowing them plenty of playtime, he hit the gym downtown, not in the mood for the fire station today.

Though he and the guys loved working out there, sometimes Mack just needed his own space. Once at the gym near his house, he hit the treadmill and the free weights, allowing himself to think about what an amazing night he'd had with Cass and how to gently nudge her to the next level—becoming the boyfriend.

He had no problem at all calling her his girlfriend, but he had a feeling she'd balk if he tried to label them an item.

As he finished up with his workout, he turned to hit the showers and ran into someone. "Oh, damn. Sorry." He looked into big dumb eyes and wished he'd risked running over icy sidewalks instead of visiting the gym.

"Hey, Revere. What are you doing here?" Ben Templeton, the same asshole he'd taken down at the station gym, asked with a wide grin on his face. Behind him, two large men waited, watching their conversation. "I don't see your boyfriends around. How you holding up?" He snickered, and his friends laughed too.

"Great. I'm sad being without them, almost lonely, but now that you're here, my whole day is brighter. Thanks, man." Mack patted Templeton on the shoulder as he passed, amused that Templeton didn't seem to know how to handle the falsity.

He recovered quickly enough and followed Mack into the locker room. His two friends followed. Enough members came in and out. They didn't have the space to themselves, so Mack didn't overly worry about a physical confrontation.

He should have known better.

Mack just wanted to get cleaned up and head over to Reggie's. It seemed Templeton didn't plan to let that happen. His friends stood by the end of the bench nearest the exit, while Templeton loomed at Mack's side.

"Need something?" Mack asked and turned to face Templeton only to get punched in the face. He saw it coming and tried to turn away in time but didn't make it, getting tagged in the cheek.

Pain exploded, and he saw red. Knowing that to go down would put him in too vulnerable a position, he acted like he was about to fall and instead straightened, only to get a hold on Templeton's arm, securing his movement. He had the guy twisted and turned and in a choke hold in seconds.

The men with him scowled, ready to move.

"What's going on?" someone asked near the sinks.

"Mind your business," one of Templeton's friends growled.

The door opened and closed. No one came to Mack's assistance.

Mack controlled the situation by continuing to cut off Templeton's oxygen. "Okay, you two, get lost. I'm going to ease your buddy down, then we're going to wait for help to arrive.

When I explain this second attack to the police, I'd advise you to be nowhere near."

They looked at each other for a second.

"My entire family is on the police department, and I'm dating an officer. Your call."

They bolted.

Templeton kept tapping Mack's biceps, trying to talk.

"Nope. You listen. I'm done with your shit. You are done with Station 44. I'm not sure what your major problem is with me, but it stops now. You keep it up, you'll end up seriously hurting someone. Likely just yourself, but still."

Sensing Templeton had had enough, Mack eased his arm from around the big guy's throat and set him down on his ass, a little less than gently. He eased back just as three large guys he recognized, two who'd been lifting weights earlier and one trainer, entered.

"What the hell?" The trainer whistled as he took in Mack's face. "That's gonna sting."

"It's all good," Mack said, not wanting any undue trouble. He figured he'd handled things. "Just a work discussion that got out of hand."

One of the big guys huffed. "Nice. That asshole was on my last nerve a few minutes ago. Kept trying to tell me I was doing it wrong. Fuckhead, weightlifting is my job. I'm on a break. I'm usually training half the guys in here."

His other thick-necked friend nodded. "Yeah. But your boy thinks he knows best. Was yapping about all his connections in town. Who cares?"

"Try working with him," Mack said, trying not to wince now that his cheekbone started throbbing. "And he's not my boy. Hey, you mind taking him out? I have a lunch to get to, and I stink."

The large guys helped Templeton toward the door.

"Watch your back, Revere," Templeton had the audacity to threaten.

"Seriously?" Mack had thought Templeton had a few brain cells, but maybe not.

Everyone watched Templeton as he shoved his way past the big guys through the door.

"See that he leaves, would you?" the trainer asked them.

They nodded and left.

The trainer turned to Mack. "You sure you're okay? That's already really red and starting to bruise. Might want to get it checked out in case he cracked bone."

"I know. I'm an EMT."

"Ah, okay."

"I'm good. But thanks."

The guy left, and Mack hustled to shower, dress, and leave, glad at least the snow had started to melt.

He made it to Reggie's in time to see Maggie and Emily leaving, the little one skipping as she held her mom's hand on the way to their car. Mack waved. They waved back, and he had a weird image of Cass holding her daughter's hand as they waved at Mack. At *Daddy*.

"I must have been hit harder than I thought," he muttered and made his way up Reggie's walkway.

He knocked once before entering, letting himself in, and found the guys centered in Reggie's living room, playing *Arrow Sins & Siege*, some streaming action game taking the internet by storm. Snacks had been laid out on the dining table, but Mack really wanted something to drink. And maybe some ice for his face.

"Soda in the fridge," Reggie called out. "Ha. Take that, sucker."

"You're cheatin'," Tex complained. "This game sucks."

Brad laughed. "Try playing my brother or his girlfriend. They spend hours on this crap."

"You're just calling it crap because you're terrible," Reggie said as he chopped someone's head off.

"Well, yeah. It's a video game. I'd rather push Avery's buttons than the ones on this stupid controller, if you know what I mean."

"Thanks for making it all sexual, you perv," Tex complained and yelled at Reggie for stealing his gold.

Mack found a bottle of cream soda in the fridge and put it on his cheek with a sigh. He then hunted down the delicious smell of meat, somewhere near the guys. He'd taken a swig from the bottle and knew he'd have to show off his growing bruise at some point.

Reggie was the first to see him and dropped the controller. "What the hell happened to you?"

Which caused the others to look over at him and stand up.

"Damn, son. Who hit first?" Tex asked.

"I'll get the keys. Whose ass are we kicking?" Brad, normally the even-tempered leader of the crew, looked livid.

"How bad is it?" Mack asked.

"Pretty dark. Can't you feel your eye swelling? 'Cause I can see it," Tex said.

"It hurts, but I don't think it's anything more than a bad bruise." Mack drank more soda. "Templeton sucker-punched me at the gym. Not at the station, the one in Beacon Hill. Don't worry. I put him down. Nearly choked him out, but I didn't leave any bruises. Tex, I think you should talk to the chief and let him know Templeton needs to go. The guy is unstable. If you don't, I will." Mack described exactly how everything had happened.

"Why does he have such a hard-on for you?" Brad asked.

"I have no idea. But when we met at the station, he seemed to recognize my name. He seems to have some personal vendetta I just don't understand," Mack said.

"Good thing those friends of his didn't jump in." Anger flushed Brad's cheeks. "You could have seriously been hurt."

"Might still be," Reggie said, staring into Mack's eyes. "Track my finger."

"I know my own body. Would you stop?" Mack sighed. When

Reggie kept moving his hand in front of Mack's face, he gave in and tracked Reggie's finger. "Happy now?" He swore when someone shone a light into his eyes. "I'm not concussed, damn it. I'm annoyed. I wanted to be here before you broke out the subs."

Reggie lowered his hand. Finally. "Saved you a roast beef. It's over there." Wrapped and on the side table near a big red bowl full of ice and bottles of beer.

Tex blew out a breath. "I'll talk to the chief. Don't worry. I was going to anyway, but this caps it. Templeton is a fucknugget."

"That's too nice." Brad fumed.

They spent the next round of *Arrow Sins & Siege* coming up with insults and swears for Templeton, which Mack found super entertaining. "Gosh, Brad. This is just like when you nearly messed up with Avery and she had that insult book about you."

Tex laughed. "I think we still have his picture somewhere, the one we put on the punching bag at the station."

Brad flushed.

They spent their time hanging out, as if nothing among the four of them had changed. Yet everything had.

Mack looked from friend to friend, seeing growth. Brad no longer acted like the world would end if he couldn't save everyone. Tex had eased past his girl-of-the-week mentality to settle down and become a terrific, stable boyfriend and one heck of a seasoned firefighter. Reggie no longer moped all the time, angry with the world. People didn't take advantage of him so easily anymore thanks to some much-needed therapy and his lovely fiancée's influence.

But what had changed with Mack? Anything?

"No. I've always been an awesome guy," he mumbled.

"Talking to himself. Yep. He's got head trauma," Brad said to much amusement.

Mack took a breath, let it out, and stood, nearly upending a bowl of pretzels. Time to start his own change so his friends could get on with their lives and not worry about babying the sad, weak one left over. He didn't think he could bear it if they turned into carbon copies of James, Alec, and Xavier.

"Hey, watch it," Reggie growled.

"Easy, neat freak." Mack cleared his throat. "I have an announcement to make." He gave it the requisite pause before adding, "I'm keeping the cop."

Everyone looked at him.

"What are you talkin' about?" Tex frowned. "Not the pretty one with the temper?"

"Her?" Reggie blinked. "Really?"

Brad stared at him. "This I have to hear."

"Yes, yes, Cass is the hot cop who nailed me at the soccer game. I decided I like her. But she's on the fence about dating."

"Oh boy," Brad muttered. "This sounds rough."

Mack ignored him. "She has no idea who she's dealing with. I'm Mack Revere."

"Amen, brother." Tex drank down his bottle. "I need another one."

Mack continued, "I'm making her fall for me a little at a time. We're a lot alike. She thinks we're just friends, which we are. But we're gonna be more. I really like her." He smiled, thinking about how great she was, how sweet she'd looked in his bed and in his arms. "Pretty soon she's going to be wondering how she existed BM. Before Mack."

Tex blinked. "Ah, BM stands for a lot of things. Maybe another acronym."

"No shit." Reggie grinned wide. "Oh, that's even funnier."

Brad wiped his face, trying to hide a smile Mack clearly saw. BM? Oh…

"Bowel movement? Really? How old are you, three?"

They burst into laughter.

When they finally calmed a little, red-faced, Mack suggested, "How about *PM*? Like Pre-Mack."

"Better," Brad said. "When do we get to meet her?"

"Dun dun dun," Reggie sang. "She needs to run the gauntlet."

"The girlfriend gauntlet," Tex added, as if Mack didn't know. "All of ours passed. Now it's your turn."

"I'm not worried. For her…" Mack grinned. "You remember she nearly killed me on the soccer field."

The guys pondered that.

Brad nodded. "A big game of Scrabble should do it. What do you say, guys? Can we get everyone, ladies included, for a party?"

"She has off next Tuesday and Wednesday," Mack offered, both excited and unnerved to bring Cass to a crew party. Something only the guys and their significant others attended. Once or twice the guys had brought a sibling as well. But not Mack.

To his surprise, that hurt a little, so he shoved it deep down inside and focused on the things he could control. He thought about how Cass would handle a competitive game with the others and grinned. Then grimaced. "Damn, my face hurts. Don't say it, Tex."

Tex gave a wide grin. "What? That your face hurts me too? Because it's killing me!"

Reggie groaned.

Brad socked him in the arm.

"Ow!"

"Bad jokes get beatdowns. Remember that." Brad left and returned with a bag of frozen peas. "Here. Put this on."

Reggie looked at Brad. "Sure, help yourself."

"I did." Brad stared at Reggie. "Hmm. You know what this calls for?"

Reggie got that stern look that signified trouble, his eyes glued to Brad's. "I do." He turned to Tex. "Clear the table."

Mack laughed. "Not again."

Tex hurried to clear the coffee table, and Brad and Reggie got on either side of it, on their knees on the ground, and set their elbows on the table. Then they clasped hands.

Arm wrestling for the seriously strong. Though big himself, even Tex liked to take a seat and watch the muscleheads on the floor go at it. At Mack's look, he grinned and shook his head. "I'm too pretty to get broken. Bree likes me all in one piece."

Mack chuckled and said, "Best of three, you idiots." At the glares he received, he corrected himself. "I'm sorry. You morons. One, two, three…"

Reggie won in the last round, but they congratulated Brad for having the strength to beat Reggie at all. Personally, Mack thought it a healthy thing Reggie finally lost. Lately, he hadn't been spending all his time at the gym, mourning a lost love. Now the guy was happy and healthy, spending time with his fiancée and her adorable six-year-old. And the dog…

"Hey, Reggie, where's Frank?"

The pit-mix puppy was so ugly he was cute and still scarred from an accident, having been hit by a car.

"Oh, my sister has him. Lisa's dating Stephen now." Reggie sighed. "She thinks Frank is a good-luck charm, for some reason, and keeps taking him over to Stephen's when they spend time together. It's weird."

"What? That your fiancée's ex-husband and your sister are hooking up?" Tex asked.

Reggie glared. "They're *dating*. I think it's weird she keeps bringing a dog on her dates."

"I found two kittens I'm fostering," Mack said, since he'd forgotten to tell them. "Copo and Impala."

"Cute names." Brad grinned. "Though I'd have gone with GTO or Shelby."

"You would." Mack sneered. "You know little about cars. Or how much Chevy outshines them all."

"Up yours." Brad started talking out his ass while Tex interrogated Reggie on exactly how Reggie had known it was time to propose to Maggie.

Brad and Mack eventually tapered off as one and all understood Tex had seriously bit the love bug. With Reggie already engaged, Brad planning to ask his pregnant girlfriend to marry him after Christmas, and now Tex thinking diamond rings, Mack knew he needed to start spending more time apart from the guys. No matter what they said, they were clearly moving on.

It hurt in a way, but Mack had already sensed the need to move on, the subtle cracks of distance in their four-man crew spreading.

Though he smiled with the others and congratulated Tex, a part of him mourned what had been. Yet another part was excited for what might come to be.

Chapter Fifteen

SATURDAY NIGHT, JED WOULD NOT SHUT UP ABOUT HOW wonderful Thursday's dinner had gone. "I mean, Shannon thought Mack was the best guy. Let me tell you, she *really* showed me *how much* she appreciated how well dinner went. Even the kids went to bed early, without a fuss, drunk off their little asses."

The cuffed criminal in the back of the car perked up at the sound of drunk minors.

"Off apple juice?" Cass couldn't help grinning.

"Best. Night. Ever," Jed practically sang.

She sighed. "Can you please stop being so cheery? I don't even know you anymore."

He laughed. "So when are the four of us going out again?"

"We technically haven't gone out the first time."

"True. But Shannon cooked the hell out of that roast, you have to admit."

Cass still drooled thinking about it. "I'll give you that."

"Well?"

She looked over at him briefly before focusing on the road, driving tonight. Thus far, they'd had to deal with one fistfight over a shoe sale, one drunk and disorderly, and one attempted robbery at a convenience store that, fortunately, had ended the moment the suspect had seen flashing lights nearing. Jed and she had run him down, leaving them both breathless yet pleased. With the offender in the back and his toy water gun taken away, they drove to booking.

Cass wondered if she'd entered an alternate dimension. Did Jed actually want her to date Mack? For real? "I'll let you know when we'll go out again. It's not as if he and I are really dating."

"Why not?" asked the young punk from the back seat. He looked barely legal to drink, a young white kid with a chip on his shoulder. "You're pretty hot. Is the dude gay?"

Cass shot Jed a look. *See? This is why we don't share personal details with criminals in the back seat.*

"Good point, kid. She's not bad-looking. He's not gay, is he, Cass?" Jed asked with a smirk.

"You, zip it," she ordered the kid, staring at him in the rearview. "Jed, you too. He's not gay, you jackass. He's nice."

The kid frowned. "Hey, gay people can be nice. My cousin is gay."

"Oh my God. I'm not saying gay people aren't nice. I'm saying the guy is nice, so I don't know if I can date him."

"Oh, you're one of them demons in the sack, is that it?" The kid laughed himself silly. "Can't take a brother who's nice and shit."

Jed coughed to hide his own grin.

"You see what you started?" Cass said to her partner. "I'm not talking about my personal life with either of you."

When they'd dropped off the young criminal and were back in the car on patrol, Jed tried again. "Sorry, but I have to know. Mack seemed like a great guy. Not your type or something?"

She could hear his honest concern and flushed. "He's just fine. I like him. We're taking it slowly. Right now, we're just friends, okay?"

"Fine, fine. No need to get huffy."

She told him where to stick his "huffy."

He chuckled. They sat in silence for a few miles.

"I'm thinking of taking him to meet my parents," she admitted. "Just to get them off my case about dating."

"Good plan. He'll impress them. He impressed Shannon and me. Funny, nice, and didn't let my kids scare him."

"Mike." She shook her head, still grinning about that. "Tell him he's my new favorite."

"Sam will be crushed, but okay." He sighed and after a few beats said, "Shannon thinks she wants another kid."

Cass swung her head to him before sighting on the road again. "*What?*"

"That's what I said. We have two beautiful children out of diapers. Little evil geniuses who keep us on our toes as it is. I'm thirty. She's thirty-two. Why do we need to start over again?"

She sat with what he'd said. "You ask me, she's seeing thirty-five nearing and freaking out. They say women have more potential for health risks with babies once they hit the age of thirty-five. So maybe she's thinking if she wants more children, now is the time to have them."

For some wacky reason, Cass had been thinking about children a lot lately as well. Those blasted kittens, the twins, and her mother had texted her earlier in the day about some cousin out east getting pregnant. She figured she'd have her own someday, but right now her career took precedence. But God, she'd be hitting thirty in just two and a half more years. Add five after that and she'd be in health-risk territory herself.

Jed still seemed uneasy, so she changed the subject to the sarge's terrible haircut and the fistfight over those shoes they'd interrupted earlier in their shift.

When they reached the precinct once more and readied for turnover, she noticed Newcastle grabbing some papers from his desk. He must have been working on a case because he usually had later hours. He saw her and smiled.

"Crap."

Jed joined her and saw Newcastle's approach. "What's up, Josh?"

Newcastle shrugged. "Caught wind of a serial arsonist, maybe. How was patrol?" He looked Cass over, and she did her best to ignore all the attention he gave her breasts. She had a freaking vest under her shirt, for God's sake.

"Ah, same old," Jed said before she said something obnoxious.

Newcastle studied her. "So I hear you're dating some guy. Is that right? 'Cause I was going to ask if—"

"Oh, hell, Cass," Jed interrupted. "Sorry. I saw Mack yesterday. He told me to tell you dinner is a go next week." Jed turned to Newcastle. "Cass is dating a friend of mine. Small world, eh?"

Newcastle mumbled a congratulations before turning away.

As they left the station, she elbowed him. "What the hell was that?"

"I got Newcastle off your tail. Guess he didn't believe me before when I said you were taken. You're welcome."

"But he'll tell everyone I'm dating someone." Gossip around the department was worse than the gossip at her mother's hospital. Like an incurable disease that spread like wildfire.

"And that you're no longer available. You're welcome."

"Oh. I guess that's good."

"Yeah." He paused at his car, parked next to hers. "When you see Mack again, tell him we'll go out next time. Dinner and a movie?"

"Wait. Do *you* want to date him? Or can I come too?" She grinned when he shot her the finger. "I'll ask. Good luck with Shannon. Just go easy with the kid talk and figure out what she really wants. And talk to her out of bed, in a nonsexual environment."

"I will. Thanks, Dr. Carmichael."

"I'll bill you later." She got in her car and checked her phone again. Mack had sent her a text earlier asking if she wanted to get breakfast the next morning. She'd told him she'd let him know after her shift.

After arriving home at five Sunday morning, she undressed, washed up, and got into bed before texting him back. Late breakfast at noon? That would give her a solid six hours of sleep and time to shower before meeting him. He didn't respond, but then, she figured he was either on shift or asleep. She'd know either way when she woke.

At eleven on the dot, her eyes popped open. Then her alarm rang. She turned it off and glanced at her phone to see a thumbs-up and a question.

Should I bring breakfast over?

Sure, she typed, smiling when he immediately responded.

What do you want?

Eggs, meat, something sweet?

He sent a bunch of emojis, and darned if one of them wasn't a devil followed by an eggplant. Kidding. I'll bring real food. See you at noon.

She gave him a laughing face and hurried into the shower.

Once clean, teeth brushed, hair sleek and in a ponytail, she relaxed in the living room reading a book. Her secret addiction—erotic romance. Cass was a sucker for a great story about love and sex because how else did a woman know if a man was worth keeping? Great conversation was all well and good, but to Cass, physical intimacy was a key component to a great relationship. She had wonderful friends for conversation and a good time. But sex—"amazing chemistry" kind of sex—had to come from the man in her life. Otherwise, why bother dating him?

She'd dated a bunch of one-hit wonders. Her last boyfriend had put her off men for a good while. How hard was it to be happy for Cass to succeed in her career? How tough to not be threatened by her job or other men? Sean had been handsome, wealthy, and hung like a horse. But such a controlling bastard.

Looking back, she couldn't believe they'd lasted as long as they had. Maybe because he'd spent a good bit of time traveling, he hadn't been around as much to show how poorly they meshed. But at least he was gone.

And now she, kind of, had Mack.

Her heart soared at thoughts of seeing him again, and she grinned like a fool as she read about the heroine in her book getting busy with the hero. In an elevator. In a park. Oh, in a hot tub.

Too bad I'm not into people watching me have sex. Because this book is giving me ideas.

The doorbell rang, and she saw Mack waiting outside. She buried her book under some travel guides on the coffee table and opened the door to let him inside.

He passed, and she got a whiff of his Eau de Mack once more. What a dork. "What are you wearing?" she had to know.

He smiled at her. "You later, if I'm lucky."

"Very funny." She'd find out one way or another. Although his suggestion of wearing her sounded ideal.

"I grabbed us omelets, bacon, and some sticky rolls from a place around the corner. It's one of my favorites." He put the food on the set table. She offered him coffee, which he refused, though he took her up on the orange juice. As she handed it to him, she noticed the big purple bruise on his left cheek.

"What the hell?" She turned his head and gently ran a finger over it.

He sighed. "Shannon found me yesterday and beat on me."

"*What?*"

He grinned. "I'm kidding. Got into a scrap at the gym. It's all good."

"What happened?"

He told her over breakfast, and she grew angrier and angrier as she thought about what might have happened if those other guys had jumped him as well. A blow to the head could do real damage, not like the way TV and movies portrayed it.

"You need to press charges."

He continued to calmly eat. "I'm not pressing charges. It was an in-house thing."

"But, Mack, you—"

"If I involve the cops, I look like I can't handle my business. And I handled it just fine. I won."

"I know, but—"

"In my place, would you report a fellow cop after you'd dealt with the situation?"

"Well, no."

"Exactly. I handled it. The guy is toast. We'll bounce him from the station. Trust me."

"Okay. But I don't like it." She couldn't explain how angry she felt. "Want me to beat him up for you? I'll even take off my badge when I do it."

He smiled, then winced a little. "Ow. No, but thanks. That's awfully sweet."

"Offering to beat up a douchebag?"

"So loving." He batted his eyelashes at her, which had her laughing. "I met with the guys yesterday for lunch. I think Tex is going to ask Bree to marry him."

"Wow. Big move."

"Yeah."

She studied him, keying in on his lack of enthusiasm. "What's wrong?"

"Nothing. I'm happy for him."

"Mack, we're friends, remember? You can tell me stuff you can't tell them. And who am I going to tell? Jed? Shannon?"

"You could tell Mike. I don't know how trustworthy that kid is." He chuckled. "But Sam likes me. I could tell."

"She's a girl. Of course she likes you," Cass said wryly. "Come on. I'm listening."

He pushed his half-empty plate away and sipped his juice. "I don't want to tell you. Because I'll sound petty, and I hate petty."

"Oh, the poster boy for Station 44 is less than perfect! Do tell."

He shot her a look. She arched her brows.

Mack sighed. "Fine. My cheek hurts. I'm tired because I had a tough time getting to sleep without someone to snuggle with." He glanced at her, saw her blush, and gave a sad smile. "But I think I'm a really bad friend, and that hurts."

"What?"

"I don't like lying. I do my best not to lie to myself especially. I'm not digging Tex getting engaged, and I don't know why. I mean, I love the guy. I want him to be happy, but I'm also bummed." He ran a hand through his hair, and the unkempt look only made him sexier. "Tex is a great guy. Seriously. The way Jed is your brother? Brad, Tex, and Reggie are mine. We're closer than I am with my own family."

She wanted to ask him about that but didn't think it the time. So she watched him and said nothing.

"I've been friends with them for nearly four years. We do everything together. Sure, they've all dated. I've dated. Women come and go. But not like this. Brad is having a kid with Avery. That's serious. Reggie's engaged to a woman with a little girl. They live together. They have a dog."

She nodded.

"Tex has always been this tall, sarcastic ass. I love him. He's like the holder-on to being single. And he's going to ask Bree to marry him. I don't know. It just hit home for me. We're all moving on." He paused. "They're all moving on. But I'm holding them back."

"How?" That she didn't understand. He'd mentioned before he thought they pitied him, but she didn't see it. That night when Tex had been out with them, he hadn't seemed to be there just for Mack. He'd been having a great time with all of them, Jed especially.

"I think I'm taking too much of their time. I need to get more involved in my own hobbies so they don't always have to invite me to spend time with them. I'm that third wheel when Tex and Bree go to a concert. Or the guy who's on Emily's team—she's six, by the way—when Reggie and Maggie have me over. Or the one who has to sit through yet another blind date when Avery tries to find me a plus-one when Brad's expected to go to some event of hers and I tag along so he's not bored."

"You think they pity you because you're single?"

"Yeah." He sighed. "Oh man. I suck. I didn't mean to burden you with my crap."

"No, we're friends, and that's what friends do." She was surprised to find how much she liked him baring himself. Not making himself look so good as he opened up about feeling jealous. Even selfish. That imperfection made her like him that much more. "God, Mack. You're human. Give yourself a break."

"Huh?"

"Everyone feels jealous now and then. It's perfectly normal not to like change, especially when something has been working for you. You and your friends are the perfect bros. You like each other. You trust each other. And then they start moving away, little by little, sharing their lives with other people. If you didn't love them so much, it wouldn't hurt so much."

"I guess."

"I was kind of lucky with Jed. I met him already married and with kids. He came with the whole package. That still doesn't mean it's not hard when they do holidays or dinners or date nights and want me to come. Because, like you, it's always Jed and Shannon…oh, and Cass. But with me, they know better than to set me up on blind dates."

"Lucky you." Mack watched her, his gaze intense. "I just don't know why I'm so down after Tex shared such happy news. I feel bad that I feel bad. I was so happy when Brad found Avery. And even when Reggie finally got his head out of his ass and grabbed onto Maggie. I like these women a lot. I love Bree with Tex. I don't know. It's just not like it was before, me being happy for them. I feel like an asshole."

"Good."

He glared. "Real nice."

"I mean it's good that you're aware of your feelings. You're in touch with your wants and needs, Mack. Mentally and emotionally healthy people feel that way."

He stared. "How do you know all this?"

"My dad's Dr. Aaron Carmichael, a clinical psychologist and best-selling author of self-help books." She shrugged. "It rubbed off."

His eyes widened. "Seriously? Aaron Carmichael is your dad? I think my mom has one of his books."

"Yeah. It wasn't easy growing up with someone who had a rational explanation anytime I argued or had a temper tantrum."

"Tantrum? You?"

She ignored his grin. "My dad is a pretty smart guy. It's annoying to constantly have him on me about my unhealthy lifestyle and stunted emotional growth."

"What's unhealthy about you?"

"Hanging with Jed and Shannon all the time. Not having much of a life outside my job. Not dating since my last disastrous relationship."

"Tell me."

She sighed. "Do I have to?"

"Yes. We're *friends*," he emphasized, a twinkle in his eye that she'd help put there. "Plus, I spilled my guts to you, looking like a loser. You should do the same so I don't feel bad."

"Wait. I have to feel bad because you feel bad?"

"Yes."

She laughed. "Fine. Not like I have anything to hide."

"Sure you do. We all have secrets." He tilted his head. "Yours have to do with books, for some reason."

She flushed, her mind in the immediate gutter at thoughts of her and Mack reenacting what she'd just read. "I have no idea what you're talking about."

"You're blushing."

"I met Sean downtown, at a community fundraiser." She pretended not to see Mack's smug expression. "He was handsome. He asked me out. I said yes. The sex was great." She paused, forcing herself not to smile at the growing frown on Mack's face. "Sean had money and liked to go out. A lot. He was a fun date at first. But then he kept wanting to change things about me. I like to dress up and look nice. But not all the time. And I'm not into being less so someone else can be more."

"Ah, one of those, eh?" Mack shook his head. "I bet he was intimidated by you."

"I think so too. It took a while though. Usually I can tell after a date or two if the guy can't handle being with a cop. But Sean lasted months. He traveled a lot for his job, so maybe that's why we were together for so long."

"How long?"

"About a year. We stopped dating a year and a half ago, so no worries that I'm not over him or anything. I broke it off."

"Poor guy."

She snorted. "He grew to be a controlling asshole. Jed never liked him. Shannon thought he was okay, but that's just because he was always on his best behavior around her."

"She liked me."

Cass frowned. "I attributed that to the wine."

He smirked.

"Anyway, Sean thought we had to like the same things. Or, rather, that *I* had to like everything *he* did. At first, having things in common was great."

"I can't see that for you."

"Why not?"

"You clearly love to argue."

"I do not."

"See?"

She gave him the finger, which made him laugh. "Anyway, the longer we were together, the more Sean tried to mold me into his perfect girlfriend. I met his parents. I met his work friends. He met my folks, who weren't as impressed as I'd thought they'd be.

I thought he was the kind of guy my dad would love, but my dad gave me a lame 'if you're happy, we're happy' spiel. I should have known better."

"Your dad sounds like he just wants you to be happy."

"Yeah, but he's not the expert on what makes me happy. I am."

"Good point." Mack paused. "So you liked Sean because he was handsome, rich, and great at sex?"

"Kind of. That attracted me to him, sure. Not the rich part though. I just wanted a guy who wouldn't expect me to pay for all the bills. I'm fine with going Dutch, but I once dated a guy who forgot his wallet on three consecutive dates. We never had a fourth."

"Ouch. I usually offer to pay for my dates. I had one woman who called me old-fashioned, but she didn't object to my paying."

"Who would? You want to buy me dinner? Fine. But if I offer to pay, don't call me names for it later."

"Right." He nodded. "Handsome and sexy. That's what you like." He looked down at himself and gave her a thumbs-up. "Got it."

"Oh stop." Yet he wasn't wrong. "I also like a good personality and a man who knows boundaries."

"Sounds like a dog. You want a guy to sit on command?"

Was he teasing her? She frowned. "Not at all. I want a man who doesn't get in a snit because I tell him no. If I don't want sex or I don't want to go out, that doesn't mean I'm frigid or I'm an introvert."

"True. And just because I might be too tired for hours of foreplay and just want a quickie, or if I feel the need to hang with the guys instead of yet another chick flick on TV, that doesn't mean I'm not a caring lover or hate the woman I'm with. It just means I'm tired and need to decompress off a tough shift. Sometimes I don't want my girlfriend to deal with my issues. She shouldn't have to."

"Good point. But if she wants to share your life, you'll have to let her see some of the ugly."

"Yeah, I know. But so many women think a firefighter would make a sexy partner without understanding the lifestyle. It's dangerous and something I have to devote a lot of my energy to. My crew is tight because we need to be. One slipup could mean we don't all go home."

"Right?" She took a big sip of coffee and grimaced at the cold liquid. She reached for Mack's glass and finished the rest of his juice.

"Please, help yourself."

"I did." She laughed at him. "Well, now are you happy we shared our uglies?"

"If you're referring to this face, know I'll be back to normal in a week or so."

"Does it hurt?"

He nodded solemnly. "It really does." A pause. "A kiss would make it better."

"Is that right?" Butterflies gathered in her belly, and she was glad she'd been too nervous to eat a lot. Sitting near Mack made her think of all kinds of things they could have been doing.

In her bedroom.

"Yep. How about you take care of this ugly for me?" He pointed to his bruise and gave her a sad face she didn't buy for a second.

"Well, if it would make you feel better."

His gaze lingered on her mouth. "Oh, it really would."

Chapter Sixteen

MACK HAD BEEN STEADILY DYING, SITTING SO CLOSE TO CASS but having to hold himself back. He'd wanted nothing more than to kiss and hug her, feeling so close as he unveiled his neediness, his selfishness, and still found acceptance.

He never could have told the guys how he felt because they'd have gone out of their way to make him feel better about himself. He didn't need that. He knew what he felt was legitimate. And negative. Not something he liked about himself right now.

But Cass let him own it. She didn't make excuses for him, except to tell him he was a normal human being with normal emotions.

She scooted closer in her chair and leaned forward to plant the gentlest kiss on his cheek.

His entire body vibrated, on fire to have her closer. He moaned and shifted, drawing her out of her seat and into his lap. "Come here."

"What do you need?" she feathered over his lips as she straddled him.

"You," he said simply and kissed her.

Her hands cradled his face gently, but the kiss was nothing short of scorching. Her lips captured his, dominating as she sipped from his mouth, pushing her tongue between his lips to capture his moans of pleasure.

Cass ground over him, and she had to feel how hard he'd become, his erection pulsing with each shift and graze of her pelvis, her thighs.

He gripped her waist and took over the kiss, conscious she let him. Cass might come on strong, but she liked it when he'd taken charge before. And he had no problem directing where they went next. "Bedroom."

She nodded and continued to kiss him.

When he stood with her in his arms, she pulled back to stare with wide eyes, her gasp audible. "What are you doing?"

"I'm being manly and carrying you to the bed," he said and huffed, then pretended to drop her.

She clung to him like a burr, making him laugh despite how he hurt, needing to be inside her in the worst way.

"Hurry up." She nipped his neck, then kissed her way to his ear. "I'm so wet."

He rushed to her bed and put her down, joining her as he kissed her until they were both moaning and desperate. He stripped her quickly, finally dragging her panties off so he could spread her legs wide and feast.

She gasped his name as he sucked and licked her sweet pussy, addicted to the sexy need building between them. She arched into his mouth and gripped his hair. "More. Oh yeah. So good."

He stroked her thighs as he kissed her, his hands moving up then down, close to her sex then away.

"In me," Cass demanded.

Not begging, not yet.

Mack grinned and sat up to strip off his shirt. Then he shucked out of the rest of his clothes and moved up her body to straddle her neck. "How about you blow me, baby? I hear you're good at it, and it's something you do to perps. You know, it's *criminal* how badly I want you."

She cringed, though her lips quirked, her flush of passion mixing with humor. "You're really not good at the sex talk."

"That hurts." He angled his cock at her mouth, watching her watch him, her lips barely parted when he pushed between them. "Fuck. Come on. Suck me."

She grinned and opened her mouth a fraction wider.

Mack grew steel-hard, her enjoyment, her teasing, making everything so much hotter.

Then she gripped his hips and dragged him closer, and he slid inside her mouth. Before he knew it, he was pumping, faster as her tongue lapped him, sliding around his shaft and stroking the underside of the crown.

He nearly lost it when she palmed his balls and sucked harder.

"Mmm." She drew down on his cockhead, and he hurriedly withdrew.

"Condom," he said hoarsely.

She handed him one out of her nightstand, and he'd never moved faster to put one on.

Once sheathed, he blanketed her body, nudged her legs wider, and shoved as deep as he could go.

She cried out, coming and hugging him so tight as he pumped faster. Needing to move deeper inside her. The tension grew, his desire combustible.

"Coming," he managed to get out as he surged and shook, jetting into her in an explosion of pleasure that seemed never-ending. He almost hurt as he emptied, the ecstasy mind-blowing.

She lay under him, still hugging him to her as she panted and he came, until he collapsed on top of her, unable to catch his breath.

"F-uck," he whispered, withdrew, and moved to the side so as not to crush her. But Cass rolled over him, the press of her soft breasts cushioned against his chest, her body heavy against his sensitive cock.

"Wow." Cass sighed and lay her head against his chest. "Your ugly is still showing. We have to do that again."

"My…what?" His brain had yet to restart, and he lay there, so incredibly satisfied, as he strove to get back to normalcy. Better than any drug, Cass had him hooked and high and smiling.

"Your bruise. That purple blotch marring all that perfection."

"You're good with words too." His voice sounded scratchy, his breathing still raspy. He reached around the small of her back to hug her to him and sighed. "God, you feel amazing."

"You too. You're a master between the sheets. Or, er, on top of them."

He chuckled, his dick now throbbing gently. "Let me get rid of this."

"I'll do it."

Before he could protest, Cass shifted and took the condom from him. He hissed at the contact, but she'd already gone and returned with a warm, wet washcloth. She bathed his dick with it, and it felt so damn good.

Then she folded it over and washed herself while she watched him.

"I should do that." He felt almost drunk. "But first I need to get my strength back. I'm weak."

"You're male. I get it." She left to dispose of the washcloth in the bathroom and returned with a big smile. "I came hard."

"No question I did." He hugged her to his side as she joined him in her bed. The feel of her next to him made everything right, and all the worries and fears he'd earlier shared no longer existed. "So, ah, are you on any birth control?"

"I was on the pill for a while but stopped after Sean. Why?"

"Curious."

She shifted onto her elbow to look at his face. "Wondering if the condom broke? It didn't."

He smiled. "You scared you'll have to make an honest man of me if it did?"

She blinked, the expression she wore one hard to read. A cross between panic and confusion.

He laughed, harder when that confusion turned to a frown. "Relax, Cass. I won't get you pregnant with a condom that didn't break. I mean, it's true I'm super, thus I have super sperm. But they have yet to leap a single building and break through latex."

Her blush caused more laughter.

She smacked his chest. "Not funny. I'm not ready to be a mom yet."

"But you'd be so good at breastfeeding." He eyed her pert breasts, perfect handfuls with rosy nipples.

She snorted. "Such a guy."

"What? It's a known fact many men are fascinated by breasts. I love sucking yours." He reached out to cup one and rubbed his thumb over her nipple, mesmerized as it hardened and a pretty pink flush stole its way over her face. Before she could stop him, he leaned in to kiss it.

He carefully guided her onto her back and kissed her nipple again. He started sucking and sighed. "I dream about this."

She whispered his name, her fingers burrowing through her hair.

Annoyed with himself for not paying enough attention to her breasts, Mack spent time massaging them, kissing them, and sucking her into a writhing, trembling mess.

"That's what I like to see. Officer Carmichael, at my mercy." He put his face between her breasts and inhaled the essence of her, such a sweet, sultry woman. He leaned up and sat on his knees over her belly, his hands still caressing her chest.

"Mack, you're a tease." She stared at him, studying his cock. "You're still hard?"

"Semi-hard and getting there. Your body is the best thing I've ever seen."

"Flatterer."

He grinned, loving how his hands completely covered her. "You're a handful, Cass. Fuck, you feel good."

"You just want my mouth on your dick again."

"Duh."

She laughed.

He'd never had so much fun with sex before. Oh, the desire had been there, but not the way it was for Cass. He enjoyed all of it—the before, the after, and, of course, the during. But talking with her wasn't awkward or something he had to try to feel comfortable with.

Being with Cass felt natural.

"I want to come inside you," he said bluntly.

She blinked. "Ah, well, we talked about using condoms." She looked uncomfortable.

"Yeah, I know. I won't come inside you. But I want to." He sighed and felt his body stir. "You're so warm. And tight. I love the way you smell. The way you taste."

She stared at him, wide-eyed. "You do?"

"You get me so fucking hard." He rubbed himself against her belly and kept palming her breasts, riding his palms against her hard little nipples. "I like watching you come, Cass. It's hot." He gave her a naughty grin. "We should make a movie."

"*What?*"

"Yeah, a sex movie. So I can watch you get off and masturbate to it while you're at work."

She just gaped at him, her face pink. But her breathing grew faster. Was she into it?

"I can go get my phone."

"No!"

He grinned. "Such a prude. I was just teasing. As much as I'd love to watch you over and over again, I don't want to share you with the world. Anything you record can and will come back to bite you in the ass. I truly believe that."

She sagged back into the bed. "That's the truth." He leaned down to kiss her. "Real truth." She sounded dreamy. "Mack, put a condom on. Right now."

"Is that an order?"

"Don't make me cuff you to the bed."

"Promises, promises."

Two hours later, when Cass should have been heading to the gym, she sat in her bed, wearing a short silk robe. Mack sat next to her, the two of them sharing a pint of vanilla caramel gelato.

"This is really good," Mack was saying as he spoon-fed her a bite.

"Hmm." She'd been dithering about asking him and finally blurted, "I want to take you to meet my parents on Tuesday. We're celebrating an early Thanksgiving."

He paused with the spoon in his mouth, still earth-shatteringly attractive with messed hair, pouty lips, and a body that didn't quit. The boxer briefs he wore couldn't hide the thick flesh beneath and only emphasized the corded abs and muscular thighs making her want.

Everything about Mack was the total package.

And that bothered her. After the many orgasms he'd given her, his intelligence, humor, and incredible body only added to a problem she hated addressing.

She didn't want him to leave and go home. Not in a few more minutes, an hour, today, or tomorrow. *Oh no! I'm growing clingy.*

Mack removed the spoon and watched her with those sky-blue eyes that had snared her and refused to let go. "To meet the parents? Sure. Why not?" He smiled and went back to eating the gelato.

"My turn." She opened her mouth.

He chuckled as he gave her more of the creamy treat. "I so want to put something else between those gorgeous lips."

"You already did. Several times."

"Yeah." He sighed. "I think you've ruined me for blow jobs. Thanks a lot."

She chuckled. "Ha. Well, you've ruined me for—" *everyone with a Y chromosome* "—gelato. Oh, and sex. That too."

He grinned around the spoon.

"So it's not a problem to meet my parents? You know who my dad is. My mom's a doctor. They're both busybodies who want their oldest daughter to fall in love and get married."

Mack paused. "Oldest daughter?"

Huh. She hadn't meant to let that slip. What an odd turn of phrase. "I don't know why I said that. My sister died a long time ago."

"Oh wow. I'm so sorry." Mack appeared concerned, tender and caring.

"It's sad, yeah, but Sofie died when I was six. She was five. Like, twenty-two years ago." Twenty-two years ago next week. "The anniversary of her death is coming up. Must have been a Freudian slip."

"I don't care what it was. I'm still sorry you lost her."

Cass didn't feel the angst she supposed she should have. "I think sometimes that's why my parents get on my case about finding someone and moving on with my life. They miss Sofie, and they want for me what she never got to have." It made sense. She felt sorry for her parents and for herself because her memories of the little girl were so faded.

"How did she die, if you don't mind me asking?" Mack threaded his fingers through hers, and it felt nice.

"A freak accident at school. She was on the playground, got hit with a ball, and fell to the ground. And never got up. Apparently, she had an aneurysm that killed her instantly. I don't remember much, to be honest. She was there and then not there. And it was sad, and then we recovered and moved on. But I was young. I know it really hurt my parents, but we're big on honesty and being healthy—mentally, emotionally, and physically.

"My dad made sure we all got the therapy we needed. My mom was a big helicopter parent for a few years after Sofie passed. That I remember." She sighed. "But she got better too."

"That's so sad."

She squeezed his hand. "I know. My sister never showed any signs. No bad headaches, nausea, or dizziness. Just a bad hit in the head that triggered her death. It took a while for my folks to realize it was something no one could have prevented. Mom, because she's a doctor and control freak who heals people for a living. And Dad because he has a rationale for everyone and everything. Me? I don't feel I was affected by it except that I lost my sister. But I was little, so I don't feel it the way they do." And probably still did, she realized. Losing a child never went away, but they loved her and missed her. And that was healthy.

"Maybe that's why you like being a police officer so much. Because there are rules that make sense. A right way and a wrong way to act. You get to protect people the way you obviously couldn't, as a six-year-old who was never a brain surgeon, protect your sister."

She stared at him. "Wow. That was very insightful." She took the gelato he fed her.

"I'm an insightful kind of guy." He smiled and kissed her. "Are you sure you're not sad?"

"I guess I should be, but it happened so long ago. I remember her through pictures, but not much else."

"Makes sense. And, no, you're not weird for not tearing up after twenty-plus years." He kissed her again. "Mmm. You taste like caramel." He stroked her cheek. "I really like you, Cass. A lot."

Her heart raced. "I like you too. A lot." She swallowed. "My parents are going to think you're amazing. Don't let it get to your head."

He smiled with full, firm lips that had caused her so much pleasure. "I'll try not to. But since I already know I'm amazing, that shouldn't be a problem." He drew circles over her knee. "I guess if I'm meeting your parents, it's just fair to say if mine decide they want a family get-together, you have to come. You'll owe me."

"Fair is fair." She tried to ignore the jitters filling her, the zap of feeling that spread from her knee to the rest of her body. How the hell could the man get her off so many times and still make her desire him?

"You know before, how you asked about my favorite number?"

She swallowed. "Yeah."

"I was wondering if we could try something. I know you need to get in a workout, and I don't think we exhausted you enough. You seem like you still have too much energy."

"I do?" She felt like a limp noodle, pliable to whatever Mack wanted.

"Yeah. I know all about being fit. You could use a better exercise routine than what we've done."

"Is that so?"

He pushed the gelato aside and skimmed out of his underwear. Then he untied her robe, smiling as he parted it to stare over her nude body. He lay back on the bed. "Now turn around. Let's get those jaw muscles working."

"You might be a closet nymphomaniac."

"Sadly, I think you might be right." He turned her around as she knelt over him, her face aligned with his crotch. "But I'm only doing this for your own good, Cass. After all, you want to be on your best at work tonight."

"So for the sake of Seattle, I should lower my lips and suck?"

"For the city, I think you have to."

She laughed and got to work, forgetting everything but the scent and taste of Mack Revere as she sacrificed for Seattle once more.

———

Mack hadn't felt so good in… Well, he didn't know when. But he did know that orgasms must be good for the soul because he'd never slept so well. After leaving Cass yesterday—and had *that* been a lot tougher than he'd expected—he'd come home and gotten a ton done. An oil change on the SUV, some deep cleaning he'd been putting off, and a terrific run around the neighborhood.

He'd slept for a solid ten hours, something he hadn't done in forever. Monday, he felt refreshed and high on life.

And maybe a little in love.

He'd wanted nothing more than to call and text Cass since he'd left her, but worried about scaring her off after their almost-spiritual sharing, he'd only texted her that he missed her twice, and that last one had been right before her shift, a be safe, miss u with a big pink heart.

As he played with the kittens, he heard his phone chime and looked down to see a text from Tex, wondering what he had planned for their day off.

Mack thought about all he'd confessed to Cass the other day, about what he felt and what he needed to do for the health of the team. With a sorry heart, he texted the group to let them know he'd be busy the next few days with some major car maintenance and his parents, and that he'd see them Thursday at work and wished them a happy Thanksgiving.

No one seemed upset he was bowing out of "bro time," which told him what he'd been suspecting—they secretly wanted to spend time with their girlfriends, not him.

He hoped this new state of being wouldn't hurt their work relationship or the way they dealt with each other. Moving on from their little family hurt. A lot. But he didn't want to be responsible for causing potential friction with their relation-ships. So when Reggie texted him later about hanging out the next weekend at his place for a group dinner, he told them maybe, knowing he'd later decline with another made-up excuse, maybe involving Cass.

Slowly, gradually, he'd exclude himself from the group. So that they'd feel better about doing what felt natural—building their new family units into their own happily ever afters.

That evening, he got a cute text from Cass to get some sleep and stop messing around with the kittens.

He smiled, took a photo of Copo climbing all over him, and sent it to her.

She sent one back of Jed with his mouth open and U win. Copo much cuter.

Smiling, he'd just found an old episode of *Knight Rider* with the incredible David Hasselhoff when his mother called. He answered and turned down the TV. "Hi, Mom."

"Hey, honey. How are you?"

They made the necessary small talk his mother liked before diving into the meat of a conversation. "We're having a family dinner Wednesday night. Can you come?"

She had his schedule, so she pretty much knew he had the night off. But talk about last-minute. "I can."

"Oh good! Everyone will be here. I'm so excited!"

"Sounds good."

"We're having an early Thanksgiving since James and Alec are working during the holiday." Yeah, and so was Mack, but that didn't seem to be a consideration. He swallowed a sigh. "I told you everyone's coming. Dean, Ashley, and Sasha." Sasha—Xavier's girlfriend. His mom paused. "If you'd like to bring anyone, you're more than welcome."

"Actually, I do have someone I'd like to bring." And since she had tomorrow night with her parents, he didn't think Wednesday with his folks would be a problem. "I have to check to make sure she can get the time off. If she can, I might bring her."

"Oh, that would be terrific! I mean, well, if she can come, that's fine. I'll leave a spot for her until you tell me otherwise." His mom sounded thrilled. She chatted about his father and a new car he'd been looking into buying. After telling her, for the third time, that he was fine and the guys were fine and *his car* was fine, Mack hung up.

He played with the kittens for a little bit, winding down from the call. Had he done the right thing, inviting Cass to a family meal? With *all* the family?

His brothers could be a major pain. But maybe this holiday they'd start to realize they were no longer immature little boys ganging up on the youngest. That the time for coming together as a family was past due and they'd enjoy each other as adults.

Yeah, that could happen. James had already mellowed thanks to Ashley, and Alec was fun, especially with Dean around. Xavier... Well, Xavier had potential to be much more than the jackass he normally was.

But all that didn't matter. Because Mack had to get through a dinner with Cass's parents and convince her to join him for dinner with the Revere clan.

He brightened. On the positive side, if his family didn't scare her away, nothing would.

He settled Copo and Impala with a few goodnight pets then tucked into his bed, missing the strong, tender woman who should have been there with him and dreaming about her all night long.

Chapter Seventeen

TUESDAY NIGHT, SITTING IN THE CAR IN FRONT OF HER parents' house, Cass didn't think she'd ever been so nervous. She felt like a major doofus for letting anxiety about the night affect her.

"Relax. I'm telling you. Parents love me." Mack patted her on the shoulder.

"Easy there, Captain Ego. I'm not nervous."

"Sure you aren't." He glanced at her fists clenched around the steering wheel. "You're super chill." He got out of her car and headed up the walkway, not waiting for her, carrying two bottles of wine.

Who knew the firefighter was an oenophile? And, yeah, she'd looked the word up after losing at Scrabble earlier in the day. Mack liked to play games, and he hadn't pulled any punches at his favorite game while she'd been distracted by furry busybodies crawling all over her.

The afternoon spent at his house, making love and playing together, had been the highlight of her week so far. And that was including the lovefest on Sunday. She had no idea when their time together had gone from "having sex" to "making love." Maybe because Mack stared into her eyes when they were together or because she couldn't separate her affection for his smiles and cheery personality from the stud-muffin proportions of his perfect, naked body.

She only knew she had totally become the clingy, possessive, obsessed woman she hadn't wanted to be. But she didn't know how to stop what she was feeling.

Or if she should.

Mack paused with his finger at the doorbell and turned to wait for her. "Well? Shall I?"

She yanked his arm down and pounded on the door. "Be good, Revere, or you'll pay later."

"I'm properly terrified."

She snickered.

Her father opened the door, looked them both over, and smiled. "Well, you are a real boy. I had no idea my daughter hadn't been lying about bringing one over."

"Dad."

Mack laughed. "Hello. I'm Mack Revere."

Her father took the bag Mack handed him, studied the bruise on his face, and shook with his free hand. "Aaron. It's a pleasure to meet you. Come on in."

Mack passed him, but Cass had to wait to pay the toll to enter with a kiss on her dad's cheek.

"Hi, Dad."

"Cass. I'm so glad you guys could come over. Your mom made her famous lemon chicken."

"Oh, nice." Cass's favorite dish. They normally had something exotic and different on Thanksgiving, none of them needing a typical turkey. But lemon chicken definitely counted as the perfect meal. "With the couscous salad?"

"Of course." Aaron walked them all past the spacious living room and dining room into the kitchen.

"Wow. My mom would go ape in here," Mack muttered and goggled at the kitchen. "This place is amazing."

"Yeah. My mom doesn't cook that much, but when she does, she has pretty much every doodad needed to make anything, from bread to macarons to soufflés."

Stainless-steel appliances, a walk-in pantry, and a huge island with a butcher-block space, prep sink, and marble countertop, which could also seat six, made the kitchen a designer's dream.

"Cooking is Mom's hobby. Well, that and Dad." Cass laughed at her father. She moved to kiss her mom on the cheek. "Hey, Mom. This is Mack. Mack, my mom."

Her mother blinked. "I sure hope Cass isn't responsible for that bruise."

Mack grinned. "A love tap. I'm kidding. Just a scuffle with a guy at work. No biggie."

"Ah. I see. I'm Jennifer. So nice to meet you." She waved at him, her hands gunked in something she'd been making. "I'd shake your hand, but mine's covered in flour."

"Hi, Jennifer." He smiled.

Cass frowned. "Flour? That implies you're baking something. Aren't we eating at six?"

"Six-thirty," her dad said. "We need time to grill your date."

"Seriously?"

Mack laughed. "Hey, at least he's honest."

Her mom chuckled. "Aaron's kidding." She gave him the death glare. "We just wanted to spend some time with you, Cass. We hardly ever see you."

Talk about exaggerating. "We talk all the time and only missed dinner last week because you guys had a thing to attend."

"It was your father's thing," her mom said. "And it was very nice, though the meat was dry."

"Terrible." Her father shook his head. "But our award dinners usually are."

"Award? Did you win something?" Mack asked, taking a seat at the counter to watch her mother work, as if he came over all the time and tonight was nothing new.

Her mom smiled at him. "Apricot tarts for dessert. And an apple one in case you don't like apricot."

"I like everything." Mack smiled wide. "Especially Cassandra."

"Oh, how sweet."

Mack hadn't been lying. Parents *did* like him. Her mother glowed as she smiled at him, and her father laughed. Sean had once made a similar comment, and her parents hadn't so much as nodded in his direction.

Her dad was saying something about being nominated for his clinic, and she turned to him. "You never told me that."

"You never asked."

She sputtered, "Well, I mean, I just assumed it was another one of those fancy dinners for the letter people." At Mack's look, she flushed and mumbled, "You know, people with letters in front of or behind their names, like DR or PhD or MD…"

Mack's eyes widened. "W. O. W."

She glared at him, but her parents chuckled.

"My clinic didn't win this year, but to even be nominated is a huge deal."

Jennifer added, "And it looks really good when you're trying to get new clients. Not that you are, honey, I'm just saying."

Her dad blushed and accepted all their congratulations. Cass noticed Mack wasn't overly effusive, just sincere. *Such a great guy,* she seemed to think just about all the time.

Her father glanced at the bottles Mack had given him. "Oh, Mack, very nice. Special reserve."

Mack shrugged. "I didn't know what you'd be having, so I brought a white and a red. I thought you might like them."

Ha. He didn't fool her. He'd asked a ton of questions about what her parents liked to drink and had apparently chosen nice blends of a richer quality.

She muttered, "Suck-up," but he ignored her.

Instead of moving into the living room to let her mother finish cooking, they all settled in the kitchen to talk while Jennifer continued to work her magic.

Her dad had poured them all drinks, though Cass settled on a nice lemonade, wanting a clear head since she'd driven over.

Her parents spent the next fifteen minutes embarrassing her, bragging about how smart and athletic she was. But

Mack seemed fascinated, not put off, and contributed his own observations.

"She's clearly intelligent. Fast, sporty. Of course, attractive." Mack winked at her, and she blushed. "You should see her in uniform though. I watched her deal with some big guys in a fight, and when one came at her, she took him down. Not excessive about it either. She used calm and some amazing physicality to bring the man down. And she was there backing up Jed and the other cops on scene. I was impressed."

"You were?" Cass looked at him, surprised.

"Yeah. I also wanted to rush in because that guy looked like he wanted to grab you again, but I didn't. I mean, you can totally handle yourself."

She smiled. "Yes, I can."

"Plus Brad was holding me back and told me not to blow it with you." Mack gave a self-deprecating laugh. "So I waited until you gave the all clear."

She liked that he told her the truth. "Mess with my job and I'll lock you up."

"I figured." The warmth in his smile made her feel treasured.

She smiled back until she realized how focused her parents were on them. She didn't think they'd blinked in minutes. She cleared her throat, and her mom elbowed her dad.

"Cass hasn't told us much about you, only that you're a firefighter?" her dad prodded.

Mack nodded, sipping from a white wine her father had already had chilling. Apparently, the white stuff got refrigerated. Who knew?

"Yep. I've been a firefighter for five years. Was in the Air Force for seven before that. I really love my job."

"That's terrific," her mom said. "So many people work at what they don't like, and it causes a lot of additional stress. Aaron could dissect the topic at length—trust me, he's done it before."

"Hey."

Jennifer smirked at her husband and continued, "But he's right that stress kills. With such a high-pressure job like firefighting or police work," she said with a nod at Cass, "you'd have to really love your job to reap the joy along with all the hazards that come with service. Trust me, I know."

"I told you Mom's a doctor," Cass said.

"A cardiologist," Jennifer specified.

"Yeah, you'd know all about stress," Mack agreed. "My family is all law enforcement." He sounded positive, but Cass sensed something off about his tone. "My mom works in administration in the police department. My dad retired after thirty years. My three brothers are all active-duty police. One's a detective, one's SWAT, and, well, you know Xavier," he said to Cass. "A patrol officer who works in Cass's precinct."

"Interesting." Her dad sipped his wine. "Cass used to have a policy of not dating anyone she works with or anyone who's related to anyone she works with."

"Well now, I realize that." Mack sipped from his glass, looking like he'd been born sophisticated. Whatever. She'd never forget the sight of him covered in mud. "But I like to think it was my incredible skill at bar games, not to mention my fine soccer legs, that had her taking a chance on me."

Her parents chuckled.

He exaggerated his win over pool and his failure at darts. Then he continued to embellish about her loss at Scrabble. He'd hit double word score twice and barely beat her by a few points.

"He makes up words," she said when her parents stopped laughing, doing her darndest not to smile. "That or he sleeps with a dictionary under his pillow."

"Your inability to choose words with care put a damp squib on our game."

"See what I mean?" she said to her parents, then turned to

Mack. "'Damp squib'? What the hell are you talking about? And don't even try fobbing me off. I know words too, you supercilious rapscallion."

Mack's eyes shone. "You should have used those earlier."

Losing had been such a treat though, especially since she'd had to obey Mack for a solid hour. And hadn't that been a mass of orgasms she'd never forget.

He winked at her, and she blushed.

Her parents exchanged smiles, and her mom asked the big question, "What does Jed think? Because he's the real bar you need to pass."

"He tolerates me, I think." Mack sighed. "But it's his wife I'm after."

"Mack." Cass would warn him later not to make statements like that in Jed's company if he wanted to keep his face in one piece.

"What? Her pot roast was killer good. I mean, I'm still thinking about it five days later. It was melt-in-your-mouth delicious. I can't help it. I like food."

Her father just stared. "You had dinner with Shannon?"

"And Jed?" her mom added. "And survived?"

Cass chuckled. "Well, he plied the kids with liquor so they'd like him."

"Don't listen to her. It was kid beer—apple juice in cans."

Her dad winked. "Smart man. Jed and Shannon are lovely. Their children are especially fun. Very smart."

"Bordering on psychotic," Cass muttered, which had Mack nearly choking on his wine.

Her dad frowned. "That's not any kind of real diagnosis, and we don't diagnose children anyway, Cassandra."

"I hate it when you call me by my full name."

"I know. That's why I do it."

She turned to Mack, who watched them all with such fascinated amusement. "Do you see what it was like growing up with them? It's a wonder I'm normal."

"Well, normal is relative," Mack said with a large smile. "But *I* like you."

Her parents died laughing.

And the night got better from there.

By the time they returned to her house, Mack was still laughing over a pun her mother had made. He really did love words.

"God, Cass. I think I'm in love with your mom." He stumbled over the doorjamb.

She shut and locked the door behind him, hearing the kittens meow as they entered. Since Mack hadn't wanted to leave them alone, he'd brought them to Cass's house. They raced to her, and she lifted one up while Mack lifted the other one, kissing it on the nose.

Warm fuzzies took up space in her brain, and she watched a man she was coming to care for, very much, as he cradled a vulnerable kitty with so much care and attention.

Oh wow. I could really grow to love this guy.

Love. Seriously? She kept spinning head over heels with jumbled affection and confusion because Cass didn't fall fast in love. Heck, she rarely felt instant *like* for anyone.

Yet with Mack, she feared she'd started falling and had no inkling how to stop before she hit rock bottom. And then what?

She set the cat down and drawled, "First Shannon, now my mom. If I make you something that tastes good, will you be in love with me too?"

He grabbed her sweater and yanked her close, the kitten in one hand, her in another.

"Hey."

Mack kissed her, and she forgot why she felt upset. "Ah, but I don't have too far to fall, do I?" He tilted into her and nearly fell putting the cat on the ground. Then he used her to straighten himself.

Mack was acting a little loopy, which she found more than

entertaining. He seemed like a man always in control of himself. She respected that because he was like her in that way. Yet she loved his endearing grin. The way he stared at her too long, showing her exactly how he felt. And right now, he seemed awfully enamored.

"Mack?"

"Put the cat down and take me to bed," he whispered, turned, and started getting naked. Articles of clothing dropped in a trail to her bedroom.

"What cat? You mean the one I already set on the floor?" She laughed and gave the furballs a treat before following Mack to her bedroom.

He lay naked in the middle of her bed, his arms outstretched, a goofy smile on his face.

Completely asleep.

She wished she had the stones to take a picture of him like this. So much for thinking he'd been a little loopy. Hell, the man was *a lot* loopy and hadn't seemed drunk at all.

With a sigh because the night wouldn't end up as she'd hoped, she put on a sleepshirt, grabbed a thick blanket to throw over them both, and joined him in bed.

She wouldn't be getting any panty-melting sex, but she'd get the next best thing. Mack, all to herself.

———

Cass woke up to someone caressing her cheek and poking her in the arm asking, "Hey, Sleeping Beauty, you awake?"

Then someone else purred in her ear and licked her.

She opened her eyes wide, only to see a tiny, furry head staring at her. The kitten licked her nose and backed away then used Cass's stomach as a launching pad. "*Oomph*." She turned on her side.

"Hold on," Mack said and left the bed to put the two kittens on the floor before returning under the blanket to spoon her. He kissed her neck, moving her hair aside, and continued his kisses up to her ear. "I opened the curtain to let in some moonlight, but it's still dark out. So it's still technically tonight."

"Hmm?" She pulled his arm over her middle and sighed when he cupped her breast through her shirt. Cuddling on their sides, feeling closer than close.

"I wanted tonight to have a great ending." He nuzzled her neck.

Something hard prodded her backside.

She smiled. "Let me help you."

She felt him tug at her waist and lifted so he could pull her panties down. He settled her sleepshirt over her hips, leaving her bare from the waist down underneath the blanket.

Mack pulled her leg over his, spreading her thighs wide, and shifted his hand from her breast down between her legs to stroke her.

Still muzzy with sleep, Cass fully wakened as pleasure arced throughout her body.

"Yeah, that's it. Just relax." He kept touching and kissing her, giving her the best wake-up she'd had in some time. He angled closer to her bottom then pushed, easing inside her already-wet sex. "*Fuck*, you're tight."

Especially in their position, on their sides. Mack thrust in and out, slowly at first, his fingers like magic over her. He knew just how to touch her, moving softer then faster, gauging her responses. And he kissed her, constantly loving her with his mouth wherever he could reach.

"So sexy. God, Cass, you make me so hard." Mack whispered naughty thing, funny things, loving things. And through it all, he held himself back, seeing to her desires. Making her feel as if only her pleasure mattered. He teased her nipples, knowing how much she loved when he did that.

His big strong hands held her tight, controlling her movements while he rode her faster. His arousal increased her own. Knowing how much he wanted her was its own kind of aphrodisiac.

His fingers danced across her flesh, tugging at her clit while he stroked that spot inside that had her seeing stars and hurdled her into an orgasm she hadn't expected. As she clamped down on him, he moved his hand back to her breast, squeezing and playing with her while he pumped harder and faster. To her shock, she kept coming.

The pleasure held her in its grip, refusing to let go as Mack groaned her name and shuddered, finally stilling inside her.

Only then did she realize she hadn't asked if he'd been wearing a condom.

"Oh, fuck, you're really hugging me tight inside. Keep doing what you're doing," Mack rasped as he pumped once more and hugged her close.

After her heart rate slowed and he caught his breath, she asked the question she'd been dreading. "Mack, ah, did you... Are you wearing protection?"

"Yeah." He kissed her neck and moaned. "If I hadn't, I would have lost it as soon as I entered you. You're fucking hot."

The tension of the moment passed, and she relaxed in his arms. "Good."

He gently eased out of her and kissed her cheek. "I swear, I'll always do my best to protect you, and, yeah, I know you don't need protecting. You're strong and smart and can kick my ass. But when I can, I will. I'd never not use a condom with you unless you said it was okay."

She flushed, feeling bad for having doubted him.

"I'm not mad you asked," he said, reading her mind. She felt his smile against her neck. "I'm actually kind of flattered."

"Huh?" She turned around so she could look at him, not that she could see much since the moonlight through the window had shifted, now angled on the floor. "Flattered?"

"That you were so caught up you didn't ask before you came." His white smile glinted at her. "I made you lose your mind, didn't I?"

"Yeah, well, you got lucky."

"Did I." Not a question but a statement with a smug grin attached.

She choked on a laugh. "Okay, you deserve a medal for waking me up the way you did. I don't think I've ever had multiple orgasms before." And hadn't that been incredible. She had no idea her body could experience so much pleasure from sex.

"Er, yeah." He rolled away and left the room, returning to join her once more under the blanket. "All clear."

"What?"

"Condom free. I wrapped it and put in the trash."

"Oh, right." She felt herself blush, which was silly.

He stroked her hair and leaned in for a kiss. "Cass?"

"Yeah?" She kissed him back, feeling closer to him than anyone she'd ever been with.

"I meant to ask you earlier about something, but I kept going back and forth on it. And well, I kind of need to know."

"What?" He could pretty much ask her anything and she'd say yes, as lethargic and contented as she now felt.

He sighed. "Tomorrow night, well, technically tonight, I guess, my mom and dad are having a Thanksgiving for the family. We almost never have all our off-time together. Mom wants us all to celebrate at dinner."

"That's nice." For as large a family as they had with differing schedules, she could see how important it would be to get together when they could.

"I'd like it if you came with me. As my date."

She tried to see him through the dark and couldn't, so she reached around him to turn on the light. "Really?"

He looked both sleepy and a little alarmed, though that could just be her imagination. "Well, yeah. But it's not really fair. I had so much fun with your parents tonight. My family dinner won't be nearly as nice."

"Why not?"

"My brothers can be a pain, and my mom's pushy."

"Not your dad?" She smiled.

He didn't smile back. "Maybe you should forget I asked."

"No, I want to come." To see him with his family and figure out the weird dynamic she could sense but hadn't yet seen.

He sighed and hugged her. "I don't deserve you."

"Aw. You sure don't."

He tickled her as payback, and she howled with laughter as she tickled him right back.

But all that wrestling woke them both up.

"Aw, hell."

She looked down at Mack from her vantage, sitting on his stomach and holding his wrists down on either side of his head. "What's your problem now? That you're losing?"

"That you woke Junior up," he complained, a twinkle in his eye. "Now you have to put him back to bed." He arched up against her, and she felt something hard against her butt.

She grinned. "Junior, huh?"

"You can call it whatever you want. A big old tent pole. God's gift to women. Your favorite beef jerky." He guffawed. "Just don't bite too hard, eh?"

"But, Mack, why use my mouth when I have something so much better?" She wriggled against his belly, rubbing back against his erection.

"Why indeed?"

They fell asleep much later. And Cass had the absolute best dreams, wrapped up in her lover's arms.

Chapter Eighteen

MACK KNEW HE'D MADE A MISTAKE ASKING CASS TO JOIN HIM for a full-family dinner. He'd gone back and forth over the idea to invite her, but after getting soused at her parents', then losing his mind buried inside her last night, he'd had to ask.

Her parents had been wonderful. Polite and intelligent, compassionate and funny. No wonder Cass seemed like such a well-rounded individual. She knew her own worth and her own mind because her parents had raised her so well. And, man, did they love her. He could hear their pride in every word of her accomplishments. And he agreed. She was fucking wonderful.

Knowing about her sister's passing helped paint a picture of a family who'd come together in grief and grown stronger. Her father had been delighted to point out several pictures of his daughters in addition to the photos of Cass winning some trophy or another. And one of her standing with Jed in their blues.

Mack's family had plenty of photos strewn around the house. Tons of pictures of their boys in blue, but not so many of Mack in his gear, with his firefighting brethren. And, yeah, that did still bother him, even after so many years. As kids, James and Alec had drawn pictures of policemen that ended up on the refrigerator door. He had drawn fire trucks and planes and cars that ended up tucked away in a binder he had to keep in his room. And Xavier, well, he just acted like the police, constantly putting Mack in jail for imagined infractions.

A dick then, a dick now.

Mack and Cass parked down the street and walked past several vehicles to get to the walkway. Everyone had already arrived.

"Nice house," she said, looking at the old two-story colonial located in Queen Anne.

"Yeah. I never lived here. They bought a nice place once their four boys moved out." He smiled. "Can't say I blamed them."

"Where did you grow up?"

"West Seattle. Nice neighborhood, but I like living on the east side of the city better."

"Me too."

They smiled at each other.

He leaned in to whisper, "Remember, you liked me before we got here. Don't judge me on my family."

"Oh stop." She kissed him just as the door opened, and Xavier of all people stood there.

His jaw dropped. "What the fuck?" His eyes narrowed. "Who hit you?"

"Xavier Anthony Revere, watch your mouth," his mother said and shoved him aside. "Mack? What happened to your face?"

"Hazard of the job."

She seemed to accept that because she turned to Cass and smiled. "Oh, hello. I'm Sandra, Mack's mom."

"Mom, this is Cass Carmichael, my date." He smiled at his mother, who looked genuinely pleased to see him with someone, so much so that she didn't grill him about his face.

"Cass, come on in." She took Cass and pulled her inside. "You too, Mack."

"Gee, thanks."

Before he got two steps inside, his brother dragged him into their father's office off the entrance.

"Cass Carmichael? What the hell?" Xavier asked.

Mack forced himself to be amiable. The role he always played when with family. *Just let it all roll off. Don't let it bother you. Breathe in, breathe out.* "And happy Thanksgiving to you too. Yes, Cass is a friend of mine. What's the problem?"

Xavier stared at him, and Mack knew the resemblance would have Cass looking at all of them all night. Unfortunately, Mack and his siblings looked like carbon copies of their father. James was the tallest, Xavier the most muscular, and Alec in between, while Mack could have been his father's twin if his father were three decades younger.

"No problem," Xavier said slowly. "Just don't be fucking around with her."

Mack paused. "Excuse me?" Before he could ask what the hell business of Xavier's his dating life was, their father entered.

"Mack, good to see you, son." His dad pulled him in for a bear hug. "I hear you bumped into a door at work." Mack rolled his eyes. *Nice, Mom.* "It's been a while."

"A few weeks, maybe," Mack muttered and forced himself not to play the dysfunction game. No blaming or shaming tonight. He relaxed his shoulders and ignored Xavier. "How's the turkey looking, Dad?"

His father laughed. "Your mom won't let me step a foot in the kitchen." He put an arm around Mack and walked him out into the grand living room, which overlooked a huge dining table with a ton of chairs and the kitchen across the open floor plan. "Who's the looker?"

Cass glanced over her shoulder at him and winked, then turned back to his mother, who was telling her about something to do with the stuffing.

"Dad." Mack blew out a breath.

He noticed everyone else in the living room, nibbling on snacks and watching a basketball game. Although Alec and Dean seemed to be talking to Ashley, James's wife, while James and Sasha, Xavier's girlfriend, yelled at the TV.

"The looker is a friend of mine. Cass works in the South Precinct with Xavier."

His father's eyes brightened. "Oh ho, another officer on site. Good to know the house is protected from criminals *and* fire," he said and squeezed Mack's shoulders. "How are Reggie and the fellas?"

"Just fine." He gave his dad a rundown of his friends while keeping an eye on Cass. He should probably head over there to introduce everyone, but it was nice to have his dad's attention, and in a positive way.

Cass didn't seem to have any problems as she talked with his mom, overlooking the kitchen.

James yelled, "Commercial break," and everyone scattered.

Mack grinned. "Wow, it's like halftime for everyone, not just the guys on the big screen."

"Yeah. I'd better hit the bathroom before Xavier gets a shot. I swear, I don't know what he eats, but it never ends well."

"TMI, Dad."

His father barked a laugh and left. Mack searched out his family and hugged everyone hello, trying to be nice as he made his way to Cass.

Almost there, he stopped when Dean cut in front of him with a smile. "Been a long time, Mack. Nice face."

Mack shook his hand and *oomphed* as Dean pulled him in for a hug.

"Hey, get your hands off my man before I bruise the other cheek," Alec warned, tugged Mack away, then smiled. "Hey, little brother, about time you came over to say hi."

"Dad was interrogating me. I couldn't get past him."

"The old man's still got it," Alec mused then laughed and lowered his voice. "I can't believe you brought Cass here. I thought you liked her."

Mack relaxed. "I do. I thought since we were having a big old turkey dinner, everyone would be too chill after eating to be too annoying."

Dean frowned. "But Xavier's here. You knew he was coming, right?"

Mack snorted. Dean, like him, could tolerate Xavier in small bursts. "I did and came anyway. That's how much love I have for this family."

"Yeah, no shit," Alec said before taking a healthy swallow of soda. "Me too." He nodded at Dean. "I told him all about our lunch. And about how long it took you to open the door and let me in." His brows rose up and down, and for some reason, Mack blushed.

Dean pointed at him and said to Alec, "I told you he *really* liked her."

"What are you talking about?" Mack should really go save Cass from his parents' version of "the gauntlet." Which would mean talking her ear off. And God forbid Xavier got to her. Mack hadn't wanted to alarm her, since she did kind of work with the guy. But maybe he should have told her how obnoxious Xavier could be when in a nonwork environment.

"You blushed," Dean explained. "You're the most even-tempered of all your brothers. You're mellow, pleasant to be around, and don't get overly excited, even when Xavier is showing off how much of a douche he really is."

Alec choked on his drink.

"Oh please. We all know it."

And that's why Mack loved Dean. The guy didn't hide behind platitudes. He had no problem with the truth. As tall as Alec but built on stronger lines, the guy was even prettier than Mack, and Mack was pretty damn good-looking. He still couldn't believe his brother had nabbed the guy, but somehow they'd fallen for each other, moved in together, and gotten engaged.

Hmm. Would Cass move in with him at some point? He did have a larger house than she did, though he admitted he liked the character of her home.

"…which is how I can tell you're really into her," Dean was saying.

"Er, right."

Dean guffawed. "Spacing out! Classic crush behavior."

"You put way too much thought into my personal life," Mack muttered.

Alec scowled at his fiancé. "Yeah."

Dean made a sad face. "Aw, baby, don't be jealous. You're still better-looking than all of them."

Alec puffed his chest out.

Mack rolled his eyes. "Gross. I'm out of here before you bury him in lies. Next thing you know, you'll be telling me he's the most athletically gifted of all of us, which is just a blatant untruth. And look at that paunch. He's not as in shape as he used to be."

"Paunch? What paunch?" Alec's eyes widened, and he looked down at himself.

Dean shook his head. "I'm glad I'm an only child."

Mack darted away as Dean soothed Alec, in search of his own partner. He found himself thinking about Cass as his girlfriend more and more. He hadn't thought he'd fall for her so fast. Heck, that he'd fall for anyone, really. He had no idea why because he'd been dating girls since high school.

No stranger to affection for the opposite sex, Mack had simply never felt a soul-deep connection before. Despite what Tex and the guys thought, he had dated women for more than a month at a time. None of them stuck, for one reason or another.

He glanced at Cass, now talking with his mom, Ashley, and Sasha. Holding her own, if that smile on her face was any indication. She didn't seem to need him for anything, but she liked spending time with him.

He still couldn't believe she'd had to ask if he'd been wearing a condom. He should have been offended that she could think he'd do something like that, but instead he felt more than satisfied. She'd been so hot for him she hadn't cared enough to stop him before asking.

God, had he ever shared that kind of chemistry with anyone before? He liked her so damn much, and for more than her smokin' body. She was the whole package, especially the competitive, snarky side of her that enthralled him.

He sighed, found a can of soda from the fridge, and popped the top for a long drink. *Better get my head on straight before everyone realizes how much I love*—like—*her.* He wiped the cold can against his forehead, needing to cool off.

Then he marshaled his features and steadied himself, prepared to be pleasant as he went in search of his *friend*. Not girlfriend, but friend. Because he had no doubt if she learned how much he liked her, she'd cut him loose. And he couldn't bear to live with a lack of Cass in his life. Not now. Maybe not ever.

Cass smiled at something Mack's mom said about canned cranberry sauce versus the fresh stuff, an argument she'd been having with her father for years.

She tried to tune in but kept getting distracted by the cheerful atmosphere.

The house was gorgeous and festive, already decked out with a few garlands and ornamental centerpieces. Sandra was super nice. She looked Cass in the eye when talking, listened to what Cass had to say, and smiled a lot. She seemed thrilled that Cass had come with Mack, which was a surprise. Cass couldn't imagine Mack had a dearth of lady friends. But maybe very few he'd brought home?

That thought pleased her. Too much.

She turned to the two women she'd just been introduced to and smiled. Ashley, married to the oldest, James, seemed as nice as Mack had said she was. A woman with light-brown skin and an expressive face, she seemed to glow with joy. And pregnancy, Cass recalled, not seeing much of a baby bump.

"I know whatever Alec comes up with will work. He's pretty particular about details though." She rested her hand on her stomach. "Oh my gosh, Sandy, I can't wait to eat. My stomach has been growling all day, and the smell of what's in the oven is killing me."

Cass laughed. "Me too. I wasn't going to say anything, but my stomach is growling overtime. What are you making to go with the turkey?"

"What *isn't* she making, you mean?" The other woman with them asked. Tall, with short, dark hair and intense eyes, Sasha appeared to be dating Xavier. From what Cass had been told, the woman worked as a 911 operator and had nerves of steel. "I hope you made a lot of mashed potatoes. And sweet potatoes too. I can't help it. I love the starch family. Can you tell?"

Sasha had a voluptuous figure, and she owned her curves. Personally, Cass felt a little underwhelming standing near her. But then, she didn't need to look ultrafeminine and sexy for Mack to like her.

She glanced over to see him talking to Alec and Dean.

"Which is why I made some of everything for you." Sandy smiled. "So you can keep that amazing figure. Honey, if I had looked like you when I met my husband, I would have made him work even harder to win me over. I still think he got off lightly."

Jimmy walked by. "What's that, Cath?"

She snorted. "You still owe me a honeymoon."

"Oh boy. Not this again," Jimmy muttered. He turned around. "Forgot my drink."

"In your hand?" Sandy yelled after him. "Wimp."

A familiar argument, apparently. The women laughed, and Cass found them all funny and sweet. She didn't have a lot of women friends. Shannon had been her first real girlfriend for any length of time. Growing up, Cass had always tended to bond with boys. She'd had her fair share of teasing, but she didn't know how to explain it. She liked being a girl, but she seemed to get along better with the male of the species. Until Shannon, another sarcastic, honest-to-the-skin, funny woman.

And now, these ladies, who treated her as if she belonged without really knowing her.

Sean's parents and sisters had been standoffish, as if always measuring her worth.

"What about you, Cass?" Mack's mom asked her. "What's your favorite dish?"

He's standing over there with Alec and Dean. "Oh, I like stuffing. It's a sickness."

"Me too," Ashley agreed. "Although lately I seem to like everything."

James appeared at his wife's side and kissed her. "Hey, Ash. You doing okay?" He put his hand over hers, protectively on her belly. "Ash Junior isn't giving you any trouble, is she?"

"Not yet. But she's hungry."

James smiled.

Cass had a tough time not staring at the gorgeous Reveres. She'd known of Xavier and Mack's resemblance, of course, but seeing all five Revere men together had given her brain freeze.

That sweet look on James's face for his wife, she'd seen that on Mack's when looking at her. She turned to see him staring at her and drinking a soda as if dying of thirst. When he saw her watching, he winked.

She felt her cheeks heating and turned back to Ashley. "When are you due?"

"Another five months. We don't exactly know it's a girl, but James seems sure."

"I can just tell." He smiled at his wife, kissed her on the cheek again, and grabbed more olives from the refrigerator. "Besides, what a nightmare if we keep having boys, right, Ma?"

"You said it." She cleared her throat. "I mean, boys are a joy. So easy to manage."

Mack joined them and laughed. "Yeah, right. I was the easy one. The others were nightmares."

"Oh please." Alec joined them. "Tell them, Ma, how I helped you all the time when I was little. It was the others who caused you so much mental anguish."

"Yeah, this one right here." Sandy put her son in an awkward, pretend headlock, which had Cass laughing since Alec clearly stood several inches taller than his mother. "So neat and orderly."

"That's a good thing." Alec escaped his mother's hold and hugged her. "I was the good son."

"You were a snot who was obsessive about neatness," Mack corrected. He said to Cass, "If you touched anything of his, he'd steal your toy cars and refused to tell you where he hid them. James would lecture you. Xavier would beat on you."

"That's my man, a brute," Sasha said with humor.

"But Alec would 'clean' your room and hide all your stuff. So traumatic. I still have nightmares," Mack ended as he stood next to Cass, not touching her but showing everyone they'd come together.

She had to give it to him. Mack had been doing pretty well about not beating his chest and toting Cass around by her hair. She grinned, the ridiculous image amusing.

"What's so funny?" he whispered when everyone started harping on Alec's fascination with cleanliness.

"Oh, nothing."

"Tell me." He drew closer, his arm on the counter behind her. Almost hugging, but not quite.

As much as Cass liked their relationship free of labels and possessive standards, she admitted to liking him so close. Would he kiss her in front of everyone? Would she mind if he did?

She was about to answer him when she noticed Xavier frowning at them.

She raised a brow, but his brother's expression didn't change. If anything, it grew darker the longer he looked at Mack.

Cass didn't like it. Before she could say anything, Dean called them back over because the game had started again. Everyone but Mack and Cass gravitated into the living room.

"Okay, you two. Shoo. I need to get organized." Sandy paused. "Ah, Jimmy, there you are. Come help me."

"Sure thing. What do you need?"

Mack drew Cass with him toward the dining area, still in full view of the kitchen and living room.

"Geez. How big is this space? It's like the size of my whole house, and it's just their first floor." Cass looked around her.

"And that's not including the office, bathroom, laundry room, and master suite down the hall."

"Great. Now I really feel like a peon."

She felt someone looking at her and glanced toward the living area to see Xavier glaring before he turned back to the TV, cheering with the group at the action onscreen.

Cass glared at the back of Xavier's fat head and murmured, "If your brother keeps looking at me like that, I'm going to punch him in the throat." She hadn't expected Mack's loud laugh. "Shh."

"Sorry. That's something I'd pay to see." He leaned closer to whisper, "How do multiple orgasms all night long sound as payment?"

She blushed. "Mack. Not here."

He grinned, the tension that seemed to grip him the moment they'd stepped foot in his parents' house gone, at least for the moment. "Don't worry, Cass. I won't get all possessive with you, even though I really want to kiss you."

She did it for him, a quick though loving kiss that told him she cared. Then, feeling embarrassed for putting them on display, she said gruffly, "Now will that shut you up?"

He zipped his lips, then ruined it by laughing. "How about if *I* punch him in the throat? What will you give me?"

"Dinner!" Sandy called out.

Saved from trying to come up with an answer, Cass discreetly patted him on the ass.

"Hey." He grinned. "Save that for later."

She would have answered with something sarcastic but saw his father staring at them. She blushed three shades of red, especially when Jimmy chuckled and said, "Yep. Mack's a real chip off the old block."

Chapter Nineteen

MACK THOUGHT DINNER HAD GONE WELL. HE IGNORED Xavier's pointed stares throughout the meal and didn't act put out that despite all the sports and wedding talk, the family once again settled into cop talk.

A major case James had worked on. Alec's exciting work in SWAT followed by Xavier's thoughts about the officers in his precinct, which had Cass chiming in, not afraid to state her opinion.

Usually, all the talk about a profession he wasn't a part of had him feeling left out, but hearing Cass chime in didn't bother him. At first.

Xavier added something about a call Sasha had taken.

"Oh yeah," Sasha said with a grin. "That big fight involving a family reunion at Wing Luke Elementary? That was something." She turned to Cass. "Weren't you on the scene of that one?"

"We both were," Cass said with a nod at Mack. "It was a mess. Family fighting, half of them drunk, over a football game."

"Well, I mean, it's football," James said.

His wife poked him. "Not that *you'd* ever get in a fight over a silly game."

Cass and Mack looked at each other, and Mack mouthed, *Slide tackle.*

She coughed. "We had three cars there to handle the rowdy players. Mack showed up to patch them up."

"Brad and I were on call," he said.

"Did you kiss all their booboos?" Xavier smirked. "Band-Aids and they're all better?"

"You know, it's not just a rumor. You really are an ass," Cass said, which shut everyone up.

"Rumor? Who said that?" Xavier glared at Mack.

Cass continued as if she hadn't just insulted his brother. "One guy lost his front teeth. It was gross. Right, Mack?"

"We had a few sprains, broken bones, and a pretty bad concussion," Mack added. "All over a family reunion gone wrong. I guess that shows you we should skip the one next year," he said to his mom.

"Nice try."

His dad cut in, "So Cass, you're a patrol officer, yes?" At her nod, he said, "Have you thought about what you'll do after patrol? Or do you want a career right where you are? Nothing wrong with serving the community on patrol to retirement."

"I'm not sure. I have the best partner right now, but we're both at that period where we can make choices. We've talked about becoming detectives, maybe."

James nodded. "It's definitely better hours. More nine to five. What shift do you work now?"

"Third watch. 1930 to 0430. It's not bad, really, but I wouldn't mind not working through the night."

Try 24/7 several times a month, Mack wanted to say. He hadn't known Cass had thought about shifting her duties. Then again, they hadn't known each other that long, which felt wrong to him because he'd swear he knew her so very well.

But maybe not because she grew more animated with his family. They seemed enthralled with her, which he could understand. But the more she talked, the further she drifted from him.

While they questioned her about the job, leaving Mack and the rest of them to talk among themselves, Mack turned to Dean and asked about any available training slots in his schedule. He could use some more arm workouts to enhance his endurance on the job. Plus, Dean happened to be one of the best trainers in the city.

He noticed Ashley and his mom talking about dinner and recipes, but the rest of the table dug into the cop life, bantering, laughing, and acting as if everyone else didn't exist.

The dinner finally wrapped up, and he'd had enough, sitting through an excruciating pumpkin pie while his brothers told stories about what a loser he'd been as a kid. So small and helpless. He laughed where he was supposed to and pretended being teased and taunted while growing up had been fun and not so often demoralizing.

Finally, he and a laughing Cass said their goodbyes, easing out the front door after being told to return, and soon. Yep, they'd loved her, as he'd expected. Unfortunately, they'd loved her a little too well.

He said little as they walked toward the car, only to be stopped by Xavier, who raced out after them.

"Hold up," he ordered.

Mack turned, holding on to his patience by a thread. "What now?"

"Cass, would you mind giving me a minute with my brother?"

She shot him a narrow-eyed look but nodded and went to the car. She started it, warming it up, and waited.

"What do you want?" Mack asked, grumpy and tired of reliving the same visit over and over. It was all about being a police officer. About serving in the Army. About being one of *them*.

"You need to back off," Xavier said in a low voice and glanced at the car. "She's a great cop. Don't fuck her over."

"What the hell are you talking about?" Did Xavier know something about Cass Mack didn't?

"She's not one of your casual girlfriends. Cass is solid."

"I'm sorry. How is this your business? And what's wrong with my old girlfriends?"

"Look, your love life is your own. I'm just saying she's a good cop. You fuck her around and it'll hurt her, and that'll reflect on the job."

"In the department, you mean." Mack nodded, thoroughly annoyed and doing his best to ignore the way his brother always got under his skin. "You know what?"

"What?"

"You're right."

Xavier smiled. "Good."

"It's none of your fucking business. She's a good friend of mine."
I think I love her. "If you were a good brother, you'd be worried she
might end up hurting me. But no, you don't care. Because I'm not
one of you assholes."

"What the hell are you talking about?"

"Exactly. Thanks for nothing." Mack turned and left before he
actually did punch his brother in the throat.

He got into the car, careful not to slam the door, and buckled in.

"What was that about?" Cass asked, the low hum of music filling the car.

"Nothing. Just my brother being an asshole as usual."

She didn't say anything. He felt her gaze on him on the ride
back to her place but didn't speak, not sure he could tell her what
bothered him without blaming her for part of it too.

She could have told everyone to stop talking about the job.
Could have included him on bits of it, but like the others, she'd
bonded and smiled and laughed while he, once again, had been
scuttled to the side.

He didn't think his family even realized they did it anymore. It
was so natural to be that big band of brothers…minus the youngest. The spouses and significant others simply ignored what they
didn't understand and seemed to have no problem amusing themselves. But Mack thought they shouldn't have to accept being shut
out. *He* sure as hell shouldn't, especially not from his own family.

They parked and entered her house, and he sought out the kittens, not in the mood to talk. "I might just go home. I'm tired." He
stroked Impala, warmed when the little guy rubbed his cheeks on
Mack's face.

"Okay, what's going on? Why are you so quiet? I thought
tonight went okay until Xavier annoyed you."

"I don't want to talk about it." He kept playing with the kittens, trying not to care, to not feel the hurt she wouldn't understand.

"I do want to talk about it," she said. "I'm not into passive-aggressive bullshit. If you have a problem with me, say it. I thought we had honesty between us."

He stood, slowly, keeping a lid on his temper. Mack rarely got mad. But when he did, he had a tendency to rage. Hard. "You really want to know?"

"I asked, didn't I?" She planted her hands on her hips.

"I'm sick and tired of constantly being shuffled to the side in any and all conversations with my family. We get like two seconds to talk about anything besides cop drama, and then it's all about James's last murder case or Alec's standoff with an armed suspect. No one gives a shit about what I do at all, and it bothers me. There. I'm a petty bastard who would just once like his family to notice that what he does is important too. Happy now?"

She stared, appearing surprised. "Oh. Wow. I'm sorry."

Great. Now Mack felt even worse. She pitied him. "Never mind."

"What did Xavier have to say?"

She'd wanted to know the other stuff. Might as well spill that too. "Officer Xavier Revere warned me to leave you alone because your state of health is so much more important than mine. That I shouldn't treat you the way I do the myriad other women I apparently treat with a lack of regard. My casual dates who are so broken when I leave them that they can't exist." *Xavier, such a fuckhead.*

Cass frowned. "He was worried I was just another casual hookup for you?"

"I'm hearing tone there." Judgment. And that pissed him off. "First of all, I've been honest with you from the beginning. I'm not a whore. I don't date nearly as much as everyone seems to think I do. And I've never, ever treated a woman with anything but respect. The fact that I haven't made any lasting connections is no one's fault. Not mine or the women I dated. It just didn't happen."

"I know."

"I don't think you do." Or she wouldn't have sounded so critical. "I've never considered you casual. We're friends, and I've always respected the way you want us to present ourselves to others. I didn't hug you or hold your hand, though I wanted to. *You* kissed *me* back there."

"I know," she repeated, but this time with a little more heat. "I didn't say you did."

"I'm really tired of everyone thinking I'm so beneath them because I'm not a fucking cop."

Her eyes narrowed. "Now wait a minute. You're putting your bullshit on me. I never said anything about that being a problem. Just because you're having an issue standing up to your brother does not mean I did anything wrong."

If he were a cat, he would have hissed right then, right there. "I'm leaving." He grabbed the kittens and headed for the door.

"Mack, you're being silly about this."

"Screw you, Cass." He left in a huff.

"Fuck off, then." She slammed the door behind him.

Mack put the kittens in the carrier in his back seat and swore all the way home. Not a great ending to what should have been a pleasant family dinner. At least the Revere clan had been consistent. Hell, he had more in common with Dean than his brothers and dad. His mom still treated him like the baby, but she never stepped in and tried to get anyone to see him as more than the youngest of her boys.

He hadn't understood how difficult it would be to see his family accept Cass but not him. Of course he wanted them to like her. But having yet one more reminder that even his girlfriend—who wasn't even a girlfriend—was more acceptable than he was hurt.

He let himself in his house, feeling the chill of solitude, and went to bed. Alone.

And missed Cass all night long.

The next day at work, he said little, telling Reggie straight out he was in a foul mood.

"You're never happy after hanging with the folks." Reggie shook his head. "No problem, bro. I got your back."

The day passed quickly. They saved a choking toddler and helped a cardiac arrest make it to the hospital. The afternoon settled down, enough for them to restock the aid units and clean. Wash had just finished making a huge pot of stew for the entire shift, which even had the LT hanging around instead of bolting home for turkey, when a call came in for immediate assistance.

With Tex and Brad already taking a call to a traumatic injury nearby, Reggie and Mack headed to the scene of a major accident.

"Crap. I really wanted some of that stew. Wash knows how to cook," Mack complained.

Reggie grunted. "I can still smell it. I've got residual drooling."

Mack couldn't help laughing at that.

"There we go. You've been in a bitch of a mood all day."

"Yeah."

Reggie paused. "Want to talk about it?"

"Maybe after." They closed in on several mangled vehicles, police cars, and more than a few people bleeding and or wounded.

They pulled in and parked and were directed to an older white man who didn't look well at all. He sat on the ground, blinking as he absorbed all the chaos. Mack didn't see any blood, but that didn't mean the man couldn't be bleeding internally.

"Sir? Sir, what's your name? Are you hurt?"

"S-s-tt-ifffn." He added something unintelligible.

A woman wearing a bandage around her head approached. "Steven, honey, are you okay?"

Reggie intercepted her, checking to find out the woman was the man's wife. He asked her questions about the patient while

Mack continued his assessment, knowing time was of the essence. "Steven, I want you to smile for me, okay?"

Half of Steven's face drooped, and Mack had a bad feeling they were looking at a stroke victim.

"Okay, now I want you to lift your arms like this." Mack lifted his arms out by his sides. "And keep them up."

The man lifted one arm. The other didn't move.

Shit.

"Reggie, let's go. We've got a stroke."

Reggie and Mack carefully eased the man onto a gurney and in the back of the ambulance. Then Reggie helped the woman inside the back. "Mack, you want to drive?"

"Got it."

Mack knew the streets better than Reggie despite what Reggie thought. He called in the stroke and had people waiting when they arrived. They wheeled the man into the hospital and handed off their notes before coming back to help the man's wife inside.

Mack and Reggie returned to the accident to see several medic units on hand and filled in wherever needed.

Sadly, the man's stroke seemed to have caused the accident, according to several witnesses, and factored into two families of four who didn't fare so well. Nor did the woman on the motorcycle, caught between two crashed SUVs, who died on the scene.

"Just think how much worse this might have been with ice on the ground," Reggie muttered as they finished up.

"Yeah." Mack sighed, glad Cass hadn't been there to see such pain and death. And wishing they'd never fought to begin with. *Hell. I miss her.*

———

Cass missed Mackenzie Revere, asshole extraordinaire. She sat next to Jed, fuming, and recounted exactly what Mack had done wrong, in detail, as they finished up their shift. The night had been surprisingly quiet, for which she was thankful.

And Jed had been a great wall of silence, letting her vent while saying nothing about what he thought. Until she couldn't take it anymore. "Well? Are you just going to sit there and not talk?"

"Okay, do you want the truth? Or do you just want to stew in your little world of 'Cass is perfect and Mack's an ass'?"

"The truth," she growled.

They sat in the car, watching a neighborhood park that had been reported as the scene of several recent teen fights. They made their presence known, sitting under an overhead streetlight, trying to prevent trouble from happening.

"Well, seems to me like you've both been jerks. He clearly has family issues."

"Yeah, I sensed that. Xavier's such a dick."

"Not a news flash," Jed said drily. "If you talk to the guy for more than ten minutes, you know he's a good cop and that he's got enough arrogance to fill Lumen Field."

She snorted. "Yeah. It was weird him sticking up for me, but acting like by being with Mack, I'd somehow come out contaminated? As if Mack could screw me over just by dating me?"

She said a few more not-so-nice things about Xavier, Mack, and the warped family dinner.

Some time later, Jed groaned. "Fuck, Cass. You've been ranting for hours."

"Please. More like twenty minutes."

"It's felt like forever."

She flipped Jed off and felt better.

He gave a ghost of a grin. "Your *friend* Mack took out his frustration with his family on you. No question." Apparently Jed wasn't buying the idea that she and Mack were merely friends.

She flushed. "Go on."

"But you should have given your *friend* the benefit of being an asshole. You said Mack was amazing with your parents, the two supportive people who always make you feel like you belong."

"Yeah?"

"He doesn't seem to have that. The Reveres are known for being stellar officers. Everyone knows that last name. It's like cop royalty. It has to be tough for Mack being the sole firefighter in the family, the guy who doesn't fit in. Can't you see how awkward that would be? And especially when they gush all about the girl he brings over and he's still not good enough to sit at the grown-up table?"

"What grown-up table?" She'd been with Jed until that comparison.

"Sorry. The kids have been bitching about sitting at the kids' table when we go to Shannon's folks' next week to celebrate a late Thanksgiving. You're more than invited to come."

"Ugh, no, thanks. I've already had two celebrations this week. Oh, in case I forgot to tell you, happy Thanksgiving."

"Don't change the subject. My whole point was Mack's date seemed to have a better time than he did with his family. And that's gotta be tough."

"Yeah." She sighed. "I told him to fuck off when he left."

"Oh, nice." Jed shook his head. "Is he coming back?"

"I don't know."

"Do you want him to come back?"

Miserable, she wanted to yell *Yes*. "Maybe."

Jed sighed. "You know I hate talking feelings."

"And yet you've done nothing but Dr. Phil me for the past five minutes."

"Remember what you said to Mack?"

"Fuck off?"

"Yeah, fuck off."

She sighed. "Sorry. I'm frustrated."

"I can tell. Look. Just talk to the guy. And before our game next

Saturday. So you have time. You do know we have a soccer match with the Burning Embers to make up for the disqualified mud fight a few weeks ago next week. Are you going?"

"Of course."

"Then figure out what you want from your *friend* before then."

"Would you stop saying *friend* like you don't believe me? Or putting it in air quotes?"

In air quotes, he responded, "What-ever."

She snorted. "Such a jerk." She paused. "So did you and Shannon ever talk about that baby you don't want?"

He flushed. "Yeah. She cried a lot. Talked about her time as a mom being over and shit. That she feels like she's shriveling into an old lady."

"She's thirty-two years old. Gimme a break."

"That's what I wanted to say but didn't."

"I'm impressed."

"Me too because I was *really* close to calling her on all her drama. Then the twins came in covered in permanent marker from a fight that got out of hand." He cleared his throat. "The word 'idiot'—spelled I D J I T— is faded but still visible on my son's forehead."

She did her best not to laugh.

"Sam has the word 'pig-face' on her cheek, but Shannon managed to erase enough of the G that it looks like 'pie-face,' and I'm not sure that's any better." He paused. "After we saw the kids, we both had a long, cleansing laugh and decided not to have any more children because we love our own so much. We really need to appreciate the ones we have."

"Smart move."

"Yeah." He blew out a breath.

"I'm happy you guys worked that out."

"Me too, Cass. Me too."

Chapter Twenty

Mack hated the fact he and Cass had fought. And he hated that he felt so uncomfortable unburdening himself to his friends because he used to feel like he could tell them anything. He'd made another excuse to avoid everyone until shift on Sunday. He'd somehow figure out how to bypass them next week too, though he could do nothing about the soccer game next week, when he'd have to face Cass again.

Mack didn't do drama. He didn't not talk to people. So he had no idea when he'd become this huge dickwad who couldn't apologize to the woman he unfortunately loved.

God. Thinking about how he'd fallen for a police officer galled him. Because he had to learn how to deal with his own issues if he and Cass could make a go of being together. And that was taking a lot for granted because one, the woman hadn't called to talk to him at all, and two, she'd never said she wanted more than a friendship. He might be expecting a lot more than he deserved.

But, hell, being without her, without even the opportunity to talk to her with his head out of his ass, was killing him.

Mack liked her, damn it. All that sass and grit and in-your-face honesty.

Genuinely sad because they hadn't talked for a whole two days, he mustered up the courage and drove to her house Saturday afternoon. He texted, Do you have time to talk?

She didn't make him wait, which he appreciated. He'd intentionally timed it so that she should be up and moving, though he knew she worked later in the evening.

Yeah.

Face to face?

Sure. When?

Now. He left his car, locked up, and walked to her door.

She opened it and stepped back before he had a chance to knock. "Come in."

He entered and stood, feeling awkward, his hands in his pockets. "I'm sorry."

She sighed. "Me too."

He paused. "Oh?"

"You first." She closed the door behind him and moved to her couch, where she plopped down, waiting.

Mack followed after getting rid of his shoes and jacket, prepared to stay as long as he had to in order to convince her to take him back. Hell, he didn't even know if they were dating, so could they have actually broken up?

He took a fortified breath and admitted, "I took out my anger with my family on you, and you didn't deserve it. It wasn't fair. You have nothing to do with how they act, and you were nothing but nice to everyone. I really am sorry."

She sighed. "I am too. I could tell there was something off whenever you mentioned them." She paused. "Xavier is a dick."

"Yeah," he said with feeling. He loved his brother, but lately, he didn't like the guy much. He had no idea why his brother held him in such low esteem.

"I could see how they talked around you. Not trying to exclude you, I don't think, but if you're all always like that, it could get super frustrating."

"You have no idea."

She shrugged. "I don't. My sister died when I was little, so I've lived as an only child for a long time. I'd like it if my parents spent *less* time on me."

"I really liked your parents. They're so proud of you."

"They are. And you deserve more support than you're getting from yours. Have you ever talked to them about how you feel?"

"No. Well, a little right after I joined the Air Force. It wasn't the Army, and they didn't like that. I'm the only Revere who goes my own way." He thought about how much pleasure that gave him. "And maybe that's my way of sticking it to them."

"Serving your country and then serving your city. You big rebel." She shook her head. "I'm kidding. I get what you're saying. Look, I was wrong to tell you that you were being silly. You have every right to feel the way you do."

"Thanks."

"Right."

They stared at each other, the moment growing more awkward before he blurted, "I missed you."

"Yeah?" She looked at him with what he could only hope was more than mere affection. "I, um." She cleared her throat. "I'm sorry I told you to fuck off."

"Are you?"

"Well, no, not really." She smiled, and the glow of humor in her eyes had his heart racing. "I was mad. But I'm sorry you felt bad about that night. When I think about it, I'm sorry I missed understanding how the dinner affected you. They totally talked around not only you but Dean, Ashley, and Sasha too."

"Sasha works 911, so she kind of fits in."

"Your dad seems nice but clueless."

"I think it's more a passive clueless. Like, he knows it annoys me, but what can I expect since I didn't join the police force like all the good little Reveres?" Mack snorted. "I deserve a lot of what you said. I am silly for not speaking plainly to my folks. Alec gets it. Dean too. But I don't think the others care."

"Or they honestly don't see it. I didn't until you pointed it out."

"I guess, but how could you? That's the first time you've ever met my family."

She patted the couch. "Come sit next to me."

"What if I don't?" he asked as he drew near. "Will you tell me to fuck off again?"

She laughed. "Maybe." He sat next to her, and she crept into his lap and hugged him. "I'm sorry, Mack. Mostly because I kind of believed Xavier's bit that you might have been treating me as a casual hookup, even though we both pledged to be friends first."

"I am your friend, Cass." He kissed her, tenderly holding her while he showed her how much he felt. He couldn't say it, fearful of scaring her away. But he wanted her to know in every kiss and caress. Loving or fighting or laughing. She had to know she meant so much more than anything casual. "But if you'd let me, I could be so much more."

She lifted his sweater, and he let her take it off him.

He stroked her cheek. "Does this mean you forgive me?"

"I'm going to work off my anger with your glorious body."

"I'm game."

She stopped. "Mack, I'm not mad. Well, not anymore. I, uh…" She seemed to be having a difficult time expressing what she felt. Her cheeks turned pink. "I missed you a lot. Like, a lot-lot."

He watched her, seeing the anger and the affection, not sure which emotion made more sense. "Were you mad because you missed me?"

"*Yes.*" She groaned. "You have been a huge pain in the ass from the beginning. But you do something to me I don't understand. I like you. I mean, I *really* like you, as a person. And I felt bad after I told you to fuck off, and normally expressing my honest feelings doesn't bother me."

He held back a grin, so glad to not be the only one unsure of what their relationship, such as it was, meant. "I'm glad it bothered you. I don't like fighting with you. Well, you're fun to argue with.

I love when we talk smack or discuss who's a better soccer team, who has better taste in music or TV."

"I do," she said at the same time he said, "It's me, clearly."

They grinned at each other.

"I know you don't want us to get all emotional and tied up in relationship definitions, but—"

She interrupted, "I think it'd be okay if we were dating. Like, just seeing each other."

He studied her, loving the shyness he saw in her eyes. "Are you sure? Because I really don't want to put you on the spot or pressure you. I …" *Love you, Cass.* "You're smart. I like talking to you about all kinds of topics. I can't look at you without wanting you. And I love how organized you are. I think it's really sexy."

"You do?" Her gray eyes looked so surprised, a tentative happiness waiting to bloom.

His heart threatened to burst out of his chest with love for this woman.

"I do. I also don't want to fuck it up, so you tell me where we are, and we'll go from there."

"Are you sure?" She blew out a breath. "I'm not great with relationships."

"I can tell. I'm about to come in my pants and you still won't give me an answer." He kissed her, full of pent-up frustration and need.

"Fine," she rasped when they parted. "We're dating. If you must label me—"

"I must." He hurried to undress, put her back on his lap, and groaned when her hand sought him out, gripping his erection before pumping him up and down. When she let him go, he wanted to cry.

"Then I guess we're dating. Exclusively." She paused, her cheeks red as she looked into his eyes. "Like, the kind of couple who don't need to worry about condoms because they're only having sex with each other, and the birth control shot she got two weeks ago is now safe."

He stared, aching. "So no condom?"

"Well, if you're okay not seeing other peop—"

He yanked her shirt off and kissed her, frantically pulling her clothes off while she laughed. He kissed her everywhere, in lust with her strength, her full breasts, the wet need between her legs.

He moved down to kiss her there, licking the arousal and sucking her clit as she cried out, then sitting down and pulling her on top of him so he could watch her bounce up and down while his climax built.

He pulled her close and clamped his mouth to her breast, totally enraptured with her rosy nipples. He teethed and sucked as she cried out. Pulling away as his orgasm consumed him, he hissed her name as he emptied into her, continuing to pump as she slammed down on him. Until he couldn't take any more and gripped her hips, keeping her still as he finished.

He remained deep inside her, hugging her close. When her shivering stopped, he eased back and leaned his head against the couch, his eyes closed. "Fuck. I don't think I can move."

And damned if he didn't feel moved to tears by the love he had for her, a confusing mass of need and care. Cass kissed him, her hands on his cheeks as she thanked him without speaking.

He opened his eyes and saw tears on her cheeks, but the tender expression on her face, something he'd never seen before, shocked him. "You okay?"

"That was *so good*."

"Yeah." He kissed her back. Her warmth filling the void that had been inside him for too long. "We have to tell each other to fuck off when needed."

She smiled through tears. "You're such a dick."

"A big dick." He shifted, still inside her. "And one that will be a giant among men again. Just as soon as I get a little recovery time."

"We should probably clean up first."

"Oh, shower sex. Yeah, that sounds great."

They raced to her bathroom and proceeded to get super clean. Just so they could get dirty all over again.

━━━━━━━━━

The next week was perfect. Mack spent time with Cass at her house or his. They played with the kittens, exercised together, and continued to try to outdo the other. He managed to avoid the guys by telling them he needed the space to figure out how he and Cass could make things work.

And for the most part, they left him alone, still laughing and acting tight at work, but Mack thought he saw them giving him odd looks a few times.

He'd ignored a call from his mother and two calls from Alec and James, not in the mood to deal with any of them. Maybe not for a long while. Immature, but he needed the emotional breather, and Cass agreed he should talk to them when *he* felt up to it.

The weather warmed up to a crisp 39 degrees, just in time for the big rematch soccer game on Saturday.

Mack dressed for the game in sweats and his jersey along with much-needed cleats. Though the cold would be challenging to play in, it wouldn't be a muddy game today. The frozen ground would be unforgiving when he fell, however.

Mack met up with his teammates, including the guys, who gave him a ration of shit for being so out of the loop lately.

"You sure you know what you're doing on the field?" Tex taunted. "The last time we played, you lost us the game."

"Only because Xavier has a big mouth," Mack muttered.

"Hey, we're all on the same team here," peacemaker Brad said. "And before you say anything obnoxious, Hernandez, just don't."

Hernandez shot Brad the finger, said something in a low voice to one of his buddies, and laughed.

Brad turned to their leader. "Okay, Captain. Any words of wisdom?"

Lori, one of their fellow firefighters on A shift, nodded. "The Top Cops are assholes, but they have size and brutality on their side. They also have a few key scorers. Today is not going to be pretty."

At least Reggie had shown up this time, not like the last time, with his lame excuses.

Mack turned to see the guys' girlfriends and Emily in the stands, all sitting together. Bree spotted Mack and waved. He noted Cass's parents too, both of whom waved at him from the Top Cops side. He waved back, pleased they'd come.

And there, up a few rows from the Carmichaels, his parents, Sasha, Alec, and Dean. Dean gave him a thumbs-up. Mack nodded then hurriedly looked away, not wanting to deal with his family even though they likely had no idea he was annoyed with them despite not having answered their calls.

And why was that? Because he didn't have the guts to tell them how he felt.

Cass was right. He had been silly about it all. More like a huge pussy too afraid to deal with the fallout of hurt feelings instead of making his family own up to the shitty way they treated him.

Tex smacked him on the back.

"Ow."

"Pay attention, boy. Lori wants you on that tough halfback of theirs. What's her name?"

"Carmichael," Lori sneered. "Such a bitch."

Mack did his best to keep his grin to himself. Cass was a bitch... on the field. He loved that about her. "I got her."

"Yeah, right," Reggie muttered.

"Mack's got her covered, don't ya, stud?" Tex grinned wide.

Hernandez looked from Mack to the Top Cops huddle and nodded. "Ah, so that's why Mack's been in such a snit lately."

"A snit? This coming from you, God's gift to bad moods?"

"Fuck you, Revere."

"Dream on, Hernandez. But tell your mom I'll see her later under the bleachers after the game."

Hernandez sputtered with laughter. "Yeah? Well, your mom can…"

More mom banter went back and forth before Lori called a halt to it with a "your dad" joke that made them all cringe. Even Lori.

"Okay, that was gross. Pretend I never said it."

Brad grimaced. "Gladly."

Tex tipped an imaginary hat her way. "You scare me, Lori. Impressive."

She blushed. "Shut up, Tex. Get those asses onto the field. Victory or death, you remember that."

After a chant and a *Go, team!*, they ran onto the field.

"Yeah, yeah." Reggie complained as he parked his butt in front of the goal. "Let's hurry this up. I'm cold!"

A little girl yelled out his name. "Go, Reggie!"

Everyone near her smiled or laughed, and Reggie waved like a crazy man at her.

Mack tried but couldn't stop staring at Cass. She lined up at the midfield line on her team's side, while he stood as a left wing, put there because, yeah, of all the guys, he was the least capable when it came to dribbling the ball. He was still pretty good, but they had a lot of crazy talent on the field. Though Brad's came from his ability to merge football with soccer, nearly tackling those who came near him.

Cass sneered at him.

He sneered back. "Good luck, Officer Cheats-to-Win."

"Blow me, Revere."

Hoots and laughter sounded just before the referee blew the whistle, and Lori kicked the ball back to Tex, who passed it over to one of the A shift guys.

The game was on.

Mack ran a ton, feeling good about getting in his share of exercise running up and down the field. Twice they kicked the ball to him, and he centered it or switched fields, not having a shot with Cass constantly in his face.

The last time the ball came near, she seemed to stumble, and he dribbled around her before passing to Lori for an assist. She scored a heck of a shot, and the teams ran back to their respective fields to face off again.

He laughed at Cass, and she smirked back at him.

Again, he managed to move around her. And a third time, until he started to wonder if she was letting him beat her. Nah. She wouldn't do that. Cass liked cutting him down to size.

Xavier yelled at her once more to get in the game, and she flipped him off.

Then Xavier yelled at Mack for getting his girlfriend to make him look good. The cops and firefighters ignored him, mostly. But Mack's crew gave Cass and Mack more than a few speculative looks.

Mack didn't appreciate Xavier's tone, so when Xavier took Cass's place on the next play, to steal the ball when it came into Mack's possession again, Mack deliberately kicked the ball as hard as he could straight at his defender, "accidentally" kicking Xavier in the nuts with it.

And damn, but that felt good.

But not great because the center halfback didn't appreciate Mack's kick and slammed into him, knocking him to the ground, flat on his back.

"Oh, my bad," the giant said.

"Hey, unibrow, this ain't rugby," Tex yelled.

"It 'ain't' Texas either, you hick."

Once again, the game spiraled into name-calling while Mack tried to catch his breath and get to his feet.

Cass leaned over him, looking down, and shook her head. "You just had to do it, didn't you?"

Mack stood with her help, wheezing. "So worth it."

She murmured, "Yeah, I bet it was."

Chapter Twenty-One

CASS DIDN'T LIKE THE WAY MACK KEPT LOOKING AT HER AS they sat in his home, playing with the kittens and nibbling on pizza. She'd overheard him make some lame excuse to his friends before leaving the soccer game. It had surprised her that he intended to spend quality time with Cass over his bros.

She didn't know how she felt about that. Good because he chose her, but bad because he didn't seem to be true to himself. He'd told her before that his friends were like family and that he spent a lot of his free time with them.

Lately, he seemed to spend all his free time with her.

"Okay, spill it. What's your problem?" she asked in a huff, nervous and not sure why.

"You tell me." He sat back, his arms over his chest, and sunk into his sofa as Impala rappelled down his jean-clad leg, paw over paw, claws out.

"You're on your period?" she asked and snickered. "You're upset we won?"

"You didn't win, we tied." He glared at her, and weirdo that she was, she found him incredibly sexy. "I'm angry with you. And I'm not kidding."

"What did I do?" She ignored the guilt she'd been feeling since letting him steal that first ball. "If you wanted to hang with your friends, you could have."

"Try again. And do me the courtesy of being honest."

She stared at him and huffed. "Oh, come on. It was one play."

"Try several. What the hell? I don't want you playing down so we can win. We would have kicked your asses again," he emphasized, "if that ref could keep his eyes off your breasts and on the game!"

She knew Shannon's cousin had a thing for her, but Cass didn't need any help to beat an opponent. "How is it my fault he's got a crush? It's not like I flashed him or anything."

"Why did you deliberately let me steal the ball? It wasn't obvious, which made it worse! If you were clowning, I'd get it. But you played like a fourth-grader out there."

That hurt. "Hey, not cool."

"No, it's not."

"I thought we were going to eat and have sex and goof around before I head to work. This isn't fun."

"I thought we promised to be honest with each other." His voice grew quiet. "You owe me that much."

Cass felt like an idiot. Never in her life would she have imagined acting like she had in high school. Or the way she had with Sean, pretending to be less to make her partner feel good about himself.

But being with Mack had put her world right again. She didn't want him to feel bad for losing. They'd just made up, declaring themselves to each other. She wanted him happy with her. With the Cass he liked cuddling with, smiling with, and loving until she could barely walk.

"It's no big deal. So I let you get the ball once or twice? Soccer is a team sport."

"That's bullshit."

She started, shocked that he seemed so serious and angry. "It was just a game."

"No, it's you."

"Me?"

"Cass, one of things I like so much about you is your honesty. When we met for pool, you tried to beat me. And I tried to beat you. Same with darts. I tried to beat you. I lost, fair and square. Today was a joke."

"It was just a game," she said again, irked and embarrassed to be called out for trying to be nice. "Give it a rest."

"Really? How would you feel if I showed up to a race and let you win? Would you like that?"

"I'd hate that, but that'll never happen. I'm faster than you."

"Are you?" He smiled. "We should have a race and see."

"Fine."

"Fine." He stood.

She blinked. "Right now?"

"Why? Full on pizza?"

"No." Yes. But the competitor within her wouldn't back down. "Where are we racing?"

"Let's go to my gym. It's got an indoor track on the second floor. Six laps make a mile."

"You're on."

An hour later, they stood on the track, panting, as he congratulated her on her win.

"Thanks. I told you I was…fast." She narrowed her eyes on him. "You…don't seem too…out of breath."

"It was a great race. You were super." He winked, but she didn't see humor on his face.

She took a moment until she could breathe normally again. "Oh, wait. Is this where you try to make me think you let me win?" She knew she was super competitive. She made no excuses for it. Cass liked to win. "Try again. I earned that."

"Did you?" He sneered. "Let's do another lap. I'll kick your scrawny ass."

"*Scrawny?*"

They lined up, annoying an older man who had to wait to pass the narrow way, and when she said, "Go," they took off.

Mack smoked her. No way she'd fairly won their previous race.

He stood waiting at the finish, breathing hard. And wow, could he *move*.

She had been flying and still came in seconds later.

"See? Doesn't feel good when you win because someone let you."

She scowled. "I have to be at…" breathe, breathe, "work in… three hours. I wanted… us to have…a nice day."

"Then you shouldn't be lying to me." He walked with her outside to his car, which they'd taken together. "Cass, I like you for you. I don't want you to *let* me do anything. I want to earn my wins and my losses."

"I… Damn. I'm sorry." She felt stupidly on the verge of tears but had no intention of showing him. She'd just wanted him to be happy about life and thought if he lost to her they'd have drama. The way she had with Sean after they'd taken those first steps toward a serious relationship.

Drama she'd now created.

"Can you just take me home? I'm tired and sweaty." She glared at him. "And not in a good way."

"Your call. I'm still happy to fuck the fight out of you, but then, if it's a race to the finish, how can I be sure I'll be the winner?"

"What?" She gasped. "Are you insinuating I fake orgasms?"

"I don't know. Do you?"

She slammed into the car and swore at him, her tears lost to the anger taking over. Mack simply nodded while she told him what she thought of his stupid ideas and bad playing at soccer.

"And you can just fuck off."

Expecting him to roar back at her, she was taken aback when he smiled and drove them home. "See? That. *That's* what I want. A woman not afraid to tell me to fuck off. That's what we agreed to." He left the car to follow her up the walkway to her house. When she would have slammed the door in his face, he pushed through and spun her to receive one angry, hot-as-fuck kiss. "Now, have a safe shift, and we can fight about this when you get done."

His honest amusement baffled her.

"See ya, Cassandra." He jogged back to his car and drove away.

"Asshole." She fumed, finally slammed the front door, and went to shower.

The night was horrible. Mrs. Cleary called about her grand-daughter, now dating some "loser" named Kenny who had a warrant out for his arrest. Oh, and he'd battered her granddaughter, giving the girl two black eyes and a busted lip, though Mandy refused to press charges.

After arresting the guy and dropping him off to be processed, Cass said little to Jed, who kept glancing at her as he drove. "It sucks, but I'm not surprised. Mandy had a run of great luck. Her luck ran out."

Cass sighed. "I know. I was just hoping never to see that happen to her. At least she's breaking up with the guy."

Jed nodded. Then a slow smile crept over his face. "But Lame Dick isn't so lame after all. Mandy's ex showed up as we pulled away. Did you see that?"

"Yeah." Cass chuckled. "Owen Dickerson to the rescue. With any luck, Mandy will start listening to her grandmother. Maybe Limp Dick will stick around and be the good guy Mandy needs."

"One can hope."

They drove around, patrolling. The night passed, and Cass wanted nothing but to go home and figure out just what had happened between her and Mack. But Jed kept her occupied, probably sensing her bad mood, with a lot of funny stories about Shannon and the kids. After they finished for the night and made their way to their cars, she learned that the twins had an even better story than permanent marker-face, one that included Samantha, a priest, and church last Sunday that Jed had forgotten to mention.

"Yep," Jed growled. "Nothing says funny like Sam asking the priest, 'What do a Christmas tree and a priest have in common? Their balls are just for decoration.'" He slapped a hand over his face.

She laughed her way to her car. "Thanks, Jed. You always know what to say to make me feel better." She laughed harder. *That's a really funny joke. I'll have to remember that.*

"I swear, I didn't know she was standing there when I told that joke to Shannon's dad over the phone. Then, of course, the kid breaks it out right after service. We hit ten-o'clock mass, the busiest of the day. Shannon's only grudgingly talking to me."

Cass stifled her laughter, and it wasn't easy. "Aw, she'll forgive you. Eventually. It can't be that bad. Who heard Sam, anyway? Couldn't be that many people."

"Everyone. The priest was shaking hands after the service, surrounded by happy parishioners, when Sam stopped to tell him the joke." Jed groaned. "He laughed, actually. He's a good guy. But Shannon… I thought her head was going to explode."

"Well, have a good time at church in a few hours," Cass said, chipper. "Give Shannon an amen from me, would you?"

He flipped her off and left.

She got into her car, still chuckling, and made her way home. The streets were usually empty so early in the morning, a few early birds rising. The die-hard joggers out with cleats on their sneakers to battle any icy sidewalks, homeless people curled up, just trying to stay warm.

One particular face caught her eye, and she headed over, popped out, and stuck five dollars in the old lady's cup. The woman grunted a thanks, and Cass continued on her way home. Despite trying to get the older woman into a shelter or, better yet, back with her daughter, who'd been happy enough to take her in, Cass had been unsuccessful. The woman wanted her independence on the street with her friends.

Cass didn't understand it, but then, she'd grown up with warmth and love. Any hint of mental or emotional distress and her father would immediately drop everything to help her get better. And with her mother so concerned about Cass's physical wellbeing, having lost one daughter to sickness, Cass had striven to exceed in the physical so her mom wouldn't worry.

She'd been tremendously fortunate growing up to know herself and her capabilities.

So why the heck had she acted so contrary to her nature to let

Mack win when even according to him it hadn't mattered all that much?

Instead of whining to Jed yet again, she'd tried to figure herself out. Even after showering and getting some sleep, she woke feeling unrested, disturbed.

So she called in the big guns. "Dad? Do you have time to meet me for lunch today? I have a problem."

"You bet. I have the day off, as a matter of fact," he teased. "How about I make us some subs?"

She grinned. "You mean you're going to buy some amazing sandwiches from a certain sub shop off Rainier?"

"Maybe."

"Thanks, Dad. I'll see you at one if that's okay."

"Perfect. It'll give me time for a nice walk with your mother. She's got a surgery scheduled later today, so we're spending the rest of the late morning together."

"Oh, okay. Tell her I said hi and I'll try to get over to see both of you next week if I can. And, Dad, I need to know what to get you guys for Christmas." Every year, it was the same thing. They had everything they needed, but just maybe she could find some obscure item she'd have to get in person downtown, amid the crowds of shoppers.

"I'll give it more thought. See you soon." He disconnected.

She threw a load of laundry in and dressed casually in jeans and a sweatshirt before heading to see her dad. All the while, she kept thinking about Mack. He'd been happy when she'd told him to fuck off yet mad because she'd let him steal the ball a few times?

Men. She'd never understand them.

She pulled up to her parents' house and entered, content to receive a hug and to see the house decorated for the holidays. At least this she understood.

"Come in, come in." Her dad wrangled her out of her coat and ushered her into the kitchen.

On the island, two plates had been set out, each with a footlong sub full of meat and veggies. And two iced teas as well.

Cass wondered if she should unbutton her jeans now or later. She sighed. "Thanks, Dad. I needed this."

"Eat. And tell me what's on your feeble mind." He grinned.

She grinned back. "I love you, Dad."

"Aw. I love you too, honey. Now tell me what's troubling you."

She told him everything, including how she thought she might be falling for Mackenzie Revere, even though it should be ridiculous, since she hadn't known him all that long.

Her father, for once, didn't look overjoyed to hear about his daughter having feelings for a man. He wore his serious therapist face. "You can't see it, can you?"

"What?"

"You're afraid of losing this one."

"I don't know…"

"Ah, but you have to ask yourself, why did you try to let him win?"

"That's an easy answer. I tried to make him feel good."

"Did you?"

"What do you mean?" She swallowed some iced tea, feeling parched. "I like Mack a lot. I tried to do a nice thing for him. But he'd rather I told him to fuck off—excuse my French—than be nice to him."

"Cassandra, please." Her dad seemed disappointed. "You're not being honest with yourself. That's why Mack is angry." He smiled. "I like that boy more and more."

She groaned. "I knew it was a little dishonest to pretend I wasn't as good on the field as I could have been. But it was just a game."

"Cass, with you, it's never 'just a game.' Mack knows that. You know that. You respect strength and integrity. As does your boyfriend."

When she didn't refute the label, her dad's grin grew wider.

"Stop it."

"Sorry." He cleared his throat and tried to stop smiling. "You and I both know why Mack was angry. But we don't know why you treated him the way you once treated Sean."

She tried to listen to herself, to see the bigger picture as she talked it out. "I guess... I guess I was afraid that since Mack and I are new, and it's so happy and fun right now, that I know the feeling will fade. And it would be easier if it faded faster. Mack didn't ask me to be less than I am. I just did it." She paused. "I was mad at myself a little afterward." She thought about it. "And that anger would fester, and I'd blame Mack for making me do something I really made myself do. So it's almost like I'm trying to break us up before we can really be a thing."

Her father bit into his sub and said a muffled, "Go on."

"It's like I'm self-sabotaging." Huh. She hadn't thought she'd ever do that. Cass had never been afraid of success. Afraid of failure, sure, but she strove to achieve victory in all things.

"Mack saw your making yourself seem less for what it was, even if he doesn't fully understand why you did it. He likes you for you. That's why when you weren't so nice, he seemed pleased."

"Isn't that a little destructive on his part? Wanting to be with a woman who cusses him out?"

Her dad just looked at her.

She flushed. "What?"

"I don't think you're an abusive partner."

"Huh? I never said that."

"You intimated you might be. We both know when you give your heart, you give it fully, without reservation. You're an honest woman, Cassandra. You always have been. Especially with yourself. How do you feel about Mack?"

"I... I, um. I might love him."

"The same way you loved Sean?"

"No. More. A lot more." She frowned. "But that's awfully quick, don't you think? I was with Sean for a year. I've known Mack maybe a month."

"People are both different and the same in their own way. Something in Mack helps you be more of who you need to be. I'd say the same goes for what you give him. Whatever it is you do for him, it makes him a better person. And if it doesn't, that's because you two aren't meant for each other."

"What? Like he's my soul mate?" Cass didn't know if she believed in such things.

Her father laughed. "Oh, God, no. Your mother believes in that claptrap, but I don't. And don't you tell her I said that."

"She won't hear it from me."

"As we go through life, we have periods where we have certain needs. And those people we keep in our lives continue to fulfill us in the many ways that matter. But the couples who stay together, those are the people who can change and grow—together. No one can see into the future. I certainly can't. But when I met your mother, I just knew. Everything about her, even the things I don't like, are what pull me to her. That woman's got a big brain and an even bigger heart. And I love all of her."

"Even her insistence on seeing Uncle Pete every year?"

Her father grimaced. "Even that. She loves that old asshole. I have no idea why."

"Dad." Cass chuckled.

"You and your partner will never be the perfect people. No one's perfect. But you might just be perfect for each other. Think about why you like Mack. I bet one of those reasons is he's never tried to change you."

"Like Sean did," she said, remembering. "No. Mack likes me as competitive as I am."

"Then why would you think he'd ever want you to give less than your best?"

"I don't know. I guess I just got scared of the thought of losing him and tried to make sure he'd be so happy that he'd never break it off with me. That's dumb." She sighed and took another bite of her sub, growing full on the good food and good advice. "What did you think of him? You only met him once."

"Yes, but your mother and I asked a lot of questions." He smiled. "He's someone I would have imagined you being happy with. He understands service, and he's funny. Laid-back. You stress enough as it is."

"Dad." Not this again.

"You need something in your life that's easy. Mack is extremely personable, smart, and fun to be around. Even your mother likes him, and not just because he has 'dreamy blue eyes.' Whatever that means." Her dad's eyes twinkled. "Didn't hurt that he's that fireman on all the Station 44 posters either. She's been bragging to her friends that you're dating him."

"What?" Cass flushed. "We, I…"

"I know. You take a little bit longer to adjust to new things and new people. But you and he fit. I could tell, and so could your mom. The question is, do you want to take that next step and let him into your life? Or are you going to back out now before your heart gets broken? And it will at some point, Cass. Life is all about loving and hurting and recovering. And doing it all again."

"Words to live by."

He nodded. "And a sub to die by." He sighed. "No telling your mother I got the full meat or she'll be on me about my cholesterol."

Cass smiled. "But you love her anyway."

"I surely do. The question you have to ask yourself, do you love Mack anyway? And if you don't, you're not wrong." He looked at her and smiled. "But if you can't imagine living without that sharp-witted man by your side, you have to ask yourself why. The only one who can tell if you if you're right or wrong is you."

Chapter Twenty-Two

MACK RECEIVED A TEXT FROM CASS TO MEET UP AND TALK later in the afternoon, which worked for him because he was just about to sign off from work on the start of his next ninety-six hours off duty.

The night had been a real bitch, and he looked forward to engine duty again come the new year.

He nodded to the LT and waved to some of guys and gals coming on D shift. Before he could slip out to his car, Tex and Reggie boxed him in.

Crap.

Brad exited close behind them and smiled, looking more like a human shark than a Ken doll. "Well, well. Mr. I Don't Have Time for My Friends. I think we need to talk."

Mack groaned. "I'm tired. Maybe later?"

Brad nodded to Tex.

"I got 'im." He yanked Mack's bag away and tossed it to Reggie. Then he had Mack over his shoulder in a fireman's carry—how appropriate—and shoved him inside his truck. "See you at your place," Tex said before roaring away.

Mack fumbled to get his seat belt on. "Kidnapping's a crime, asshole."

"Shut up. We're worrying about you. Time to talk."

"I'm saying nothing." He tried not to be amused, but Tex kept laughing like an evil mastermind and turning up his country music.

By the time they arrived at Brad's condo, going the long way, Mack would have happily told them everything they wanted to hear if only to save himself from more Kenny Chesney.

"Git on with ya."

"Easy, Hee Haw. I'm going," Mack grumbled as he walked up to Brad's place. He didn't bother knocking and entered with an attitude. Better to be on the offensive because when he told them what they actually didn't want to hear and they acted all offended, he could insist on doing what was surely for their own good.

The open floor plan of Brad's place meant the living room to the right and dining area just ahead gave Brad plenty of space for parties. The kitchen, sectioned off by a few overhead cabinets and a counter behind the dining area, showed Brad and Reggie getting out chips, dip, and some drinks.

So not a total waste of Mack's time then.

He sighed. Loudly. "I'm tired. Can we please get this over with? Whose feelings did I hurt? And can I just say right now, I'm sorry?"

Brad and Reggie came out with the food and drinks and plopped them on the dining table, where the guys used to have poker games.

Mack felt a pang of wistfulness but suppressed it. "I'll have a cream soda." At Reggie's look, he sullenly added, "Please."

"That's better." Reggie set it in front of him, doling out the other drinks before taking a seat himself. The one nearest the door.

Meaning Mack would have to go through Reggie to leave. A not-so-subtle threat.

Tex and Brad sat as well, and Brad—of course it would have to be Brad leading this feel-good meeting—said, "We've been talking. All of us. The girls too."

Mack refused to acknowledge the heat crawling over his cheeks. Instead, he took a big sip of soda. And sneezed when he felt bubbles coming out of his nose.

Tex just shook his head, trying to hide a grin.

"We all realize how you feel."

"I don't think you do."

Reggie sighed. "Mack, please. Before Maggie and Emily, I felt the same way. Odd man out. Always the third wheel. Wondering when we could just have guy time without all the girls around."

Mack hadn't thought Reggie would ever admit that aloud to the guys. "Oh?"

"Yeah, oh." Reggie gave him a dark look. "Stop being a pussy and tell us the truth. Are you avoiding us because we're all coupled up and you aren't?"

"Or because you don't think your new squeeze will stand up to the rest of us?" Tex asked. "Because we ain't blind. We know you have a thing with the monster soccer gal."

"Officer Mighty Kick," Brad added with a sneer.

Mack frowned. "Hey."

"Sorry." Brad's sneer vanished. "Tex said I had to insult her to get your goat, but I couldn't think of anything nasty. And she does have a mighty kick."

"She does." Tex nodded. "So what's up? Why have you been avoidin' us? Are you choosing the chick over the dick?" He looked around at them. "We all said we'd never do that."

"I'm trying to make it easier for you idiots to move on," Mack blurted. There. He'd said it, no matter how much it hurt.

Brad sat up straighter. Maybe Hernandez had a point and Brad really did have a poker up his ass. "Explain that."

Mack groaned. "You guys are making this uncomfortable."

"Kind of like the way we felt when you were blowing us off without a reason."

Mack flushed. "I'm sorry about that. I just thought if you didn't have to keep babying me because you thought I had nothing else going on in my life, you'd start enjoying yourselves more. I mean, it's kind of obvious you only hang out with me when you have nothing else to do with your girlfriends. Fiancées. Whatever." He sucked down more soda, feeling stupid.

"I knew it." Tex slapped a hand on the table. "I knew that's why you've been lyin' and keeping away. It was me getting engaged, right?"

Mack blinked. "You asked her?"

"Well, not yet. But I'm going to."

"And, no, that's not it. I like Avery, Bree, Maggie, and Emily. I love the fact that you guys found women who actually love you, and isn't that a shock."

Brad scowled. "Hey."

Reggie rolled his eyes while Tex smirked and said, "It's true. Bree loves her a Texan."

"But I can see where things are heading. You guys always feeling like you can't be with your new families because Mack needs help. Mack needs attention." He shook his head. "Hell, even Avery and Bree were giving me pity looks when they ditched the last time we all hung out together because they could see I needed you guys more. It made me feel stupid."

Brad's expression softened. "Damn, Mack. We've all felt that way at some point. But did it ever occur to you that we like hanging out with each other, not just you?"

"I... What?"

Reggie nodded. "Look, I love my sisters and my dad. And sometimes I need core family time. Now I'm living with Maggie and Emily, and I love them dearly. But they're not my buds. You guys are. I like just hanging out with the crew sometimes. And that's for me, not you, Mack."

Mack hadn't thought about their get-togethers in that way.

Tex nodded. "Yeah. I mean, Bree's amazing. I love the sex."

Brad sighed. "Tex..."

"But I like hanging with you guys too. It's different and necessary. I miss my brothers a lot. But I got you fellas. Or at least, I did before Mack started breaking things up."

Brad nodded. "We all knew eventually we'd grow up and find girlfriends, get married, maybe even someday have kids." He smiled at Reggie, who smiled back. "But we are the core of our family, Mack. All of us. Not just you." His voice gentled. "I know your family treats you like you don't matter. Like you're not as important as the good little soldiers who follow your mom and dad. But we're not them."

Mack sucked in a breath, startled. He'd let the way his parents and brothers treat him impact the way he looked at his friends, through that same lens of unacceptance. But the guys here had bled for each other. Literally. They watched each other's backs.

"I'm sorry. I should have told you how I felt. But I didn't want the pity." He glared at Tex, who pretended to wipe a tear from his eye. "You, cut it out."

Tex coughed and drank his soda.

Mack tried to hold back a laugh. "I'm serious. I, well, maybe I was indulging in a little self-pity."

"A little?" Reggie murmured.

"I heard that."

"Good." Reggie glared at him. "I'm tired of stepping around your tender feelings. Look, you hate being on the outs because you don't have a girl. I get it. But we're here for you, dumbass. And we always will be. Get that through your pretty little head."

Brad cleared his throat. "I think what Reggie means to say is we're your brothers. The ones who get you and who will be with you through the good times and the bad."

"Ain't that a song?" Tex asked.

Mack snorted. "You are such a pain."

"There you go." Tex grinned then grew serious. "Mack, I love you, man. I'd never throw you for a chick. Never. I love Bree with everything I got. But if she told me it was either you or her, I'd toss her."

Everyone looked at him in disbelief.

Tex colored. "I mean, she'd never say that because she's Bree and I love her. The kind of woman who would tell a guy not to have friends isn't who I'd be with. Besides, Bree has someone she thinks you'd like if things don't work out with the mean chick."

"Can we stop calling her that?" Mack asked.

"I don't know." Reggie looked thoughtful and said to Brad, "Brad, have you met her? Because I haven't—and no, Mack, the soccer field doesn't count. I only know her as the mean chick. Now, if I *met her*, things might be different."

Brad nodded, his gaze narrowed on Mack. "That's a good point. I haven't met her either. All I know is she practically handed us the game on Saturday. And I doubt it was for my benefit. Or Tex's."

"Or mine," Reggie added with a huge, insincere smile.

"I think she has a crush on our little guy here."

"Up yours." Mack glared and shoved a handful of chips in his mouth, making an obnoxious mess as he crunched all over Brad's table, dropping bits of food.

Brad cringed. "You're disgusting."

Tex laughed. "Yup. Mack's in love with the mean chick. I can tell."

"So what if I am?"

They all stared at him before slowly smiling. "Yeah?" Brad asked.

"Well, I might be." Mack's mouth was too salty, so he escaped the table to drink some water before returning. "Look, I like her a lot. Then my family got in my head and made me act like an ass with her. Then *she* turned around and tried to throw the game because she didn't want me to look bad."

"Well, it could be worse," Tex said kindly. "At least it wasn't a pity fuck. Or did you get one of those too?"

"No, I didn't." Mack hated blushing, especially when the guys laughed like loons. "Okay, okay. I'm sorry for lumping you in with my family. I just got—"

"All butt-hurt?"

He glared at Tex and said, "A little *too sensitive* for a while. But I've been dealing with family, Xavier especially, this idiot Templeton, and... Well, I don't really have an excuse. I was just a bad friend for ignoring you guys, I guess."

"Not bad," Reggie said kindly. "Just a guy with his head stuck up his ass. As you've accused all of us at one time or another. Especially in regard to the women in our lives."

"Was that rehearsed?" Mack asked with a laugh. "Because that sounded scripted."

Reggie rubbed the back of his neck. "Well, I had some things on my mind for a while. Maggie said I should write them down and talk to you about them. Nicely."

Mack snorted, relieved to have his friends back. Which was funny because they'd never been gone. He had. "She's the best thing that ever happened to you. With the exception of me."

"Here we go." Brad sighed, but the relieved smile on his face spoke volumes. "Mack's back and talking big. This calls for a real game."

Tex looked excited. "Soda pong?"

"Yep. Get the Ping-Pong balls and cups. They're in the cabinet."

Tex raced off. Reggie stood and pulled Mack into a bear hug. "Idiot."

"I know. I'm sorry. I just didn't want to get in the way of your happiness."

"Like I'd let that happen." Reggie shoved him at Brad, who put him in a headlock.

"Uncle," he said on a gasp. Geez, Brad had been seriously bulking up. Talk about killer biceps.

"Damn right." Brad let Mack go and thumped him on the back. "We all have issues, Mack. Next time let us help them get better. Together, we'll deal with Xavier. A dark alley, brass knuckles…"

Mack laughed. "Right. Though I have to get to him first. Where he gets off counseling me about Cass? What a jackass." Saying it made him feel so much better.

As they set the table with wide cups and prepared to shoot on both ends, Tex asked, "So what's with you and Cass? You guys a real item then?"

Mack sighed. "Yeah. Except she's being weird. We need to straighten a few things out."

Brad nodded and sunk a ball. "Good. Do that. Then we'll see you guys at Reggie's on Sunday. I know your girl is off duty because Jed gave Tex her schedule."

Mack frowned. "What?"

"Big mouth," Tex muttered. "Nothing. Just me and Jed getting to be friends from hangin' at the bar that night."

Mack studied him, and Tex refused to meet his eye. "Oh my God. Her partner set her up with me?" Mack laughed and laughed. "She's gonna be so pissed when she finds out."

"Maybe pissed at *you*," Brad said, "for something not your fault. Be smart and shut up. If Jed wants her to know he set her up, he'll tell her."

Mack brightened. "That means I have the partner's okay. I already ran her gauntlet."

"That's right. Now it's time for her to run ours." Reggie grinned. "Don't worry, buddy. I have no doubt she'll fit right in. A woman who works to let her man win in front of his friends must really love you."

"I could have taken her."

Tex snorted. "You keep thinking that, Mack."

Even Brad disagreed. "Mack, we love and support you. But no. She'd have kicked your ass if she wanted."

"Only at soccer," he muttered. "Because I trounced her at pool."

Tex nodded. "You did at that." He paused and asked with a smirk, "So what's the deal on those kittens you're fostering? I talked to Gerty about adopting them out, and she's got some interest."

"They're mine. The woman's mine. And this game…" He sank all six Ping-Pong balls in all six cups. "Is mine."

Brad sighed. "You sure it was a good idea to bring him back into the fold?"

"We ain't playin' for money, Brad." Tex chuckled. "It's fine."

Mack grinned. It was. And it would be. Just as soon as he and Cass had a meeting of the minds. He loved her. He had to tell her. And she had to tell him some of her own truths.

———————

Except the blasted woman had to work, and she texted him that she had some real thinking to do. So she asked him to wait.

Mack didn't want to wait. He wanted their issues settled now. Getting all the ugliness out with his friends had been more than necessary. He could only thank his lucky stars they hadn't given up on him and his stupid notions of what people needed.

Being honest, something he had trashed Cass for not being, mattered. It always had. Not telling his friends the truth had bothered him. As had not telling his parents where he stood. He couldn't control their actions, but he certainly could control his.

On a roll, he called his mother and asked to come and talk to her and his father.

When he arrived, he noticed James's truck in the driveway as well. Great. Another person to deal with. Whatever. He'd get the job done.

He marched up the walkway, knocked, and entered when his father yelled for him to come in.

It had just reached six, and Mack had hoped to be in and out after speaking his peace before his parents sat down to eat. His mother had insisted his father wouldn't be home until close to dinner, so Mack, wanting to get it all over with, arrived to the smell of homemade spaghetti.

One of his favorites.

He frowned. What was his mother up to?

"Hi, Mom, Dad." He swallowed a sigh when he noted James setting four glasses on the table. "James. Is Ashley here?"

"No, she's spending the evening out with some friends. I thought I'd pop over to see Mom and Dad." James shrugged.

"I'm not eating," Mack tried, but his stomach chose that moment to grumble.

James smiled and set the fourth plate and silverware at the table.

His parents had set out more decorations, making the house look like Christmas had already arrived. As they typically did the weekend after Thanksgiving. There could be comfort in some things that never changed.

"I need to talk to you two," he said to his parents. "And you," he told James. *Might as well tell him how I really feel.*

"Okay." His mother smiled. "Is this about Cass? We all really liked her."

"I'll bet." He sat with the three of them at the table but didn't take any of the food his mom had prepared. "You liked her because she's just like you. And I'll never be." He kept his smile in place, so it took his parents a moment to realize he wasn't exactly happy.

"What do you mean?" his dad had the nerve to ask.

"Seriously?" Mack sighed. "I'm the happy kid. The one who goes along with all the teasing and the ignoring and the doubting. I'm done."

His mom blinked. "Honey, I don't understand."

"I do," James said, his expression surprisingly contrite. "I could see last week that you were upset. I thought a lot of it had to do with Xavier."

"Xavier's just being Xavier," his mom said.

"Being himself is not an excuse for the way he acts," Mack argued.

James cut in. "Ashley and I talked about it, and I saw that we weren't that nice to you over dinner. And I'm sorry. I didn't mean to make fun of you, and especially not with your girlfriend there."

"Girlfriend?" Their dad perked up. "Finally. One I like."

"No." Mack wouldn't let James apologize and sweep everything under the family rug. "James, thanks for saying that. But it's not just one dinner. It's *all* the dinners. All the breakfasts, the family gatherings. It's me joining the Air Force instead of the Army. And you all finally accepted it because I was SF—a cop. But it wasn't for me. I found something I'm good at. Something I love. Fighting fires. Being an EMT. But again, it's not what you wanted for me, so it doesn't count."

His mom frowned. "Honey, I'm not sure where this is coming from. We're very proud of you."

"Are you?" Mack saw his mom looking concerned, his brother quiet, and his father...bored. "Sorry, Dad. Am I keeping you from something more important?"

"Watch the tone, Son."

"Seriously? I'm trying to have an open conversation about why I always feel like a piece of shit when I leave this house, and you're worried about my tone?" His voice rose. For once, Mack let it, feeding the anger, not falling back into his role as family omega.

His father frowned. *Good. Get as upset as I am.*

"Everything with this family is judged on how it fits into what you and Mom think or want. I brought a woman I care for very much to dinner, even knowing it was a mistake." His mom looked hurt by that, but he kept going. "The five of you—yes, you too, Mom—talked around me or about me as if I was still some stupid little kid getting in trouble and having to be saved by my big, strong brothers." He sighed. "I know, I'm probably overly sensitive about this. But if you'd ever just sit back and listen to the way you talk about me... None of you seem to respect me. And that hurts."

"Jesus, is this how they run the fire department? Everyone getting their feelings out and oversharing?" his dad asked.

"Jimmy." His mom looked upset. "Honey, I never knew you felt that way."

"Because I'm supposed to laugh it off and accept it when you guys sit around sharing Army stories or talk about how much the South Precinct has changed. The past ten years, it's always been the same. The only thing Dad and I have in common is cars. If we can't talk about that or football, there's nothing to be said."

"Not true." His dad scowled. "I love all my boys the same."

"Yeah? Then why didn't you come to my probie graduation, Dad?"

"That was four years ago!"

"So?"

"Bud Jackson retired. Thirty-five years on the force, Mack. What did you want me to do?"

"I don't know. Put me first?" Because for damn sure he'd been there to see all three of Mack's older brothers graduate from the Police Academy. "I'm a grown man. I have a house, make my own money, have my own job. It might not be what you wanted for me, but it's what *I* want for me. I'm a firefighter in the city of Seattle, for God's sake. People are on waiting lists to join up. Did you know that?"

His father shook his head. "Mack, you're taking this the wrong way. We're proud of you."

"So proud you didn't ask more than how Brad and the guys were doing before jumping into James's next case or Alec's last requal at dinner? Hell, even Sasha's 911 calls are more interesting to you guys than anything I do. And she's not even your daughter!"

Okay, that pettiness had poured out despite him wanting to keep it locked up.

"You don't like Sasha?" His dad frowned. "She's a lovely girl."

"Yeah, she is, but she's not the point. You are. You and Mom and your three sons. I never seem to count."

"So you want my attention, is that it?" his dad asked, nodding. "Mack, it's not easy to be the youngest." *Condescending much?*

"Fuck me, you're not listening."

His mother scowled. "Watch your mouth."

"Or what? You'll strike me from the family Christmas card? The one you send out each year that lists my brothers' and father's and mother's many accomplishments, with one line about me still fighting fires?" He snorted, glad to see her blush. "Yeah, I read last year's. And the year before that. You guys probably think this is stupid, that I'm making a big deal out of nothing."

"You are," his dad said plainly.

"Am I?" He turned to James. "You heard all of it. You sat there, and you laughed and asked Cass more about her day-to-day than you ever ask me about mine. I'm proud of Cass and what she does. I'm also proud of what I do, but no one seems to care." And hearing that, he knew they would only remember this as Mack not getting enough attention.

Hell, he was veering off in a direction he hadn't wanted to go.

"You know what? Forget about the dinner. Forget Cass. This is about so much more than that dinner," he insisted. "You hate that I don't toe the party line, doing whatever you tell me to. That's why I get the subtle punishments, the exclusions, the last-minute invitations," he said to his mother, who blushed. "And it's not just this past Thanksgiving. I'm talking about the Halloween party you guys forgot to invite me to. And the anniversary party for your police retirement, Dad, this summer. Really? You only remembered I wasn't on the guest list the day before?" He'd been lucky they'd had space on the yacht they'd rented.

His dad flushed. "Now, Mack, I didn't know if you'd feel comfortable attending. You seem to hate law enforcement."

"That's crap, Dad," James said before Mack could, shocking the heck out of Mack. "I told you to invite him or it would cause hurt feelings."

"Yeah, hurt feelings," Mack agreed, feeling them all over again knowing his father had almost intentionally not invited him. "I'm saying it. My bad for not telling you, for years, how I feel. Well, now you know. You guys hurt my feelings all the time. Go ahead, Dad. Call me a weakling for showing emotion. And Mom, you sit there and say nothing, the way you always do. Because it's all about being strong. Army wife, Army life. Police living is hard. Yeah, I know. I can never forget it. I'm proud of all of you and all you've done. I'm not bitter about my Blue family. But I'm tired of being forgotten. If that's the case, why don't we all save ourselves the hassle and I'll stop coming to events and holidays? I can be the estranged son and uncle you see at funerals and the occasional wedding."

He stood up, breathing hard, in the silence.

James wouldn't meet his eyes.

His mother looked hurt and furious, and his father seemed not to care.

"Mackenzie, you are just wrong." She stood, walked over to him, and poked him in the chest, tears in her eyes. "So wrong." Then, as usual when confronted with something she didn't like, she walked away.

"I'm out of here." He turned and left, not surprised when no one stopped him.

He'd said his piece, and he was proud he'd stood up for himself.

But still, it hurt. It hurt a lot.

Chapter Twenty-Three

Thursday morning, Mack had just finished working out and cleaned up. He dried off and threw on a pair of sweats and a T-shirt, wondering if and when he'd talk to his family again.

He didn't think they'd completely cut him off. But in his current mood, he didn't care if he never spoke to them again. Well, maybe James because he'd apologized a little. And Alec, who'd called yesterday to say how proud of Mack he was.

"About time you stood up for yourself. Sorry, man, but that had to be your battle. Not mine." He'd paused. "Dean agrees. He's tired of all the cop talk. Totally boring." Alec had laughed, and Mack had felt warm. Included. And loved.

But the others could take a short walk off an even shorter pier, and that hurt to even think. He loved his mom a ton, but he was tired of her just ignoring the family problems. And, yeah, maybe he was oversensitive about all of it. But, damn, he had been talked around and talked down to for years. James and Alec admitted it. Why the hell couldn't she just apologize so they could move on?

He was done turning the other cheek all the time. And annoyed and still hurt because despite all the family crap, he missed Cass like crazy. Talking to Brad about the drama with his folks last night had helped a little. Brad, having dealt with even uglier family drama, had plenty to say about Mack's folks not believing—or showing belief—in their son.

The texts from Tex and Reggie had made him feel even better. He might not have all the Reveres at his back, but he had his full crew on his side. Who didn't feel at all bad about nagging him the past two days not to forget Sunday's game day—with Cass and crew.

That's if I can get her to talk to me again. He didn't like her avoiding him. They had things they needed to talk about. Mack felt good about finally taking charge of the problems in his life. He was still the laid-back guy of C shift, the one who could get everyone laughing, the amiable one in the bunch.

But he had a backbone that until lately he'd ignored. Not anymore. Just because he was easygoing didn't mean he had to be anyone's doormat.

He grabbed the kittens and lay in his bed. "Okay, guys, the truth. Copo, Impala, I'm keeping you. You are now official firefighting kittens. We're going to have to get Christmas photos taken. And yes, I'm lame and embarrassingly lonely because the woman I love can't bother to pick up the fucking phone."

Copo danced sideways, his tail puffed up, and batted Mack's hand. Then Impala smacked him down, and the kittens raced around the bed, pretending Mack was a mountain. Occasionally they'd stop to sniff his face or utter a small trill or chirp.

He sighed. *At least someone likes me.*

He spent the day running errands. Later in the evening, he helped out at a Pets Fur Life adoption event at a pet shop on Queen Anne with Reggie. Maggie and Emily stopped by with Frank on his leash and bought some toys for the little guy.

They'd set up in the back, several pens and tables prepped to showcase the animals, with helpers like Mack, Reggie, and several other volunteers managing the pets.

While Maggie greeted Reggie with a kiss, her daughter and the dog crept closer to Mack and the dog he was holding, an adorable tan-and-white two-year-old Chihuahua named Noodle.

"No," Reggie said before Emily could open her mouth. "Noodle already has someone interested in him, and Frank already has a brother."

"He does?" Mack asked, aware Reggie had been speaking the truth about Noodle, who already had several people signed up to possibly adopt him. The dog licked his hand, and he smiled down at him. "You're such a cutie."

"Yeah, who, Reggie?" Emily planted her hands on her hips. She looked just like Maggie, he thought, and wondered what it must feel like to look at a small person with your DNA and see yourself in them. Or to see your wife in them. Like, say, Cass.

Gah. Stop thinking about her.

Reggie planted his hands on his hips and stared down at the little girl. They looked cute together, the burly firefighter and the scrappy kid with her puppy on a pink leash. "Ahem," Reggie said. "Vader?"

Maggie snapped a quick picture.

"Frame that one," Mack said to her.

She nodded, smiling.

"Who's Vader?" The name sounded familiar.

"My cat," Emily said at the same time Reggie said, "Her cat."

"Jinx! Buy me a Coke." Emily smirked at Reggie.

Mack had to laugh because the kid clearly had Reggie wrapped around her little finger.

Emily turned to Mack. "Can I just hold him? For a second? *Pleassse?*" She blinked at him, her lashes so long, her eyes so dark in that cute face.

"Okay, but just for a second or two."

"Sucker," Reggie muttered.

Around them, people streamed, looking over the many cats and dogs available for adoption. A terrific turnout for a Thursday evening.

Mack took the leash, holding on to Frank, who didn't really move. The leash might as well have been for show. Emily carefully cradled Noodle, who seemed to fall in love with her.

Mack elbowed his buddy. "Looks like a match made in heaven," he said before something spooked Emily and she turned quickly. The Chihuahua jumped to the floor and took off toward the front, threading through a sea of legs. Unfortunately, the door opened at the wrong moment, and Noodle escaped.

"Shoot. Hold this." Mack handed the leash to Reggie and hurried after the pup. Late at night, no one would see the little guy if he darted into the road. Though the cute Queen Anne neighborhood had a lower speed limit, even a car going ten miles per hour wouldn't save the dog from being crushed.

Outside, he nearly ran over one of their other volunteers, a huge, beefed-up guy covered in tattoos who often helped home unwanted strays.

"Yo, Sam, have you seen a white Chihuahua?" Mack asked, frantic.

"Follow me." They raced down the sidewalk and across a thankfully empty street, up into a residential area off Queen Anne Avenue. As they ran, Mack spotted a flash of white and heard a familiar yip.

"Noodle!" he yelled, but that blasted dog turned his head, his tongue out, laughing, and moved down a driveway that led to an alley behind some really nice houses.

"Shit. Come on." Sam ran, but Mack was faster.

Not loaded up with all that muscle, some of us can move.

He heard sirens and swore, seeing all over again a puppy nearly run down, a woman lying in the street, having been hit saving it. Exactly what had happened to Maggie and Frank a few months back.

He'd outraced Sam but still didn't see Noodle. And now he'd entered someone's private backyard. Not cool.

"Noodle," he whispered. "Come out."

It took him a few minutes, but he finally spotted the escapee chewing someone else's bone about the size of his body.

After tugging the dog out from under some bushes, he tossed the bone back in the yard and left, climbing back over the wooden fence he'd been forced to scale.

And found two annoyed police officers, one holding Sam by the upper arm, his wrists behind his back...as if in cuffs.

The taller of the two officers smiled wide. "Well, well. If it isn't the love bandit, stealing another heart. What you got there, buddy, lady bait?"

Sam looked from Jed to Mack and rolled his eyes. "Obviously, you know Mack. How about uncuffing me, Officer?" he said to Cass.

The hard-ass looked from Sam to Mack and shook her head. "They both look like criminals to me. Jed, drag Revere back to the car. I have this one."

"Yes, ma'am." He yanked Mack with him, following a cuffed Sam and Cass as they walked toward flashing lights. "And you, make things right. She's been a huge pain lately."

Mack cradled Noodle, still panting and overjoyed from his escape. "Me?" In a louder voice, he said, "She's the one being a pain. She crushed my poor heart."

Cass glared at him over her shoulder.

Sam looked over and grinned.

"What's up with your boy?" Jed asked. "He looks like he just escaped from King County."

"Nah, Sam's a mechanic who runs a lot of the Pets Fur Life adoptions. His wife owns the massage shop on Queen Anne. Bodywork."

"She doesn't own it, Mack. She's a partner there." Sam asked over his shoulder, "And what's the deal with you and that dog? Are you taking it too? I heard you found some kittens you're keeping. Nice."

"You adopted a dog?" Cass asked, pulling Sam back with her to walk next to him and Jed.

"No, I didn't adopt a dog," he said. "But I did find this sly escape artist. Tell them, Noodle, how fast you are."

Sam nodded. "He's a bullet. So's Mack. Mack outran me, and I'm pretty good at running from the cops." Sam grinned.

Jed hadn't been wrong. The guy did look dangerous. But seeing him with any of the animals or his wife you'd know he was a softie at heart. Despite the tattoos. And the muscles. And the killer glare…

They arrived at the car, where Cass uncuffed Sam. "Sorry, but we had a few calls about possible burglars in the area."

"I'm sure you did." Mack gave Sam a once-over and grinned at the gesture the guy shot back. "You want to take Noodle with you? I need a minute with Benson and Stabler here."

Sam snickered. "Sure." He took the dog in his arms, and the thing seemed to melt. Animals knew good people. "Aw, come on, Noodle. Let's go find you a home."

Sam walked away.

"I'm Stabler, by the way." Jed slapped Mack on the back. "We're on for dinner on Sunday. Thought I'd let you know." He pointed at Cass and ordered, "Fix it. I'll meet you by the pet shop." He walked away, whistling, and got back into the car.

Something occurred to Mack. "This isn't your area. What are you doing up here?"

Cass blushed but said nothing.

Mack waited, but she just looked at him as they continued down the alley toward the street. "You have nothing to say? Really?"

He turned away from her, uber annoyed. Because his heart wouldn't stop racing and the love he'd been trying to ignore was overwhelming.

"Stop, stop." She pulled him to a halt and tugged him under the darkness of an overhead tree, out from under a streetlight. "Look, I made a mistake."

"With…?"

She blew out a loud, exasperated breath. That made him feel slightly better.

"I'm sorry I didn't do more to crush you at soccer."

He crossed his arms over his chest and tried to look stern and not as if he were drinking in the sight of her. She looked so damn sexy in her uniform.

"I just… I talked to my dad, and he thinks maybe I was trying to sabotage our relationship."

"If you want out, you only have to say—"

"Will you shut up? I'm trying to tell you I love you, okay?" she snapped.

He blinked, not sure how to follow that and doing his best not to appear as joyful as a kid at Christmas.

But Cass seemed stressed and unsure because she started pacing in front of him, not meeting his gaze. "I told you before I'm not great with relationships. I like myself, and I don't think I should have to change to suit anyone else's needs."

He started to tell her he'd never asked her to change but instead kept quiet, doing his best to just listen. Something he wished his parents had done instead of treating him like a little boy wanting attention he didn't deserve.

"But you never asked me to change. The one time I did something that, frankly, bothered even me, you told me to stop and just be myself." She met his gaze. "For the record, I just wanted you to have fun with the game. I didn't want you to be mad if I crushed you in front of your friends."

"I hate to break it to you, Officer Hotness, but I did steal the ball from you at our mud game."

"Yeah, because I slipped in the mud," she said drily. "You got lucky because David Beckham you are not."

He sneered. "And yet you still didn't win."

"We tied, doofus." She walked up to him and put her hands on his shoulders. "I'm sorry, Mack. I got weirded out by what I feel for you. It just snuck up on me. And when I get nervous or—"

"Scared?"

Her eyes narrowed. "Or *anxious,* I don't react well. I'm sometimes quick to get angry—"

"Sometimes?"

She talked over him. "Usually think I'm right because I am right, and have a tough time confronting those I love, which is why I keep avoiding you."

"It's driving me crazy," he said and pulled her in for a kiss. He broke away, breathing hard, his whole body one live wire, and leaned his forehead against hers. "God, Cass. I love you so much. I've been trying to keep it to myself and not scare you off. I know you're independent and tough and smart. And any guy would be lucky to have you." He pulled back to look into her gorgeous gray eyes, swearing he could see the love in them even in the shadows. "But I'm the best you'll ever get."

Her lips quirked. "Is that so?"

"Yep. Everyone likes me. Well, except for my folks. And Xavier. And apparently Ben Templeton, and I have no idea why. But everyone else, yeah."

"Does it matter that *I* like you?" She cupped his cheeks, careful of his bruised one, and kissed him again.

"It sure the hell does. I know it feels like we just met and it's sudden. But you get me better than anyone else. And I get you. I'm a single father now. I need help supporting my kittens."

She laughed. "So you did adopt after all."

"Officially, I did. I'm also keeping you. And if you must know, I decided that after you nearly killed me at soccer the first time."

"It was a legal slide tackle, you big whiner."

"Keep thinking that. I'm sure the sight of your bare legs and clingy top—"

"It was a sweatshirt."

"—didn't affect that ref with the crush on you at all."

They started walking back to the car, him with his hands in his pockets to stop from hugging her, all the way to Jed. They continued to argue about who had the better team.

"You're just so darn cute when you're wrong."

She laughed. "Moron." She paused by the passenger door to her patrol car.

"Hurry up, Cass," Jed called, his window rolled down. "We need to do another drive by Mrs. Cleary's."

"Hold on." She glanced around, seeing the many people in and round the pet store. "Nice adoption going on."

"Yep. They come to see Reggie flex and leave with an animal." He nodded to Reggie inside, who could be seen laughing and holding a mature cat in his big old arms.

"And Sam, hmm?" She stared at the tattooed giant also holding some animals and being very careful as he showed a few small children how to properly pet the rattled dog.

"Eyes up here, woman." Mack poked her in the shoulder and pointed at himself, smiling. "That's better. I'm told I can be a possessive kind of guy."

"Well, apparently, I'm clingy." She smiled.

"Will I ever see you again? Or is this it? Do I have to take a mental picture of you in that uniform for use at night?" He ignored Jed's groan. *Big ears.* "Or can I expect to see you at my place tomorrow after your shift? You know, for the kids and all."

"For the kits, you mean." She grinned. "The sacrifices I make for this city. Okay." She kissed him, right there in front of everyone. "I love you, Mack. See you tomorrow at noon." She leaned closer and whispered, "Clothing is optional."

She got in the car, and they left.

Mack stood there, grinning like a fool, until Reggie clapped a hand on his shoulder. "Put your tongue back in your mouth, Mack. I could see your panting from inside. The kiss looked good. Your desperation, not so much."

"She loves me." He turned that silly grin on Reggie. "She told me."

"I'm glad." Reggie's sincere smile only added to Mack's joy. Until the big guy slapped him in the back of the head. "Of course she loves you, dumbass. You're Mack Revere. Now get that scrawny butt inside and help us adopt out some animals. And pretend you're still available. I'm pretty sure we get more older dogs adopted when you handle them with all the single moms."

"Why don't you do it?" Mack said with a laugh.

"Maggie's in there watching me like a hawk. No way I'm getting some poor women hurt when my gal lights into them."

They both looked at sweet, petite, innocent-looking Maggie.

Mack knew better. It was the quiet ones you had to look out for. Well, and the ones in uniform.

He grinned. "How about we just let the animals sell themselves, so to speak?"

Noodle sat in an older man's arms, looking delighted with himself.

"Sounds good. Now, for the last time, invite the woman to the Sunday gauntlet or you're in real trouble."

"I'm supposed to do a dinner—"

"If you two aren't there, you'll partner with Tex all week long. And it's nothing but Jason Aldean and Keith Urban all day every day."

Mack frowned. "You're pretty familiar with country artists for a guy who hates country."

Reggie darted away awfully fast after one last threat.

Mack followed him back and put his happy mood to extra good use. He had some animals to help and a woman to wait for.

One he'd been waiting for his whole life and had finally found.

Chapter Twenty-Four

CASS DIDN'T KNOW WHY SHE FELT SO NERVOUS THE NEXT afternoon. She loved Mack. He loved her—and didn't it still give her a thrill knowing that. It wasn't just her. The dork loved her back.

Jed had teased her all night long because she'd been giddy and not shy about sharing why.

Even the graffiti artist and illegal pugilists they'd picked up commented on it when she'd arrested them with politeness and a smile.

"Cop is smokin'." The twenty-something graffiti artist had said. "Yo, hon, you are lookin' fine. Like, glowing. I'm gonna do you up downtown. Check it out next week."

Jed had sighed. "Jay, just don't. Try to keep yourself on the straight and narrow, okay?"

"Yeah, but dude, she's hot. Like, scary when she stares at you and sexy when she smiles."

Cass would normally have set him straight. All she said last night was, "Aw, thanks, Jay. But you're still going to jail for vandalism on private property. Get permission from the business owner next time."

Now she knocked on Mack's door, wondering where they would go, from like to love to…togetherness?

He opened the door, and she handed him a bouquet of flowers. "My apology," she said and flushed. "I hope that's not weird. I like flowers. I thought you might too."

"I do." He smiled, and she had to kiss him.

And then they were both naked in his bedroom, and he was making slow, sweet love to her and driving her mindless with need. His mouth trailed a blaze from her lips down her neck to her breasts. He lay over her, rubbing that huge cock between her legs, not penetrating but caressing her clit with every delicate thrust.

He sucked one nipple, then the other, playing with her with those huge, callused hands. "I love you, Cass." He continued to kiss her, one hand cupping her cheek while he used the other to push himself down, positioned at the entrance to her sex.

He watched her as he pushed inside, and she started coming, sighing at the pleasure that radiated throughout her body and soul. "I love you, Mack," she cried when he shoved hard and deep.

He continued to take her, loving her with his body, his words. Until they were coming together and she knew a perfect moment, a feeling of pure togetherness.

They spent the early afternoon making love and sharing hopes and dreams, both content to enjoy each other's company, keeping the world at bay.

Mack told her about his parents, who had yet to contact him.

"I'm so sorry." Cass kissed him, naked and just fine with her state of undress.

He stroked her body, enamored with her breasts, she noted with amusement. "I'm sorry too. I wish they could understand that I'm not upset about one night but about a decade of disappointment."

She nodded and rubbed his solid chest, fascinated with his strength. "What we need is to sit them down in a room with Dr. Aaron Carmichael. He'd have them straightened out in no time."

"Maybe before the wedding."

She froze, and he laughed. So she tugged at his nipple.

"Ow. I'm kidding. Not that we'll be married, of course. Next year, when I've had time to ease you into the idea. We'll start smaller, figure out where to live. Then in the far future, we'll talk about kids. I have no problem being a house husband, just so you know."

"Yeah, right." Yet the thought of future children didn't panic her the way it once would have. "I'm not scared of a life with you, Mack."

"I'm terrified of a life without you, Cass." He drew her closer for a kiss. "There's only one other thing I'm scared of."

"What?"

"The amount of pain you'll bring to my friends when they run you through the gauntlet."

She laughed. He'd described how important it was for the right ladies in their lives to get along with the crew. But Mack wasn't worried at all. Cass knew what being in service meant. And she already liked Tex. She figured Brad and Reggie would be just as fun to decimate in a competition.

═══════════

An hour later, they'd decided to go out for lunch. They hit one of the best sandwich shops in town. Normally, the line out the door would preclude anyone from getting a spot. But Mack was friends with the owner, a prior Air Force buddy, and had called in a favor. So when the indoor seating closed, leaving only a pickup window for call-in orders, Mack and Cass sat in the back and devoured their steak sandwiches.

"He's really from Philly," Mack said around a mouthful. "That's why his sandwiches taste so good while also telling you to go fuck yourself."

A middle finger appeared from around the corner near the kitchen, causing them both to laugh.

They had just filled their drinks from the soda fountain when Xavier, of all people, showed up in civvies and sat down with them. Uninvited.

"Okay, we're gonna have this out," he said through gritted teeth.

"How'd you know I was here?"

"I followed you from your house."

"Stalk much?" Cass muttered.

He glared at her. He glared at Mack. Xavier Revere, the epitome of attitude.

"Well, hello there, Xavier." Cass gave him a fake smile. "How absolutely lovely to see you."

"Yeah, yeah. Hi, Cass."

"Look, Mack. An honest-to-goodness police officer out of uniform. So handsome and honest, sworn to defend the public and to uphold a code of honor."

"Except when he's maligning his own brother to some chick he works with," Mack muttered. At her look, he cleared his throat. "I meant some amazing officer he's lucky to be in the same room with."

"Better."

"Though I'm not sure I'd call him handsome."

"But he looks like you."

Mack relaxed a little. "Well, okay then."

"Hey, Mackenzie. Ignore her for a minute, okay? I'm sorry for warning you off." Xavier seemed to bite out the words. "James lit into me last night. And Alec told me off the day after our Thanksgiving dinner. Apparently, he and Dean are done with me until I clean up my act." He snorted. "Whatever that means." Yet it obviously meant something, or Xavier wouldn't have hunted his brother down.

Cass looked him over, seeing the similarities between the brothers. She preferred Mack's smiling eyes to Xavier's more serious ones. Her lover's giving soul to his brother's needy one.

"You're interrupting my lunch. Get to the point." Mack was no longer smiling.

Before Xavier could answer, a giant stormed up to the table and glared down at them. "*You.*"

"For fuck's sake, I thought this place was closed." Mack groaned. "I'm eating, Templeton. What do you want now?"

"Wait. Is this the guy who punched you?" Cass stared. This man was *huge*, at least several inches taller and broader than Mack.

Xavier stood. "You punched my little brother?"

Mack sighed. "Xavier, hold on."

"Fuck off, Revere." Templeton looked ready to take them all on. And then she noticed the bat he carried by his side.

Cass and Mack looked at each other then at Templeton.

Mack stood next to his brother. "Are you talking to me or him?"

"Does it matter?" Templeton hefted the bat in his hands. "You're both Reveres."

She slowly slid out of her chair and moved away from the Revere brothers, hoping to get an advantage when she moved in to disarm the giant.

"It matters to my family," Mack said and turned his gaze to his brother. "You see, I'm not a *real* Revere. I only exist to be the butt of jokes at dinner and to be conveniently left out of the important things, in addition to being the runt of the litter, apparently."

Xavier turned, now also ignoring Templeton, who frowned in confusion. "Seriously? Is this because we didn't pay you enough attention at dinner? Did I embarrass you in front of your girlfriend?"

She didn't like the way he sneered "girlfriend."

"Hey, I—" Templeton barked, but Xavier cut him off.

"Hold on a minute," he snapped, holding up a finger for the big guy to wait. To Mack, he said, "I have no idea how you can say no one is proud of you or cares about you. That's shit. I care. Hell, I brag to all my friends about the idiot on the Station 44 posters. And I was right up front when you graduated from BMT."

"BMT?" Cass asked, her attention still on Templeton, who looked like he didn't know what to do while the brothers argued.

"Basic Military Training," Xavier and Mack said as one.

Mack swore. "Then what the fuck is your problem? I am *so* sick of you riding my ass for every little thing. You make fun of me, you mock me, you act like you're God's gift to the police force and like I'm barely good enough to be the gum under your shoe."

"You really do, Xavier," Cass had to agree.

Templeton yelled, "*Hey*. I'm the guy with the bat. And if you're pissed about him," he said to Mack with a nod to Xavier, "then that's really like looking into a mirror, isn't it? Mr. My Shit Don't Stink. You're both assholes. *You* got me in trouble with the lieutenant. They're kicking me out because of you," he spat and turned to Xavier. "And because of *you*, my best friend's in jail," he roared and lifted the bat.

Before Cass could step in, Mack countered the big man by grabbing onto his shoulders, fitting his ankle behind Templeton's, and jerking the man off-balance. Mack slammed him down to the ground, one hand on his right arm to keep his shoulders and head from bouncing off concrete. Then he twisted and stomped his foot right next to Templeton's head.

"Be glad this is just a demonstration," he growled before leaning down to slug Templeton in the gut.

Templeton wheezed and curled into a ball.

Mack straightened and once again glared at his brother, as if the takedown hadn't been a thing of utter beauty.

Cass wanted to mount him then and there. "I love you so much."

Mack shot her a wink.

"Holy shit," Xavier said, staring at the downed giant. "Wait. Ben Templeton? Yeah, I did lock up your bestie. You saw him, dickhead. What did you think was going to happen?" He looked up at Mack, for once with approval. "Nice moves."

"Thanks." Mack shoved Templeton back down when he tried to stand. "So what is he talking about? His best friend?"

"Two months ago the guys are at a dive bar drinking. His fucker of a best friend kicked the hell out of some kid who was out celebrating his twenty-first birthday. And why? Because the kid disrespected him. I think he called him an old man."

"He said other stuff too," Templeton argued. This time when he gingerly rose to his feet, Mack let him, though Cass grabbed the bat and held it tight.

"It couldn't have been bad enough to cause all that damage. Your friend and you are twice the size of that guy. Your dickish friend broke the kid's ribs and almost ruptured his spleen."

"That's not what happened. You set him up when he tried to explain things."

The mulish look on Templeton's face told Cass he was in denial.

"Are you kidding me?" Xavier gave angry laugh. "The whole thing was caught on video. Hell, it's even on YouTube. A few of the bar patrons posted it, and the fight went viral."

"Yeah, and now Ted is in a fight for his life with a lawsuit from hell," Templeton growled.

"So what is this? You coming after my brother as payback?"

"What if it is? What will you do about it?" He cradled his ribs and grinned. "I'm gonna scream police brutality so loud you'll still be hearing it twenty years from now. And it's my word against yours, stupid. My dad's cousins with the state senator. Who the fuck do you know higher than that?"

"My dad is friends with the police commissioner," Xavier said with a smile. "And the governor's a golf buddy. Your move."

Templeton paled.

Cass almost felt bad for him.

"Um, Templeton, is it?" She nodded to the owner and cook holding their cell phones out and recording. "We have video of you attempting to assault not only a firefighter but a police officer. That's an automatic jail sentence."

"You're lying."

"You're not that smart, are you?" Mack sighed. "Templeton, just go away. No one wants you in jail. We just want you gone."

"I want him in jail," Xavier growled, glancing again at Mack's purple cheekbone.

"Fuck you. I—"

Cass had had enough. She tugged Templeton down by the ear and whispered, "If you don't get out of here and get away from my man, I will personally make it my mission to put you, your friend, and anyone else close to you away for a long time. Every time you speed. Every time you jaywalk. Every time you don't signal before turning. I'll be there. Or a friend of mine will be there. And I have a lot of friends. We'll be watching and waiting. And when you eventually lose it and try to beat on someone else who can't defend themselves, I'll be there too to slap some cuffs on you and take you to jail. Where a few big, brawny inmates owe me some favors. And they like big, strong men like you. A lot."

He blinked and backed up. "You know what? I'm done. This city sucks. And so do all of you. Stay the fuck away from me. And Revere?"

"What?" Mack and Xavier said at the same time and glared at each other.

Men. Seriously.

"I hope you burn." He turned and left, favoring his right side.

"Like, burn in hell?" Mack asked Cass. "In a building? Was that meant for me or the idiot next to me?"

"Okay, I'm out." She kissed Mack on the cheek, then pointed the bat at Xavier. "Stop being a dick. Be nice to your brother. And stop picking on him at family dinners. Mack, I'll see you on Sunday. Text me tomorrow when you get a minute. And have a good shift. Be safe."

He kissed her. "Will do." He looked at Xavier. "But maybe I should go with you. You need a ride."

"I'll grab a rideshare." She pushed the bat into his gut and shoved him toward his brother. "Talk it out."

Then she left, feeling pretty darn good about her day.

Mack stared at Xavier, who stared back. He sighed and sat, hungry enough to finish off the rest of his sandwich and Cass's, which he pulled toward him before Xavier could touch it.

"Selfish," Xavier muttered.

"Tell me. Why such a prick all these years?" Mack frowned. "You've always been annoying, but not so nasty. Not until a year ago. What the hell, man?"

Xavier looked down, and his cheeks turned pink.

Mack had no idea why his brother would be embarrassed. Xavier seemed to thrive on the idea he never stepped a foot wrong.

"I get Mom and Dad ignoring me. I wasn't Army. Then I wasn't a cop. So I disappointed them on two fronts. But I usually got along with my brothers." Growing up he had. He supposed he really had been overly sensitive about all the teasing lately. As children, they had protected him, always rallying around the youngest to keep up or stay strong so no one might pick on him at school.

It had worked. Until he'd graduated and gone his own way. Then nothing he did seemed right.

But Xavier hadn't been as mean until about a year ago.

"It's Sasha," he finally admitted, all choked up.

Mack blinked. "What about her?" Did she hate him too?

"I love her."

"Ah, okay. Good for you."

"I plan to marry her."

"Congrats?"

Xavier swore. "Fuck it. You remember Daphne? The woman I dated for a year and a half before we broke it off?"

"Yeah." He'd thought at the time his brother might marry her, but apparently they hadn't been able to go the distance. Then Xavier met Sasha, and that was all she wrote.

"Daphne had a thing for you."

Mack paused in the middle of chewing, his mouth open. He hurried to swallow. "What?"

"She thought you were hot," Xavier said, his face tomato-red. "She wanted to date you. And it hurt. A lot."

"I, uh…" Though he and his brothers had only six years, from the oldest to the youngest, between them, they'd always been very clear about not poaching girlfriends. Mack had had no idea. "That's why you broke it off?"

"Yeah. She used to get all weird around you. You don't remember?"

"No." Mack had always treated her the way he treated Ashley. Like a sister.

"Well, she thought you were so funny and sweet. I was just the stud she used for sex."

"O-kay." Mack stared at his brother, seeing a side to him Xavier never exposed. "You really loved her."

"And she wanted you instead."

"That's not my fault."

Xavier seemed to sink lower in his chair. "I fucking know, okay? But when I clicked with Sasha, I just couldn't go there again."

"Wait. You treated me like shit for a year because you were jealous?" Mack would never, in a million years, have expected that.

Xavier rested his face in his hands, his elbows on the table. "Yeah."

Mack didn't know what to say. "Xavier, that's nuts. If Daphne didn't want you, for whatever reason, then she wasn't good enough to be your girlfriend."

Xavier lifted his head. "That's what I thought."

"I mean, maybe she saw the dickish side and couldn't deal. I get that." He continued past Xavier's angry expression. "But you need someone who gets the real you. And that wasn't her. Even if she'd come to me, which she never did, I wouldn't have dated her."

His brother grunted and picked at Cass's leftover fries.

"Cass, now, she gets me. We click. And I can tell you right now she's going to be the love of my life." Mack smiled, feeling so free.

Xavier just stared at him. "You really love her, huh?"

"I do. And she loves me back. I have great friends, a great job, and maybe someday I'll have a family who'll back me."

Xavier groaned. "Mom was crying because she thinks we all hurt your feelings for so long. James and Alec are sorry. Dad is... Dad. He still can't see what all the fuss was about. But we get it." He paused. "We're still going to make fun of you at family dinners. But maybe we can do a better job including *everyone* at the table. Not just with cop talk either." He sighed. "Christmas is going to be a shit show, I'm just saying. But I'll do my best to stop picking on you." He smirked. "Sissy."

"You're such an ass."

Xavier chuckled. "Well, maybe you're not such a sissy. That was a grade A-takedown you gave Templeton. But how did he get one over on you?" Xavier nodded at Mack's face.

"Sucker punch with two beefcakes to back him up." Mack explained what had happened at the gym.

Xavier nodded, asked him questions. Then Mack asked some back.

Before he knew it, he was talking and laughing with his brother again.

He couldn't wait to tell Cass.

Chapter Twenty-Five

Sunday afternoon, Cass laughed with a few of the women present, thoroughly impressed by the little girl Emily's knowledge of planets.

"How old are you, Emily?" she asked.

The party at Reggie's was raging. Mack's best friends, Brad, Tex, and Reggie, had brought their A games. Their dates were enjoyable and amusing, and Reggie's almost-stepdaughter was a true joy. Adorable and intelligent, with a serious attitude and tons of questions about tasers and weapons.

"I'm almost seven." Emily smiled, holding a fuzzy brown bear with an ax strapped to its back. A scarred pit bull puppy sat at her side and watched her with adoring eyes.

"And too young to be tasering people," Mack said as he lifted Emily in his arms and held her upside down as he tickled her.

She giggled and tried to zap him with her fingers while yelling, "Zap zap," until Mack set her down.

Then she growled and warned, "You'd better be nice, or Reggie-Dad will decimate you with contusions."

Cass and Mack stared after her as she raced back toward the cookies.

Mack shook his head. "Don't ask. Yes, she's a little genius. And yes, she's more than a little scary."

"I might have to look up the word 'decimate' later," she said, grinning.

"Naked Scrabble? Yes." He kissed her.

Next to them, two women *awed*.

"Look, Avery," Tex's gorgeous girlfriend said. "We didn't even need to set him up with our friends." Bree looked at Cass over the rim of her glass. "And I have model girlfriends, woman, so treat him right."

Avery, the pretty reporter in glasses who put Cass in mind of Clark Kent, nodded. "And I know all the aliens, monsters, and weirdos in this city. I can hook him up with the Queen of the Dead in a snap." She snapped her fingers and laughed. "Or Mummy Dearest. She'll be in the next issue of *The Needle*. Don't miss it."

Personally, Cass loved the wacky free paper, though she had yet to see the latest Seattle Psycho, a canine/feline mix who screeched during the night. Supposedly if you heard it, you'd lose a tooth the next day.

Now hundreds of young children claimed to have seen the dastardly dog/cat. Brad's girlfriend was a little zany but warm-hearted. She made Cass's parents laugh since they tuned into her segment every Friday. She couldn't wait to tell her parents she'd met Avery Dearborn.

As she glanced around, she saw nothing but joy and laughter. "You know, your friends will really like Jed and Shannon. I have a feeling we're opening up a whole new friend group."

Mack blinked. "What do you mean 'will really like'? That implies they will all meet at some point."

She'd cleared it with Reggie via Tex yesterday. For some reason, Jed had had Tex's number on hand. *The two must have really bonded at that bar a few weeks ago*, was all she could think.

"Well, sweetcakes, I wanted to celebrate tonight with you and me all alone. Together." She leaned closer and whispered, "Without clothes."

"Ah." He cleared his throat and blew out a breath. "Keep it clean. There are kids present. And I don't mean Brad."

Hearing his name, Brad looked toward them and frowned.

Cass swallowed a laugh. "Right. Well, I thought we could kill two birds with one stone."

The doorbell rang.

Emily yelled, "I can get it!"

Her mother sighed. "Use the peep... Oh, forget it. Hold on, Emily."

Cass soon heard Jed's deep voice followed by Shannon's exclamation.

"See? The gauntlet plus Jed and Shannon. They go home happy, and your friends stop crying because I whooped them at Cards Against Humanity. Awesome game, by the way."

He laughed and hugged her. "You're such a poor winner."

"Yeah, she's just like you." Tex moped. "Bree, honey, I need some lovin'. Cass done broke my spirit."

"Oh my God. Would you take that hat off already?" Bree huffed.

Tex pushed his Stetson back and sighed. "A little togetherness and she's takin' me for granted." He grabbed and spun her, making her laugh.

Cass shook her head. "He should definitely not lose the hat. It's hot."

Mack frowned then looked at her. "I was in a calendar. With puppies."

"Shirtless?" She wiggled her brows.

"Yeah. With puppies."

"Yep. You win." She was kissing him just as Shannon and Jed approached.

Before Jed could say hello, Tex yanked him aside and introduced him to the room. "This is the guy who don't know a thing about the Cowboys."

Brad rolled his eyes. "Welcome to the party. And please, let's only talk about the Seahawks."

"But—"

"No, Tex," Brad said.

Shannon stared wide-eyed at the room.

Cass understood the feeling. So she yelled to her friend, "My man was shirtless on a calendar. With puppies! *And* he's the poster boy for Station 44!"

Everyone booed, and Cass and Mack laughed before Mack said loudly, "And I got the mean chick to admit she loves me!"

Jed nodded. "She is mean. Good luck with that." He winked at his wife. "Then again, mean chicks do it better."

Mack kissed Cass breathless. When he pulled back, he put his hand over his heart, the love clear in his eyes, and said, "Do they ever."

A year later, on a muddy soccer field, firefighter Mack Revere asked Detective Cassandra Carmichael to marry him.

And she said yes.

"Oh, now that lady's looking fine. Yep. You could do worse than that redhead, son."

Firefighter Brad Battle ignored the Texan eyeballing the crowd and looked up, praying for rain. Spring in Seattle brought the wet weather, but not today. The temperature had warmed to a mild 54 degrees, the sky bright with the occasional fluffy cloud dancing across the sun when the wind deigned to blow. The Dog Days of Spring Festival, in Green Lake Park this year, had a decent turnout. Such a turnout, in fact, that a man with a microphone flitted around, asking people questions.

Just what Brad didn't need. He *hated* reporters.

"We're here to work, not flirt, Tex," he said to his partner.

"You need to learn to multitask, Brad."

"I'm listening to you while not punching you in the face. How's that?"

Tex chuckled.

Brad glanced at his partner. They both wore Station 44

long-sleeved shirts tucked into dark-blue trousers accompanied by black boots. "Where's your hat?"

Tex typically wore a station ballcap when on duty and his Stetson on his off-hours.

With a sad sigh, Tex said, "LT wouldn't let me bring it today. Wants everyone to see my pretty face."

"Pretty face, right."

They both chuckled. With the lieutenant on them to be personable and *friendly*—directly aimed at Brad—there was no way Brad could duck out and avoid the press they'd been inundated with since opening up the new fire station.

Press like the man with a microphone striding toward him and smiling.

Tex saw the incoming reporter and drawled, "I got this. But you owe me drinks after."

"You're the man."

"Damn skippy." Tex intercepted the reporter and poured it on thick. "How do, friend. How about this amazin' weather, eh?"

Brad casually walked away from his buddy and lost himself in the crowd. He watched families cozying up to a few felines under one tent. To the right, a petting zoo had been set up, and the sight of small children smiling while riding ponies eased a bit of his stress.

He saw dogs everywhere, appropriate since it was called the *Dog* Days of Spring Festival, and wondered how the last stray he'd fostered was doing. His work for Pets Fur Life satisfied him, helping the helpless. His mood lifted even more.

Brad continued to meander, smiling and shaking hands with the locals. This he could do. But even so, after a while, he wanted to pare down on all the people.

He dragged a hand through his hair, counting down the hours until he could go home. At the beginning of his two-shift rotation, he worked twenty-four hours then earned two days off. He had plans to hang with the guys for a few beers tonight and a hike up Mt. Rainier on Sunday. Anything to stay outdoors and away from crowds.

A commotion just beyond a copse of bushes drew him, and he nodded at folks in greeting before moving closer to watch a short woman talking to a small group about adoption. She stood on a small stage under an arch of balloons in a shower of reds and blues, dressed in colors to match. Next to her stood a dark-haired woman in glasses holding a microphone—another reporter.

He stopped at the periphery and noticed a cameraman focusing on the group, but Brad's attention swayed toward the reporter. Beautiful, taller than the woman next to her, and smiling, she captivated with ease. He frowned. She looked familiar. But he couldn't see so well from his distance, so he drew closer.

"Mr. Fluffy Paws loves his catnip, long walks in the garden and mice, and is a raging Aquarius. So please, water signs need apply," the shorter woman quipped to much laughter. She had cropped blond hair that added to her all-around cuteness and wore slim-fitting jeans and suspenders over a long-sleeved red Deadpool T-shirt. She held the cat up like an offering.

The reporter sneezed. And sneezed again.

"Oh, sorry." The blond didn't sound sorry. Especially when she held the cat closer to the poor reporter. "But let this be a lesson, everyone. Do *not* adopt a cat or dog if you're allergic. You'll only end up giving the animal back, and everyone will be sad." She handed the cat to a nearby helper and brought out a large yellow Labrador retriever. "Meet Banana." Several children in the crowd perked up. "He's a three-year-old Lab needing a good home. He's friendly and sweet. And he loves to lick."

That wasn't all he loved.

Brad tried not to laugh as the dog sidled up to the reporter and rose on his hind legs.

"Look, he's dancing!" a little boy cried.

The dancing dog started humping the reporter's leg, much to the amused snickers of those around her.

"Dang it," she muttered as she tried to get some distance from the enthusiastic canine.

The laughing blond was no help. Nor were the amused onlookers. Brad couldn't help joining in. The "dancing" dog and helpless reporter were cracking him up.

She tried to make the best of it by taking the dog by the paws and dancing with him; not so easy to do with one hand still holding her mic.

Brad decided to help her out since no one else seemed inclined to do so.

The reporter laughed, keeping a good attitude, and addressed the crowd. "And this is why you need dog training."

Brad frowned as he drew closer to her. *Where do I know this woman from?*

"That would be my area of expertise." A tall, older woman next to the stage nodded. "Yep. We teach the little ones how to care for their dogs and take care of a dog's needs." She pointed to a large stuffed dog and a monster pile of fake dog poop on the stage right behind the reporter. "Come on over and I'll show you how we help our canine friends behave."

And that's when the situation went from bad to worse. Or, as Brad had the sudden thought, *it all went to crap.*

Oh no. Get off me! Please, not today.

Avery Dearborn's best friend was being no help whatsoever as the randy Lab kept trying to advance while Avery did her best to push the beast back and keep her microphone out of its mouth.

The colorfully dressed, short blond who should have been

helping and wasn't finally choked back her laughter. In a low voice, Gerty said, "Uh-oh. Your dad's here. And he's looking at you."

"This is all your fault," Avery whispered back, wishing to be anywhere but in her particular circumstances just then.

The sun sparkled as a light wind whisked a few scattered clouds overhead. The weather was lovely. A little brisk, but the jacket she wore kept out the cold. A perfect day to film a short segment for the online e-news site *Searching the Needle Weekly*.

The opportunity to star in the piece that another reporter would normally be covering had been a gift from Avery's editor. And a chance to show her father she was more than just a glorified junk-piece reporter.

Unfortunately, the excitable dog kept trying to hump her leg. The crowd seemed to grow as children and parents alike gathered to watch the spectacle she continued to make of herself. So *of course* her father had actually shown up to the festival in time to see her looking like a moron. His horrified expression spoke volumes.

Avery backed away and tripped over plastic poop.

Gerty burst into hysterical laughter along with the crowd. Banana woofed and licked Avery's face.

"I hate you," she muttered at the Lab and her best friend.

The dog cocked his head then turned to follow the trainer, who'd grabbed his leash. Behind him, Avery saw a mammoth Great Dane giving her legs a speculative glance.

She hurried to stand and pasted a smile on her face, aware her cameraman had been snickering and filming the entire time. She mentally added Alan to her revenge list.

Wiping the grass off her jeans, she pointed at the plastic poop and said to the amused audience, "And *that's* why we need to clean up after our best friends do their business. Because falling into that is something nobody wants, am I right?"

Several parents nodded, grinning. The children seemed

enthralled with the animals up for adoption, letting Avery off the hook. She hoped.

"Dance with the doggie again," one of them pleaded.

"Yeah, dance with Banana. I think he likes you," Alan said.

Gerty looked over at Avery's dad and gave him a thumbs-up. "Keep going, Avery. You're doing great."

Avery's father took one look at Avery, grimaced, then turned and, dragging her mother with him, made way for the food trucks.

Avery swallowed her embarrassment and launched into an introduction of Gerty's newest furry friend. A gerbil, thank God. With any luck, this one wouldn't make her sneeze.

As Gerty talked about Jerry the Gerbil, Avery happened to glance at the crowd.

And spotted *him* next to the stage.

The man who had been the star on her journalistic walk of shame. She'd made him a household name, and he'd been so incredibly nasty about one lousy article that he'd managed to make her question everything about herself in the process. An emotional trial from which she was still recovering, even five years later.

Bradford T. Battle. Jackass Extraordinaire. No, *Sergeant* Jackass Extraordinaire.

He stared at her in bemusement before his eyes narrowed and his expression turned to one of loathing.

Ah, so he does remember me.

Acknowledgments

Thanks to all the great first responders out there. I've taken some liberties with imagined altercations and the day-to-day serving the public. I don't know how you do it, but thank you!

About the Author

Caffeine addict, boy referee, and romance aficionado, *New York Times* and *USA Today* bestseller Marie Harte is a confessed bibliophile and devotee of action movies. Whether biking around town, hiking, or hanging at the local tea shop, she's constantly plotting to give everyone a happily ever after. Visit marieharte.com and fall in love.

Also by Marie Harte